WORK
IN
PROGRESS

WORK IN PROGRESS

A Novel

KAT MACKENZIE

AVON

An Imprint of HarperCollins*Publishers*

WORK IN PROGRESS. Copyright © 2025 by Kat Mackenzie. All rights reserved. Printed in the United States of America. No part of this book may be used or reproduced in any manner whatsoever without written permission except in the case of brief quotations embodied in critical articles and reviews. For information, address HarperCollins Publishers, 195 Broadway, New York, NY 10007.

HarperCollins books may be purchased for educational, business, or sales promotional use. For information, please email the Special Markets Department at SPsales@harpercollins.com.

Avon, Avon & logo, and Avon Books & logo are registered trademarks of HarperCollins Publishers in the United States of America and other countries.

FIRST EDITION

Interior text design by Diahann Sturge-Campbell

Spiral notepad illustration © zeynurbabayev/Stock.Adobe.com

Library of Congress Cataloging-in-Publication Data has been applied for.

ISBN 978-0-06-337903-9

24 25 26 27 28 LBC 5 4 3 2 1

To my endlessly generous and supportive parents.
Thanks for helping me pay for all those degrees in the
UK. This is what you had in mind, right?

WORK
IN
PROGRESS

CHAPTER 1

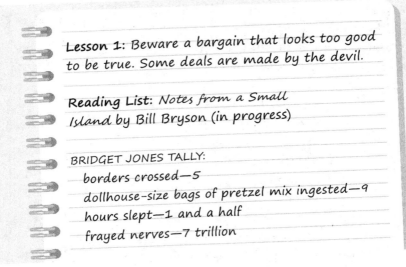

Lesson 1: Beware a bargain that looks too good to be true. Some deals are made by the devil.

Reading List: *Notes from a Small Island* by Bill Bryson (in progress)

BRIDGET JONES TALLY:
borders crossed—5
dollhouse-size bags of pretzel mix ingested—9
hours slept—1 and a half
frayed nerves—7 trillion

I could never have imagined that I would be so happy to see the inside of Edinburgh Airport. Surprisingly small and unmemorable, to me it was heaven: a beautiful salvation after my quick, seven-hour hop over the pond had become a thirty-six-hour circle of hell that would have chilled even Dante to the marrow. I have a hazy memory of trying to suffocate myself in the velour depths of my travel pillow, but I was too tired to die, and gave up.

When finally I arrived in the UK, I was dangerously underslept and underfed, and my entire body was one giant cramp. Only a maniac could have been happy as they trudged off the plane, wove through endless yellowed hallways, and got at the back of a line so long it looked like James McAvoy was giving away free hugs at the Scottish border. But to my surprise, I found I had a smile on my face.

An unfamiliar ember of joy sparked and began to warm my chest.

I zeroed in on it and tried to let all the pains and miseries of the past day and a half fall away. I put an upbeat song on my headphones and coaxed my smile to grow. Sometimes happiness needed to be fought for. That's why I was here, and I was ready for my adventure to begin.

While I waited in the customs line, I took the opportunity to dig out my notebook and make a list. Because lists make everything better.

WONDERFUL BRITISH THINGS I'M FINALLY ABOUT TO EXPERIENCE IRL:

1. Crooked thatched cottages with curls of smoke rising from the chimney
2. Cobbled streets with painted shop fronts
3. Crispy fish and salty chips wrapped in paper
4. Cozy old pubs with open fires
5. Mossy stone walls that you can run your hand across as you set out for a chilly country walk
6. Stately English lawns where I can imagine Mr. Darcy on a horse with the wind in his hair
7. Rugged Scottish vistas where I can imagine Jamie Fraser on a mountain with the wind in his kilt
8. The accents—every single one of the confusing, sexy, adorable accents
9. Castles
10. Actual freaking castles!
11. Red phone boxes
12. Double-decker buses
13. The word *loo*

A stern lady stamped my passport, and the sound of it sent a little thrill to my stomach. This trip was going to be life-changing. I just knew it. Every damn minute of it was going to be spectacular!

That is until almost immediately after stepping on British soil, when disaster struck.

My suitcase was missing. While others grabbed their bags off the carousel and skipped away arm in arm, I stood looking at the clock, trying to hold out hope as the last few bags squeaked past, inch by excruciating inch. An eternity later when the empty carousel finally shuddered to a stop, so did my desperate little heart.

This was going to be bad. I just knew it. And I really needed this trip to be perfect. I needed it so badly. My feet hardly left the linoleum as I dragged my body toward the customer service desk, bowed and beaten. Over my earbuds, the first few miserable strums of R.E.M.'s "Everybody Hurts" came up in the shuffle to provide the soundtrack.

Touché, universe. Touché.

"Good morning, madam. Thank you for flying with Blue Skies. How can I help you?"

I stood for a weighted moment and just stared at the woman's candied smile, trying to hold it together.

"Hello. It has . . . *not* been a very good morning, actually. My flight got canceled, and I was . . ."—*tortured, stripped of my dignity, had my soul ripped very slowly from my body, leaving only the dried, lifeless husk you see before you*—"very much delayed. I have a tour that's leaving in an hour and a half from the city center, and my luggage hasn't arrived. Please. Please tell me where it is."

The woman was poised, pink, tidily attired, and perfectly coiffed. At that moment, she was my antithesis in every way. Her lips tightened before she opened them a crack to push out a little sigh.

She scrunched her nose. "An hour and a half is a bit tight, isn't it? It's always best to plan for a little extra time when traveling."

"But I was supposed to arrive yester—"

"Do you have your luggage tag, madam?"

For a blessed moment I imagined grabbing her by the striped

lapels and shaking her bodily until her teeth clacked. Instead, I produced the luggage tag. The woman took it, and then proceeded to click endlessly at the keyboard until the end of time. *Can she actually be typing, or is this just for effect?* I couldn't be sure, but every tap chiseled at my raw nerve endings.

"So . . . it looks like you traveled from Washington, DC, to Atlanta, then Atlanta to Nashville, Nashville to Reykjavík, Reykjavík to London, and London to Edinburgh."

I closed my eyes, wincing, each stop like the lash of a whip.

"I did, God help me."

"Unfortunately, it looks like there was some problem with your luggage between Reykjavík and your final destination." My spine drooped, but she went on to deliver the death blow. "Yes. It appears to have been crushed."

"*Crushed?*"

"Correct, madam. That's what it says here. Crushed."

"Crushed? What do you mean, *crushed*? How did this happen?"

She finally stopped tapping and met my eyes, unblinking—the look of a cat who is about to push your favorite mug off the table.

"I really couldn't tell you, madam. We didn't have video surveillance on your particular bag as it traveled across four countries."

"But it was never supposed to travel across four countries. I booked a direct—"

"I do have some good news for you. It has arrived to Edinburgh, and we have taped and wrapped it to keep your belongings safely inside, free of charge. It'll be waiting for you just here in the back."

"Taped? There must be some mistake. My suitcase is unbreakable. It's polycarbonate. I bought it from Brookstone. It's called Air Armor because it's so strong."

She gave me a pitying look. "They'll say anything to make a sale these days, won't they?"

I considered making a flamethrower with a lighter and hairspray, and then remembered that those items were being held hostage in my suitcase. I turned away to collect myself. *It could be worse, right? At least they have my luggage here in Edinburgh, and my undies aren't already being tried on for size by a goatherd in Kazakhstan.* I could work with this! I just needed to hurry.

"Alright. Can I have what's left of my bag, please? If I leave now, I can just about make it to my tour bus."

"Of course. But you'll have to wait for Keith to bring it round for you, and he's on his break."

I checked my phone—6:55 a.m. The tour would leave at 8:00, and here I was, being toyed with by this hot pink sadist. If the past two days had been hell, then this woman was hell's gatekeeper, barring my exit.

I turned around and forced my face into outward calm.

"Is my suitcase in that room just behind you?"

"Yes."

"Can I go get it myself?"

"Well, we can't let just anyone wander about picking through people's luggage, now can we."

I looked down at her name badge and made an appeal to her humanity. "Please, Muriel. This trip is very important to me. I've been having a . . ." My voice threatened to crack. I swallowed hard and tried again. "A *really* hard week. Could you please grab my suitcase and bring it out for me? I would be so grateful."

"I couldn't possibly. That's Keith's job." She splayed her two hands and held them out in front of me to show off her pink manicure. "And I just got these done yesterday." She gave me a little wink.

She had no humanity.

I used to be great at handling difficult people, but I'd since discovered that when you're already teetering on the edge of a precipice, all it takes is one tiny nudge to push you over the edge. I felt tears prickle. *Shit.*

I breathed deeply for a few seconds and tried to calm myself down the best way I knew how: baked goods. *That's right, Alice, there are real British scones waiting for you out there, and all you have to do is get past Waterboard Barbie.*

"Right. Okay then. Who else can I speak to who could get my suitcase while Keith is on break?"

She made a little pout and then checked her watch with the heavy sigh of a woman who is being forced to do her job. "I suppose I could make a few phone calls."

"Thank you."

It was 7:10. I had fifty minutes to get my bag, make my way into Edinburgh city center, and find the meeting location for the tour. While she picked up her phone, I tried to connect mine to the Wi-Fi so that I could send an email to the tour company and beg them to wait.

Suddenly someone shoved past me hard enough that it sent my phone clattering to the floor.

"Sorry. I need help here, please." A man pushed in front of me at the counter.

Pushed.

In front of me.

At the counter.

"Excuse me!" I grabbed my phone. It was still in one piece—thank God. I moved past him and retook my place, my shoulder staking my claim as first in line. "Look. I'm sorry but she's busy helping me right now. You'll just have to wait your turn."

He ignored me completely. He stretched past and attempted to get the gatekeeper's attention, his Scottish voice low as he leaned in. He didn't even spare me a glance while our elbows jostled for counter space.

"Excuse me? Can you help me please?"

To my annoyance, a blush warmed the gatekeeper's cheeks as she nodded and held up a *just one second* finger.

"Hey. I'm in a huge hurry. She's trying to get my suitcase, and then you can—"

"Shh."

He shushed me. The man actually shushed me. The clipped, gusty sound of it was the bellows to the burning fire in my belly. I wasn't sad anymore. I was angry. It was the wrong day to mess with me. This egomaniac needed someone to cut him back down to size. *And guess what, buddy, that somebody is me!*

I spun around, squeezed between him and the counter, and looked him full in the face, nothing more than an inch of crackling hatred between us.

"Excuse *me*." I was quiet but dangerous with a face like thunder. "It cannot have escaped even *your* attention that this woman is clearly busy helping someone else. Now, you can get behind me and form an orderly line and wait your turn as you, no doubt, learned to do in kindergarten. What you do *not* want to do is continue pushing me around. Would you like to know why? I'll tell you why. Because, my indestructible three-hundred-dollar suitcase has apparently been crushed beyond recognition. My relaxing, boozy, transatlantic flight turned into a thirty-six-hour shitshow made of nightmares. I had to spend the night in the Nashville Airport. Nashville! Have you ever been to the Nashville Airport? This woman is trying to retrieve my bag which I have been informed has had to be *taped* together to keep its contents from spilling out like a gutted animal. And now I have got to get to Edinburgh city center in less than an hour, or I'll be stranded and alone in a strange country. So in case it still isn't clear to you, let me spell this out. You will move back, keep your damn shoulders to yourself, and remember your manners, or I will be happy to give you a crash course."

I am a force to be reckoned with. I am a dragon woman breathing fire. He will cower before me. He will snivel, and apologize, and scuttle away like the rat he is.

But he did none of those things. Instead he continued to act as if I didn't exist, hurriedly pressed some buttons on his phone, and pushed it to his ear as he moved around me back to the counter.

I grabbed his shoulder, prepared to catch him in a neck hold and slam us both into the ground, Hulk Hogan–style. But we were interrupted when a large man emerged from the door behind the gatekeeper. He was carrying a parcel—a minifridge, a body, I couldn't be sure. It was bandaged in copious layers of plastic wrap and a thick layer of bright yellow police tape for good measure. A little corner of silver poked through the wrapping and glimmered at me—it was my Air Armor.

The man laid it gingerly on the counter and backed away with his hands outstretched, lest it somehow manage to break free from its bindings and bury us all in an avalanche of socks and bras. The gatekeeper put the phone down with a snap.

"There . . . now that wasn't worth getting upset over, was it?"

This *thing* was my suitcase? How was I going to travel with this for the next three weeks? Before I could even open my mouth to wail, or protest, or even just sit there with my mouth ajar—all things that I had earned the right to do—the flaming hemorrhoid next to me made another bid for attention.

"Hi. Sorry. I am here to pick up a passenger on the 433 from Cardiff, and I can't find her anywhere. It landed nearly an hour ago. She's not answering her phone. She's ninety-eight years old, and I'm really starting to worry."

"Oh." Her eyes grew big and doe-like. "Of course, sir, I can understand your concern. If you just give me some information, I will do a bit of research for you here to make sure that she arrived. I'm sure we'll find her safe and sound."

Well, that put me in my place a little bit. I hoped that the old lady was alright, but people got turned around in airports all the time, didn't they? Surely a brief search would find her at the back corner of the bookstore, squinting over the large-print copies of Barbara Cartland.

I wrapped my arms around my suitcase and was preparing to lift it down when the gatekeeper's claw shot out and dug pink talons into its wrapping.

"Before I can give this back into your custody, I'll need to go over some things with you, get you to sign some paperwork, and inform you of the protocol for requesting compensation, should you find that there has been any damage to your luggage or its contents. But *first* I must see to this gentleman and his emergency."

"I appreciate that," he said.

Her face changed entirely as she turned to him, batting false eyelashes and flashing a row of dazzling teeth. *Aren't the British famous for their hideous teeth?* Her voice came out all serious and throaty. "I'll do everything I can for you."

Good God, I most certainly do not have time for this!

"I'm sorry, and I hope you find your friend soon, I really do," I said without sparing him a glance. "But my suitcase is right here. I need to get to Edinburgh urgently. Surely you can send another staff member to help this . . . person." I refused to say *gentleman—Take that!* "While you please give me my luggage, and give me the forms I need to fill out, so that I can get the hell out of here."

She pouted. "Unfortunately, there is only one of me. We will have to deal with issues one at a time."

"Alright. Look. I'm taking my suitcase and I'm leaving. I'll email to sort out the paperwork later."

The Scottish scrotum turned to me then, finally looking me in the face for the first time. He paused for dramatic effect, trying to zap me into oblivion with his ice-blue laser eyes. Then he stared me down, from my airplane-bedhead mess of hair to my boots. I fought the urge to punch him in the throat.

"Listen, you have *obviously* had a very bad day. I'm sorry if your *luggage* went missing, but I am missing a *human being.* An elderly woman. This could be serious, so I'll thank you to just keep it together a moment longer, and schedule your tantrum for after we've located her."

The look on his face, the tightened jaw, the narrowed eyes, told me just what he thought of me. I wanted to smush it with a steamroller.

A smug little smirk from the gatekeeper was the very last straw.

I leaned closer, took out my finger, and jabbed it into the center of his chest. "No. *You* listen!" But before I could let loose a deluge of expletives, a sound from behind made us all turn.

"Yoo-hoo!" An ancient woman about half my height was holding a hanky aloft and waving it to and fro. "Yoo-hoo, Robbie dear!"

His face crumpled in relief. He sidestepped my finger, caught midpoke, and ran to her. She had a wild dandelion fluff of hair, and she hobbled with the help of a cane with four sturdy little feet. Next to her trotted a small dog in a bow tie and vest, nails tapping on the shiny floor as it ran to sniff every passerby without exception.

"Oh, Doris. Thank God! You had me worried sick, you wee troublemaker."

"Oh, I am sorry if you were looking for me. But you see, I had a spot of indigestion. I've been visiting the lavatory since I got in. Plane food—you know how it is, don't you, dear?"

He laughed and gave her a hug—apparently his hideous behavior, my poking finger, and our shouting match completely forgotten. Taking her handbag from her shoulder and the roller bag from her hand, he put her arm firmly in his and began to lead her out.

"We've got to get our skates on, love, or we'll have everyone waiting on us." The little dog with the vest jumped up and pawed at his shins. "Yes, hello to you too, Percy. How could I forget?" He bent down and scratched him behind the ears.

I let out the breath I'd been holding. This little old lady and her graying terrier were so adorable they could have stepped right out of Doc Martin's waiting room. I was glad that they were safe and sound and on their way. I mean, she waved her hanky in the air—no one has done that since the *Titanic* left the dock in 1912. As I watched the three of them leave together, the ice in my heart thawed a degree or two. If this lady had been my friend and I couldn't find her, I would have been frantic too. I almost began to forgive the guy for being an abominable, world-class douchebag. *Almost . . .*

Until he turned around and did the unforgivable.

"Okay, now you can go ahead and treat yourself to a little tantrum." He winked at me, shot me a one-sided grin, and then disappeared through the glass doors.

My blood boiled into hard candy.

CHAPTER 2

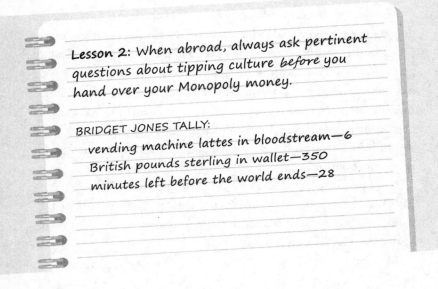

Lesson 2: When abroad, always ask pertinent questions about tipping culture *before* you hand over your Monopoly money.

BRIDGET JONES TALLY:
vending machine lattes in bloodstream—6
British pounds sterling in wallet—350
minutes left before the world ends—28

I filled out some paperwork; received phone numbers and instructions; hugged my suitcase around its middle like an awkward, overweight toddler; and heaved it to the floor with a thud, one wheel gone altogether, the other spinning at a comedic angle. *Of course.*

I missed the tram and didn't have much choice but to shell out for a taxi, so I jumped into the nearest one and instructed the driver to put his foot down.

I had a headache, and each time it throbbed I saw that detestable little smirk and wished I had slapped it right off his stupid Scottish face. I imagined all the cutting things I might have said if only the glass doors had taken a little longer to close. At least I would never have to see him again. Thank God for that. I wished upon him an unsightly rash, and worked to put him behind me forever. I wasn't going to let that horse's ass ruin my first day in the UK.

My soul calmed as the cab made its way through the countryside and suburbs surrounding Edinburgh. I took in the beautiful rolling hills, the clusters of little stone bungalows, the elegant Victorian houses. The air was fresh and cold blowing in through the cracked window, and the sun was out and making a show of kissing every bare inch of Scottish soil, coaxing buds to bloom.

It was surreal to be zipping through Scotland in the back of a black cab. This entire trip had been arranged less than a week earlier—the one and only spontaneous decision I had ever made. My whole life I had *longed* for the UK, and suddenly here I was, and my adventure was already beginning.

I took out my notebook and flipped through the well-turned pages, my hands knowing the way, to look over my list again. I knew it by heart, of course, but I ran the words over in my head like fingers across a talisman.

UK BUS TRIP GOALS:

1. Crawl out of pajamas.
2. Get over cheating bastard and his stupid ironed jeans.
3. Have my first real adventure!
4. Achieve stability, strength, and growth.
5. Adjust life plan, and prepare to kick butt upon arrival home.

I'm doing it already, aren't I? What could be more adventurous than surviving the last day and a half, and nearly murdering a strange man in public?

Regular pep talks were needed. The past six months of my life had been a colossal poop tornado, and I was the little trailer: swept up, turned upside down, and dumped in the desert somewhere, jobless, hopeless, and fianceless. I needed something big to shake me out of my all-consuming funk quicksand, and this was going to be it. It was a desperate move to snap myself out of it, learn from my injuries, and make a new plan to get my life back on track.

For as long as I could remember, I had dreamed of traveling to the UK. When I was a little girl, my English grandmother had looked after me when my parents were busy working, which was most of the time. Together we watched British TV, and she read to me from Beatrix Potter, Paddington Bear, and later, Roald Dahl and C. S. Lewis. In high school I discovered English literature, and it was Mr. Rochester, Heathcliff, and Mr. Darcy who seduced me nightly and inflamed my love for Britain into obsession.

I had always planned to travel to the UK, but with college and then work, somehow something always got in the way. For six years, that something was my ex-boyfriend, Hunter. He was afraid of flying, so I convinced myself I was satisfied with simply reading and watching all things British, from Bridget Jones to Jane Eyre, from *Downton Abbey* to *Happy Valley*.

And I suppose things might have stayed that way, at least for the foreseeable future, until one fateful night when I got a nasty surprise. A photo on Instagram of a ring. My engagement ring. On another girl's hand.

I had finished an old bottle of butterscotch schnapps I discovered in the back of the pantry, opened my laptop, found a flight from DC to Edinburgh at such a good price that it would have been criminal *not* to buy it, clicked, and treated myself as a little early birthday gift.

Before I could sober up and chicken out, I also booked a non-refundable three-week literary bus tour. It was going to be my lifeline. I was going to *Eat, Pray, Love* the crap out of this! But rather than meditation and moderation in an ashram in India somewhere, I chose tea, castles, and book chat in Britain.

The tour would start in Edinburgh, travel southward through England, then scoop along to the southern coast up to Wales, through the mountains back to Scotland, zip along the Highlands, and finally return to Edinburgh in one giant, picturesque loop, hitting major landmarks along the way as well as several spots off the beaten track.

Normally, I would have spent untold lengths of time researching and planning the trip—making charts, schedules, maps, and spreadsheets; carefully ensuring that I made it to every single spot on my Great British Bucket List—but this was so last-minute that I hadn't had the time. *It's fine*, I told myself. *This tour is going to be perfect.*

For one thing, I've always been a bookworm, and the focus of the tour was on historical sites of literary interest, from classic to contemporary works. It even included filming locations for some of my favorite films and costume dramas. It was no small enticement that there was *also* a notable focus on good food, making use of stops to visit tearooms and award-winning restaurants, as well as many a pub plus a Highland distillery. Toward the end of the tour, we'd even be sleeping in a real Scottish castle after a rousing country dance, where I fully intended to gossip with my new friends behind a fan, like every Regency heroine ever written. The pièce de résistance—it came with a reading list. A reading list!

Sure, I obviously didn't have enough time to read the books all in the week before I left, but some I had already read. I brought *Notes from a Small Island* in paperback, put audiobooks of *Once There Were Wolves* and *Three Men in a Boat* on my Libby, and hoped for the best. Mostly, I couldn't help but commend the organizers for the spirit of the thing. It was a good sign!

Another thing that swayed me was that this was a tour for women only, with an "emphasis on comfort and female camaraderie." I found that a little bit strange at first, but soon decided it was just perfect. I didn't want to get distracted and confused by the first sexy accent that walked on to the bus. Men? Who needed them?

As far as I could tell, women would soon be able to continue the human race through cloning and just let the males of the species eradicate themselves—mostly from being crushed to death under an avalanche of unwashed dishes.

Three weeks did seem a long time to spend trapped in a box with a group of strangers, but that was all part of the adventure, right? I liked this idea of a tour designed for strong women who wanted to embark on an adventure with other like-minded souls, and focus on strengthening female bonds without the perpetual drone of mansplaining.

Besides, these women weren't going to be strangers for long. They were going to be new friends and kindred spirits. I was certain of it.

Now all I had to do was let this trip work its magic. That, and not miss the tour bus!

"There we go, love. That's St. Andrew's Square. Forty-two pound sixty, please."

I handed him a fifty and told him to keep the change.

"Wait . . . I'm American. Did I just overtip?"

He laughed heartily, pocketed the cash, and drove off without another word.

CHAPTER 3

Lesson 3: Never start a battle you cannot win, neither with a cobbled street nor an equally cold and immovable man.

BRIDGET JONES TALLY:
blood spilled on Scottish soil—4 drops
thoughts of maiming—27
tampons—34
short, sensible hairdos—7

As it turns out, St. Andrew's Square was fairly large—large enough at least to not know where the heck I was supposed to be waiting. Christ, I was already ten minutes late! I *hated* to be late. I was never late. Soon I would find out I had missed my bus and immediately combust into a pillar of over-caffeinated flames on the sidewalk.

I scanned the parts of the square that I could see. It was a vast square of beautiful Georgian buildings enclosing a large park, with a massive phallic monument adorning its center. I had thought it would be obvious where to go, but saw nothing. Nothing indicated the pickup point: no signs, no large group of women with backpacks already bonding and cackling freely, no large green buses. *Was it green?* I pulled out my confirmation email and quickly skimmed the instructions.

Look for the green bus with a sign in front that says BOADICEA ADVEN-
TURES. It will be parked near the bus station and tram stop next to
Harvey Nichols. Please have your documents ready for inspection. We
appreciate your choosing Boadicea Adventures and look forward to
the pleasure of your company. Your adventure awaits!

At this moment I'd like a little less *adventure, thank you very much.*
Then I spotted the HARVEY NICHOLS sign. It was on the other side
of the square. Because why wouldn't it be? I girded my loins and
prepared to book it over. Sadly, the following four things conspired
against me:

1. I had worn my tall leather boots with the heels to
   cleverly save space in my luggage. [Note: Not so clever
   after all. Do not do this.]
2. My ridiculous-beyond-reason Air Armor was a useless
   padded boulder with only one wonky wheel.
3. The combination of starvation, stress, and sleep
   deprivation was finally taking its toll.
4. Cobblestones.

I had imagined myself sprinting like a gazelle and making it in
record time to arrive elegantly windswept and a little pink of cheek.
The reality was that dragging my heavy Air Armor was like pulling a porpoise by a leash down a gravel road. All my personal items
that weren't in my suitcase were strapped to my person, and they
thumped and jangled against me as I frantically scrambled at the
speed of Vaseline. I did not press the button at the crosswalk, I did
not wait for the light to change, I did not cross at the designated pe-
destrian crossing. *Who has time for that? Safety be damned!*
One minute I was Frogger, dodging between moving cars, and

the next I was a heap in the middle of the road with scraped hands and knees and a line of traffic behind me.

I waved from my prostrate position to signal that I was still alive, and silently implored drivers and onlookers to politely ignore me and go about their business, for the love of God.

I stood myself up and saw that the worst had happened. My leather tote had dislodged from my shoulder and toppled over, liberally spewing its contents all over the street. Little jars of hand lotion, bottles of contact solution, hand sanitizer—all of which had been measured and decanted for carry on travel—twirled and rolled around in front of me, under cars, and into gutters. All my carefully printed and highlighted itineraries and information took flight, billowing romantically through the rain-slicked street. My tampons (yes, tampons!) hadn't gone far, however. They laid there littering the area about me in alarming abundance, dutifully absorbing the gray street water.

I took one single, calming breath and then began the humiliating business of squatting and crawling in high-heeled boots to collect my very personal items in a very public display.

"Sorry! I'm so sorry!" I said to the drivers and the universe in general. "Just one second, please." To my horror, a car horn sounded from behind me, and others began to chime in.

"Need help, hen?"

"No, thank you."

"Come on, princess. Get out of it! Some of us are in a hurry."

Dear. God.

I quickly surveyed the remaining items, did some rapid triage calculations, grabbed items deemed most important, and left the rest to their fate. I clambered the remainder of the way toward Harvey Nichols in pain, and nearly in tears. *The tour was sure to have left by now*, I thought. It was almost twenty past, and I didn't see the bus parked anywhere.

Then a light green bus caught the corner of my eye. It was only just pulling up! I stood there amid a cluster of cute little old ladies (*On a walk to buy some stamps*, I assumed, *how nice for them*) and thanked my lucky stars.

A vaguely familiar form swung lithely out of the driver's seat and put up a wooden sandwich board in front of the bus that said BOADICEA ADVENTURES underneath their logo of the epic Celtic warrior queen. I was so flooded with relief and gratitude that I started to laugh. They hadn't left without me. It was all going to be fine. My great plan was still on track. I could buy more tampons in transit.

Suddenly, all the fresh joy, the happy chemicals, the optimism about this trip evaporated in one wretched moment of recognition. It was him: the basket-full-of-assholes from the airport. *How? Why? Will he be along with us for the whole tour? Could I get a refund and then just lay back down in traffic?*

I watched as he pulled out a little wooden step and placed it in front of the door of the bus—needless, surely, when the bus already had a built-in step only a foot from the ground. Then my horror deepened and solidified into a cannonball in the pit of my stomach. The little gaggle of gray and papery centenarians shuffled on to the bus one at a time, some giving Scottish slimeball a kiss on the cheek as they used his outstretched hand for leverage in the mighty effort to hoist themselves up to the four-inch-high step.

This couldn't be right. Was there another bus? One with all the cool, young, globe-trotting women with piercings, meaningful tattoos, and passport inserts as thick as a sandwich? Where were those kindred spirits that had an insatiable lust for adventure? The walking archives of the best travel stories you'd ever heard? Where were the gap year students? Where were the cool chicks from the website photos? Where were all my new friends?

I stood stock-still while they each took their time over the task of getting onboard and settling down. The overbearing ass with the Scottish accent took out his clipboard and started marking off names. With a little crinkle of his brow, he began looking around for the last attendee. *Crap! Is it too late to hide? Should I abandon my bags and run?*

This couldn't be happening. I would rather drown myself in the gutter next to my tampons than get on that bus. Of course, he eventually noticed me standing there right in front of him. Perhaps the only reason he had not done so sooner was because I did not resemble Miss Marple on her way to solve a mystery, and was, therefore, rather different from his usual clientele. I saw a flicker of something cross his face—shock, recognition surely, and then amusement, all quickly hidden away.

"Alice Cooper?" He looked down at my name again, and his mouth tightened at the corners. *Here we go.*

In high school, there was one year that people would sing "School's Out" at me every single day as the final bell rang. One time I fell asleep at a party and woke up with Alice Cooper's diamond eye makeup drawn on me in permanent marker; it had taken a week and several layers of skin to scrub it off completely. If there was a joke about my name, I'd already heard it, and I hadn't laughed the first time.

"Yes. Obviously. Should I assume you are the bus driver?"

"Yes. Obviously," he repeated but without my menace. "Robbie Brodie." He stepped in to shake my hand, but I ignored it. *Burn!* He cleared his throat and squared his shoulders. "Thanks for booking with us, Miss Cooper. Do you have a copy of your trip documents so we can complete the registration and get started on our trip?"

He was all business now, as if nothing unpleasant had transpired between us. The gentlemanly thing would have been to acknowledge it and apologize for his poor behavior. I stared at him, waiting. The moment stretched out between us—the moment where he would prove himself to be a decent human being, so that I could explain that I had been testy because I'd had the worst day in human history and then shake his hand while I magnanimously muttered something about bygones.

He checked his watch. "Or did those go the same way as your suitcase?"

The moment passed like a kidney stone. He obviously had no intention of apologizing. And clearly he was no gentleman.

I looked at the old bus with the ancient ladies inside and then back at his stupid face. A familiar smirk tugged at the corner of his mouth. He thought this was funny. It was lots of things—funny certainly wasn't one of them. The very idea of spending three solid weeks in the company of the mothball mob, and this, the most detestable man in Christendom, dashed every hope I had, every plan I'd made, every list I'd written, to smithereens.

I had foolishly assumed that my heinous thirty-six-hour flight, the gatekeeper, the broken suitcase, the airport asshole war, being late, and falling in the middle of the street, where my toothbrush landed on a wad of prechewed gum, was the absolute limit for the amount of calamitous fuckery the universe would allow before spacetime ripped apart. Evidently I was wrong.

I had to get out of this. I would fight like the trapped rat I was. Fight or flight—I was hoping for both.

"Wait just one minute." I tried to sound threatening. "I have some questions." He cocked an eyebrow without the slightest bit of concern.

"Do ya now? What a surprise." *Rude!*

"*This*"—I waved my hand toward the bus—"isn't the tour that I booked."

"That's odd. I've got your name right here. It's hard to miss."

I scowled. He grinned.

He crossed his arms and leaned back against the bus, eyebrow raised, with a look that teetered between exasperation and boredom. I had tried to work myself up for a fight, but now I didn't have to. His smug, arrogant face made me angrier with each passing second.

"This is false advertising. This tour was described as a . . . what was it?" I opened the wet confirmation I'd salvaged from the road. "A 'history-based British adventure designed for the young at heart looking to foster strong bonds with an international and dynamic friend group.' Does that particular group of ladies look youthful and dynamic to you? The banner on your website has a photo of outdoorsy twentysomethings climbing on castle ruins. These women had trouble climbing the step on to the bus! And I'm the only one here that isn't British, aren't I?"

"Not at all. One very nice lady has come all the way from Germany."

"So just the two of us then?"

"Yes. But she's *very* German." He smiled. "And you're clearly *very* American."

Anger coiled its way up my throat. "What is *that* supposed to mean? This trip has been grossly misrepresented. And this bus is an antique! Are you seriously planning to hold us hostage in that unreliable clunker for three whole weeks? It's not going to make it across Britain—I'd be surprised if it manages to roll out of that parking space. *And* this is *supposed* to be an all-woman tour, but clearly you're not a woman, are you?"

He smiled—a slow, spreading thing. "Noticed, did you?"

"Oh my God! This is so unprofessional. *Nothing* about you is professional."

Now it was my turn to look him up and down in judgment. He wore old Converse and faded jeans and, despite the cold wind, a plain, gray T-shirt that had been washed so many times it looked like a second skin. His dark hair was a tousled mess, and he had scruffy stubble that was lazily on its way to becoming a beard. I waved my hand around. "This isn't the uniform of someone who takes pride in their job. It's the uniform of someone who lives in smoky back-alley bars, drinks too much hooch, and busks for money. You look . . . like a wastrel." *Oh God. Did I just say* wastrel?

He bit back a laugh and had to cough and rub his stubble to hide a smile. He took a breath and schooled his face.

"Alright. I've taken note of all your complaints. Now can you please give me your papers and get on the bus, Miss Cooper? I know you only just strolled up, but if you haven't noticed, we're now half an hour late."

"*You* just got here! Which, by the way, is a great way to start the trip. Late, messy, rude, and unreliable before the bus even rolls off the lot."

He wasn't getting upset or angry. In fact, he was remaining perfectly calm. *Aggressively* calm. And it was edging me off the cliffs of insanity.

"About how long is this going to take, do you think? Perhaps we could save some time if you put all of this melodrama in a letter for me to read later."

One of my eyes twitched. If I hadn't bitten all my nails down, I would have scratched his stupid face off. I stepped closer and growled like an animal.

"Oh, you want some melodrama, do you? Well, buckle up, asshole. You pushed me at the airport—you *shoved* me and knocked my phone to the ground—without an ounce of shame or a word of apology. Who acts like that? And now you want me to just keep quiet and join the Golden Girls up there on that rust bucket and forget it ever happened? To spend three damn weeks trapped on a bus with you? I can't think of anything worse! You couldn't pay me to step foot in that damn—"

A low rumble of laughter broke my stride. He may as well have slapped me. "Wow. When I suggested that you schedule your tantrum for later, I didn't mean now."

I seethed. "You can take this phony little tour of yours and cram it right up your ass! I want a full refund!"

He let out a breath and stepped closer. "Look. This tour isn't about me. Why, you'll hardly even notice I'm there."

I scoffed. "Impossible."

"It's about having an adventure and meeting new friends. Like this group of vivacious ladies. I have been guiding these tours for three years now, and I can personally attest to the fact that most of the women who book them are just as youthful and dynamic as twentysomethings, with a good deal more wisdom and experience. You're concerned that you can't find value, interest, and friendship with this particular group of women because of their age? I think that says more about you than it does about them. You've not even given them a chance, have you?"

I opened my mouth to protest, but no words came. I floundered. *Damn! How dare he be right!*

"And as for a refund, I'm afraid it's impossible. You'll find it all clearly laid out in the terms and conditions, which I am sure you read thoroughly before booking. It will all be in the confirmation email you have clutched there in your wee hand."

"Well, that's hardly valid after you—"

"Now, you're free *not* to join us, of course. The choice is yours. But you'd be missing out on a memorable trip with a wonderful group of people. So why don't you go ahead and hop on? The fun is about to start." He put his hand near the small of my back and tried to guide me toward the door. I stepped out of his reach, all the angrier for being treated like the sheep to his border collie.

He and I stared unblinking, neither of us willing to back down. My breathing was heavy and ragged. His was completely tranquil, though his gaze was so intense that a lesser woman would have crumbled under the weight of it.

Curiosity forced me to break eye contact and throw a glance up to the windows of the bus. A few of the women had been drawn in by the ruckus and were peering down at us with unmasked interest through Coke-bottle glasses, while others appeared to be sleeping already, and yet another had gotten her knitting out.

"Do you need a hand getting up?" He gestured to the four-inch step. I hated him.

My mind raced for a winning maneuver but came up empty-handed. If he wasn't going to give me a refund, what could I do? It would cost another small fortune to travel the UK on my own. I had no plans. No reservations. No itinerary. No spreadsheets. I would either have to return home with my tail between my legs or try to make my paltry budget stretch for three weeks traveling on my own, risking a panic attack, homelessness, destitution, certain depression, haggis poisoning, and lord knew what else.

I was counting on this holiday. I couldn't allow this weapons-grade irritant to ruin my journey of self-growth before it had even begun to work its magic.

Damn it!

I stood there breathing a minute longer, still unwilling to back down. Some old lady at the back of the bus rattled off a Gatling gun fart. Our eyes narrowed, as if in response to a war cry. It was a showdown. A battle of wills.

Unfortunately, as much as I loathed him for it, he held all the cards.

CHAPTER 4

Lesson 4: You cannot judge a book by its cover, but you can still hate the book nonetheless.

Reading List: *The Da Vinci Code* by Dan Brown (read)

BRIDGET JONES TALLY:
   deeply mysterious corn cobs—dozens
   thoughts of homicide—16

Stepping on to the bus came as quite a surprise. It wasn't at all the run-down pile of scrap metal I had imagined it to be. The small, retro school bus had been renovated inside and looked more like a ladies' tearoom than a tour bus. The walls and ceiling had been painted a softer version of the minty green outside, with white trim. The floors were gray, glossy, and immaculate.

The original wooden bus benches had been spread out to offer more room, and each bench had cushioned backs and seats upholstered in a tartan of lavenders and grays with a light thread of green that complemented the paint. There were extra cushions on each bench, as well as folded blankets to cover one's lap should one catch a chill.

In front of each seat was a little padded foot rest that could be pulled down to support dangly legs, and a variety of pockets and hooks to store your things. In the spaces between windows were brass sconces with tiny white lampshades glowing away pleasantly. It was really quite cute. Perhaps I had judged too hastily.

As luck would have it, the only seat available where I would not have to share a bench with one of the other women, who would no doubt talk my ear off about her latest mole removal, was the one directly behind the driver's seat. He watched me settle my smaller bags on the overhead rack and then sit down behind him, flashing me a self-satisfied grin.

"You see? You're warming to me already."

"The only way I'd warm up to you is if I set you on fire first," I mumbled, too quietly for the others to hear.

His smile stretched in gratification.

Moving to stand between the rows at the front of the bus, he placed a hand on the benches at either side and leaned forward to address us all in the relaxed and confident manner that smacked of arrogance.

"Good morning, ladies. Welcome to Boadicea Adventures. I'm so happy that you're all here."

Armed with the rolled *R*s and soft vowels of his Scottish accent and a warm smile that made his blue eyes crinkle at the edges, he tried to trick a bus full of women into finding him charming. It might have worked, had I not already known him to have all the charm of a wool thong.

The ladies were taken in, however, and began to applaud while whispering to one another in sotto voce about his dazzling good looks and which granddaughter or grandson they were going to set him up with. I heard the phrase *bobby dazzler*, and even though I didn't know exactly what it meant, I was disgusted all the same. I rolled my eyes so hard that I burst a blood vessel.

"Now, I apologize that we're setting out a bit late, but I've a fantastic day planned for you, and I'm eager to get started. I'm called

Robbie, and this lovely lady"—he patted the bus bench—"who will be whisking us away to some of the most beautiful sites in the British Isles is affectionately called Rosie. Why don't we have a quick round of introductions so we can start being friendly right away?"

Ugh. What is this? Summer camp?

"Where should we begin?" He pretended to look around the bus as if he hadn't already marked me for sacrifice. "Let's see . . . why not right here in the front with Alice Cooper? Can you stand up for us, please, so that everyone can see you?"

I waited a beat or two and stared at him in defiance, just to make him sweat it before I gave in.

"Hello. I'm Alice. I've just arrived this morning from Washington, DC. This is my first time in the UK, and I'm very excited to be here." I sat immediately back down to discourage any questions or comments.

"Could we have that again a wee bit louder please, Alice Cooper? So that they can hear you right the way at the back."

I narrowed my eyes menacingly to leave no question that he would pay for this, and then took my time over it, enunciating the words slowly and loudly. The smile on his face showed far too much pleasure than was decent.

"Very nicely done, Alice Cooper." *He got my last name in there. Of course he did.* "Who's next? How about you, Helena, and then we'll work our way back from there?"

An elegant woman, whose silky platinum hair fell in fashionably messy waves just past her shoulders, sat behind me and smiled. She was tall, even in her seat, though I noticed she made no effort to stand. She must have been in her late sixties or early seventies, but the years had done nothing to diminish her statuesque looks. She was dressed casually yet very expensively, as only the truly rich can manage.

"Hello, everyone." Her English voice was low and smooth. "I'm

Helena. I live in Bourton-on-the-Water in the Cotswolds with my husband and our two lurchers. We have five children and nine grandchildren, some of whom are now starting to have children of their own. I'm here for a bit of 'me time,' as they say."

"Thank you, Helena." Our gargoyle guide gestured behind her to a sturdy-looking woman, probably in her midsixties, with an Angela Merkel haircut.

"I am Berrta" came a sharp, loud voice. "I am from Heidelberg, Germany. This is my third time to visit to the UK. I am here to learn, and to bird-watch." She held up the binoculars that hung around her neck for illustration but did not bother with a smile.

Next were two ladies who looked to be in their midseventies and who sat side by side on the bench: one wiry and angular, the other plump and soft with a pleasant and amiable look about her. It was the wiry one who spoke up first. "I am Agatha. This is my sister Flossie. She never was a genius, but in her old age she's grown as batty as a march hare. She's perfectly harmless, provided you tune out her nonsense."

The pleasant one batted her round blue eyes and smiled sweetly. Then she raised her hand and confidently ordered the trout.

Next was another pair of women sitting together. They were both in their late sixties, I suspected, but the two couldn't have looked more different. One had a massive rope of silvery hair piled artfully in a messy Gibson girl bun and was wearing a colorful, flowy dress and eccentric jewelry, while the other one, a Black lady, had very neatly cropped short hair and wore a simple black top and jeans.

The tidy lady spoke first. "Hi, I'm called Madge, and this is Lorna. We're originally from Edinburgh, and—"

"Well, actually, I'm from Lanark, and Madge is from Glasgow, but we did meet in Edinburgh," interjected the eccentric one.

"That's right. We lived around Canonmills for twenty-some-odd years before we bought a little place in North Berwick and moved over."

"Now that Madge is retired, we have a lot more time to travel."

"I was a social worker for thirty-five years, and Lorna is an artist—a sculptor and painter."

"Yes, we're hoping to see a bit more of the world now that we have the time to do so."

"But we haven't really so much time as all that. We're starting an art therapy center for at-risk youth."

"No, we haven't much time, but we should still take a holiday every once in a while," said the artist. This last bit was more to her partner than to the rest of us, airing some ghost of a former argument, it seemed.

"Anyway, we're happy to meet you all."

"Yes, we are."

They smiled at the crowd and then at each other, and seemed to decide that that was enough for now.

Finally, last in line was the tiny lady whom I could not possibly have forgotten from the airport that morning. *Was airport pickup an option? Well, that could have saved me a triple heart attack.* On the bench next to her, the little vested dog sat atop a cushion and scratched at his ear. She spoke energetically with a broad Welsh accent that singsonged its way over to us.

"Hello, everyone! My name is Doris. I split my time between Betws-y-Coed and London, where my great-grandchildren run me ragged. I'm ninety-eight, but I've never let that stop me! My friend Beatrice ran a marathon at a hundred and one. Although that sounds bloody boring, if you ask me. Instead I take senior's aerobics, and I started a book club for steamy romance novels. This handsome devil is my Percy. He's a service dog and goes with me everywhere. Very helpful. He's a very good boy, aren't you, Percy?" She patted Percy's head and he dangled his tongue out contentedly.

"Probably has fleas," the wiry sister said in a displeased whisper loud enough for everyone to hear.

Undeterred, or hard of hearing, Doris went on. "I never got to travel much when I was younger, so I'm doing my best to make up for it now. I have been on every tour that Robbie has operated since this company opened three years ago. And I can personally guarantee that we have the cleverest, sweetest tour guide in all of Britain. Plus, he's awfully easy on the eyes, isn't he?"

Good God. What is he paying this woman? Oops. He caught me rolling my eyes again.

"Aww, thanks, Doris!" He laughed. "Great! So let me see if I have this all straight." Our despicable driver clapped his hands together and pointed at the women one by one. "My buddy Doris, of course, and the dapper Percy. Lorna, Madge, Flossie, and Agatha. Then Berrta. Then Helena. And finally, Alice Cooper." He said my name quickly, as if it was one word.

I loathe him with the burning fire of a thousand UTIs.

"Please just call me Alice, actually." I half stood to address the bus. "Cooper is my last name. It's not a double-barreled first name or anything like that." I slumped back in my seat and refused to acknowledge his smile.

"Ah, but it sounds so well together," he said. "It suits you better that way."

I was back in middle school.

OLD LADIES:

1. Helena—quintessential English rose
2. Berrta—perfunctory Prussian bird-watcher
3. Agatha—the type of old lady that would pop your ball if it landed in her yard

4. Flossie—likes trout and has already improved the trip immensely
5. Madge—bickering social worker
6. Lorna—bickering artist
7. Doris—little Welsh lady who likes saucy bodice rippers
8. Percy—best-dressed male on the bus

I THOUGHT IT would be a good idea to sleep a bit, but I just couldn't bring myself to do it. Edinburgh was far too beautiful to close my eyes on. Even when we left the city, the surrounding area, with its little stone towns and villages, was so picturesque that my heart swelled with the roll of each hill.

We were at our first destination within half an hour: the enigmatic, fifteenth-century Rosslyn Chapel, with its ties to the Knights Templar and the supposed resting place of the Holy Grail. Like the rest of the world, I had read about Rosslyn Chapel in the early 2000s in Dan Brown's novel *The Da Vinci Code*, and it had piqued my interest.

We all toddled off the bus, with some ladies stopping to stretch as if they'd been traveling for days, and then ducked in under a low doorway. To my surprise, Percy relieved himself on the chapel wall and then trotted right in alongside us in his little vest, nails tapping along the hallowed flagstones.

The chapel was much smaller than I had expected. The vaulted ceilings were relatively low, but every spare inch of the stonework was carved and adorned. Smelling of dust, cold stone, and incense, it had an ineffable air of ancient secrets that grabbed hold of me as soon as I walked into the chilly shade of the space.

A clever-looking bespectacled woman approached and offered us a guided tour.

Our torturous tour guide declined with a polite smile. "That's kind, but no, thank you. I generally like to do the honors myself."

I was disappointed yet again. The website had promised expert historians guiding us through the wonders of British history, not some driver whom they had clearly scraped off the streets selling plasma for booze.

He saw my face. "Something the matter?"

"I thought we were supposed to be getting an expert historical tour at each site?"

"And you will be."

"By you, do you mean?" I scoffed and rolled my eyes. I couldn't stop myself. "Great. This should have about as much historical substance as a Happy Meal."

He turned his body then and looked pensively up at the stone carvings not far from where I was standing—quite close, but seemingly separate to any onlookers.

His voice was quiet, nearly a whisper. "Oh, come on, Alice Cooper. I don't come to Washington, DC, and heckle you while you're turning puppies into fur coats, now, do I?"

I narrowed my eyes to blade-thin slits. He was such a child. Well, I was too mature to play that game. No, I wasn't.

"Actually, I am great at my job. The question is, can you do yours? Because it looks to me like you're far more of an expert at flouting traffic laws, ignoring your personal hygiene, and seducing the old and infirm than an expert of fifteenth-century architecture." We moved around slowly, knitted together in battle while keeping up the façade of appreciating the incredible stonework.

"Ah well, did no one ever tell you that you can't judge a book by its cover? After all, if I did that, I would have pegged you as an uptight control freak who doesn't own a hairbrush and likes to kick up a fuss when she doesn't get her own way."

"A fuss is not the only thing I'd like to kick right now," I said quietly. I turned to him, locking eyes, and added sweetly with a saccharine smile, "Preferably right off a cliff after choking you with my hairbrush."

He took his time looking down at my thin frame. I squirmed internally. "Don't be silly. We both know that you haven't the bodily strength to be much of a threat to anything." He tilted his head to the side. "Except for eardrums, of course. Mine have been bleeding since the moment I met you."

Then he turned swiftly away and denied me the retort already on my lips. "Alright, ladies, if you can please make your way back to me, we'll start the tour here, thank you."

A smug little grin pulled at the corner of his mouth. He was pleased with himself. What an idiot! I would have to make more of an effort to eviscerate him next time.

WELL, I HAD to admit (to myself, at least) that I was shocked and impressed by how engaging and professional his tour was. His smooth, accented voice echoed off the stones with clarity and authority as he described in detail the complicated history of the chapel and made its stories come to life. His cadence sounded natural and unrehearsed, and he threw in some well-timed jokes that delighted the ladies.

The stonework boggled the mind. There were Masonic symbols, saints, pagan green men, and Lucifer himself scowling down at us. Some mysterious symbols were believed to be in code, and anachronistic anomalies—like depictions of corn, a New World food—had been carved some fifty years before Columbus's crew even set sail. The whole building was a mystery. I loved every minute of it.

Our own personal Lucifer was careful to point out the more curious and significant carvings and urged the group to search and find them amid the overwrought abundance at our every side. The German woman, Berrta, decided it was a competition and shouted with enthusiasm whenever she located a carving before the others. The sweet trout lady pointed out what she said was "a great big fanny" and later, Michael Jackson. Her sister swatted her, but I had to agree.

Afterward, we all filed into the little chapel café for a quick spot of tea to fortify us before moving on to the next location. My antagonist walked by to take a phone call outside, and I was careful to take great interest in the postcards and avoid his eyes, lest he have the opportunity to give me a look of triumph. A better woman might have complimented him on an excellent tour, but I was not a better woman, and had no plans to become one for the rest of the day, at very least.

Next we stopped by Rosslyn Castle, which was built by the Masonic Sinclair family. It was half in ruins and bewitching, the crumbling "lamp tower" still managing to stand these past seven hundred years. Unfortunately, it wasn't open to visitors, but we strolled over the high-arched stone bridge to get a closer look as we learned about the castle's history and the enthralling exploits of Henry Sinclair.

"For those of you who feel up to having a bit of a scamper around the grounds, I'm going to take a little side tour through the meadow and under the bridge to get a different vantage point. Otherwise, you're welcome to stay here and enjoy the view in the sunshine before we head out to lunch." *Lunch! Thank God.*

We were down the road and onto the path when he looked back to address the group but stopped short. A wry smirk curled his lip. I had been snapping photos in my own little world as we walked, so I looked behind me to see why. No one else was there. We'd both unwittingly set out alone together. Like two fucking idiots.

CHAPTER 5

"Oh," I said lamely. "Umm. No . . . I don't want to . . . Let's just head back."

"Course not. Come on, shake a leg. We'll be back before they've even noticed we're gone."

"No, wait. I . . ." *Would rather complete the Tour de France with a yeast infection!* But he ignored me as usual and set off so quickly down the path that I had to hurry to catch up with him. At least I had had the foresight to change out of my boots on the bus and into something better suited to meadow rambling at top speed.

I paused to take photos of the river or the castle, but no matter how long I stopped to change lenses or fiddle with settings, I couldn't shake him. He was only ever a few feet ahead of me. But the spring air was cool and crisp, and the sun felt good on my skin as I walked briskly between the wildflowers. I felt my mood lighten, despite the company. I was glad I hadn't waited on the bridge to wallow in thoughts of home and my empty bank account and other women wearing my engagement ring.

When he finally stopped, we were far below the bridge. It was cooler down here in the small valley between the two steep hills. The only sounds were the chirps of birds and the wind rustling the leaves. A pair of small, white butterflies chased each other in the stray beams of green sunlight that had filtered in through the trees.

I felt a sudden wave of gratitude. I could be stuck in my apartment looking for jobs in my underwear, but here I was basking in the Scottish sunshine under the picturesque ruins of a medieval castle.

We descended the old, uneven stone steps that sloped down the other side to get a better view. It was *so* neat.

Waiting for me to take a few more photos, he took off his sweater and tousled his dark hair, leaving it handsomely disheveled in a way that I decidedly did not notice. I moved my camera to make sure he wasn't in the shot.

"This steep trench was dug for protection. This was originally a drawbridge. Fairly adept at keeping the English out."

"Oh really? I would have thought that the threat of bagpipes and haggis would have done a fine job of that." *What are you thinking? Do not engage!*

He laughed. "Now it's an American invasion that we have to worry about." I rolled my eyes. "It's true. Armies of them arrive in droves every summer, camera-laden, clad in plastic ponchos, and asking what time the one o'clock gun goes off in a loud, nasal war cry that sends a chill through every red-blooded Scot." He gave a little shiver.

"It's no wonder you catch a chill when you people run around wearing little plaid skirts with nothing on underneath."

He raised a suggestive eyebrow. "Why do you think the Americans are in such a hurry to get here?"

"Gross." He wasn't wrong. But I'd be damned if I'd admit it.

"And just so you know, I'm going to personally make sure that you try haggis while you're in Scotland. And you're going to thank me for it."

"No thanks. It's true that you Scots have been very innovative with your sheep stomachs, but I think it's highly unlikely that you and I share the same taste in anything."

"Well, you did pick this tour over all the others, so I'd reckon we've got a bit more in common than you'd like to admit."

I scoffed.

"For instance," he went on, "I love Highland cows, and you've styled your hair just like one."

Was he playing with me? Or was he trying to put me down for demeaning his little tour in front of the others? Either way, his smile told me he was enjoying it, and I just couldn't let that happen. The smart move would be to ignore him. But I was too sleep-deprived for smarts.

"You should talk. Your hair looks like you drove here with your head out the window—the first of many doglike qualities, now that I think about it." I gave him a scornful look to convince both of us that it wasn't attractive.

He laughed. "And I take it you're a cat person. Like most witches."

I sighed. "Look. I don't know what you're doing, but you really don't have to try this hard to make me miserable. Just being near you is enough."

He laughed again, and I ignored him and went back to fiddling with my camera settings, hoping he could take a hint.

He crossed over to lean back against the stone of the bridge right next to me and looked down at my camera. I am on the tall side for a woman, and while he was only a few inches taller, his shoulders were broad, and he had a capable, masculine frame that managed to make me feel small.

"Can I see?"

"No." That felt good. I tried to ignore him until he went away. Instead he watched me.

"So what is it that brought you all the way to Scotland, Alice Cooper? You just booked a few days ago, didn't you? Why so last-minute?"

Something unpleasant stirred in the pit of my stomach. A flash of dread that I worked to ignore. I lifted a shoulder. "Temporary insanity, obviously. Can you not stand so close?"

"Hmm . . . interesting. Let me guess—you're running away from something, aren't you?" I felt the words deep in my gut as he went on to make a list of options on his fingers. "Wait. Don't tell me. Did the men of your country chase you out with pitchforks for being an overbearing hellcat? Were you left at the altar when some poor pillock came to his senses? Were you hired to assassinate me with nonstop complaints and moody looks?" He flashed white teeth in a wide grin. "All feasible scenarios."

I felt a little swoop of nausea. My face grew hot. He'd unwittingly stepped on a landmine. I didn't want him to know how close he had gotten or how much it hurt.

"Shut up. I'm not running from anything. I've just always wanted to see Scotland. I obviously didn't know *you* would be here."

He spoke through his smile and crossed his arms over his chest. "Aye, I saw you there getting a *real* close look at the Edinburgh cobbles this morning." He gave me a nudge.

"Wait. You saw me fall on the street? And now you're mocking me for it?"

"Oh, come on. I'm only having a laugh." I hated that lopsided smirk of his. Like everything was funny. Like everything was a joke to him and everyone in the world just there for his amusement. I didn't need this. I'd had a day from hell, and yet I was trying my damndest to focus on something positive, to enjoy the fucking butterflies, and this asshole was doing everything he could to bring me back down. Heat crept up my spine. I felt the exact moment control slipped away from me.

"My God, you're the fucking worst. I can't even believe this. How on earth does anyone put up with you for three whole weeks?"

"Oh, they don't just put up with me—they pay me for the privilege."

"Look. Can you just leave me alone? I have had—"

His eyes rolled upward.

"Oh, don't you dare roll your eyes at me."

His eyes snapped back down to mine.

"And why not? Do you have a monopoly on eyerolling?"

My voice came out shaky. I raised the volume to make it stronger. "I am *so* done with this. You have been outrageously rude since the first moment I stepped foot here. If you think that for the next three weeks, I'm just going to sit by and—"

His eyes rolled skyward again. "Umm." He interrupted, lifting a petulant finger in the air, as if that would stop me. It was all I could do not to grab the thing and snap it off! "You might want to keep it—"

"What? Keep it down? Because I'm just *so* hysterical?" I raised my hands and shook them above my head like a threatening crazy person. He started to laugh. I honestly think steam started coming out of my ears. "No. I won't keep it down! You don't get to tell me what to do. You're so used to old ladies crooning about how wonderful you are all the time, but you don't have any idea what to do if someone actually calls you out on your—"

I was gesticulating dramatically when my hand hit something falling through the air. We both looked down between us and saw a thick pair of reading glasses, attached on one side to a little broken pink chain. I looked up. Above us, all the ladies were leaning over the side of the bridge watching the show.

I died and waited for the white light at the end of the tunnel.

Could they hear us? It was likely that the sound was echoing up the walls of the bridge loudly enough for their hearing aids to pick up. Even if they couldn't, it was plain to see from my body language that I was losing my temper. Again.

Damn it! I'm making a terrible first impression. And it's all his fault!

The pointing. The eyerolling. "You knew, didn't you? That they were there."

"Course I did." He smiled and waved up at them sweetly.

"Yoo-hoo!" called the same voice from the airport. It echoed along the stone, plenty loud enough to reach us.

"I did try to tell you, but you were too busy having one of your tantrums."

There was that fucking word again. If the old ladies hadn't been watching, I would have made sure he regretted ever being born.

They waved down at us. My cheeks grew hot. And I marched off in the direction we had come from without saying another damning word.

CHAPTER 6

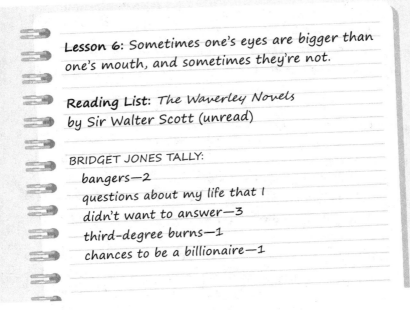

Lesson 6: Sometimes one's eyes are bigger than one's mouth, and sometimes they're not.

Reading List: *The Waverley Novels* by Sir Walter Scott (unread)

BRIDGET JONES TALLY:
bangers—2
questions about my life that I didn't want to answer—3
third-degree burns—1
chances to be a billionaire—1

We all piled on to the bus and rode exactly one minute down the street to our next destination. With all the fussing and rearranging that the ladies did, it was long enough for me to fish my notebook out of my bag and start a new list.

HOW I LOATHE THEE, LET ME COUNT THE WAYS:

1. Rude. Unaccountably, unprofessionally, unforgivably rude.
2. Knocked my phone to the floor.
3. Flirted with the gatekeeper (revolting display).
4. Made inarguable points about ageism when I was angry.

5. Public humiliation/childish reoccurring name jokes.
6. Stupid, messy hair that he probably spends half an hour waxing and teasing into peaks each morning.
7. Goaded me into causing a scene in front of the ladies . . . twice!
8. Dead set on making my life a misery.

We arrived at the pub—the pub, thank God. Since that morning, I had gone from starving to nauseous to ravenous. I hadn't eaten in . . . well, I was too tired and hungry to calculate how long it had been in this time zone, but I was certain that it was longer than the entire lifespan of many of Earth's insects.

Could it be low blood sugar that's making me grumpy? I considered this briefly and then huffed and crossed my arms. *No, it's the douchebaggery.*

We all piled back out of the bus—surely it would have taken us less time to walk—and the ladies began their stretches and ankle-rolling again. The German lady braced her feet, stretched way up, and then doubled over, reaching presumably for her toes but only getting as far as the knees. The little dog ran to look for fallen scraps under the outdoor tables.

The pub's interior was all black beams, red walls, and exposed stone, with a nicely glowing fire despite the season. We sat ourselves around a large table with a view of the village, and I stayed quiet as the others chatted away. I didn't want to appear unfriendly to the ladies, but I was fuming, hungry, exhausted, and embarrassed. Hopefully they all had poor short-term memory.

The artsy lady, Lorna, held her menu as far away as her arms would allow, stretching her neck back to get that extra inch, while her partner, Madge, had her glasses pushed to the very end of her nose and was peering over the top of them at the menu she was holding a hair's breadth from her face. I wasn't sure how either of them could read anything. I wondered if I should offer to read things aloud, but I didn't want to risk insulting them.

"Just look at those prices!" said Agatha, the grumpy one, to her sister. "Eight pound for a jacket potato. Who's ever heard the like? This is daylight robbery here. We're being robbed."

"Are we really? Oh, how exciting!" The pleasant sister, Flossie, pulled her blouse down an inch and looked over each shoulder with an expectant smile—on the lookout, perhaps, for dashing, swash-buckling highwaymen.

When the server finally arrived, I ordered the biggest things that I could find on the menu—bangers and mash with sage and pork sausage from a local farm and mushroom and onion gravy, a pint of a honey beer called Waggle Dance that the server recommended, followed by the sticky toffee pudding with ice cream. These were classic foods I'd seen on British TV and read about often but had never had the opportunity to try.

While we waited for our food, our truculent tour guide engaged the group in a talk about *The Da Vinci Code*, and just like that, he turned lunch into a book club meeting. He seemed to be making them all laugh, but I couldn't manage to focus on the conversation. Following his accent took more energy than I could spare, and I didn't want to run the risk of finding anything he said amusing.

When the food came, I was convinced it was the best thing I had ever put in my mouth, and I zoned in and out of consciousness, shoveling it into my body as quickly as possible, occasionally catching a snippet of conversation here and there.

"Be careful you don't swallow the plate as well, dear," Doris said good-naturedly, and then her glasses with the broken chain fell into her steak and kidney pie.

"Leave the girl," scolded Agatha. "This is a large part of American culture. We will be treated to this display of our cultural differences at each mealtime, so we may as well get used to it."

"Well, the poor thing, she must be starving." Lorna joined in from across the table. "Look at you—you could snap in the wind!"

I took a couple of large gulps from my pint and let loose a sheepish smile. "I'm sorry—it's been an incredibly long trip for me to get here, and I don't think I've ever been so hungry in all my life. Plus"—I pointed with my fork—"this is delicious! What's a girl to do?" I bookended this with another wobbly smile that earned me a couple of grins and chuckles from around the table, and a motherly pat on the arm from Welsh Doris, who had a sheen of gravy on her hand.

"That's right, dear. You carry on."

There was a little frustrated yip from below, so Doris dug her fingers into her pie, pulled out a glistening piece of meat, blew on it, and then passed it to Percy under the table. I wasn't convinced that this was proper support animal behavior, but perhaps standards were different here.

I did slow down eating after that and made an attempt to listen to the conversation. I even answered a few questions. I had assumed no one would want to talk to me after my public outbursts, and that was okay—I would start making a better impression first thing in the morning. But it turned out I was wrong. These ladies were clearly a forgiving bunch, and the more they talked to me, the more I felt my shoulders relax.

"What part of the US are you from?" asked Madge.

"I'm originally from Boston, but I studied in Connecticut, and now I live in Washington, DC."

"Really?" asked Lorna. "Madge and I took a road trip around the US many years back, and we just loved it. I think Santa Fe is one of my favorite cities in the world. I just felt an instant affinity with it, you know what I mean? When a place just mirrors your innermost spirit? I hope to retire there some day."

"We've already retired, my love, to North Berwick, remember?" Madge countered, but Lorna went on unhindered.

"We never did get to Boston, though, and I would so love to see it."

"We've been to Boston," Agatha informed us in her clipped tone. "I hope never to return to the place. The people there are shockingly rude."

"That's rich," Doris mumbled beside me, giving me a conspiratorial little elbow that made me smile.

"I met three of my lovers in Boston," Flossie chimed in, with a dreamy look in her watery eyes.

Agatha's face puckered like Maggie Smith tasting *store-bought marmalade.* "You did nothing of the kind! We were together every second of every day, as we always are. You are my constant burden wherever I go."

"A soldier, a barber, and a candlestick maker," Flossie went on happily. "Do you think the water closet in this establishment offers the services of a bidet? I pride myself on a fresh and fragrant under-carriage at all times."

"If it does, I should wash your mouth out with it," snarled her sister. "Now be quiet this instant, before you get us all turned out for indecency."

The beautiful lady—Helena, I think it was—had been deeply engrossed in a side conversation with my aggressor since we had ar-rived, but I happened to notice his eyes light up as they flicked over the scene the ladies were making. His face melted into a grin that confirmed that he had heard the best of it.

"I have traveled to twenty-three states," Berrta said loudly to me. "North America is most excellent for birding. I saw sixty-four species there in just four veeks. I have seen three hundred and seventy-two species this year, and I have most here on my camera. I vould like to show you if any of you vish to see them."

"A fascinating offer. Perhaps we will seek you out if we have any trouble falling asleep tonight," quipped Agatha, but she had been quieted by the shame of the undercarriage comment, and luckily Berrta didn't appear to have heard her.

"I'd love to see them, Berrta. Thank you," I said. "Perhaps a little later when I can focus properly?"

I didn't really have any particular interest in spending hours look-ing through her extensive catalog of bird photos, but no one else had accepted the offer, and I didn't want her feelings to be hurt. I was rewarded by a tight-lipped German smile and a firm nod that made me feel good, even if it meant that future me would discover a new fear for Hitchcock's *The Birds*.

Before dessert arrived, I was also asked how long I had lived in DC (five years), how long I would stay in the UK (just the three weeks, and I would fly out of Edinburgh soon after the tour had ended), was I single (yes), how did I stay so thin (stressing calories away, I guessed, and anxiety was a natural laxative), which *Pride and Prejudice* adaptation did I prefer (BBC), and did I listen to Barry Manilow (umm . . . sure).

While it was nice having a conversation with these ladies and get-ting to know one another, it was harder to talk about myself than I had anticipated. It was not something I had ever felt before. I had always been proud of my achievements, rather than ashamed of how my life was going. It was a sharp thing, with jagged teeth and a tight grip. I hadn't been single for over six years, and answering yes to that question felt worse than I had expected.

By the time we got to the question of what I did, I chickened out. I wasn't ready to admit the truth, so I kept my voice even, and told them that I worked on the outreach team at a large nonprofit fo-cused on ending poverty in the Global South. It was what I used to do and what I hoped to be doing again soon. I gave myself permission to bend the truth a little bit. I wasn't really capable of anything else.

"Oh, how noble," said Lorna. "I could just tell you were a good person." She gave me a little wink, and I smiled back.

Doris hadn't eaten her roll, and before they took her plate away, she wrapped it up in a slightly used paper napkin and snuck it to me under the table like a drug deal.

"Here, love. Put this in your handbag for later," she whispered. I thought about it for a second and decided that "later" I was unlikely to want a stale dinner roll wrapped in someone else's napkin.

"Oh. Good idea. Are you sure you don't want it?"

"No, no, dear. That's for you."

I tucked it away in my bag with a covert smile.

The sticky toffee pudding arrived in a mass of glistening, golden goodness that smelled intoxicatingly of butter and burnt sugar. I grabbed the spoon with childish glee and fed myself a portion the size of my own fist before spitting it out into my napkin and launching into a spasmodic coughing fit. It was as hot as boiling tar. Molten toffee coated my mouth and continued to cook it mercilessly even after I had spat it out.

Before I knew what was happening, the object of my contempt had rushed to the bar and returned with a glass of ice water—worried about an American lawsuit, no doubt, lest I see an opportunity to make my fortunes via toffee injury.

"Be careful. It's hot."

"Thanks for the warning." I gulped the water greedily.

"No trouble," he said, and then quietly added, "It would be a terrible shame if you really hurt yourself and then found it too painful to speak for a few days . . . or weeks even."

After a moment of genuine deliberation, I came to the regretful conclusion that I couldn't stab him in the leg with my fork in front of everyone, so instead I shot him a look of unfettered disdain I hoped would have the same effect. To my frustration, this seemed to amuse him, before he quickly changed his face back to the overdone mask of concern to fool the ladies.

I ignored the way his stupid little smirk made me feel like my entire body was a piñata filled with hornets and went back to my magma cake. It was worth it. Sticky toffee pudding was my new favorite dessert, even with a side of third-degree burns.

THE MINUTE I slid onto my bus bench, I fell into a deep and dreamless sleep, the type achieved only through the consumption of beer, copious amounts of mashed potatoes, and large, sugar-soaked cakes. I came to only after the bus had stopped, roused by the haunting voice of my enemy. I appeared to have drooled a little. I checked his face quickly to see if he'd noticed but could discern nothing.

"So we are now in the Scottish Borders, ladies, as I'm sure many of you have noticed from enjoying the stunning views of the changing landscape as we drove south. In fact, this is one of my favorite drives in Scotland. Alice Cooper had her face pressed against the glass the entire drive down. Would you like to share with us your favorite part?"

My stomach tightened. "Umm. Well," I said with the voice of James Earl Jones. I looked out the window for an answer, any answer. "I liked the hills."

I don't deserve this. Do I deserve this? Okay, maybe a little. But I just had a thirty-six-hour flight—what's his excuse?

"Ahh, yes. The hills. A fine choice. Wouldn't you agree, ladies?" he said with a smile. I scrubbed a hand over my face. This. Was going to be the longest three weeks of my life.

Abbotsford, the stately home of Sir Walter Scott, was our next stop. It was a sprawling, baronial castle, the opulence and splendor of which I had never seen in real life and only occasionally on-screen. The fairy tale was complete with spires and turrets and huge windows looking out upon what must surely be the most perfect garden in existence. Inside was no less breathtaking, Scott had had his home built with all the romance of a poem.

The library was enough to make a bibliophile weep openly. The elaborately carved wooden paneling, the painted ceilings, the Gothic marble fireplaces, the mullioned windows, the walls of gorgeous leather-bound antiquated books—I loved every inch of it. Even the smell was perfect: wood polish, old paper, and pipe tobacco.

I walked from room to room, selecting one favorite item from each that I would move into my bedroom after I inevitably bought Abbotsford from the National Trust with my toffee-burn billions and moved in.

Voldemort gave us what was another excellent tour. Scott, it seemed, liked to collect curiosities, and his castle was full of fascinating oddities—witches' cauldrons, decorated human skulls, Rob Roy's knife—and he had lots of stories and mysteries to share.

We spent a couple of hours in the house and then another on the grounds and in the gardens. We were left free to wander of our own accord, sans contemptuous Caledonian cretin, to spread out and explore the enchanted woodlands and converse with the gentle babble of the picturesque River Tweed. I forgot my exhaustion and really enjoyed strolling around the gardens alone—and later on, alongside the ladies. I learned about the plants and flowers from Lorna, Helena, and even Agatha, all of whom enjoyed gardening at home. I took photos of everything from every angle so I could remember what it all looked like for the rest of time.

A few hours later, we were at our bed-and-breakfast. As the hostess fixed us a roast supper, I looked at some of Berrta's bird photos and the ladies talked about what TV shows they were missing.

"That was a nice day, but I sure missed me *Countdown* at 2:10," said Doris. "Although it hasn't been the same since that sexy Richard Whiteley left."

"Well, I missed *Neighbours*," said Lorna. "And today we were supposed to find out what's been going on with Toadie! I'll have to call my friend Selma tomorrow to find out, but she'll be asleep now, it's nearly half eight."

"Don't get me started on *Coronation Street*," said Agatha.

I thanked Berrta, stood up, and backed away quietly. The roast smelled delicious, but I could no longer keep my eyes open. Besides, I didn't think anyone would commiserate with me that I was only halfway through *Squid Game*. My room called to me, where I could sleep the well-deserved sleep of the dead.

I spotted my Air Armor at the bottom of the stairs. Well, how could anyone miss it? I had opened it earlier to get to my walking shoes, and now it was a blossoming bundle of ripped yellow tape, crushed and defeated, clothes of all colors spilling out, a soldier after a brutal battle. A battle that I had also fought and looked similarly destroyed by.

I grabbed what was once the handle and tried to lift it up, but it was impossibly heavy. Gravity was against me, weighing the heavy outer casing down to spread further open and spit my socks out onto the floor. Even if I was in a fit state to carry the thing up the stairs to my room, which I can confirm I was not, I would inevitably leave a trail of toiletries and underwear behind me. I tucked the socks back in and tried again, turning around and dragging it up the stairs backward, one step at a time, while attempting to hold it together with my free hand.

The problem with this method: as the bag scraped each step, more tape was pulled off, disrupting its fragile integrity. It was impossible. At this rate, I could carry my belongings to my room one bundle at a time, like a mother cat moving her kittens, or I could just light the whole goddamn thing on fire. It was a tough choice.

Just when I was contemplating the latter, our detestable driver arrived. I'm sure this was an enjoyable still life for him—me doubled over, balancing the huge broken case on the steps, hair obscuring my face, rump raised high.

Anyone. Anyone but him.

He chuckled low when he saw me but moved quickly to help.

"Here, let me help with that." He put a hand out to stop the case from falling, but I didn't let go.

"I got it," I said like a fool.

"Don't be silly. I'll bring it to your room."

"No thanks."

"It's okay to accept help when you need it, Alice Cooper."

"Accepting help from you would be like accepting a ride from Ted Bundy. I'd only regret it later. Thanks, but I got it." I knew I didn't have it, but the words spilled out nonetheless, like I had no say in the matter.

He laughed. "Yes, I can see that. It's quite a sight, actually. I was wondering if I could get a photo for the website. 'Stubborn American victoriously carries own luggage upstairs before trip to chiropractor.'" He laughed again, clearly enjoying his own insufferable brand of humor.

"Only if I can get one of you. 'Smug Scottish Neanderthal finds women incapable of looking after themselves.'"

"Oh, not *all* women."

I shot him a look that would have eviscerated his manhood if it could have.

"Look, Gloria Steinem, I'm not offering to help because you're a woman. I'm offering to help because you've had such a long day that you're barely even human at this point."

We stood there in limbo, between war and surrender, the Air Armor between us, him at the bottom of the steps, leaning up to brace the case, me a few steps up, still bent over double. I couldn't put my finger on what it was that drove me up the wall whenever he smiled that cocky little grin of his. No, I *could* put my finger on it. He had been goading me all day. On purpose. Like it was his job. And he'd been enjoying it. I blew the hair out of my eyes and glared down at him before it swung right back into place.

"Look, your suitcase has become a comedy routine. Do you want to get up to your room now, or do you want to spend the next half hour or so grappling with your own stubbornness? And the suitcase, of course."

I turned and looked behind me up the stairs. They were infinite, like an Escher painting. I had only made it up about four. A little bit of my heart died as I gave in.

"Okay. Thanks." I sounded more like I was doing him the favor. He moved to grab the case and I tried to help him, thinking to split the weight between us.

"Nah. You just go ahead and take it easy while I do the heavy lifting." He saw the fight on my face, but before I could say anything, he laughed and hoisted the massive bag easily up onto one broad shoulder, looping his arm around it to hold it shut.

"Show off."

We got to the room, and he placed the case down on a chair. As he did, my lacy blue silk nightgown slithered out onto the floor, moving like mercury and falling in a suggestive display. *Oh, come on! Of all things!* He swooped down automatically to pick it up, but I snatched it before he could touch it and stuffed it back in my bag. He cocked an eyebrow at me over a set of dimples.

"Funny. I would have guessed you slept in a suit of armor."

"Shut up." I was too tired to think of anything better. A great comeback would probably come to me tomorrow, and then I'd spend all day fantasizing about a repeat situation.

"Well, Alice Cooper, this suitcase is clearly not going to work. I've a bag you can borrow—I'll shift some of my stuff around until you find another for the way home."

"Nah," I said like a child. "You can keep your trash bag. I'm sure they have others in the kitchen I can use without the irritating commentary. I'll figure something out." He laughed at me and then went on to make the decision without my consent.

"You'll have it tomorrow. Now get some sleep so that we don't have to use the defibrillator on you in the morning."

I tried to smile and thank him like a mature adult person, but it came out more like a pained snarl.

Oh well. Tomorrow I'll be a mature adult, I told myself. But something deeper down knew it was a lie. With the ladies, sure—they were lovely. But this man was like poison ivy—the more I scratched, the more it spread, and the worse it itched.

CHAPTER 7

Lesson 7: There are many things that romanticized British dramas hide from you—like the shocking stupidity of British bathrooms.

BRIDGET JONES TALLY:
lights—0
hot water—0
fucks to give—about a million

That night I waged war against my own en suite bathroom.

I had longed for nothing so much as a hot shower to wash away the days of grime and festering indignities from my sagging bones. Half comatose, I fumbled for the light switch on the wall inside of this, the blackest of all soulless abysms. Left side: nothing. Right: zippo. So I checked the wall outside of the doorjamb. Nothing but an empty stretch of switchless wasteland. I checked inside a second time, but found nothing.

Then something tapped my face and flew away! In the dark of that old place, it could have been anything: fly, roach, restless spirit, feather held aloft by some pantless pervert. I felt my face and found nothing had landed there. Then it tapped again! I flailed my arms in front of me and connected with a string. I grabbed it and fondled the end, which was capped in a little plastic Hershey's Kiss. Was it a trap? I tugged experimentally. Suddenly there was light, and I sighed with relief when I found no Lowlands Norman Bates waiting for me there.

Hurriedly, I peeled away the layers of garments sticking to my unwashed skin and hopped into the shower. There didn't seem to be any knob to pull or twist but rather a white plastic box high on the wall, sporting a number of buttons and dormant lights, and a white plastic showerhead attached to a long, ropey umbilical cord. I pressed what looked like it might be an ON button. The coldest water, piped directly over four and a half thousand miles from the snowcapped peaks of the Himalayas, spat and dribbled incontinently onto my nakedness.

I crushed myself into the cold glass corner, trying to spare as many inches of bare skin as I could, and waited it out. And then I waited. And waited some more. Was it getting warmer? Or was that just the freezing hot burn of frostbite? Nope. If anything, it was getting colder.

I pressed the buttons on and off, but to no avail. I looked for knobs. There was a dial that you could spin with markers for hot and cold, but this seemed to exist purely for mockery's sake. It was after at least ten minutes that I finally accepted defeat. If I positioned my body under that, it was sure to be the last thing I ever did.

I turned it off, cried a little bit, and then used the one free, individually wrapped wet wipe I had gotten from the airplane. I scrubbed at my most odiferous areas in receding order of cleanliness, folding the rectangle over and over again, until it was a postage stamp clutched between two pincerlike fingers with which I dabbed at my nethers.

I wondered then if all the water was cold—perhaps there was a hot water curfew? But it was only 8:35 at night, so I tried the sink tap, turning the left of two small spigots for the hot water. Lo and behold, water gushed forth, and in no time at all it was as if fresh from a boiling kettle. Thank God! At least I could wash my face and soothe my throbbing temples.

I realized quickly that there was an issue here too. Because of course there was. It was so very hot that it was cooking my skin from the bone, and I couldn't stand to cup it in my hands, let alone splash my face in it. Rather than one central faucet that combined both hot and cold, from which one could adjust the temperature with a turn of the knob to better suit the limits of the human body, there were two small separate taps, each with a knob that spoke only on, off, and pressure wash.

Why, I asked myself. Why would they do this? Why, when we can fly a man to the moon, and Netflix can send nonstop bingeable entertainment *through the air* with the single click of a button— why has Britain continued on in the dark ages of plumbing when the technology for combined taps exists? I turned on the right spigot and got the Himalayan water. I cupped my hands, moving them quickly between the two faucets to try to mix the water—searing, glacial, searing, glacial—and splashed my face while I sucked in air and shouted obscenities. This did not soothe my nerves.

My hair had gotten wet from the flapping, and I couldn't sleep with a wet head, so I dug around in my bag and retrieved my brand-new, purpose-bought, AV-adaptable hair dryer and a round brush for smoothing, so that I wouldn't look like Don King in the morning, but was there a power outlet to be found anywhere in the bathroom? Yes. Yes there was. *But* it had ugly little plugholes and a sign that read SHAVERS ONLY. I tried to jam my dryer in anyway, not caring anymore if I short-circuited the electricity for the entire wretched town, but it wouldn't fit, no matter how I pleaded with it.

Again I asked myself, why? I would discover on my trip that there were no power outlets in the bathrooms, in *any* bathrooms in the whole country, for safety reasons. However, I wondered then, and wonder still: If the entirety of the US is still alive and kicking, and has somehow managed, with their combined IQ average of "bumpkin," to escape frying themselves into extinction with a great bathroom electrocution pogrom, then surely so too can the UK? Is there nothing to be said for natural selection?

I unplugged my bedside lamp and used the hair dryer in the dark, which didn't much matter, because the only mirror in the room was in the bathroom. I ended up looking like a downcast Don King anyway.

I was later informed that there is *another* white cotton string that dangles from the ceiling, and this must be pulled in order to get hot water in the shower. Was it near the shower? No. No, it was not. It hung lazily in the corner attached to an unassuming white box on the ceiling the size of a mouse trap, with no sign or indicator of any kind. Another thing that I learned was that the bathroom is not called a bathroom, but instead the room—in its entirety—is most often called a "toilet."

It's times like these where I sing out in grateful thanks for the Revolutionary War.

CHAPTER 8

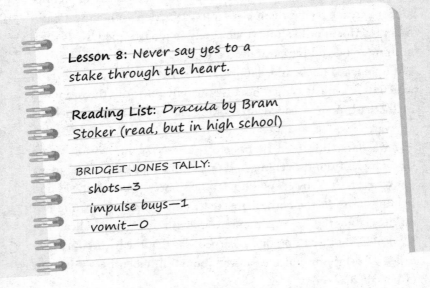

Lesson 8: Never say yes to a stake through the heart.

Reading List: *Dracula* by Bram Stoker (read, but in high school)

BRIDGET JONES TALLY:
shots—3
impulse buys—1
vomit—0

"Ahoy!" he said with a morning zeal that I found repugnant. "How are you feeling, Alice Cooper? Did you manage to get some kip last night?"

"I did. You'll find that I'm not as easy to rile up today."

"Aww, don't spoil all the fun." His tone seemed to be good-natured, but I knew it for what it was—a threat. He would try extra hard.

"Here. Try this." He held out a black canvas duffel bag as the corner of his mouth ticked up. "It won't withstand direct cannon fire but is also significantly less likely to inflict spinal damage."

It was nice and helpful. I knew it was. And yet his smug tone rankled me. I had always thought of myself as a mature sort of person—an adult, surely—but somehow in front of this man and his stupid smirk, I was no more self-possessed than Veruca Salt on a tour of the chocolate factory.

"I don't want this. It smells like . . ." I stuck my face near the open zipper and breathed in. *Heaven. Cedar. The inside of Jamie Fraser's shirt collar.* "Like feet. And smug sanctimony." I held it out to him, but he made no move to take it back. In truth, I didn't want to give it back. What I wanted was to take it to my room and zip my whole head inside of it. *Well, that's unfortunate.*

"Here. I'm sure you need your bag. I'll buy something along the way."

"Ach, go on, ya wee numpty. Surely no one could actually be this stubborn. Go on back to your room, repack your cauldron and broomsticks, and then throw your ridiculous tank of a suitcase in the bin. Okay? See you outside in fifteen minutes."

Annoyingly, he walked off before I got a chance to make any other stupid objections or demand that my father buy me the whole chocolate factory. He was right, obviously, so I did as I was told. But why did he have to be so bossy and superior about it?

It was a new day, and I had slept, I reminded myself. I could do better. While I would find it physically impossible to thank this man verbally, I resolved to be a better person and buy him a thank-you coffee or beer, or whatever the beast drank—children's tears? human blood?

THE PLAN WAS to start day two at the gorgeous ruins of Melrose Abbey, drinking coffees and eating pastries as we wandered the grounds. And that is exactly what we did, but only after a bit of a scuffle.

We found a little café in town and had put our drink and cake orders in before waiting outside, when Doris's little terrier, Percy, took an instant dislike to a passing German shepherd, despite the much larger dog minding his own damned business.

Percy took to the air in attack mode. Time slowed like in *The Matrix*. Percy flew toward the shepherd's face, mouth open, teeth bared, and Doris, leash in hand, went flying right along with him. We all gasped and yelled *Nooooo!!*, also in slow motion. I grabbed for Doris but wasn't fast enough. Luckily, our guide snatched out with lightning speed and caught a windmilling arm, stopping her before she could fall on a bad knee or hip.

While we worried over Doris, the dogs began a fight that sounded like they were ripping each other's throats out. The other dog owner—another tiny, fluffy-white-haired lady—was screaming as if she was witnessing a decapitation.

Both leashes had been dropped, and now the dogs spun in a bundle of fur and fury, saliva slinging in all directions, lassoing tables and chairs with loose leashes and knocking over two large planters. The little woman looked down at the ruined pansies and screamed again at the humanity of it all.

I came to my senses and leaped forward to try to do . . . *Crap. What now?* They were spinning so quickly that I didn't know where to grab without being caught in the crossfire. With Doris secured, our guide came over, threw himself in the scrum, and managed to tackle Percy. This gave the shepherd a chance to shuffle away sideways with his back arched and his tail between his legs. The little lady grabbed his leash and shuffled away sideways as well, while she and Doris shouted out random apologies to each other, to the café owners, and to everyone else within a mile radius.

We checked Percy over afterward, who looked very proud of himself. There wasn't even a scratch on him. I did at this time notice that Percy's official "service dog" vest looked suspiciously like a regular harness with the words SERVICE DOG embroidered by a shaky hand.

"Oh, they never do draw blood, do they? It's just a lot of noise and bravado."

"Fool dog!" Agatha said straight to Percy. "You should have been left at home."

Flossie reached down to Percy and covered his ears. "Oh. Aggie, don't. Poor dear. I think he just wants to be taken seriously." Her brows pinched. "I know exactly how you feel, Percy." She scratched his ears until his foot kicked. "I think you're very big and brave."

"That's right. Think he's probably got something to prove since I had his nuts chopped off, haven't you, Percy?" Doris laughed. Agatha's face pursed like a lemon in the sun.

ONCE OUR NERVES settled and no one was any longer at risk of fainting, we went along to the ruins of Melrose Abbey and looked up in wonder, letting the warm drinks soothe us. The weather was beautiful, and the birds were singing. Berrta, of course, was elated to tell us all about the birds that roosted in the arches. Then a light shower came along and nudged us on our way.

I felt . . . lighter. Better than I had in a long time. It was a beautiful morning, I had gotten some food and sleep, and these ladies (and their loathsome leader) were keeping me too busy to worry over what my life had become and where it was going, or to picture Hunter down on one knee holding my ring out to Misty's boobs. This could still work. Perhaps it wasn't exactly what I had pictured, but it was already starting to work, wasn't it?

We crossed the border into England and drove on through Northumberland National Park, past Newcastle, and stopped in Durham for lunch and an afternoon's wandering. A wide river hugged along the city's curves and cliffs, its large stone bridge welcoming us in. Carved into the bridge was a passage from Sir Walter Scott. After the intimacy of exploring his library, it felt like a note from an old friend.

I went wild taking photos. I had to pinch myself. So this is what a vacation felt like. I was beginning to understand what all the fuss was about.

We continued south to finish our day in the charming fishing town of Whitby. Just before we made it into town, our driver pulled off the road to make an unexpected stop. It was dusk. Eerie purple light filtered through the dancing trees, and in the bus we needed the glow of the lamps to see properly. He turned around slowly in his squeaky chair, stood dramatically, pulled an old book from behind his back, and, with no intro or explanation, began to read us a passage from Bram Stoker's *Dracula*.

Stopped there on the side of the road with the sky darkening outside, and the bus deadly silent but for his deep voice resonating low and heavy, he read us a creepy passage with a grim theatrical flair that made the hairs raise on my arms, his blue eyes dark and flashing with mischief. When he was done, there was a full minute of silence. Then the group began to applaud enthusiastically, and even I had to give in and join them. He swept an invisible cape into a deep bow.

"Now, for those of you who have traveled with me before, you'll know that every once in a while I like to surprise you with something that is not on the itinerary. Tonight is one of those nights. Whitby served as inspiration and partial setting for Bram Stoker's *Dracula*, and a festival was created to celebrate the connection—the Whitby Goth Weekend. Perhaps this isn't a festival that many of you would go to of your own accord, but it will be a perfect opportunity for a spooky tour, and an evening stroll to a night bazaar. The people watching will be the best bit. Attendees work all year on their costumes. They're really quite extraordinary.

"So . . ." he continued with a hint of challenge in his voice, "for those of you brave enough to participate, we will be arriving at the inn shortly, where you will have a chance to change and gather your things before we head out." After a moment he added, "I would recommend wearing your darkest clothes and heaviest makeup." All the ladies started to chat excitedly while we got back on the road. A smile stretched so wide across my face that I didn't even try to hide it.

WE WERE TOLD to meet at the bar in the inn. As I waited to see how many of us would show, I began to fret. *Is this going to be just the two of us again? Oh God.* I had worn my heeled black leather boots with gray skinny jeans and a black silk top with a trim of eyelash lace lining the deep V of the neck. *Why on earth did I have to wear this stupid smokey eyeliner and blood red lipstick? Maybe I can still sneak out.*

Across the bar, he was laughing while talking to some older local man, and I saw him falter when I arrived. He quieted for a second or two before remembering that he was in the middle of a sentence. *Crap. He's seen me now. No escape.*

To my relief, every single one of the ladies turned up over the course of the next ten minutes, all in dark clothes—some casual in jeans, while others who put in more effort looked decidedly spooky, like reverse Miss Havishams, in black instead of white. I loved it! Berrta, true to form, wore khakis, sensible shoes, and a brown sweater.

Our ghoulish guide wore a smart, dark gray tweed jacket and a pinstripe vest, with buttons opened at the white shirt collar and his hair coiffed at an angle like a rakish Victorian gentleman. Under different circumstances, perhaps in a parallel universe where he was mute, I might have admitted to my heart stopping for just a moment. As it was, however, his personality had precluded me from feeling even the slightest stirring of lust. Well . . . perhaps just one tiny stirring, but it was quickly snuffed out by the irritated indignation that I had been storing and stoking carefully since our first encounter.

We were led to a nearby seafood restaurant on the wharf with stunning views over the water. Striking curved beams in light wood provided a dramatic ribcage to the room. Before the food even arrived, I had already inhaled two of the most heavenly cocktails I had ever tasted. They were serving a special cocktail list for the festival, and I chose one with blood orange, thyme, and gin called The Blood Vow. It was a luxurious, deep-garnet color, in every way the perfect complement to the salt air, seafood, and electricity the festival brought to the evening.

By the end of the meal, I had had four cocktails and a deadly Stake Through the Heart shot that Helena had treated us all to a round of. I wasn't usually so heavy-handed with the drinks, but I had been building steam like a pressure cooker, and it felt good to finally relax and celebrate the beginning of my first ever real adventure.

Like it or not, I was starting a new chapter in my life. Why not turn over a new leaf? I wanted to be the girl who did all the things she wished she could do, instead of the girl who just wistfully wrote her wishes down in a sad, premature bucket list. And there I was, traveling across Great Britain, finally the heroine of my own story. It was worth commemorating.

Besides, I would stop before I lost control, as I always did. And I was having fun with the ladies. We were all getting to know one another better, and their personalities were starting to shine through. I no longer had to check my list to remember their names. As we all relaxed into our cocktails, sharing stories and telling jokes, our volume turned up and so did the laughter.

Afterward, we walked slowly through the streets and listened to stories about Bram Stoker and the bloodlust of the Victorian era. I floated along merrily on the fumes of blood orange cocktails as we discussed our favorite Gothic tales, old and new, from *The Turn of the Screw* to *Mexican Gothic*.

The costumes transported us to an underworld whose inhabitants reveled in a strange and ghoulish beauty. Big, billowing corseted gowns, silk top hats, elaborate hair, masks and makeup—they were incredible, from the gorgeous and opulent to the truly terrifying and everything in between. On the hill, the sharp teeth of the ruined Whitby Abbey bit at the sky above us, lit up in purples, greens, and blues.

We found our way to the bazaar and split naturally into groups that merged and divided again as we perused the offerings: black lace parasols, creepy antiquated medical equipment, corsets, hats, Victorian taxidermy, and rows upon rows of books.

I found a beautiful copy of *The Picture of Dorian Gray* from 1892, bound in dark sapphire leather with faded gold gilding and gorgeous marbled edges, and fell helplessly under its spell. It smelled divine, like a shadowy library with a roaring fire. I paid a small fortune for it in a giddy rush of longing. I probably would have been able to prevent this if not for the blood cocktails. But every time I remembered it there in my handbag, I got a little excited flutter of buyer's ecstasy in my stomach, like a new romance waiting to be explored.

It was a short walk back, and we decided to stop for one last drink before turning in. We picked an ancient pub that was all worn stone flagging and black wood. We had to duck to get in.

"Our shout," called Madge. "What's your poison, Alice?"

"Hmm . . . a half-pint of cider, I think."

"Just a half?"

"'Fraid so. Whitby is getting a little bit spinny."

She laughed and clapped me on the back. "Half-pint it is, then."

We were there just long enough to finish one drink, but in that time my voice began to slur at the edges and the room slid under my feet.

Oh boy, what did they put in those cocktails? Gin. The answer was gin.

I got up to use the restroom and bumped hard into the doorway with my shoulder, reeling off like a pinball in the direction of the toilet. I don't know how long I sat there to pee, but my eyes were stinging from my tussle with the doorframe, and before I knew what was happening, tears were sliding down my face in earnest.

It had been a long time since I had gone out like this . . . without Hunter. I was having a great time, but it felt odd and disconcerting to not have him at my side. The gin was really soaking in now, and as the room swirled past, so did my poor excuse for a life, each failure present in vivid detail.

What would I do when the trip was over? When all the busy magic of traveling had come to an end and I had to go back home to no fiancé, no job, no prospects, and having squandered most of the little savings I had left? I just didn't understand how I had gotten to this place. I had worked so hard. I had done everything I was supposed to do. Now it was all gone.

Booze sometimes makes me a bit emotional, so there I was, resting my head on the side of the cubicle, pants around my ankles, crying heartily, when I heard the door creak open. I sniffled and gulped in a useless effort to be quiet, but I heard a little tap on the door.

"Alice, dear? Is that you in there?" a voice that was Helena's asked.

I tried to answer but succeeded only in making various squeaks and wet noises.

"What's the matter, darling? Why don't you come on out here, and we'll wash your face and have a chat? Hmm? Doesn't that sound nice?"

I weighed my options, but knew I didn't have many. I could sob in there on the toilet with the door locked until the barkeep finally broke it down at closing, or I could pull my pants up, blow my nose, dry my eyes, and go back out there before I made a melodramatic opera of myself.

A few minutes later, I was slightly drier and standing in front of the mirror next to Helena.

"There . . ." She washed my face with a damp hand towel. "Now, do you want to have a little heart-to-heart about what has made you so upset, or do you want to head back out there and talk about it another time?"

I knew if I talked to her that I would spiral all the way back down, and we'd spend the better part of an hour here in the stale, pee-tinged air of the women's lavatory.

"Thank you, Helena. That's so nice. I think I'd rather talk 'bout it another day, and go head on back to the inn now." *Wow—I sound super sober! I'm doing a really good job. I wonder if she can tell I'm swaying. Probably not.* "You're s'beautiful," I added. "So elegant." I began touching her hair uninvited. "I hope I look like you when I'm old."

She laughed. "Well, part of that was nice. Let's focus on the positive, shall we? Now, let's fix you up so that you're ready to face the world. Stand there, and let me see what I can do."

She took out an expensive compact, and expertly dabbed my face back to a normal hue. "I've certainly got a lot to work with here. Porcelain skin, lovely cheekbones, Cupid's bow lips . . ." She blotted on a beautiful shade of Chanel lipstick in a soft rosy pink that made me look as if I'd just been thoroughly kissed. I smiled a shaky smile at her, thanking her for the compliments while she pulled out her mascara. ". . . the biggest, most beautiful almond-shaped hazel eyes I think I've ever seen . . . and this thick, glossy mane of auburn hair that makes every lady on the bus green with envy." She combed her fingers through my messy waves, forcing them into submission. It felt good.

"Thank you." I hugged her, and almost cried again, but before I could she marched me out of the restroom and back to the table with a fresh glass of water. I tried my best to blend in with the wall while the ladies collected their purchases and readied themselves to leave.

"Robbie, dear. Would you be a gentleman and help the gorgeous Alice back to the inn? She's a little unsteady in those boots after such a long day." She kindly avoided the descriptor *sloppy drunk*, which would have been far more accurate.

His mouth tightened. "Of course I will." He stood up and offered me his arm, but I hoisted myself up onto my heels and waved him away.

"No, thank you. Totally . . ."—*what's the word again?*—"unnecessary. I'll do jusfine on my own, fank you very much."

He stood disbelieving, arm held out to me until I pushed past him. I heard him call out my name and took it as a cue to move faster.

Some of the hills are steep in Whitby, and unfortunately in my lifetime I had earned myself the reputation as a toppler, even when sober. I don't know why, but every once in a while, one of my ankles goes rogue, and I collapse in a heap. I also do not always look where I am going. If to this mix you add high heels and alcohol, the chances that I will topple shift squarely from possible to inevitable.

When I did trip, I came down hard and into a puddle. *Why is the ground always so wet here when I fall on it?* The ladies hurried over flapping and screeching like worried geese, but he was there in a flash, quickly lifting and moving me to a step where I could sit and lick my wounds.

"I think . . . I think I just need a minute here. To rest. You sh'go on. Get the group home. I'm really okay. I'll be there in . . . a minute."

He laughed at that. "Christ, you're stubborn. No chance. Just wait here. Don't even think about moving." He raised his eyebrow then in a stern threat, waiting to see if I would disobey. I nodded, and he went to talk to Helena, telling them to carry on the short distance back and making sure that they knew the way.

He sat by me and draped his jacket over my shoulders. It was nice to have a human body next to mine, warming me on one side, even if it was *his* (mostly human) body. I'm not sure how long we sat there in silence, him eventually flipping through a book he had bought at the market, and me with my eyes closed, trying to make my head stop spinning. Did I fall asleep at some point? I don't remember. But of one thing I am absolutely certain: I did not vomit there down the stairs, nor at any point that evening, and it is, to this day, a glowing source of pride for me.

We hobbled home. I'd ripped a small tear in the knee of my jeans, and though both knees were wet from the fall, one stuck fast to the fabric and pulled a bit painfully at each step with what I suspected was drying blood.

After another threatening look that made me think he would have made an excellent schoolteacher, I put my hand in the crook of his arm to hold on to in case my ankles should conspire to fell me again. He put his other hand over mine to make good and sure that it wouldn't slip away unexpectedly. The warmth of it traveled right up my arm.

I gave his bicep a bit of a feel through his crisp white shirt. It was so solid and smooth, and my hand was already right there. How could I help myself? I had hoped the grope would go unnoticed, but I saw his signature smirk on his lips before I turned away.

We managed the stairs slowly, but saw none of the ladies milling about the bar or hallways; they must all have gone to bed. He dropped me off at my room, opening the door for me. He knew I'd never manage the fiddly keys.

"Alright then, there you are. Now promise to drink plenty of water before bed. We don't want any sore heads the morrow. Okay? I'm just down the hall in room fourteen if you need anything."

I nodded and went in as he closed the door behind me. It wasn't long before I realized I couldn't get my jeans off. They were tight and wet and stuck to the scab on my knee, and I was very drunk indeed. I had gotten one boot off. It was too painful to bend my knee to remove the other one. I tried to unzip the long boot zipper a few times with the toes of my other liberated foot, but only succeeded in falling over very slowly.

I sat for a minute or two and considered my options. I couldn't get into the bed with a shoe and muddy jeans. I could sleep on the ground, but the old wooden flooring was terribly cold and uneven, and even with the booze and exhaustion, I knew I would feel like death in the morning. I needed the bed.

All the ladies would have been sleeping soundly by then. I didn't like it, but there was nothing I could do. The alcohol had long ago flushed away the majority of my inhibitions. I needed help, and there was only one person I could ask.

CHAPTER 9

Lesson 9: Dress for the job you want,
but avoid aspirational underwear.

BRIDGET JONES TALLY:
impure thoughts—6? no, 8

I put my top back on, walked a few doors over, and rapped quietly at his door before heading back toward my room. He came out, buttoning his shirt back up and calling softly after me.

"Alice? What's the matter?"

"I need help," I slurred in a stage whisper as I walked back to my room, leaving the door open behind me. I didn't want to have to explain in the hall. Also, I knew it would annoy him to have to follow without an explanation, and this brought an added bonus to the situation.

When he walked in, I was already unbuttoning my jeans. A dark flash of something indiscernible crossed his face. Then his brow furrowed, and a sudden frown made his mouth austere.

I laughed and then started hiccupping. "Look at you! Oh, don't be such a prude. It's nothing *lascivious*." I drew out the word, teasing him. "I just need help getting undreshed." I hiccupped again. "That'sall."

"You said you needed help. Is this what you meant?" Not moving an inch closer, he stretched an arm against the doorjamb and gave me a steely look.

"Well, I can't go to bed with one boot and muddy clothes on, can I?" My diaphragm betrayed me with another hiccup. "My jeans are wet, and it hurts to bend my knee, and I think . . . *hiccup*. I think a scab healed over with my jeans attached, and I can't pull 'em off."

He said nothing.

"It hurts," I added for good measure.

"We'll have to get one of the ladies . . . I'll wake Helena."

"No, don't wake anyone. It's late, and they're sleeping. I'd rather juss stay awake all night than drag Helena outta bed and make her pull the dirty scab off my knee. I may as well ask the queen to floss my teeth!" I waved my arm theatrically and punctuated it with another hiccup for emphasis. He looked unmoved. "Look. I need a favor. I'm asking you . . . Please."

He let out a big sigh and walked over. "Fine. I'll have a look at your knee, at least."

"Well, close the door. I can't just get undressed with the door open."

"No." His tone told me there would be no argument.

He turned on the bedside lamp, pushed me carefully by my hips back against the tall bed, and kneeled down to take a look at the wound. He worked his fingers into the ripped hole in the denim and tried to pull it away to get a better look, but stopped at a hiss from me.

"Okay. Don't move. I'll be right back."

He returned with a glass of cool water and a warm, damp face cloth. "Drink this, all of it, and don't move your leg." His commanding tone made my stomach flutter. He gave me a look of warning as if he expected me not to listen, but I was far more biddable when drunk.

He knelt down and held the warm cloth against my knee with a firm hand. His other hand cupped around the back of my leg to keep me still. It warmed my whole body through. I sank further back, closed my eyes, and enjoyed the moment. He began very gently to wipe at the wound with the cloth, pulling the denim away little by little. It didn't hurt so much now, and it was over quickly. He stuck his fingers in the hole of the cloth and tested again, finding that it pulled away easily.

"Can you do the rest from here?"

"Nope. It hurts to bend my knee."

He searched my face before letting out a reluctant sigh. "Right." He crossed over and turned off the lamp, plunging the room into near darkness. Only the soft light of the hallway helped us make out the shape of each other.

"What are you doing?"

"Shh." He shushed me for the second time in as many days. But this time it sounded different.

He was very careful getting my boot off. Then he stepped closer and put his hands on my hips. "Stand straight for me." He pulled me a few inches away from the bed and put my hands on his shoulders to steady me. I caught the smell of him—spicy and warm, like the woods after a summer rain.

I had already unbuttoned and unzipped my jeans, and he curled his fingers under the waistband and started to pull them down. In a frantic moment of dread, I remembered I had worn my red thong to avoid any visible panty lines, and wished fervently that I had worn something with full-cheek coverage. *Oops*, I thought, and then giggled a little.

"Quit that."

With his hands on either side of me, careful not to pull my underwear down with the jeans, his fingers moved between my skin and the tight denim as he slid them slowly down my body. I felt his warm breath on my exposed thighs. My pulse raced while everything else in the world slowed down, each second playing out languidly—strong hands, slow breaths, exposed skin.

The muscles of his broad shoulders shifted under my hands as he knelt in front of me, his face, his mouth, so close. Electricity combed over my skin with a sharp, almost painful scratch and settled with a live current at my middle.

I hadn't realized it would be like this. I hadn't meant to feel this way. Thank God the lights were off so he couldn't see the longing written across every line of my face.

When he got to my knee, he stopped and stretched the leghole wide so that it didn't scrape against my wound as he pulled the jeans further down. Both hands slid over the long length of calf before releasing one leg, then the next. Then he stood up and pushed me carefully back against the bed, folded my jeans, and put them aside.

"Thank God." My voice was a throaty sigh.

Rather than me clambering into bed with one straight leg, showcasing my thong-clad behind in the scuffle, he sat me on the bed, picked up both legs, and swung them easily up to the mattress. He put me under the covers and made sure that I was decent before turning the lamp back on. The smell of him was an opiate.

"I'm gonna get you another glass of water."

I nodded.

After returning with the water, he instructed me to drink, then untucked the sheets from the bottom of the bed and folded them up to expose my legs to the knees, keeping the rest modestly covered. With the light on and the jeans off, he brought the warm cloth back to my skin to wash the wound, carefully wiping away bits of dirt and fuzz from the open sore. I closed my eyes and forgot everything else.

"You smell like . . . a really sexy lumberjack."

He looked up at me for a moment, taken by surprise. Then all the worry and seriousness that had tightened the lines of his face and body suddenly melted away. His shoulders began to shake. A quiet chuckle rumbled deep in his chest. I was laughing too. Then I collapsed back on the pillows and covered my eyes with a hand while I gave in.

We said nothing else. He carried on cleaning my knee and laughing to himself. It was so blissful being looked after that I drifted off to sleep, and stirred only when I heard the latch of the door close softly behind him.

"Thank you," I whispered, but he was already gone.

CHAPTER 10

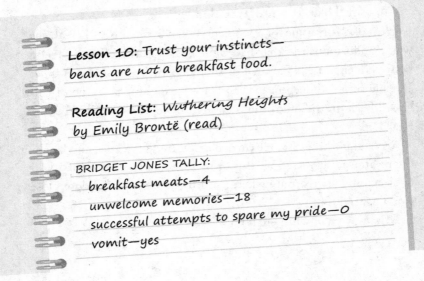

Lesson 10: Trust your instincts— beans are *not* a breakfast food.

Reading List: *Wuthering Heights* by Emily Brontë (read)

BRIDGET JONES TALLY:
breakfast meats—4
unwelcome memories—18
successful attempts to spare my pride—0
vomit—yes

I was awakened the next morning at what must have been the crack of dawn by a persistent knocking at the door. I sat up quickly, my head pounding in angry protest.

"Just a minute." I sounded like a frog with a smoking problem. I swung my legs down and gasped at the unexpected pain in my knee, then threw on some pajama bottoms and opened the door.

It was room service. A young man wheeled in a tray, lifting the cover to reveal an obscene amount of food: a full English breakfast with eggs, toast, sausage, ham, bacon, roasted mushrooms and tomatoes, more meat, and I don't even know what else. *Are those baked beans? Beans?* Also included in the feast were a large glass of orange juice and a huge mug of strong coffee with a note next to it. *Fuel up! We've got a full day, and we leave in one hour sharp.*

Something began to tug uncomfortably at the corners of my memory.

"It's from the gentleman downstairs," the server said in a thick Yorkshire accent. I mumbled something even I couldn't understand and tipped him one of those huge two-pound coins before sending him on his way.

With the room to myself, I went to the bathroom to wash my face. That's when it all started coming back to me, one nonsequential jigsaw piece at a time, falling in place to create a most humiliating image.

Oh, the crying in the bathroom! The fall! I looked down and saw a bandage on my sore knee.

OH.

MY.

GOD.

I forced him to undress me! The red thong! Oh, holy crap! This is bad . . . this is very, very bad!

This was even worse than that time I drunkenly sent several boudoir shots of myself in sexy lingerie to my boyfriend David and then woke the next day to a very cold and displeased professional response from Dr. *Davis* underneath my typo-ridden *Howm do you like my new linguine?* I didn't often get drunk, and this was exactly why.

My first reaction was denial: Maybe I had dreamed the whole thing. But no, all the evidence was there in my room. Next was flight: Maybe I could just feign serious illness and tell them to go on without me. Then I would only need to find my way back to Edinburgh, change my plane tickets, and get home just in time to die slowly of mortification and excessive Tater Tots consumption.

I thought over my options while I choked down my delicious breakfast. By the end of the last sausage, I had come to the sorry conclusion that I had no real options. I would just have to suck it up and stick it out.

I came downstairs wearing all black to mourn my dignity, and with sunglasses on to hide my red, swollen eyes. I heard some greetings and saw some waves as I got on the bus and sat on my usual bench. My own personal terrorist turned around in the driver's seat to look at me.

"Good morning, Alice Cooper," he said. Then more softly, "How are you managing?"

"Mm-hmm," I mumbled from behind my sunglasses.

I felt my cheeks redden. I wanted to own my poor behavior. I wanted to thank him for helping me against his better judgment. I wanted to explode into a fit of gasping laughter and have a laugh with him at my expense. But now that I was in front of him, I was on fire from head to toe and squirming under a fresh surge of humiliation as flashes of last night's depantsing danced to the front of my mind. So instead I just crumpled in on myself.

He looked at me a moment longer.

"Thank you . . . for breakfast." I wanted to curl up and die.

I saw a mischievous smile play at the corner of his mouth, but he seemed to think better of teasing me, because he turned back around to hide it.

"Welcome." He started the bus and drove off. And yet somehow I felt the reprieve was temporary.

Still slightly drunk and spinning, I slouched down on my bench and promptly went to sleep. I don't know how long I slept, whether it was hours or minutes, but I was woken rather suddenly by a lurching. A lurching of the stomach. One that cleared its throat, politely tapped on my shoulder, and whispered into my ear with the voice of Benedict Cumberbatch: "Hmm hmm . . . umm . . . excuse me, but I thought I should inform you that I've chosen to reject this, your most recent deposit, and will be ejecting it posthaste from whence it came."

Oh no, you damn well won't! I hissed back to my stomach. *Betray me now and so help me God, I will get a gastric bypass.* I squeezed my eyes shut and tried to go back to sleep. If I could ride out this wave of nausea, then I'd wake up later having been through the worst of it, and would be able to handle myself admirably with decorum and grace—rising above in the face of adversity. Mind over matter was all that was needed here. Totally achievable.

Just then, the bus began to hug the corners of a particularly windy stretch of single-track road, and all the sausages in my stomach rode on a tidal wave of blood orange cocktail and baked beans from side to side.

I opened my mouth to speak but shut it immediately, not trusting that I could successfully control the floodgates. Instead I reached a shaky, damp hand and clasped on to the shoulder in front of me with a death grip.

"Yes?" When I didn't respond, he looked back in his mirror and saw the look on my face. "Right, ladies. I've just got to make a brief pit stop and check the . . . washer fluid. I think the view over the fields to the right side is a lovely one. I would recommend gazing out in that general direction to ponder life's greatest questions."

The second the door opened, I flew out of it to vomit zealously into a regretfully spiny bush with yellow flowers that smelled of co-conut.

I was a scene from *Poltergeist*. There was no earthly explanation for this. I looked over between bone-cracking, full-body heaves to see that he had lifted the hood of the bus and was making a show of looking under it. He really needn't have bothered. I had waved goodbye to any hope of self-respect the night before, and shot it several times in the back for good measure.

His voice reached me from another world. "Are you gonna be okay? Can I get you anything?" I heard him draw near, and then felt a hand on my upper back.

The very last thing I would wish for at that moment was for him to see me vomiting. Had I not debased myself enough in front of the man that he should see—and hear—this?

"I need you . . ." I said, stopping to gag.

"Yes? What can I do?"

"To go away. Now."

"Ach. Don't worry yourself. I was a teenager in Glasgow. I've seen and done far gruesomer things than this."

I didn't care about his teenage vomiting sessions. I would do anything to just make him leave immediately and not see any more of the horror. I prayed that a tsunami would come suddenly to Yorkshire and scrub me from the face of the Earth.

"Would you . . . shut up? Leave me alone."

"But . . ."

"Go away," I gasped. "You fool."

For a moment he said nothing, but when he did speak, his tone had changed. And I could *hear* the smirk in it.

"Fine then. Just be careful not to make us late *again*, will you?"

Is nothing sacred? Can't a woman be shown respect while vomiting down the side of a mountain these days?

"I hate you." It was all I could muster to convey the depths of my loathing.

"No, you don't. It's sounding a lot like you hate those blood orange cocktails, though." He laughed.

I turned around and let my scowl do the talking for me, mostly because I couldn't think of anything to say that sounded superior while I was busy throwing up. He laughed at my anger, the respectful reprieve and distance he had chosen before clearly forgotten.

Heaving my way into oblivion with my face getting poked by a really thorny bush while some sadistic megalomaniac looked on and teased me was most certainly not included on my list of things to do on my trip to the UK.

I waved him off wordlessly and silently dedicated all upcoming upheavals to him.

"Vy are some of us getting out and not others?" I heard a German voice from the open door of the bus. "Are ve supposed to go out?"

"No, Berrta. Please stay in. I'll not be a moment."

"Alice is out. I think either ve should all be allowed to go out, or all of us stay on the bus."

"I'm sorry, but there's not much room at the side of the road just here, and I want everyone to be safe, and ready to go soon. Alice just needed a little fresh air."

"I don't see vy it should have different rules for different people. If some are allowed to break the rules, then this is not a rule."

Couldn't they hear me retching? I could hear them.

"She had her camera with her," Agatha said. My eyes widened. Was she purposely stirring trouble? "I'm sure I heard her say something about a rare chaffinch."

"Vhat?" Berrta exclaimed loudly. "There is no rare chaffinch. She doesn't know vhat she's talking about." I heard the squeak of her window being pulled down so she could shout out of it. "Alice! Vhat bird did you see? Is it still there? Alice, there is no rare chaffinch. Your identification is wrong! Describe the plumage to me."

In mounting frustration, she updated the group. "She is not responding to me. I see her there with her head in the bushes. I am sure she is looking at something. Alice! Alice, can you hear me? Has it got a yellow crest? Vhat color is the breast?"

Finally finished with my grand performance, I struggled just to stand upright and walk back to the bus like a convincing biped without also trying to convince Berrta that none of what I had seen in the last five minutes would interest her.

My head was throbbing. I grasped the railing and used the last vestiges of my fortitude to hoist myself back on to the bus. I could have used that little step this time. I heard the hood slam shut as I slumped onto my bench.

"Did you get a photo, Alice? May I see the photo? Robbie, ve are all here to see the sights, and it is not fair that you allow some of the group to see more than the others."

"I'm very sorry, Berrta. It was an unexpected emergency stop. I understand why you're upset, and I'll try to make sure that nothing like this happens again. Don't worry, I'm sure once Alice Cooper is finished with her nap she will regale us all with detailed descriptions and photos of everything she saw. So that's something we can all look forward to." He winked at me in the rearview mirror.

It was official. He was taking the proverbial olive branch that had momentarily bridged the gap between us and setting the damned thing on fire. I pledged a solemn oath to myself then, floating as I was on the exhaust of last night's cocktails, that I would reap my revenge on this pea-brained moron, or die trying. I dug out my notebook and began to brainstorm.

THINGS TO TORTURE THE TERRIBLE TOUR GUIDE:

My head swam. I dropped my pen, placed my hot face against the cold window, and went to sleep.

WE HAD BEEN driving through the Yorkshire moors, though I had not been conscious enough to enjoy the stark and wild delights they offered. My comatose state, however, did nothing to protect me from being bodily hoisted from the cozy bus bench and dragged around the moors after the group, like a dying mouse clutched tight in the jaws of a wandering tomcat.

Oh, but they were beautiful, and after an hour's hike at the speed of banana slugs in winter, we stopped atop a rock to have a break and look over the vista.

It swept out from us in an unfathomable expanse of heather-covered rock and barren crag: untamed and unforgiving. The wind chapped our cheeks and whipped the hair about our heads like banshees. It was so easy to imagine how *Wuthering Heights* and *Jane Eyre* had sprouted and grown from this soil. Simply to sit here in silence and look out in any direction was to be consumed whole by the drama of the place.

After a time, a Scottish voice broke the reverent silence, and competed with the wind so as not to be swept away altogether.

"Charlotte Brontë wrote: 'My sister Emily loved the moors. Flowers brighter than the rose bloomed from the blackest heath for her. Out of sullen hollow in a livid hillside, her mind could make an Eden. She found in the bleak solitude many and dear delights, and best loved was liberty.'"

His talk on the Brontë sisters was interesting and inspiring and had more than a slight feminist slant, which, if offered by any other human, would have won me over to their endearments. It was a shame that this particular human was entirely devoid of endearments. Resting against the rocks, we all weighed in on which sister and which novels we liked best and why, and speculated what life would have been like for the Victorian woman in so rural a setting.

We meandered back to the bus in silence, each one of us lost in our own little world, feeling at once solitary in the universe and yet intrinsically connected to it. The effect was quite sobering and led my mental state firmly by the hand from hungover unconsciousness to pensive introspection, with a dash of melancholia.

I stared out the window and watched Britain rush by as I thought about my place here, and my place in the world at large. I felt like an untethered balloon set loose on the wind with no direction or purpose and no power to influence my course, while I watched my friends and colleagues succeed and win every milestone and accomplishment I had wanted for myself.

Being untethered was not freeing or inspiring or liberating, like Emily Brontë on the endless expanse of the moors. The result had been vertigo: terrifying and paralyzing, and so very alone.

Percy, who occasionally left Doris's side to visit his other friends, trotted over to my bench and wagged his tail. I patted the cushion next to me and he hopped up, curled at my side, and put his head on my lap. I wrapped us both up in a woolly blanket, and as I stroked his head, I felt a little bit less alone. How did dogs always know?

Percy licked my hand, and I smiled softly down at him. An hour on the moors, and I had become as morose as a Brontë character.

CHAPTER 11

We spent our afternoon in York, and I chose to wander the city on my own while the other ladies broke off in groups to explore, trading recommendations on their favorite shops and cafés, maps clutched in their fists. I heard several of them remark delightedly at how the wind of the moors had been masterfully effective at volumizing their hair: "Better than a day at the salon!" They elbowed each other, cackling merrily, as I slung my headache over my shoulder and strode in a quieter direction.

The city was enchanting. I couldn't help but take photos as I wound my way along its alleys and streets and walls. Every view was a postcard, but my focus was lackluster. My head was home in DC, trying, fumbling, and failing to untie and set straight all the knots and loose ends of my life.

I ambled through the Shambles and found myself at a picturesque little tearoom out of the way. The ceilings were low, and the walls were papered with a linen print of roses, framed by painted wooden paneling. The tablecloths were crisp, white, embroidered linen, showing off a hodgepodge of perfectly mismatched teapots, cups, saucers, and polished silver.

The warm, sharp scent of fresh tea mingled with a swirl of baked goods. I could almost taste the butter just from breathing in. A fire crackled behind a tiled Victorian grate, and there, taking advantage of the best spot in the room, was a picture-perfect English rose, perched upon a dainty perfusion of chintz, entirely at home.

Helena peered at me over her gilded teacup, a soft smile curling from her lips like the steam from her tea, and she nodded to the chair across from her. I had ducked in here to sit alone and quietly ruminate over the splintered wreckage of my life, but I could hardly refuse, particularly not when I was so grateful to her for looking after me the night before.

"Alice, how lovely. Will you join me, dear? This is my favorite café in York, and try as I might, I simply couldn't prevent myself from ordering a tower of petits fours, as well as scones and cream. I need to recruit help if I'm to make even the slightest dent." Helena's was a soothing voice, and I was comforted by the sound of it. That and the promise of hot tea and cakes.

"Thank you, Helena. I think this is just what I need." And maybe it was.

"Undoubtedly. The healing properties of piping hot tea is widely known throughout the British Isles. I'll never understand why you Americans haven't caught on."

I smiled. "I think after we dumped it in Boston Harbor, we never looked back. But my grandmother was English, from Lancaster, so I grew up with a teacup in my hand."

"Did you really? She sounds like an upstanding woman."

"She's probably the reason why I've always longed to be here. Her stories made me feel homesick for a place I'd never been."

A warm smile spread across Helena's face, and her voice changed to honey. "Then you are right where you need to be."

I grimaced. Nothing in my life was right where it needed to be. I hid my deflation in a sip of tea until I could muster a wobbly smile. We sat quietly for a moment, and I selected a few petits fours from the lacy tiers of the silver stand.

"So. Are you feeling better, dear? Would you like to talk about what has been creasing that pretty brow of yours? We can't have you making wrinkles, now can we?"

"Uh." I focused on my tea and thought over how to respond. I wasn't in the habit of unburdening myself to strangers. I wasn't even in the habit of unburdening myself to my loved ones. Typically my way of handling hardship was to grit my teeth and get on with it. But to my surprise, I felt like maybe I did want to share my troubles with this woman. The fact that she was a relative stranger made it easier somehow.

"Are you sure you know what you're getting into?"

"Oh, I'm quite sure I've heard far worse. Let's see if you can shock me." She wiggled her bottom in the chair and leaned back, as if tuning in to a juicy soap opera.

"I've just . . ." I sighed heavily. The weight of the words pushed at my chest. "Always had this plan for my life. You know? And I worked hard for it." My nose prickled. I stopped.

"Tell me."

"I used to be proud of myself. I had a good job doing things that mattered. Last spring I got engaged to my college boyfriend, Hunter. We'd been together for seven years, and we knew we would eventually get married when the time was right, so it was no surprise. The venue was booked. Invitations were sent. We were also apartment hunting to buy our first place together. Or at least I was. I did all the organizing and planning. I suppose I should have seen the red flags." I tried at a crooked smile. "When the shackle on the ball and chain began to close, Hunter started going out every night to 'blow off some steam,' and before I knew it, well . . . I was the one he was blowing off."

Helena laughed humorlessly. "Men."

"It all just fell apart, Helena. For two months, I dragged him to couples counseling and pleaded with him not to throw away the years we had spent together, the beautiful future we had been building. That didn't work, obviously. I found out later that he had been seeing a girl named Misty and her enormous breasts for months."

"What a tiresome cliché. Can't they at least get a little creative once in a while? I am sorry, dear, but good riddance, I'd say. Better to find out now."

I let out a long breath. "I suppose. But I'm about to turn thirty, and I wanted children by now. I'm going to have to start building something from scratch with someone new. All those years wasted."

"Oh, I disagree. Years are never really wasted. This seems like a good time to take a moment to focus on yourself and make yourself happy with friends, new hobbies, in your work."

I grimaced. "I have a little confession to make. Turns out it was a poor time to let my relationship woes distract me from work. I'm sorry for the lie. I couldn't bring myself to tell everyone the first time I met the group."

"Oh, Alice."

"Yeah. Before the end of the month, I had lost my fiancé, my job, the ring, the wedding, the apartment, my entire life, and my future, and I was sending out cards to inform all our wedding guests that we would not be getting married anymore, thanks for all the toasters."

With a soft smile of consolation, Helena served me another petit four. "Poor dear. When was this?"

"About six months ago now."

"And what have you been doing since then?"

I hated that question. The answer was such a painful, humiliating admission to make. I didn't want to be this person—a person to be pitied. All the same, I opened my mouth and let the truth out.

"Sleeping, mostly. You know things are rock bottom when your daily wardrobe consists of only daytime pajamas or nighttime pajamas." I laughed—dry, humorless, forced—and ducked my head. "At first I tried to fix things. I started looking for a new job immediately and went to as many interviews as would have me, but my heart wasn't in it. All I got were rejections. I decided that I needed time, so I took a little sabbatical of two months to regroup and pull myself together, which just spiraled into a six-month period of full-on depression. A couple of weeks ago, I was making some headway. I'd started making to-do lists, cleaning the apartment, and scheduling job-hunting tasks. Then I got a phone call from a mutual friend—Hunter had proposed to the woman he had cheated on me with, with my ring."

"He didn't! The cad."

I took another sip and shrugged. "Thanks. It's fine, actually. I think I'm more jealous that they have the things I wanted for myself than jealous that another woman has Hunter." It was true. I was glad of that, at least. "Anyway. I've been, well, pretty down. I think this trip is probably the first time I've left the apartment in months. If Hunter and I had ever gotten around to adopting any pets, they would have given up and eaten me."

She chuckled. "I see. So this little trip to Britain . . . it's to shake off the cobwebs?"

"Exactly. I've never been a wallower. I've tried to pick myself up and get my life back on track, and it just hasn't worked. I've just lost . . ." I felt tears sting the back of my eyes and worked to swallow them down and keep my voice steady. "Everything. All my hard work. All my careful planning. I feel like I'm left with nothing. And the longer this goes on, the harder it feels to get my life in order again." We sat in the quiet while that statement resonated, but Helena didn't move to pick the conversation up. "This trip . . . I never do things like this. It was spontaneous and unplanned and expensive. But I didn't know how else to break free of this funk I've been in. I came here to center myself, to force myself out of my comfort zone and get into the right headspace to fix my life."

I squeezed my eyes shut a moment. It was always more difficult to speak your fears aloud—it put meat on their bones somehow. "But now I'm here, and I think maybe it's all just been a big mistake. Don't get me wrong—I love it here, and the trip has been amazing so far . . . well, mostly amazing. Last night's plans for a sophisticated and educational evening may have gone *very slightly* awry." We both laughed a bit at my expense before my smile faded. The soft look returned to Helena's face, and she topped up my tea, urging me on in her quiet way.

"The thing is, I feel even more lost and confused than before. I'm afraid to face going home, because I've still got to start my life all over again, and I know when I get back everything will be just the way it was, only worse."

I stopped for a breath and crammed a chocolate petit four in my mouth to stem the tide of despair. Tears blurred the edges of my vision, and I tried my damndest not to let them fall. Helena seemed to think for a moment, sipping her tea.

"Life is . . . very hard on women, Alice. Don't make it any harder than it already is. Be patient with yourself. Good things will come."

They were nice words, but they were just platitudes, weren't they? "But everyone I know is moving on with their happy families and glittering careers and beautiful homes. And it's going to take years and lots of hard work to get back to where I was."

"Then perhaps you shouldn't be trying to get back to where you were. Perhaps it's time for something new. Find things that make you happy. A new job, a new place, a new man—or woman, for that matter. Why not see where the wind blows you for a little while?"

"I can't do that." She didn't understand. She couldn't. "I can't just throw all those years of hard work away and become someone I'm not."

"Even the most dedicated plans and heartfelt ambitions are still vulnerable to the whims of fate. Life does not always take us from point A to point B. It follows its own course. The sooner you can learn to accept this, the better." She took another sip of her tea, and when she spoke again her tone had changed. "Life is sometimes random and unexpected, and even cruel—it can give things, and take things away."

She softened then, pouring more tea for both of us before settling back into her chair. I wasn't sure what to say, so I stirred another sugar lump into my cup.

"I felt the same once, when I was young. I was very ambitious. I had a fire in my belly. It was the late seventies, and I had gotten a place at Cambridge, reading art history. I wanted to become a museum curator. But then, after my second year, I was offered a modeling contract. I didn't even think about it. I left university and began living for what felt like the first time."

"Wow." Cambridge and a modeling contract—I was impressed, but not surprised.

"I *knew* that fashion was what I was made for, and I must have had the right look at the right time, because before I knew it, I was traveling for fashion shows in Paris and photo shoots in the Mediterranean, and I was in magazines and a few television commercials for a new makeup line."

"I can only imagine that kind of lifestyle in the seventies. I'm sure you've got some amazing stories to tell."

"Oh, a lady never tells, Alice," she said, completely deadpan. I couldn't help but laugh. "But I also had my feet on the ground. I knew even then that youth and beauty fade quickly, so I took every job I could, collecting business cards as I went. I was making a name for myself. I wanted to start my own fashion magazine. By my mid-twenties, I had it all very neatly planned and had recruited a partner and a group of investors.

"So focused was I, that when a man whom I was seeing at the time . . . oh, such a terribly handsome man he was. And powerful, and so very rich. An American business tycoon. One weekend he flew me to Paris, told me that he couldn't live another day without me, and asked me to marry him."

"Paris! How romantic." I crammed more cake into my mouth. "What did you say?"

"I turned him down. I think I could have loved him; I probably would have been very happy. But getting married wasn't part of my plan yet. I was free and ambitious and enjoying the sexual liberation of the seventies—we all were. I thought that marriage would mean that I would have to make room in my life for someone else's plans and ambitions, and that it would mean children and giving up everything that I had worked for."

"I can understand that. A family always means a career setback for a woman, no matter what they say."

"And that's today. I'm sure you can imagine what it was like in the seventies. The thought of pregnancy terrified me. It seemed like a life sentence . . . servitude by a sweeter name. And it would have ruined my body for modeling. I would have to give up everything I had earned and worked for, all of my dreams, to focus on my child's life instead of my own. My own life would be over."

I knew these thoughts as intimately as if her words were mine.

"I broke his heart that day and never saw him again. That same week I was off to a photo shoot in India, and I didn't look back."

I nodded. I could see where this was going. Choosing one's career over love, and then looking back with regret. A painful story perhaps, but not a new one.

"By the end of that year, my career was going splendidly. Then one day, I was in New York for a job when I got a phone call." She stopped and stirred her tea, and I saw a flash of pain wash across her face. She cleared her throat, sipped, and went on. "It was my sister. She had gotten a cold, and the next morning her little girl found her dead in her bed—meningitis. Just like that. No warning, no explanation, just a senseless waste."

"My God." I was completely stunned. "I'm so sorry, Helena. How tragic . . ."

"She had two little girls—one was four, and the other was in her terrible twos."

"And the father?"

"He hadn't been on the scene since the divorce and had made it clear that he didn't want them, and my mother wasn't well. There was just no one else. It had to be me, and none of the railing and bargaining that I seethed with those first few months could bring her back or change a thing. I flew home the next day, and my life changed forever."

"Was there no way to keep modeling? Or get the magazine up and running?"

"I tried. I simply couldn't figure out how to salvage my career and still provide a normal, happy life for the girls. So I did the only thing I could do. I gave up everything and became a mom. I took the money I had put aside and left London for a cottage in the country. I gave myself over to raising those babies for my sister."

My mouth was open. I closed it. "How did you manage it? How did you let go of everything?"

"At first I was bitter—and furious and desperate and depressed—but of course I had to keep moving for the girls. They still had to eat and get dressed and go to school. They had to play and be happy.

And they needed me. Before I knew it, I wasn't pretending anymore. Being a mother is hard work, believe me, and I simply didn't have any time to feel sorry for myself. But—and here's the thing, Alice. I want you to listen carefully."

She paused a moment. I couldn't help but lean in across the table.

"I didn't just manage. I flourished. I was wrong when I thought I had been happy before. Maybe this doesn't sound terribly feminist or modern, and I know it's not right for everyone, but for me, I had no idea what joy and fulfillment were until I was a mother. And it was a thing that had always terrified me, something I had never wanted for myself. I would give anything to have my sister back, but if I hadn't lost her, I may never have been a mum, and that would have been a tragedy too."

"Wow. Did you do it all on your own?"

"Oh no. Well, I did at first. But I met a man a few years later, and we had three more children of our own. I simply couldn't get enough of them!"

I blew out a lung full of air and sat back in my seat. "But what about your magazine? All your plans? You don't ever regret what you lost?"

"Not for one second," she said with slow relish. "I did build another career eventually, after all the children had left home. I had become such a happy homemaker, I opened my own little interior decor shop. I love it. Everyone needs different things, and what I needed found me. I wasn't open to it, but it bulldozed its way into my life anyway. My point, my dear, is that life is chaotic and unpredictable, and sometimes through pain and tragedy we can be given something beautiful. Maybe instead of focusing on what you lost, you could focus on your newfound freedom."

I shook my head for a moment in awed disbelief and finished my tea. "I don't . . . I wouldn't even know where to start. I wish I had an ounce of your fortitude."

"Oh, you do. I know you do. I just wish you could let go of the reins a little bit."

"I've always been on this track. Frankly, anything else seems like failure."

"It sounds like you're so focused on what you think that your life is *supposed* to be that you're not giving yourself the room to find out what you *could* be. Your anxiety is calling all the shots."

"I thought that was how everyone lived."

She smiled and pushed the plate of scones nearer to me.

"It isn't fair to put yourself under so much pressure. Maybe you'll do exactly as you always planned, or maybe your life will take an unexpected course, but either way, *you* should be in control, not your anxiety."

I took a moment. I wasn't sure I agreed. If you just let your life blow around with no plan or control, then what you ended up with was a fun, relaxed life, perhaps, but nothing substantial.

"What do your family say?" she asked.

"Well, my parents have always been very career-driven. When I was a child, they uprooted us and moved across the state to get me into a better school district. When I got into Yale, they cried and threw me a massive party. My education and career are what they lived for. They want to see me back on the horse yesterday. Hell, they'd like to see me president yesterday."

"Mm-hmm . . ." She nodded, popping a petit four neatly into her mouth and looking unsurprised. "And what did they think about the fiancé?"

"Well, they cared for Hunter only as far as they assumed he made me happy, but I think they secretly thought he was a bit lazy. They'd be just as pleased to see me with someone else, or going it on my own, for that matter."

"Not a bad idea, actually. Some time to focus on yourself might be just the thing."

"Yes. Apparently I thought the focus would be much clearer here in the British countryside, but I think the only thing clearer is my bank account," I said with a wince.

"Don't be hasty, dear girl. You've only just arrived. Did I not just tell you of the miracles that can be worked by a pot of strong English tea?"

HELENA AND I spent the rest of the afternoon meandering around York together, enjoying the sites as much as we enjoyed each other's company. In the late afternoon, we met the others for a guided tour through the city. I enjoyed myself quietly but was withdrawn, and I turned in early afterward. The tour guide made a face at this, but there were many things left heavy on my mind, so I decided to skip dinner and be by myself for a while.

Unfortunately, sleep did not come willingly, and my mind grinded on like a set of gears that refused to stop turning. Talking about my life had been a strange sensation. My parents knew what had happened, but apart from "Are you alright?" and "Is there anything we can do to help?," we didn't talk much about feelings. This was the first time I had really discussed it with anyone, and it felt painful, vulnerable, but also freeing. It felt like a move in the right direction.

This made me realize that I had let my friendships drift away from me. I had strong friendships during my college years, but after graduation, I suppose I had spent more time focusing on my career and building a life with Hunter, because those two things were vital to achieving my goals. I had let my friends sort of slip away without even noticing. I had some work friends, of course, but that wasn't the same. They were good for having a drink with after work and venting about deadlines, but not so much for crying on when I hadn't showered in five days.

Helena's advice confused me. I wasn't sure I could adapt the way she had. But it felt wise. She was a woman who undoubtedly knew more about life than I did. And when my problems were viewed from her side of the table, they didn't look quite so insurmountable.

Yet as the sleepless night wore on in a haze, things looked different, and I felt unaccountably blue. I chided myself for having run from my problems rather than face them. Was that what I'd done? I didn't even know any more. Was Helena right? Should I rethink what I'd always wanted and maybe move somewhere else, try something new? Not everyone was Helena. Maybe I wasn't as resilient or adaptable as she was.

CHAPTER 12

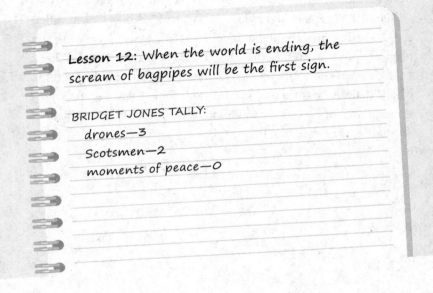

Lesson 12: When the world is ending, the scream of bagpipes will be the first sign.

BRIDGET JONES TALLY:
drones—3
Scotsmen—2
moments of peace—0

When my alarm went off, I cracked my eyes open and wished violently that there was someone whom I could bribe to allow me to stay in bed all day. I reset my alarm, closed my eyes, and rolled over.

I couldn't miss the day, but I could at least skip breakfast. I drifted off again, half-asleep, half-awake, half-consumed with my worries, half not caring anymore. When the little retro phone in my room rang, I rolled my eyes behind my closed eyelids and put my hand to my forehead. It could *only* be one person. I picked up the receiver and hung it back up. I wasn't a child. I didn't need a wake-up call.

I might not have needed a wake-up call, but I sure as hell freaking got one.

A siren wailed, and I nearly fell out of the bed. *Danger!* My heart pounded out of my chest. My body shook with adrenaline. Surely it was an air-raid siren. Surely it was the end of times! Surely it was . . .

a jig. It was a fucking jig. The siren was bagpipes, and if I wasn't mistaken, the cursed things were being squeezed directly under my window.

"Alice Cooper!" a voice called over the noise.

I swore.

Percy started howling.

I had a charming cottage bedroom with old windows set deep into thick, whitewashed walls that overlooked a circular drive and front garden. I whipped the curtain back. There in the middle of the grassy circle was a man I had never seen playing the Highland pipes. Next to him was Beelzebub himself, with a shit-eating grin. Behind him was the entire assembled tour group of ladies—and Percy, eyes squeezed shut, singing his little heart out.

The man finished the tune, the pipes deflated in an inelegant whine, and Satan's smile widened even further.

"There she is!" he said, and the women cheered. "Time to get a wriggle on, Alice Cooper."

I groaned. "I was getting up. We have twenty more minutes," I said lamely, tamping my hair down and pulling my pajama top up. "Where did you even find bagpipes anyway? We're in England!"

"Halluuu!" called the piper amiably, with a big warm smile. "I'm Ian, Robbie's mate from Glasgow." He had a deep brogue and waved with his free hand. I had seen him, actually. At check-in. This was his B&B.

"Of course you are. Nice to meet you, Ian."

I assessed. After this noise I resigned myself to never going back to sleep, possibly ever. "Alright, alright. I'll be down in a minute."

When I got on the bus, the women clapped and cheered, faces smiling. Nosferatu looked altogether too pleased with himself. I smiled down the bus and took a little bow.

"I hate you," I said low through my smile.

He laughed. "Nothing new there then."

"You will pay for this."

"I don't doubt it. Here ya are. You skipped dinner." He handed me a napkin with something warm inside.

"I don't want your . . . what is this?"

"It's a bacon butty," he said. "You'll like it."

I frowned. "A bacon buddy?" I said, as if it was some kind of child's toy. *Bacon Buddies: When your best friend just isn't greasy enough.*

"A bacon *butty*." He laughed again. "Ya daft Americans with your *D*s and *T*s. Outrageous."

"Well, I don't want it," I lied.

"Course ya do. And here's a scone and jam for after. Now have a seat, and let's get rolling."

He was right. The bacon butty was delicious, and I was ravenous. I hated him for it, but I had a little bit of a smile while I ate. I couldn't tell if I was furious or amused by his stupid prank, but I knew one thing for sure: I wasn't thinking about my problems anymore.

When I finished all my delicious carbs, fats, and sugars, I wiped my mouth and got out my notebook to brainstorm my revenge.

THINGS TO TORTURE OUR TERRIBLE TOUR GUIDE:

1. Point out his mistakes. (Note: This works with all men.)
2. Roll eyes often.
3. Refer to him as British or even English instead of Scottish.
4. Incite and inspire complaints from the oldies.
5. Ask often for bathroom breaks and make sure not to go until he calls everyone back to the bus.
6. Refer to *Braveheart* for historical accuracy.
7. Give Percy his farty snacks.

8. Bring it to Agatha's attention if he goes even a mile over the speed limit.

9. Yawn theatrically during presentations.

10. Refuse to laugh at any and all jokes.

11. Mention offhand that ~~Trainspotting~~ was a horrible film.

12. Pronounce Edinburgh as ed-in-BURG (hard G), and Glasgow as glas-GOW (rhymes with ~~cow~~).

Yes. I felt quite brightened and rejuvenated with this renewed purpose.

ON THE DRIVE to Chatsworth House, our tour guide set a cat among the pigeons.

"So I wondered if you ladies could help me out with a little quandary. If you were to choose . . . would it be Mr. Darcy and Mr. Knightly, or would it be Mr. Rochester and Heathcliff?"

War broke out.

"Well, obviously Darcy and Knightly. Right, ladies?" Madge said. "No competition, really. Nice, handsome, honorable men with lots of money."

"Speak for yourself," said Helena. "Sure, Austen men are lovely, but where's the passion? All the heroes are dry and reserved, and all the passionate men are the baddies: the Willoughbys and Wickhams. They were the cautionary tales. The men to stay away from. But that made me like them all the more."

"So instead you vill choose a disturbed man with half a face and a burned-down castle who likes to lock women in the attic?" asked Berrta, getting worked up about what she clearly thought was a nonsense opinion. "Or maybe you like an obsessive psychopath who kidnaps people and kills dogs?"

"Heathcliff seems far more lickable than Darcy," said Flossie.

"Likable! She means *likable*," interrupted Agatha.

"No I don't."

"I'm sorry, Madge," Lorna weighed in. "Sure, the Austen men are reliable. But what is life without passion and drama? I'd bet Darcy would spend most of his morning doing the crossword puzzle, whereas Heathcliff would make love to you outside in a thunderstorm."

"Oh, ridiculous," said Agatha through a tight mouth. "None of them are real. And if men were actually like that in reality, then we wouldn't be out here, just a bunch of old women without them."

"Maybe they're not real," I said. "But they sure felt real enough to me when I read them."

"Me too!" said Lorna.

"And what's more, I think I started reading these stories so young that they shaped my perspective of men, and of what men should be. Do you think that's possible?"

"Certainly," Helena agreed. "I'm sure I probably married my husband because he reminded me of Gilbert Blythe."

"Ooh, I love Gilbert Blythe!" I gushed.

"Ladies! We've lost the thread here," said Doris. "It doesn't matter whether they're Austen men or Brontë men. The only thing that really matters is Colin Firth coming out of that lake with his shirt soaking wet."

No matter where we were going or what we were doing, there was always the sound of someone somewhere blowing their nose. This meant that tissues were forever in short supply, an issue no one realized would soon become pertinent as we walked ourselves into the closest thing to Jane Austen's Pemberley that existed on earth.

Helena let out a low whistle. "Is it too late to change my answer to Darcy?"

Chatsworth House was a glittering jewelry box. Every spare inch shone with gold gilding, marble tiles, sculptures, painted ceilings, and furniture finer than I knew was possible. Abbotsford, I realized, was a small, intimate space for Sir Walter Scott. I had thought it was so grand, but really it was a place to write and be cozy. Chatsworth, on the other hand, was built by a duke and duchess to impress royalty. It was widely accepted that Pemberley was based on Chatsworth, and I could see why. It was opulence made earthbound.

"Madam. The house is dog-free, I'm afraid. But you're welcome to walk him in the garden."

I whirled around. A young man in a uniform was addressing Doris and looking very uncomfortable.

"This isn't just a dog. This is Percy. He's my support animal, as you can see on his vest, had you bothered to look."

The young man looked at Percy's hand-embroidered vest dubiously. "Umm . . . I will have to check with Mr.—"

"I'm ninety-eight. He is necessary for my health and safety. Are you going to take away my support animal?"

"Well, I . . ."

"No, I didn't think so. Stand aside. Come along, Percy."

His nails tapped the marble triumphantly.

"This is my first time visiting Chatsworth." My morning executioner walked toward us with tickets. "So I've booked us in for a tour with a guide who will know the history far better than I do." He gestured at the uncomfortable-looking young man. "This is Anthony." He walked over and parked himself next to me. I would not squander the opportunity.

"Thank God he's English. At least I'll be able to understand some of it."

"Oh, I don't know. You seem to find a way to misunderstand everything, regardless of the accent."

"I think it's just you, actually. You see, I don't speak jackass."

"Really? You surprise me. You're certainly picking it up like a native."

"I'm a quick study. And anything is easier than Scots. The question is, when are *you* going to learn English? Perhaps Anthony could help. Excuse me, Anthony. Can I ask a favor please? Could you pronounce the word *worm* for me?"

"Umm . . . *worm?*"

"Yes. Perfect. See how it's done, Braveheart? Just one syllable."

As WE WENT from one room to the next, I was rendered speechless, and forgot entirely about my scheme for retribution. I listened to Anthony's stories of the sixteen generations of the Cavendish family, and I imagined parties, banquets, and balls swirling by in a prism of rustling skirts. I imagined myself as Lizzy Bennet, seeing Pemberley for the first time with her aunt and uncle, falling under its spell, bumping into Darcy (probably in a wet shirt), and wondering how on earth she turned him down, when she might have been mistress of all this.

"Oh, come here, love. You've got a bit of jam on your face. And a bit on your lovely cardi as well." I turned around and saw Madge speaking to Doris. Doris rubbed at her face with her arthritic fingers, but the purple smear on her cheek stuck fast. Madge dug around in her handbag. "Lorna, sweet. Have you got a spare tissue?"

"Bugger. I don't think I do."

I walked closer, digging in my own bag, but not finding anything to help.

"Oh, I'm sure I've got one in here somewhere. There now, that'll do." From her purse Doris pulled out a large, wadded-up napkin, and started to rub her face with it. As she did, something crumbled and began to fall out and all over her bosom. Not noticing, she continued to smush and rub. Larger chunks bounced off her and rolled onto the pristine carpet.

"Wait, Doris. What's all this?" Lorna moved in closer. She grabbed the napkin and opened it.

"Huh?" Doris looked at the napkin, then at her chest, and then, with crumbs clinging to her chin, began to laugh. "It's my leftover scone." She laughed harder. "From Tuesday." Scone crumbs had turned the expanse of her bosom into a winter wonderland, a ski slope, and as she laughed harder the crumbs bounced to the floor. "It's me scone." It was everywhere.

Lorna and Madge started laughing, and Doris began to wheeze as her laugh deepened. I was trying to be discreet and not draw Anthony's attention to the mess we were making, but I couldn't help myself. Doris's dry hiss of noiseless laughter was contagious, and it grabbed hold of me all the tighter for my trying to struggle against it.

From nowhere, our tour guide swooped in and silently delivered an unopened package of travel tissues into Lorna's hand, then made a quick play to distract Anthony to the other side of the large room and away from the carpet.

"Anthony, can I trouble you with some questions about this map?"

Lorna laughed harder. "Oh no. It's all over the beautiful floor." She took a tissue out, licked it, and proceeded to wipe Doris's face with the spitty part. At this, Doris, holding on to her cane, crossed her legs as her knees bent under her. *Is she alright? What is she . . .*

That's when I began to laugh so hard that my chest hurt. She was trying not to wet herself!

Percy ran over from wherever he was and whatever he was doing. Doris was wheezing and gasping, but he wasn't there to check on her for signs of distress—or, say, a heart attack. He was there for the scone. This made Doris laugh so hard that she crumpled even further, and I rushed in and grabbed her elbow to keep her upright. I was glad she was wearing her black pants.

"It was me scone." This sent her into another grip of laughter. I put my arm around her shoulder and we leaned into each other—one helpless, heaving animal. I couldn't remember the last time

I'd laughed this hard. She squeezed my hand, and I gave her a big, smacking kiss on her newly cleaned cheek. When I could be trusted to move my limbs again, I stretched out and kicked a large chunk from under an eighteenth-century writing desk over to Percy, who made smart work of the evidence.

WE MIGHT HAVE thought that the rest of the tour would be comparatively uneventful. And it was. Until the end, at least, when Anthony was wrapping things up.

"Chatsworth remains a modern house that is very much alive and an integral part of the community. We have performances and events throughout the year, as well as a health and fitness club with a pool and tennis courts . . ."

"Oh, I love tennis. It helps to slow the southerly descent of my derriere. My husband and I play twice a week. Does anyone else play?" Helena asked the group as we were released into the gift shop.

"I used to play tennis," said Berrta, "but now I prefer pickleball."

"Pickleball, really? I tried it once, but I got so confused by the rules. Have you been playing long?"

"About two years now."

"How nice. What got you started?"

"Well, there was a local Nacktkultur community group that started to have pickleball games for naturists every Sunday."

"How lovely, and did you have to buy . . . I'm sorry, did you say for naturists?"

"Ja."

Doris pushed over with a squeak of her cane. "Naturists? I know what that means!"

"Yes, we play pickleball together."

"In the nude?" Doris shouted, eyes enormous behind her thick glasses. People from across the room turned their heads.

"Yes."

No. Way. This cannot be happening.

"What, with all your bits and bobs bouncing around?" asked Doris.

"Natürlich."

Lorna and Madge had come over with their eyes alight. Doris squeaked a few inches closer. "Is it women only?"

"No. It is free for any who vant to play."

Doris sucked in a breath. "You mean that you watch men running around with their . . . pickle and balls swinging about?" Doris laughed.

"Of course," Berrta said unflappably.

I muzzled into the circle with my mouth open. "Tell us everything."

Agatha appeared, as if summoned magically by the opportunity to castigate someone. "People are staring at us. Those *children* are listening to everything you're saying. Where do you think you are, Doris? Your trashy book club?"

Doris spun around with surprising agility, nostrils flaring. "Good smut is not trashy, Agatha."

"And vat is vrong vith the naked body? I vill answer. Nothing at all. You may be ashamed of your naked body, but I am not ashamed of mine. It is natural and healthy. It is good to get the flesh out in the cold air. Once you get used to all the bouncing, pickleballing in the nude is very freeing. I think you should try this one day and see for yourself."

"Why not now?" Flossie asked. "I'm not wearing any underpants."

CHAPTER 13

Lesson 13: Revenge is a dish best served with a big fat smile on your face.

BRIDGET JONES TALLY:
Alice—1
Robbie—0

On our way out of the Peak District National Park, smoke began to billow from the hood of old Rosie in great gray plumes of ominous prophecy.

This part of the tour provided an educational oration that had not been in the brochure. I got to witness firsthand the infuriated Scot in its natural habitat and learned an entirely new set of expletives alongside some of the old classics.

Of course there was *bugger me*, and *bollocks*, but there was also *dobber*, *scunnert*, *fuck a duck*, and *bawbag*, which I carefully recorded in my notepad to catalog such fascinating cultural gems. Most of this was said outside, when his face was under the hood and out of earshot of the others whose hearing was not quite as reliable as my own.

"Alright, ladies. I'm so sorry for the wait. Rosie's having a bit of trouble with her engine, and it's not going away anytime soon."

"Is it the washer fluid again?" Berrta asked, eying me suspiciously.

"No, it's most certainly not the washer fluid this time. I've called the insurance company, but I'm afraid it's going to be a few hours before they can find something big enough for the lot of us and bring it out to us here in the middle of nowhere. I tried to get someone to give us a ride into town, to at least wait with a warm cup of tea, but those people are just about as useful as tits on a fish, if you'll excuse my saying so." He rubbed a hand over his face and ruffled his hair in a gesture that looked like defeat. "I'm truly sorry, ladies, but I'm going to have to ask you to sit tight."

"Did I ever tell you that I caught a fish with tits once? Yes! That's right. I was in my twenties. They called it a mermaid, and they took it round the country in a traveling circus so that *everyone* could see the tits, and they had a parade and they called it Titstacular—"

"Honestly, Flossie!" Agatha interrupted. "The filthy rubbish you come up with! Why, just the other day she told the postman that our cottage was a house of ill repute and that he could come in to be serviced so long as he promised to keep his socks on. The *postman*, for Christ's sake! With those jowls? There aren't enough socks in the world."

I watched my enemy's mounting frustration with a childish glee.

"Can we get an exact time for when the new bus will arrive? I think we deserve to know that at least." The time had come to pay him back for the vomit heckling, and the bagpipes, and his stupid messy hair. I had waited for it. I had earned it. It was just too good an opportunity to pass up in favor of maturity and decorum. What had maturity and decorum ever gotten anyone?

"I don't have that information, obviously, or I would have already given it to you."

"How old will the new bus be?" I asked next. "Newer than this one?"

"Well, it seems unlikely that it'll be older, now doesn't it?" He ground it out, trying hard to keep his voice slow and calm while the deepening furrows in his forehead gave him away.

Before he could stop me or stomp off, I fired another one at him. "What things will we be missing today on our tour? Will adjustments need to be made? And if so, will anything be left off the itinerary?"

"I'm not sure. It'll depend—"

"Will there be a vote about which things we will miss and which to see?"

"Yes. She's right. I think ve vill all like to know this," Berrta chimed in. "I like to vote."

I saw him take a moment to master his face and voice, and then he very calmly said, "No decisions have been made at present, Alice Cooper. But when they are I will be sure to inform you and everyone else immediately, if not sooner." At that, he turned on his heel and got off the bus before I could hit him with any further nagging.

By God, this is the best part of the tour so far! My blood was up. I needed more.

If there was anyone on the planet who needed a taste of his own medicine, it was this guy, and I was only too happy to oblige. He was tinkering some more under the hood, so I crept down the steps and snuck up quietly behind him.

"*Hello!*" I said loudly just over his shoulder. I stepped back as he jumped and bumped his head on the hood. *Three points!*

He rubbed his head, squeezed his eyes shut for a long breath, and then turned around slowly. As he did, I snapped a shot of him with my camera. "For records, you know," I said with an innocent shrug.

"*Yes*, Alice Cooper?" He used my full name slowly and with a sharp clip at the end that I did not much like the sound of. "How can I help you?"

"I just thought I'd get some pictures to commemorate this exciting part of our tour."

He rolled his eyes, the image of seething frustration, and I quickly snapped another photo. At that moment my only wish in the world was that I had brought my old Polaroid so it would have made the annoying whining sound as it spat out the photo, and then I could have flapped it vigorously in front of him to "help it develop."

"Perfect! It'll be great to attach photos to my Tripadvisor review. Can I get one of you standing closer to where all of that smoke is pouring out of the antique engine over there?" His eyes flashed dangerously, and it sent a little thrill to the bottom of my stomach. "Oh, who am I kidding? There's plenty of smoke right there where you are. Any more and people might have trouble seeing that sour little pout of yours."

"What is it, Alice Cooper?" His voice was tight. "Do spit it out, so that you can go back to scraping your nails against a chalkboard somewhere."

I made my voice sugary sweet. "What are you doing in there? Are you sure you know what you're doing? Because it kind of looks like you're just making a mess. On the plus side, at least you'll finally have an excuse for being so grimy." I crinkled my nose.

"Get your arse back on the bus, you raving besom." His accent was growing thicker by the second. His jaw was tight and furious, but I could see in his eyes that he thought it was a little bit funny. I would just have to try harder.

"Oh! Is that Scots Gaelic? I was hoping that I'd get to hear some on this trip. How exciting! Can you spell it for me so that I can write it down in my notebook?" I pulled it from my back pocket. "I already have *bawbag* and *fuck a duck*."

"You'll be hearing a lot more than that if you don't leave me to get on with it." He stepped closer, a wrench clutched in his hand.

"Next question: When we get the new bus, will it have a working radio? The radio on this old thing must be stuck because it's played nothing but bagpipes since we left Edinburgh days ago."

"The radio isn't stuck. Those are my CDs. Scottish folk music. It's perfectly suited to the tour."

"It's the absolute worst."

"Sure. I guess it's silly of me to expect that you could enjoy the sounds of anything other than the screams of men as you crush their spirits."

"Well, if that sounds anything like your CDs, then I'm not that interested, thanks."

"Get back on the bus right now, and behave yourself."

Something in his tone made my stomach flutter. He stepped in closer and looked down at me threateningly. He was warm from working outside, and his T-shirt clung to him. His strong arms and hands were smeared with streaks of black grease. He even had a little on his forehead and under a cheekbone. That same smell of cedar and spice mixed with his sweat and turned it into something more primal. I fought back a sudden flash of craving.

"I'd very much like to, but the thing is, the sun is strong and it's getting really warm in there, just like a greenhouse. We would open the windows, but as you may or may not be aware, there are only two windows on the entire bus that still function enough to be opened and closed. *Two*." I held my fingers up. "So what should we do? You can't just let us all suffocate in there."

"Don't tempt me." I saw the corner of his lip twitch. *Is he enjoying this? Or is he just picturing me dead of suffocation?* "Perhaps if you weren't dressed for a tour of the tundra today, it wouldn't be such an issue. It is spring here in Britain after all, Alice Cooper. Why don't you just change into something more seasonally appropriate? Or are you incapable of undressing yourself without assistance?"

I put my hands on my hips. It was a low blow. I was getting to him. It was thrilling. "How kind of you to offer your assistance in undressing me while covered in oil and leering at me openly on the roadside. I'll be sure to include that little tidbit in the photo caption on my review."

"Oh, it was a complaint, not an offer. I'm surprised that an Olympic complainer such as yourself doesn't recognize one when it comes up and bites you on the arse."

I flipped open my notebook again, and wrote as I said aloud: "*Mentioned my ass. Again. Makes three times already today. Obvious obsession. Check for criminal record.*"

"My record is entirely clean, or it will be until I slowly choke the life out of you with these jumper cables."

"Well. At least *something* about you is clean." I gave his clothes and face a disappointed look, and tilted my head to the side to make a concession. "Actually, I think I prefer your face this way. It's so covered in grime that it's difficult to make out the shapes underneath."

He opened his mouth, but before he could get out his next remark, we heard Berrta's booming voice from the bus. "Robbie. Are ve all now able to get out?" His eyes widened in terror, and he looked at me as if he might actually kill me after all.

"No, Berrta," I said quickly. "He said that I was the only one who was allowed to get off the bus. I don't understand why. But I'm coming back now. He's really grumpy for no reason."

"Unacceptable!" Berrta shouted, annoyed. "Robbie? Vhat is the meaning of this?" I ducked away quickly and skipped back to the bus before he erupted like a volcano.

Magnificent. Sheer perfection. Performance art.

BACK ON THE bus, the ladies and I talked and exchanged travel plans and stories, but after an hour or so, hunger set in in earnest, and the chatty amiability plummeted in direct correlation with the blood sugar levels. People quieted, and I thought to retreat for some time alone with my podcasts when an idea struck me.

"Would anyone be interested in listening to some stories?" I asked, and heard some inquisitive mumblings in response. "I like to listen to a podcast called *The Moth*. They go to different cities all over the US and ask people to get onstage and tell true stories about themselves live in front of an audience. It's just wonderful, and you see, I've got these travel speakers with me and a battery pack, so it might be a nice way to kill some time if anyone is interested. Of course, we don't have to if it doesn't sound good, but I think you might like it. What do you ladies think?"

"Yes, alright," said Berrta.

"Good idea, love," answered Doris, with a look that told me that she would have patted me on the hand if she was close enough. "It'll distract us from the hunger."

The others agreed to give it a try. Agatha grumbled. "I prefer the silence, but I imagine many of you can't bear to be left alone with your own thoughts."

Flossie smiled like a little girl with a lollipop. "Yes please, Alice. I just love stories!"

I took that as a consensus, and we started listening. The theme was "Escape," and first up was a hilarious story of a woman getting trapped inside a bathroom in Borneo in the middle of the night with a threatening gang of giant cockroaches. Next we heard an uplifting story about a veteran who lost his legs, and the physical and emotional journey of getting his first prosthetics. There was a tale about a woman who attempted to run away from a horrendous first date and managed to escape out of the restaurant kitchen, but in her haste to leave got into a fender bender in the parking lot, thus drawing the attention of the people inside the restaurant, including her unsuspecting date.

We laughed and we cried and gasped and rooted for them every step of the way. At the end, everyone applauded (except for Doris, who had fallen asleep, and Agatha, who had her usual look of a lemon—because she didn't like it, or because she *did* and hated to be proven wrong, we may never know).

They asked me to put on another set of stories, and I obliged, deriving, as I always did, disproportionately abundant pleasure from someone taking one of my recommendations and enjoying it.

It was a chocolate-glazed doughnut of a day.

CHAPTER 14

Lesson 14: Sometimes people are only staring at your face because there's food on it.

BRIDGET JONES TALLY:
pints—2
sandwiches—2
pirates—2

We had arrived late to our pub/inn in a village in Nottinghamshire called Barnby in the Willows. How cute was that? But some hours after I went to bed, my body roused itself against my will, and all efforts to meditate, count sheep, or simply will myself back into sleep's warm embrace were for naught. Eventually I got out my book and kept the light on low, hoping that my eyelids would grow heavy in a soporific trance and slide back down under the covers. Unfortunately, Bill Bryson's exciting descriptions of his British travels had me looking up sites and making lists, which had the opposite effect. I was never going to sleep.

My stomach grumbled. I had tried to ignore the growing hunger pangs in the hope that they would pass, but no such luck. I was starting my period soon, and it always made me ravenous. I could stand no more. I hopped out of bed, wrapped myself up in my robe, and put my slippers on.

Crap. 2:23 a.m. Well, there's nothing for it. I'll wither and die here if I don't go downstairs and find something to scavenge. I hoped there was a nice barman closing up who would be kind enough to let me buy a bag of chips or something. *Crisps—I must remember to call them crisps.* Although at that point I would have offered a lap dance for a few dry saltines.

I tiptoed, trying my best to be quiet, but the bowed, two-hundred-year-old floorboards creaked and tattled on me as I made my way gingerly down the hall. I heard Percy bark, curse him. I crept down the stairs and peeked around the corner. I didn't want to traipse down in the middle of a lock-in at the little pub in my pajamas, but I heard no voices, and the lights were off. I did see one light on in the kitchen behind the bar. I'm not normally one to be flexible where rules are concerned, but there's a certain point in starvation when my stomach overrides my sense of propriety and better judgment, and I was there.

I tapped on the swinging door, then pushed it tentatively open, an apology on my lips, ready to plead for any available scraps. But what I saw stopped me. Our tour guide was in the kitchen, riffling through the fridge and speaking quietly on the phone.

When the hinge squeaked and gave me away, it looked as if I had been eavesdropping.

He hung up the phone and pulled his head out of the fridge.

"Ahh . . . look at what skulks in the shadows."

"I'm not *skulking.* I'm just . . . well, I'm starving."

"Of course you are. You ordered a salad for dinner, did you? Come on in, and let's fatten you up."

"Was my order wrong too? However did I keep myself alive this long without you?" I poked, but I was too hungry for any real menace.

As I walked in, he came over and stretched his hand out. "Truce?" he asked. "Well, only temporarily, of course. Until we refuel. Then we can go back to trying to kill each other with renewed vigor."

"Truce," I agreed. "But only with the proviso that any and all kitchen utensils—for, say, tenderizing meat or fileting fish—be considered fair game as soon as we're done."

He laughed. The sound of it filled the kitchen. I could have sworn the temperature rose a few degrees.

"How about a sandwich and a pint? Will it do, do you think?"

"Well, I'd really prefer hot boiled haggis in a fresh, steaming sheep's stomach, and warm scotch served in a ram's horn, but I suppose sandwiches and pints will do in a pinch."

"A lady of refined tastes." He laughed. "On you go then."

Together we moved around, busily slicing bread, shaving chunky cuts of roast chicken, washing and chopping the tomatoes and lettuce, and sourcing various cheeses and condiments. We stepped back and surveyed our provisions.

"A feast!" I licked my lips like a cartoon cat staring at a canary.

He laughed. "Do you need me to hold you back, or can you manage to restrain yourself until the sandwiches are assembled?"

"At this point, you may have to tie me to that chair."

Something flashed in his eyes, and in that moment my mind played a scene, a very vivid scene that sent heat to my cheeks, but he didn't skip a beat.

"I may just do that . . . because you'll have to wait a bit longer to give me time to make a proper mayonnaise, and after seeing that look on your face, I don't trust you enough to turn my back on you for even a second."

"Make a mayonnaise? Mayonnaise isn't something that's made . . . it's something that's bought . . . in a gallon jar . . . at Walmart."

His eyes widened dramatically, and he scoffed. "I rescind the former compliment. You have no taste. Come on, then." He took me by surprise, grabbing my hand and pulling me over to the table. "I suppose it's my duty to educate you."

"It sounds unlikely that a person like you would be capable of teaching me anything worthwhile."

"Oh?" He raised an eyebrow, and my cheeks heated again. "Are you a particularly slow learner? Well, this recipe is simple enough for even the thickest American." I gasped out some indignation, but he pulled me forward. "Okay—egg, bowl, whisk, lemon, tiny bit of mustard, salt. Now I'm going to separate the yolk"—which he did sensuously with his bare hands like a TV chef—"and then I'll start beating this yolk rapidly."

"Rather a practiced hand, I don't doubt." He barked in surprise at my rudeness and laughed unreservedly, then *tsk*ed me through a grin. "Lowering the tone will only distract me and break the mayonnaise." He shifted his focus to the bowl and began whisking the egg into a lighter color. The grin, I couldn't help but notice, felt like a small victory. "Now what I need you to do is pour the oil in very, very slowly while I beat the egg, and we'll see the mayonnaise thicken—*noooo!!* Slowly!" he cried, and we both laughed as he ramped up the beating and little bits of egg flung around the kitchen.

After a minute or so more, he dipped his finger in and tasted it, then pushed the bowl at me to do the same. Now, I am no great lover of mayonnaise, and I can't say that I was excited about eating mayonnaise out of the bowl with my finger. But I didn't want to be a killjoy, so I reluctantly obliged. The creaminess spread across my tongue with a savory decadence: salty, with a bite of fresh lemon. I swallowed and stuck my finger back in for more. This wasn't mayonnaise . . . this was something I'd never tasted before.

He laughed at me and snatched the bowl away, running around the table as I chased after him. He grabbed a spoon and brandished it at me like a sword, cradling the bowl of mayonnaise protectively to his chest.

"Back, back!" he shouted, a lion-taming act. I grabbed a blue plastic spatula, knocked his spoon from his hand and sent it clattering to the floor, then lunged forward in an old university fencing move and jabbed him in the stomach in what would have been a lethal stab. The spatula bent against his hard stomach, and we laughed, both punch-drunk with hunger and exhaustion.

"Oof!" He rubbed his middle. "Where did you learn to swash-buckle like that?"

"Oh, I was a pirate on the high seas for a few years until I got a desk job."

"Can't say I'm surprised." He laughed. "Come on—let's go get something to drink, you scurvy dog." I followed him out through the swinging door and into the bar. "Right, Redbeard. What do you like to drink?"

I stifled a bubble of mirth. "Are you sure we can really just help ourselves?" I whispered.

"Oh, sure. Old Sal would do it herself if she were awake."

"Well, beer would be nice, I guess."

He laughed. "Ale, lager, stout, cider. Dark or light? Hoppy or malty? Flat or bubbly?" I bit my lip and shrugged my shoulders. "Okay, well we'll start with the local ones and see if we can find something you fancy." He seemed to enjoy playing the bartender, pouring me lots of little tastes and describing them as I sipped.

"This one is the color of a light reindeer urine on a crisp winter's morning and has subtle notes of elderflower, followed by Jammie Dodgers and undertones of raw bacon," he said, swirling the glass like a sommelier. "This one here is more the color of boggy loch water and has a bouquet of melted Jolly Ranchers, hairspray, and wet, hibernating bear."

It felt strangely nice to laugh together. We found a local brown ale that I loved; he commended my choice and poured us both a half-pint, and we went back to the kitchen to make our sandwiches.

I hopped up on the counter, and he joined me, sitting close with our plates and glasses, a bag of kettle-cooked crisps between us. The thick slices of bread were home-baked, the chicken was juicy, the cheese was sharp, the lettuce and tomato crisp, and all was slathered with his homemade mayonnaise. It was nothing short of transcendent. We ate in a reverent and amiable silence. I closed my eyes and hummed as I chewed.

"I think this is the best thing I've ever eaten." I sighed, washing a bite down with a sip of rich, malty ale. He turned to me and smiled a genuine smile that crinkled the corners of his eyes, then went back to eating.

The pleasures were simple and the company surprisingly unguarded, and after our silliness in the kitchen, I felt like a kid again as we kicked our dangling feet back and forth and chewed quietly. The hall clock chimed 3 a.m., and he hopped down to refill our half-pints.

I brushed off the crumbs and leaned forward with my hands on the edge of the counter, elbows locked, an old casual pose from high school gym. When he returned, he didn't hop back up, but stood nearby leaning against the counter with his drink.

"So, dread pirate Cooper, tell me about yourself. Are you a regular jet-setter?"

Something tightened in my chest. I didn't want to talk about me. Especially not to him. But I looked over at his face as he ate a few more crisps. It was light and open, relaxed. I took a breath.

"First time, really. I've only been up to Canada twice for a long weekend. I'd like to go *everywhere*, though." He looked interested and ate another crisp, so I kept going. "Deep down I always thought of myself as someone who loved to travel. I've made lots of plans and itineraries for trips that I want to take. My bookshelf at home is full of travel books. But I just never had the time. Or never *made* the time, I suppose."

"Why not?"

"Too focused on school, or my career, or my ex. Now I'm almost thirty, and I haven't really been anywhere. It's sad. All those missed opportunities. Imagine the sandwiches that I'll never know." He laughed softly but didn't take the bait.

"You say thirty like you're over the hill."

It was. I hated the sound of it. My full stomach felt suddenly hollow and cold, while the whole list of things that I was supposed to have and have done by thirty flipped through my mind like a paper-cut Rolodex. I could have made a joke, my standard deflection, but what came out instead was genuine and surprisingly frank.

"It feels that way. Like I'm running out of time and missed my chance to be spontaneous. Like time is speeding by so fast that my life has forgotten to catch up with it."

"Hasn't traveling with all of those vivacious ladies taught you anything? You've got your whole life ahead of you. You can go anywhere you want."

I hissed through my teeth and shook my head. "Yeah, but I need to save for a house, or I'll never be able to buy anything in DC. And I've got to keep on track with my career—it's kind of a long slog in the nonprofit sector. Actually, one of the reasons I took my job is because I thought I'd get to travel with the development team and help people on the ground, but I got stuck doing admin work behind a screen."

"How'd that happen?"

"My boss said I had a 'rare talent for organization' that would be wasted in the field, so she gave me a promotion and kept me in the office as an assistant."

"Sounds like she was impressed, if she wanted to keep you close."

"It's probably because I'm a bit of a workaholic. I was always one of the last to leave the office. I should have been happy that I was moving up the ladder. And I *was* happy, but it was also stifling somehow."

I sipped my beer. "Next thing you know, five years have gone by, and nothing has changed. Same job, same city, same spreadsheets. There was . . ." I paused. "There were some changes in my personal life, but that's not . . . well, that doesn't matter anymore."

I stopped, flushed, and looked down at my slippers. I didn't mean to say so much. I didn't want to discuss getting fired, my broken engagement, or my stagnant cesspool of a life. I reminded myself that just because we had spent a half an hour together without wanting to disembowel each other with corkscrews, it didn't make us friends.

"Anyway, the answer to your question is no, I haven't done much traveling."

"Well, I'm glad that you're here then. I think it's exciting that you're taking some time off for yourself."

"Thanks." The warmth had gone from my voice.

Yeah, I've been taking a lot of time off these past six months. Then it got worse.

"Tell me more about your job. What do you do?"

I didn't want to lie. But I also *really* didn't want to tell the truth. It was still too raw and embarrassing.

"Well, I work for a large NGO in the nonprofit sector. We focus on global food security. My team is pretty cool, actually. I got really lucky—it combines two of my passions."

"Which are?"

"So." I settled into my old spiel without having to think. "My team looks at gender, and how its role in the cultures of the communities we work with impacts the distribution of funds, labor, and resources. Then we consider how that information might be used to work more sensitively and effectively within these communities to bring about measurable, sustainable change. I really like my job," I said, looking away. "It's hard work and long hours. But I get to help women who are struggling in poor communities. It makes me feel useful. Like I'm helping. A tourniquet for my bleeding, liberal heart."

But I don't do that anymore, I didn't add. *I don't do anything anymore.*

"Wow. That's amazing, Alice."

I didn't feel amazing. "What about you?" I forced a tight smile. "I imagine you've traveled around quite a bit."

"Yeah. I used to travel all the time. I loved it. Did a lot of backpacking with friends in Southeast Asia. Spent some time drinking beer and mountain climbing across Eastern Europe. I even did this mad Monkey Run thing with some mates across North Africa, on this rickety little motorbike that broke down nine times and had a top speed of thirty kilometers an hour."

"Wow. That sounds crazy!"

He laughed. "Name your stupid risk, and I took it. Cave diving, skydiving, dumpster diving, I used to do it all."

"I'm jealous." I was. I was gripped by it. It made my life look so much sadder by comparison. I should have just been happy for him. I really didn't recognize myself much anymore.

"Yeah, I was . . . well, young. I hadn't a single worry in the world."

"But you don't travel like that anymore?"

"Nah."

"Why not?"

"Oh, you know. Sometimes life comes along, and . . ." I saw the shadow of some old, familiar pain in his eyes. "Well, things change. Anyway, I don't do any of that stuff anymore. I'm happy where I am. Now I just take things a day at a time. I don't have to go far or do anything crazy if I truly appreciate each day I have here."

He sounded worldly and wise.

"I never learned to live in the moment. I'm not sure I ever could."

"How could I not? I'm a lucky sod! I still get to travel. I get to spend time with you ladies. It's not hard to see the joy in every day if you love what you do."

"That's great. Not many people get to do something they love."

"That's true. And here we both are saying that we love our jobs." He held his glass up and clinked it with mine, and my throat tightened. "We're living the dream!"

When I looked back he was staring at my mouth, a small, quiet smile on his own. To my complete shock he stepped toward me, standing between my knees at the counter, and reached out a hand. He gently cupped my face. With his thumb, he rubbed at the corner of my mouth in a slow, smooth glide.

My stomach flipped, and my heart raced so fast I heard it pounding in my ears. My brain melted. I melted with it. It only lasted a second. Then I pulled myself together and flinched my face out of his grasp. "What are you—"

"Hold on, you've just got a bit of food here." He laughed. Hot shame flooded my face in an instant. "I'm not surprised with the way you devoured that—"

"I've got to get some sleep," I said harshly as I jumped down from the counter.

I turned and left without giving him the chance to respond.

It was mayonnaise, it turned out, at the corner of my mouth.

I LAY IN bed and pleaded with myself to sleep for the second time that night, if only for the merciful reprieve from my own thoughts. But I had never been more awake. My heart was still drumming a panicked symphony in my chest, and the thought of the way he touched me sent butterflies to my stomach as I pictured it over and over again.

Was he hitting on me? Do I want him to hit on me? It did seem like quite an intimate and romantic gesture for two people who had only just met and had spent most of that time holding themselves back from committing grievous bodily harm.

Yes, damn it, he was very handsome, and the smell of him was intoxicating, but he was definitely not my type. He was pushy and rude and argumentative, and probably lots of other terrible things I didn't yet know. Maybe I had misunderstood the gesture. He hadn't been lying; food had, in fact, been on my face. Which was mortifying.

And yet if my colleague Frank had food on his mouth, I wouldn't move slowly into his personal space, cup his cheek in my warm hand, and caress his lips with the pad of my thumb. I'd say "Hey, Frank! You've got a little schmutz there," so that he could wipe it off his own damn self.

What was he thinking?

I just ran out of there like a frightened school girl! How embarrassing! I should have stood tall and asked him what he was doing. Let him explain himself, and if he tried to make a pass at me, I would have politely informed him that he had misread the signals. I should have handled it with maturity and confidence.

That's what I should have done, right? I didn't want a fling. A fling would definitely be bad for me. A fling would make me lose sight of the point of this trip. I wasn't ready for a fling. I didn't want one. Especially not with him of all people.

Right?

I searched my brain for an answer, but all I found there was mayonnaise.

Ugggh, the mayonnaise! I could die.

Food on your mouth was the facial equivalent of toilet paper on your shoe. It was the ultimate shame. My epitaph would read: *She died a pitiful, untraveled spinster with a glob of mayonnaise at her mouth.*

CHAPTER 15

Lesson 15: Never trust the word of a Scotsman when food is on the line.

Reading List: *A Midsummer Night's Dream* by William Shakespeare (read)

BRIDGET JONES TALLY:
lying douchebags—1
snouts—indeterminate

"Morning, Redbeard. Sleep well?" His voice was warm as I arrived to breakfast. He was speaking to me as if the awkwardness of last night had never happened, and there was a newfound burgeoning friendship between us. By the light of day, it felt like I'd imagined the whole damned thing—the chemistry, the awkwardness, the almost kiss. No one kisses a woman with a glob of mayonnaise smeared on her mouth. No one.

I had overreacted and overanalyzed. That was okay, I decided. I was still a bit fragile, and I needed to give myself time.

I decided to match like for like.

"Like the dead," I answered, "because being around you is utterly exhausting." We grinned at each other, and then I went to grab some food and sit somewhere I could keep a little distance.

WE WANDERED ABOUT while our tour guide was busy making phone calls and organizing for a new bus. I had a surprisingly wonderful time puttering around a little sleepy village with a group so ancient they personally remembered Hadrian's army and thought they were a nice group of dashing young men.

To be fair, now that I was getting to know them all individually, they didn't seem that old anymore. They were certainly more adventurous and high-spirited than I had originally given them credit for. They each had their own strengths: Where some were strong and spry, others were sharp-witted or good at solving problems, and yet others were wise and knowledgeable. And (almost) all of them were in perpetual good spirits, no matter what happened. And of course, there were those that played pickleball nude.

They all seemed to have a wealth of stories and experiences. I had just scratched the surface, but the few I had heard so far had been fascinating: different eras, different countries, different wars, different loves. I had stopped thinking of the tour as them and me—two separate entities—and had grown to think of myself as part of the group. I was happy to count myself among them, and proud to recognize that they were warming to me with equal speed and fervor.

AFTER OUR MORNING walk, we all went for a long and gluttonous lunch, where I hoped to wash forever from my mouth the lingering soapy taste of some violet candies that Lorna had given me. I had a yummy homemade veggie burger and chips with a gargantuan wedge of banoffee pie for dessert. The pie was decadent and sinfully delicious, and the ladies explained to me how to make it at home with only four ingredients, one of which was an unopened can of condensed milk that you boiled for six hours, of all things! It sounded to me like an easy way to need a skin graft.

BRITISH VOCAB LIST WITH SENTENCES
THAT I'VE HEARD THE LADIES SAY

1. *fusty*: stale or dirty. "Oh, I hate to wash my own hair, but on a trip like this, it does start to get a bit fusty after a while." —Doris

2. *pudding*: any dessert. "Should we go for a pudding then?" —Helena

3. *pants*: underwear. "Ooh, the pants they make these days are barely there. Give you a wedgie in the back and in the front! Not for me, thank you. I've gotten the same style from Marks and Sparks for thirty years now. Beige. Full coverage. Can tuck them right up into my bra if I want to." —Doris

4. *chuffed*: thrilled. "Just got a free scone because it was a day old. I'm well chuffed!" —Lorna

5. *muckle*: big (Scottish). "Well, that's a muckle slice of cake!" —Lorna / "Well, that's because you've got a muckle mooth!" —Madge

6. *fanny about*: to fool around or waste time (*fanny* being the term for a woman's reproductive bits). "Well, I thought we were all there to talk about *Fifty Shades of Grey*, and I was ready to discuss all the gritty details, you know, but all they did was blush and fanny about for an hour looking down at their tea. That's when I knew I had to leave and start my own bloody reading group." —Doris

7. *steady on*: a way to tell someone to calm down and be reasonable. "But if ve all vake up early and leave before five, then ve can make a hike and vatch the sun rise vith a good view." —Berrta / "Oof. Steady on!" —Madge

8. *shuggle*: to shake. "And it wasn't until I got to the Tesco that I noticed my pink pants from the day before had shuggled right down my trouser leg and were just waving around like a flag for all the world to see." —Lorna

9. *got a face like a*: a fill-in-the-blank-style insult that encourages improvisation. "He's got a face like a two-day-old lasagna." —Agatha, "He's got a face like a bulldog chewing on a wasp." —Agatha, "She's got a face like a ripe peach that got kicked down the stairs." —also Agatha

10. *twat*: also a woman's reproductive bits (pronounced like *flat* and used liberally). "It was only a few teeth marks. Percy does like to chew. And they told me I'd have to speak to the manager, but he was a right twat! So I told him he could take his precious ottoman and cram it right up his backside." —Doris

11. *Nowt* (or *naught*): nothing. "It was nowt but the neighbor's boy tapping on the window, and there I was piddling myself thinking it was vampires again." —Flossie

12. *gutted*: devastated. "They stopped making my favorite lilac talc because it was giving some women cancer downstairs, can you imagine? Discontinued! I was gutted." —Doris

13. *lost the plot*: become confused. "Is that your bra? How the devil did you get it off? Merciful heavens! Have you completely lost the plot?" —Agatha

14. *taking the piss*: joking, or taking advantage. "Two pounds fifty for a plain scone? You're taking the piss!" —Agatha

15. *ta*: thanks. "Oops, your skirt's tucked into your nylons. There we go." —Helena / "Ta, my love." —Doris

16. *bugger all:* nothing. "We've done bugger all since this morning but drink tea and eat cakes. We'll be fat as hogs when this tour is finished, you mark my words." —Agatha

17. *waffle on:* to talk endlessly without purpose. "Oh no, Flossie, why didn't you say so, love? Here I am waffling on about the industrial revolution, and your bladder is about to explode." —Robbie

THE NEW BUS was . . . well, what do you know! . . . an actual tour bus! And not just a rolling metal death trap accessorized by Queen Victoria. There was heat and air conditioning to warm or cool our human bodies should the need arise—a novel notion. The seats reclined. There were USB outlets. There was even a flushing toilet. What a time to be alive!

Our grisly guide had forgotten his extensive library of Highland bagpipe CDs in the other bus, so we resigned ourselves to the disappointment of listening to *actual music* on the radio that had a wide variety on offer, from classical to oldies to pop. The ride was smooth, so the ladies who suffered from osteoporosis didn't have to worry about their skeletal integrity rattling away. And all the windows were wondrously fully functional. I know this because at my earliest opportunity, I went around the bus checking that they worked, while our driver looked on and rewarded my antagonistic efforts with an annoyed eyeroll.

WE GOT TO Stratford-upon-Avon a little later than expected, but still had time for a tour of Shakespeare's birthplace and Anne Hathaway's cottage. The fact that these sixteenth-century structures still stood was incredible to me. Half-timbers, thatched roofs, and flowering gardens that were crooked, winding, and utterly, perfectly charming.

We stopped for a late lunch, and I chose some footlong, rectangular, flaky stuffed pastry thing without bothering to ask what it was. My tormentor came in from a phone call and sat down next to me with a chocolate muffin.

"Is that a Bedfordshire clanger?"

"Um." I chewed. "I think so? I didn't ask, I just pointed at the biggest thing in the case."

"I haven't seen one of those in yonks. Brave choice." He took a bite of his muffin, and his eyelids fluttered closed.

I ate a couple more bites. "What do you mean, brave?"

"Bold choice." He swallowed. "I didn't know you were an adventurous eater."

"It's just fruit. Apples mostly, I think." I showed him the inside of it. "I guess *some people* find fruit adventurous. I *have* heard that the average diet in your hometown consists mainly of Irn-Bru and deep-fried Mars bars, but I didn't think it was true."

"Well, half of it is fruit. The other half is pig snouts." He ate another bite of muffin.

I choked a little bit, but tried to hide it. "Shut up. You're such an idiot."

"I'm serious."

"This is stupid. It's a fruit pastry. If this is meant to be a prank, it's a really dumb one, even for you."

"What do you think a clanger is?" He tapped my nose with the tip of his finger. "Half of that pastry is fruit, half of it is stewed potatoes and pork. Pork snouts to be exact." He did a little pig snort, grinned, and then took another bite of his muffin.

"You're just trying to get back at me for yesterday. I'm not falling for it." I took another confident bite.

"It's called a Bedfordshire clanger because it was first made for the Bedfordshire Regiment when they were engaged in the Western Front. The men were starving. Food was scarce, apples were going bad in the fields, so the chef started cooking up a two-course meal—half meat, half fruit—so they could eat while they marched. Pig snouts were all they could get in large quantities on a dwindling budget. People found them tasty. There's nothing wrong with snouts. You're going to like it."

I scoffed. "I know you *English* people eat some weird and gross food, but you're going to have to do better than that."

He narrowed his eyes into blades. "Careful not to choke on those snouts, Cooper."

"I'm not falling for it."

"You don't have to. You'll find out in another bite or two."

I took a big showy bite to prove I didn't believe in his stupid story. There was something strangely salty at the end. I had probably imagined it because he wouldn't shut up about snouts. I took another bite, this one experimental. It wasn't apple. It was potato. And meat. I gagged. And then I spat my bite out into a napkin. I took a big gulp of my fizzy Appletiser and tried to wash it away. He laughed.

I snatched his arm in a pincer-tight grip, and he laughed even harder. "Tell me," I growled.

He laughed so hard that he almost couldn't respond but managed to gasp out, "Tell you what?"

I pinched harder. "Is it snouts?"

At this, he doubled over the table, laughing so hard that the others started to look.

"Is it snouts!" I shook his arm nearly out of the socket. "I'm going to be sick."

"No. No! Calm down." He laughed some more. "It's not snouts. It's just regular pork."

"Ugh! What? I feel sick. What is the matter with you people? Why are pork and potatoes in an apple pastry?"

"Who knows? I don't know the history. I just made that up." He took another bite of his delicious-looking, absolutely normal chocolate muffin. "I mean . . . I guess it *could* be snouts."

I let go of his arm and then took my hand and smashed what was left of his muffin flat against the table. He took a moment from his laughing to shrug and eat another bite of the smashed muffin anyway. When I looked up, I saw Berrta making her way to the table with a sandwich.

"Berrta!" I waved. "I was just getting up. Come sit here. Our charming tour guide was just telling me that he's been thinking of doing a new history tour for nudists, but he wasn't sure if it could work. I'm sure he'd like to hear *all about* your experiences."

"Oh, how vonderful, Robbie. Yes, ve have some like that in Germany. I vent for a trip with my pickleball tour just last year. I vill tell you everything."

"Do you have any photos? He said he wanted to know how to keep the bus seats clean." I leaned in and whispered in his ear, "Enjoy the rest of your lunch." I stood up, and Berrta shuffled on to the bench next to him. I smiled. Then I threw the rest of my pastry away. I couldn't eat it now. What sort of deranged sicko would want that anyway?

As I walked to get another drink to choke down the taste of snouts, I heard Berrta's voice. "Ah yes, I have some photos on my phone that I vill show you." The look on his face was worth a thousand words. I lifted my camera, took a quick shot, and then gave him a thumbs-up. Berrta got her phone out and started scrolling.

Later, when we got back on the bus, he handed me a little box.

"What's this? A bomb?"

"An apology. You didn't get to eat much."

It was heavy. I opened the box and saw a strange lump of something that looked like cake with spots that might have been raisins. "What is this?"

"Spotted dick." He tried to fight the smile off his face, but it was no good. "It's only a small one, but size shouldn't matter."

CHAPTER 16

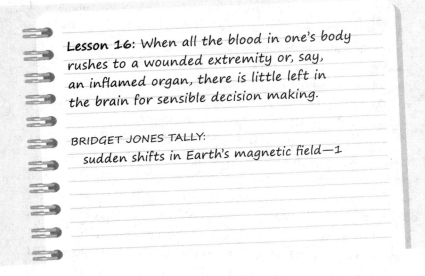

Lesson 16: When all the blood in one's body rushes to a wounded extremity or, say, an inflamed organ, there is little left in the brain for sensible decision making.

BRIDGET JONES TALLY:
   sudden shifts in Earth's magnetic field—1

Kenilworth Castle was a brooding, beautiful ruin dreamt in red sandstone. It was the magic hour when the day turned to evening, and the sky was melting into soft purple blushes, the last golden rays of the sun bursting free from the gilded clouds to set ablaze the great yawning mouths of the castle's twelfth-century windows. It was the best time of day to take photos, and I didn't stop for breath.

The others were enjoying the beautifully kept Elizabethan Garden, but I left to climb to the other side of the ruins for a more dramatic view. I stretched forward to get a tower in the frame, and my foot slipped.

Suddenly I went tumbling downward, cradling my camera and shielding it from the blows with my body. The world turned upside down. I landed with a thud on my back. Pain shot up the length of my leg. I couldn't breathe for a few long seconds. Hot tears welled in my eyes.

When I caught my breath again, I took stock of my camera and found it to be intact, as far as I could tell. The relief that it had survived made the physical pain subside a bit. I could move my arms and legs, thankfully, but when I tried to move my right ankle, it felt like someone had replaced my foot with a cattle prod. The foot was still there, and the parts still moved, so I counted myself lucky.

Next on the agenda: how to get the fucking hell out of there.

I had fallen a couple of feet and rolled down the hill toward the castle's outer wall. The sun was setting now—and, of course, it was beginning to rain. Not the tiny flecks of spitting rain that I had quickly learned was the near-constant state of British weather, but big drops of gaudy, splashing, show-off rain. Bastards, every one. It soaked me in no time, finding cunning routes to direct rivulets of water through the folds and layers of my clothes. I had a waterproof case for my camera so I nestled it back in there, hoping that water hadn't already found a way through its soft spots as it had done mine.

The rain was ice cold. I began to shake. Soon it was a full-body, teeth-chattering, painful shiver. I pushed up on my elbows to see if I could somehow cajole my body into standing or even crawling back to the group. I tried to put myself in the right position to stand. Searing jolts of red-hot pain took my breath away. I certainly wouldn't be able to put any weight on my ankle, and hopping on one leg up a rocky, wet hill seemed like a good way to knock one's two front teeth out.

I checked my phone, but there were no bars, of course, not that I could have called anyone anyway. I tried a few times to shout for help, but I hadn't seen a soul on this side of the castle, and now it was raining and growing darker. No one could hear me.

I decided that I could curl up into the fetal position and bawl my eyes out until someone found me (quite tempting, actually), or I could get on with the business of saving myself.

I was going to have to try to crawl up the steep embankment. Adrenaline had been known to endow superhuman strength. *Maybe I will make it up the hill, and then lift a car right up over my head when I get there. I mean, not an American car, but I could probably manage a European car.*

I gritted my teeth and got up on all fours. It was nearly pass-out painful, but I found I could use both knees if I kept my right shin up off the ground so that my ankle didn't touch anything. The going was slow. It seemed like every damn pointy rock in Warwickshire had rolled over for a pointy rock convention directly under my bony knees. I girded my loins and moved with great determination at the astounding speed of an arthritic sloth.

Though the rain pelted me from above, and the mud and stones hindered me from below, I had moved several feet and was feeling quite proud of myself. Then I slipped. I automatically put my hands and feet to the ground, trying to stop myself from sliding. I cried out like a wounded animal, fell to my side, and began rolling back down.

In crippling pain and frustration, I shed a few angry tears and steeled myself to get back up. That's when I heard it. A voice. A Scottish voice. His voice. Calling my name over the sound of the rain.

"Alice!" He ran down the hill, jumping and sliding to get himself down as quickly as possible. He fell to his knees, looking me over frantically to find the source of trouble. "My God, Alice. What happened to you? Are you okay? What happened?"

I shivered and pulled my lips back into a gritted smile. "I was just soaking up this beautiful British weather."

"I've been looking all over for you." His voice was tender as he pushed the wet hair from my face and tucked it behind my ear. "If I'd known you were down here playing in the mud, I would have stopped to get my swim trunks." I laughed, so relieved that he was there with me. "Alright, darlin'. Let's get you out of this rain. Tell me what hurts."

"It's my ankle. And my pride."

"Oh, hush now. Let's not pretend you have any pride left to wound."

I wanted to think of something funny to say, but then he bent down and put his arms around me. Gently, with one arm under the knees and one around my back, he lifted me up, and I forgot every stupid little thing I was going to say. I wrapped my arms around his neck. Warmth flooded my body as I curled into him, cradled so close to his chest that nothing else mattered.

He was soaking wet. Water dripped from his chin onto me, and he shook his head to get the wet hair out of his eyes. He carried me up the hill like it was the easiest thing in the world, and then he found a place where the overhang sheltered us from the rain, and the ruined wall cut out most of the wind. He sat us down and lowered me with his arms still around me. Pain hummed through my body. I was still shivering, and my teeth were chattering, but not as badly as before.

"Are you alright? Let's rest a minute before we make the long trip to the bus. Is that okay?"

I nodded, arms still around his neck, not quite ready to let go.

"Christ, you're frozen solid." He pulled me closer, rubbing my arm to warm me up, and looked down at me. "Now are you going to tell me what happened, you silly wee thing?"

"Well . . . you see . . . I was trying to take this picture—"

"Good God, Alice. A picture? Did you break your ankle? It looks like a snake swallowed a melon."

"No. It's not broken, but it's definitely not very happy with me. I tried to crawl back up the hill on my hands and knees, but it was so muddy that I slipped back down and landed on it again."

"Christ. How long were you down there? At first I thought it was another prank, but then I began to worry. You've been gone for ages."

"I don't know. Fifteen minutes, I guess. I wasn't sure anyone would ever find me. I figured you'd speed away and leave me for the crows at the first opportunity."

"If I had any sense, I would have done." He laughed. "You're tough as nails, though, aren't you? You would have eventually chased us down, and then I'd really be in for it."

"Robbie." Emotion and gratitude thickened my voice. I looked into his blue eyes as the rain ran down his cheekbones and along his chin. I said simply but earnestly, thinking of all the times I should have said it and couldn't: "Thank you."

The expression I got in return was one I hadn't yet seen on his face. "You've never called me Robbie before. I like the way it sounds." His arms tightened and pulled me even closer, our bodies and limbs wet and cold but sharing warmth with each other.

I looked from his eyes down to his mouth. Without a thought, I reached out and brought my hand to his face, cupping his cheek the way he had done mine the night in the kitchen. I moved my thumb across his lips, curious to know what they felt like. I felt a jolt run through him.

Before I knew what was happening, my lips were at the corner of his mouth, tasting the rain. He crushed me to him swiftly and his mouth came down on mine. He tilted my head back and kissed me deeply, like he needed it, like he'd waited too long for it. His lips were soft, and the scratch of his stubble sent electricity coursing through my bloodstream. His tongue in my mouth made my head swim.

Our wet clothes made us feel all the closer. I felt the muscles in his arms and chest tense and move through the wet fabric. Water dripped down our faces and into our kiss. I ran a hand through his hair, grabbing and twining my fingers into the wet mess of it, needing to feel more of him, needing something to grab as I pulled him closer, our tongues and teeth exploring the taste of each other.

I lost myself. Entirely. If the world still existed outside of the place where our lips and breath collided and merged like waves on the sand, I hardly knew it.

Perhaps it was the crazy situation, or maybe the heightened sensitivity from the pain and fear, but I felt I had never been kissed like that by anyone. My head spun, my skin tingled, my bones melted and dripped like hot wax.

I didn't think of all the reasons not to, I didn't make a list. The only possible thing that my mind was capable of thinking at that moment was that I wanted, needed more of him.

Suddenly there was a sound, an insistent and familiar yapping. We broke apart to see Percy running toward us at full speed. Robbie pulled away with a long, contented sigh and closed his eyes. He kissed my forehead softly and touched his head to mine, forehead to forehead, nose to nose, in a gesture so intimate, I felt as if we'd been lovers for years. Then thirty-five pounds of wet dog launched himself at us and started licking us all over.

"Alright, Percy. Alright, we hear you." He said softly to me, "We'll need to be getting back before the ladies start sending out more scouts to come find us. Besides, Percy is getting his little vest wet, and we can't have that, can we old boy?"

I nodded. I had no quick line or dumb joke, only a smile. I hardly knew who or where I was anymore. He looked at me with those eyes once again, and the world spun so fast I feared I might slide right off it.

"You know that I'm going to have to take you to hospital, don't you?"

I nodded to that too.

"Good," he said gently. "Because I'll have no more of your trouble, Alice Cooper."

This time when he said my name, it had none of the jeering ring it was typically laced with. Somehow this time it was sweet and comfortable—an old nickname, like a warm sweater.

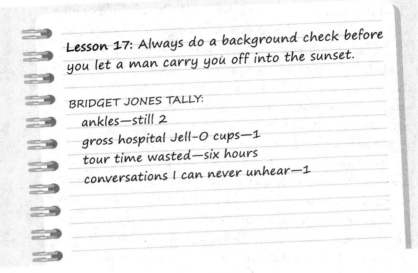

CHAPTER 17

Lesson 17: Always do a background check before you let a man carry you off into the sunset.

BRIDGET JONES TALLY:
ankles—still 2
gross hospital Jell-O cups—1
tour time wasted—six hours
conversations I can never unhear—1

After much cooing and nuzzling by the gaggle, we made our way to the hospital, where I was informed that it was a sprain and I would soon be on my feet, but I would need crutches, a brace, and plenty of ice until my ankle felt strong again. Robbie stayed with me and made a valiant effort to keep me distracted and feeling looked after. Maybe it was the painkillers, but everything he said made me smile. I couldn't stop. I laughed so much I nearly forgot the pain.

I was returning with the nurse from a pee break when I heard him on the phone down the hall. "Yeah, it was pretty terrible. They're just about to send us home from hospital now . . . Oh, just one of the ladies. A new one, you wouldn't know her. American . . . Yeah, I know. Exactly . . . Of course I'll call you before bed. I always do, don't I? Send me a shot of those new pajamas, I've gotta see them. We can have a cozy Netflix night as soon as I'm back . . . I love you too, gorgeous . . . Wish you were here . . . Yeah, I'll be home before you know it."

All that warm comfort, and suddenly I felt as if I'd been drenched with a bucket of ice water. *"I love you"? "Gorgeous"? "I'll be home"? Does Robbie have a girlfriend? Is that who he's always on the phone with?*

My memories were hazy with pain and lust, but when I replayed the tape, I knew that I was the one who had gone in for the kiss. I was the one to make the move. I hadn't asked—I just listened to my adrenaline and attacked him.

But he had kissed back.

And it wasn't a polite kiss to save a wounded woman some embarrassment. It was a full-body, rip your clothes off sort of kiss. If he wasn't single, he should never have done that. He should never have grabbed me and kissed me until I melted completely into him, until I couldn't see straight, until the whole world was knocked off its axis and revolved around the two of us.

It hurt. I didn't want to admit it to myself, but it was painful. I knew it was just a kiss. A kiss with someone who was insufferable and who I didn't even like, while I was under the influence of adrenaline. It meant nothing. It was never going to go anywhere. And maybe for him it was just a little bit of fun, but my heart was too fragile for this. I should never have been so careless with it.

And while he was there kissing the life out of me, he had a girlfriend at home missing him. He was a dirty cheat. Just like Hunter. He probably did this all the time. The more I thought about it, the angrier I got. My hands were starting to shake. He should have stopped me.

Guilt rose in my throat like bile. I didn't want to be the other woman. Perhaps they had an open relationship. That was a thing these days. But still. Even if it were true, I sure didn't want any part of it. And he should have told me. My thoughts raced. I felt sick.

"Sorry about that. I was having a talk with the doctor requesting they just take the thing off and get a peg leg for you to go with the whole pirate theme, but they wouldn't do it. Something about a hypocritical oath. But don't be too disappointed, I'm sure we can do a quick DIY job when we get back to the B&B."

I gave him a tight smile. "Can we go now?"

"Of course, darlin'," he said sweetly, and kissed my forehead. "How do you want to do it? Do you want to give these babies a spin around the block?" He held my crutches out. "For the record, I would be quite happy to carry you out. Hell, I'd be quite happy to carry you all around town even without the bum leg." I grabbed the crutches. He sure was good at making me feel special. And I was mad at myself for falling for it.

When we got back to the B&B, I went straight to my room—without being kissed, or cuddled, or joked with. I just wanted to be alone.

Later, once I was warmly tucked in bed with a nice cup of chamomile, I looked at it all again, and decided that I would take it for what it was worth—a fun and exciting fleeting moment of mad romance at a castle ruin, in the British rain, with a handsome Scotsman, heightened by the age-old aphrodisiacs of pain and jeopardy. This was something I could tell new friends over cocktails when I got home. It was something that they would swoon over and be envious of. It was an adventure. It was fun and exciting.

But that was all it was. I wouldn't wish away the memory, nor would I lose my head over it. I knew that if we kissed again, if we followed the path to see where it led, things would get out of hand quickly, and I would end up getting hurt. Also, I knew well enough that I would spend too much time focusing on Robbie and our time together, rather than focusing on myself, which is what I had come here to do. It would derail my objective. And that was *if* he was in an open relationship, and not just a cheater.

Perhaps he was feeling the same way and would go on as if nothing had happened. But either way, I would need to distance myself from him. I drifted off to sleep planning my battle strategy.

CHAPTER 18

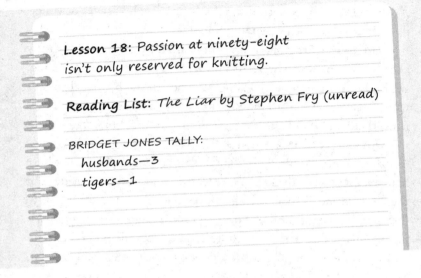

Lesson 18: Passion at ninety-eight
isn't only reserved for knitting.

Reading List: *The Liar* by Stephen Fry (unread)

BRIDGET JONES TALLY:
husbands—3
tigers—1

We were off to Cambridge. Cambridge! The seat of so much history, the wellspring of inspiration for so many great minds and great novels. I wanted to scream. I wanted to snap photos with wild abandon. I wanted to run laps around the city like a golden retriever through a sprinkler. My ankle brace and crutches had a different plan.

Now Doris and I walked at the same speed, so we lumped in together and forged a slow-moving camaraderie, chatting and laughing and helping each other hobble along the Gothic lanes with a glacial gusto, while Percy zigzagged across the streets looking for fallen chips (or other far less savory unmentionables).

Robbie and the ladies seemed to take it in turns to check on us periodically, but we were getting along just fine, and I took the opportunity to decline Robbie's offer of help in an effort to establish reserve and quietly transmit the notion that yesterday had been a mistake.

My brain, as it so often did, refused to comply. Scenes of yesterday's erotic rescue kept popping unbidden into my thoughts, sending butterflies to the pit of my stomach and blushes to warm my cheeks. The memories were so intimate—being carried in his big, strong arms, our bodies pressing together through wet fabric, his warm breath snaking around the nape of my neck until goosebumps rose. That incredible kiss. It was all so close to the skin, scratching at me with an incessant persistence.

I did my best to file these thoughts under "nice things that have happened which shall never be repeated" and put them aside. But they hunted me. They chased me down the streets and teased me to distraction. Having Robbie hovering on the edges of my periphery, feeling his eyes on me, did nothing at all to help the process of tempering my lustful mind. I made a grab for all the very many reasons why I should not be feeling this way, but they sped and dodged from my grasp like mosquitoes in the night.

I was surprised at myself, actually. It had been a long time since I'd felt this chemical charge, like I'd been hooked up to a battery. It had been different with Hunter. Of course I was attracted to him. He was tall and blond and very handsome in a polished New England sort of way—he could definitely model for, say, an L.L.Bean catalog. But looking back, I don't think I felt the butterflies and vibrating tension with him even at the beginning. He was nice, he was attractive, he took me to one nice dinner, and then another, and things progressed the way they tend to do, but I was never dizzy with longing, and I don't think we were ever infatuated with each other. I had felt that way about people in my teens, and sometimes my early twenties, but I had chalked it up to young hormones and an unrealistic worldview.

But now, I just couldn't stop looking at Robbie, and every time

I did, I got a high from it. I didn't trust it. It was dangerous. More than likely it was just the natural result of being deprived of male contact for half a year, and I wasn't going to allow my ovaries to trick me into thinking that this sudden erogenous rebirth meant anything more than it should.

As DORIS AND I trundled along, we chatted about architecture, books, and things we had learned on the tour. Beautifully decorated shop windows implored us to gaze at them in wonder as we passed. Between talking about chocolates and handbags, we spoke about our lives in a steady, comfortable ramble. Doris always had pointed, well-thought-out questions to ask about my personal life and childhood between sights and stops. For my part, I felt I could talk to Doris for a lifetime and still have much to learn and exciting stories to gush over. She had lived close to a century. She was like a living, breathing documentary—with juicy interludes. She was the goddess of wisdom.

Then she sneezed and a little toot trumpeted out.

"Oh, pardon me, dear. When you get to be my age, you sneeze out of both ends."

I laughed. "That sounds satisfying. I'll have to give it a try."

"Better out than in! Let's move along before it catches us up. And, since we're talking of moving along, tell me more about this Hunter."

I laughed again. "What a segue! Well, let's see. We were together for about six years. We met at Yale. He was doing an MBA, and I was doing business and international development, so we had some overlapping friends. He came from a nice family, and he was liberally minded and wasn't threatened by ambitious or authoritative women." I frowned a little. "He's tall, he dresses well, he has good teeth—quite handsome, but not *too* handsome. Not a smoker, gambler, or heavy drinker. I mean . . . he's perfect, really—just the sort of guy you should build a life with."

She harrumphed.

"What is it?"

"Well." She looked sideways at me, as if giving in against her better judgment to keep her nose out of other people's business. "Since you ask. It's just that, in my humble opinion, your description was very pragmatic for someone who you were willing to marry till death do you part."

"Well, he was nice to me, and he made a good salary . . . he wasn't a wanted felon . . ." I tried to think what else could be missing.

"Where's the *passion,* girl? Did he make you laugh until you couldn't breathe? Could you stay up all night just talking? Did he inspire you?" She leaned in and whispered loudly, "Did he make you want to spend all weekend locked in the bedroom?"

"Well . . . I mean, there was"—I tried to think—". . . I guess not so much passion."

"I see."

"But things were stable and comfortable and promising. Not everything has to be crazy, unbridled passion. Most long-term couples are comfortably affectionate, and not consumed with infatuation. There's more to love than that."

"Yes, you are right. There *is* much more to love than that. With mature love there is pain, and sacrifice and support and joy, and yes, of course there is comfort and stability. But without passion, you will find that you have married your friend, or worse, a business partner, and not a lover. Some people are happy with that. But for others it's not enough. We can have lots of very close friends we share our lives with, but I think a partner should be something more than that. They're the person you pick over all the others and give your freedom to. They should be someone that you can't imagine the rest of your life without."

I thought about that for a while. It seemed a bit too romantic for

my practical brain, and I was surprised to hear such saccharine senti-
ments from a woman of her years.

"How was it with your husband, Doris?"

"Which one?" she asked, with a sly smile.

I laughed. "How many have you had?"

"I've had three. One at seventeen, one at twenty-eight, and one at
sixty-seven. And a fancy man here and there along the way."

I gasped and gave her a conspiratorial little elbow. "Fancy men,
huh? Just how fancy are we talking?"

"Oh, sequined from shoulders to boots, one was. They called him
the Tiger."

"Wait. The Tiger?" I had heard that before. I had a grandmother.
"You can't mean . . . Tom Jones?"

"Can't I?"

"What? Doris! You dated Tom Jones?"

She laughed. "That was a lifetime ago. He was too young for me,
but, well . . . you know how these things go."

"I can't believe this! I want to know everything. How did you
meet? How long did it go on? What happened in the end?"

She winked. "Stories for another time."

"Can I have that in writing?"

She laughed. "But that's not the story I wanted to tell you. What
I wanted to tell you was about my first marriage."

"Did you say you were a teenager? I think I was still playing with
dolls then."

"Yes, we were young, but times were very different back then."

We walked past college quads and gardens, and little rays of sun
broke through the clouds and warmed us while we strolled. I stopped
looking in shop windows. I even stopped taking photos of the colleges. Doris had my undivided attention. "Tell me about him."

"He was called Gerald. He was my childhood sweetheart." She

sighed, lost in her memories for a beat, and her soft, lined face came to life. "I had always wanted to marry him. Our parents were friends, we lived in the same village, and we were a natural match. He had the bluest eyes I've ever seen, even to this day. We had a happy marriage—he was a good man, and it wasn't long before we had a baby boy in the nursery, little Timothy." She quieted for a moment or two as we shuffled along. I waited, hooked on her line. "Then one day he brought a new friend home from work . . . and that's when I learned what passion was."

"Whoa! Doris!" I had not seen that coming!

She saw the happily scandalized look on my face. "No, no, it's not as saucy as all that. We never betrayed Gerald. We both loved him, you see."

"Wait, tell me what this friend was like."

"Roy. I've never known anyone to be so easy around others as Roy was. Anyone who met him loved him. He wasn't as handsome as Gerald was, his face a little too long, nose a little too sharp, and his family was poor, but he had an infectious charm that took over the room. He could make even Sister Mary Joseph laugh so hard that tears came to her eyes."

I smiled and slowed my pace, hoping that she would carry on.

"He could have had anyone, but he loved me. We both knew it from the very beginning. Even though the words were never spoken, there was never any question. It was just something that we lived with. He came to visit more and more often. He loved Gerald as well, and he wanted to be near us, even if he knew that was all it could ever be, somehow it was enough.

"Just having him in the same room set me on fire. It was intoxicating and exciting and so deliciously painful. Sometimes they'd put a record on after dinner, and they'd take turns dancing with me well into the night. We were young, and it was such a happy, carefree time."

"Did you ever think that you weren't strong enough? That maybe you'd give in to temptation?"

"Sure I did. Many times. But I had the love of a good man who trusted me. Silly, foolish girl that I was, I wasn't fool enough to hurt him, thank God. Sometimes I look back and wonder if Gerald knew. He must have seen it. But if he did, he never said a word, and he never was jealous or angry, bless him."

"Is that why . . . I mean. Did you ever feel . . . like you married the wrong person, that if you'd only waited . . . ?"

"No, no. I loved Gerald. And he'd given me my Timothy, and I wouldn't have changed that for anything. I was content. That was enough. Until the war came, and they both went off to fight." We walked a few slow steps in silence, and with each passing second, my heart climbed its way into my throat. "My Gerald never came back."

"Oh, Doris."

"Roy came back to me, but he was never the same after the war. He had shone before, so brightly that we glowed just because we were near him. But after the war he was a stranger to me. Dark, withdrawn, troubled, always somewhere else. Unreachable. He looked after me for Gerald's sake, but not his own. He had no love left for me or anyone else."

"What did you do? Did you marry someone else? How did you look after the baby?"

"Well, I had worked during the war as a land girl. I was one of the lucky ones who had family to help with the baby. And after the war was over, I tried to find paid employment, but once the men had returned, there were no jobs for women anymore. So Timothy and I left our house and moved back in with my parents. I used what I had learned to grow vegetables on my parents' plot. I grew enough to feed the family and sell the extra at market. I sewed and knitted. I made sloe gin. Whatever I could do. It wasn't much, but we scraped by right enough."

We rounded the corner and ambled slowly down the next picturesque street where we'd seen the others turn not long before, but didn't worry much about keeping up with them. I was like a fish on a line, feeling every emotion with the rise and fall of Doris's voice.

"For years, Roy came to visit us every Friday afternoon. He would bring groceries and toys for Timothy, and help to provide for us. I was too proud to take his money, so he brought small gifts of things that we desperately needed and couldn't refuse—meat, fruit, butter, flour, canned goods. He saved all his rations to spend on us while I watched him waste away."

"I'm so sorry. I had a cousin in the Gulf War who was someone else entirely when he came home."

"Then you know how it can be. We didn't even have a name for it back then. Men were taught never to show weakness or talk about their fears, never to cry. It took Roy years to even begin to heal."

"But . . . he did heal though? Eventually?" My heart caught.

"Oh, yes. He was never the same carefree boy I had fallen so in love with, but he did learn to be happy again. After he got over the guilt he felt for what he thought was betraying Gerald's memory, he learned to love me again, and I learned to love this new, beautiful, complex version of him."

A warm smile spread over my face, like I had just watched the happy ending of a movie that had pulled at all my heartstrings. "How did it happen?"

"It took him six years to finally ask me to marry him. We taught each other to laugh again. Oh, we were happy. My love for him was sweeter and deeper for having thought that I had lost him. We had three more children of our own. Roy was the love of my life, and I don't think even Gerald would have minded my saying so." She was quiet for a moment as we paused to let Percy sniff a lamppost. "It was the very best part of a *very* long and wonderful life. And I want that for you, Alice."

I was taken aback.

"Well. I want that too." I had never thought much about it. But wasn't an epic love what everyone hoped for, but only Disney princesses got? I didn't say that, though. It seemed disrespectful after she had shared so much. And anyway, perhaps I was wrong. Here was Doris telling me that I was, in no uncertain terms.

"You may just have to wait a little bit for the right person to come along." She gave my hand a little squeeze, and my heart squeezed with it.

We found ourselves at King's College Chapel then, and we shared a meaningful look before slipping into the door and finally catching up with the others.

The atmosphere was so quiet and reverent that we all stood apart, no one speaking, each of us taking in the chapel in their own way. I gazed up at the remarkable Gothic fan vault ceiling while our footsteps echoed along the stone.

Sliding into one of the creaky pews, I sat alone and just absorbed it all. It is no wonder that chapels and cathedrals used such striking architecture—stained glass pouring in pools of light and color, impossibly high ceilings reaching up into the heavens, walls thick with carvings, gold gilding. It put one in a state of awe.

I sat there in my own world apart. What Doris had said was still resonating quietly at the center of my mind like a small bell that had been struck.

CHAPTER 19

Lesson 19: Pimm's and sunshine can lead one dangerously to lusty thoughts.

BRIDGET JONES TALLY:
tight white T-shirts—1

We toured the Wren Library, where perfect, mullioned-windowed symmetry and a shining chessboard floor framed the endless dark-wood shelves of leathery literary perfection. Cambridge felt as if we'd walked through a painting into another time, where academics bustled through streets full of ideas we could never fathom. We were just passers through, wandering the cloisters, peering through the window at the otherworldly Corpus Clock, where a winged metal demon greedily pulled the giant wheel of time, one shining notch at a time.

For lunch, we piled into Fitzbillies. The café, already crowded with students, had a simple interior, with glass bakery cases filled to the brim. I got a warm carrot and coriander soup with avocado toast, and followed it up with a rich cappuccino and a decadently sticky Chelsea bun.

I was careful to secure an available seat bracketed in between Berrta and Agatha, where I could be sure that (a) I wouldn't have to sit next to Robbie, and (b) I wouldn't have to make too much conversation. I just wanted to sit and ruminate on Doris's story again, chewing at each part to suck out the meaning.

Robbie took a seat across the table from me. Not in a place where we could share private confidences, but still where I was always in his line of sight. Some small, disloyal part of my lizard brain wanted nothing more than to share a cozy chat with him over a delicious lunch, our eyes flashing across the table, our feet touching by accident, or not by accident, tension building. But I held strong and put some distance between us.

Several times I felt his eyes on me. It sent a wave of prickles over my skin that I couldn't ignore. A few times I looked up and we locked eyes—accidental on my part, at least—but when he shot me a cheeky, knowing grin, it flipped my stomach upside down.

I had always had the type of fair complexion that was eager to blush with even the slightest of stimuli. For years I desperately attempted to train it otherwise. As a misguided teen, I tried to shield myself from this showy display with a thick, cakey layer of foundation. But I never did find a solution.

He flashed that smile of his, and suddenly the cold rain was on my skin again, his rough hands around my waist and his stubble rasping against my lips, and I was breathing him in breath by breath as my lungs worked faster, drunk on his scent. My cheeks turned strawberry red. He saw this and beamed with self-satisfaction.

I didn't want the others to see. I tried to disguise the telltale interaction with a feigned coughing fit, which earned me a lively beating on the back by Berrta. I wondered if the other ladies were noticing all of these blushes and micro-exchanges. Surely they were too obvious to miss. I sincerely hoped that their nearsightedness was working in my favor, because I felt like I was wearing a bumper sticker that said MY OTHER CAR IS A SCOTSMAN.

PUNTING WAS THE next thing on the itinerary. Robbie carefully helped each of us down into the boat, which was disconcertingly low in the water. Many a questioning or worried comment could be heard among the gaggle.

"Well, let's hope our driver can man this contraption better than he did that old bus," snipped Agatha, "or we'll all be down at the bottom of this filthy river in no time. He gets his jollies risking our lives every day."

Robbie laughed good-naturedly. "Don't worry, ladies. I'm an old hand at this. Normally in Cambridge, a rented punt comes with someone to do the punting, but I love to do it myself."

"Hold tight, girls—this could be your last hurrah," said Agatha.

I laughed. And whispered to Helena, "Robbie should consider rebranding: *Shuffle off with Last Hurrahs!*"

She laughed and added, "*Scratch off your bucket list while we help you kick the bucket.*" I had to turn my back to the group to keep from losing it.

Robbie helped Doris on next and made sure she was sitting safely.

"Come on, big guy," he called to Percy. "Come on. Good boy." But Percy just backed up, locked his legs, and whimpered until Robbie went and gathered him up tight in his arms and brought him directly to Doris. *I feel ya, Percy.* I was tempted to ask for the same treatment.

"First intelligent thing that animal's done all trip," Agatha said.

"Oh yeah?" said Doris. "And when are you going to give it a whirl?" I looked down into my handbag to cover a laugh.

Before long, the ladies had settled in and were oohing and aahing at the breathtaking scenery as we bobbed down the slow river, reclining against the wooden benches that weren't at all comfortable, but felt leisurely nonetheless because someone else was doing all the work.

"Lorna, would you mind opening that basket for us?" Robbie called from the back of the boat. Inside were tiny cucumber sandwiches, fresh baked cherry tarts, and a very large pitcher of Pimm's Cup with strawberries, cucumber, and mint. Lorna and Madge doled out the Pimm's to all of us as we basked in the sun eating our cucumber sandwiches and absorbing the beauty all around us.

"Prunes?" Lorna offered, and passed around a bag of little individually wrapped, shriveled brown things that did not in any way look tempting.

"Oh, yes. I could use a couple of those, thank you," Doris said. She took two before passing the bag along. "Ooh. Those are good. I wouldn't mind another, please, Lorna."

"Oh no, Doris. Two is the limit," she said quite seriously. "Never three."

We talked books. So many fantastic books and television series were based in Cambridge, and as we reminisced and debated about them all, the list seemed never-ending. We glided under bridges, weeping willows dripping their foliage prettily into the water at either side. We passed by the Wren Library and were treated to a different view of a now familiar friend after the memorable afternoon we spent in its arms. On the banks of the river were the Backs, and we drifted by, peering in to the more exclusive bits of some of Cambridge's most beautiful colleges while Robbie told us stories about their histories.

We floated under the unspeakably beautiful Bridge of Sighs. The iconic Gothic stone bridge stretched low over the river, lacy stonework surrounding pointed arches that looked for all the world like something a wizard would run across, wand aloft, robes flapping. Robbie informed us that it was said to be Queen Victoria's favorite spot in Cambridge—the very one we were drifting lazily under, a century and a half later. I had to agree with the queen. It was a resplendent moment, picturesque, like living in a painting.

"Does anyone know what a Prince Albert is?" Flossie shouted.

Agatha shushed her violently, and we all shared a little giggle.

I dozed and watched Robbie for a while as he steered the boat with ease, using a long wooden pole like a gondolier: pulling the pole up, dropping it back down, and pushing us along, moving it side to side like a rudder when he needed to change course. He'd warmed up with the work in the sun and shed his green sweater to reveal a white T-shirt underneath, his arms and chest thick and muscular and shifting with effort.

I nearly gawked openly. *Holy crap! Avert your eyes. It's like the sun—don't look directly at it!* And like the sun, it warmed me instantly and reddened my face with another embarrassing, telltale blush.

Shut it down! I scolded myself harshly. I pictured Donald Trump pantsless and perched atop his golden toilet—a visual I used only in dire emergencies to immediately dampen lusty thoughts.

When my breathing had returned, I decided that I could use a distraction.

"Can I try . . . to punt?" I said loudly over the ladies' chattering.

Robbie raised his eyebrows at me. "Really? I'm not sure that's a good idea."

"I am." I flashed a winning smile.

"And what about that wobbly trotter you've got there?" I looked down at my brace. I had stopped using the crutches after the morning. My ankle did slow me down, but had been much less painful than expected.

"Oh, I reattached it with duct tape this morning, so it'll probably hold."

"It's not easy."

"Good." I stood up and started making my way over.

Some of the ladies grumbled warnings, and I heard Agatha say something about a head stuffed with sawdust, but they were all too cozy and Pimm's-filled to stop me.

"Alice Cooper, have you any idea how likely you are to fall into the water and swallow half of the River Cam?"

"I do, as a matter of fact. I ran the figures earlier."

"You could do your ankle a mischief."

"Oh, for heaven's sake, stop nannying me. It doesn't look that difficult. I have a brace on. That's going to keep everything where it's supposed to be."

He laughed in a way that let me know he was skeptical but accommodating, and I made my way over the last bench to the back of the boat. When I got there, I put my hands out to grab the pole, but he was in no hurry to hand it over.

"You're going to need to pull this up a good deal out of the water, like this, and then let it plunge back down, and give it a bit of a push before you start pulling it out again. You steer like this when you need to." He showed me. The whole thing was surprisingly erotic. "But hopefully we can coast along without too much turning."

"Uh-huh." I nodded, doing a *Let's speed this up* motion with my hand. "I've been watching you do it. It looks pretty simple." I felt confident. I was good on the water, and stronger than my slim frame let on. I used to row. I figured I could manage this. "I mean, if you can do it . . ."

"This is actually quite heavy." His face was serious. "Don't let it sweep you off. Look . . ." he said, letting go with one hand offering me the pole. When I grabbed it, however, rather than letting it go, he held on, and moved his other hand around me to my back. His large hand was firm, and it kept me in place while I got used to the weight of the heavy pole shifting under my hands. He was unnervingly close. If I turned my head now, my face would be a mere inch from his. He spoke into the back of my hair, holding me tight as he gave further instructions. I looked down at the nook at the base of his throat and felt the urge to press my mouth there and taste the salty sweat on his skin. *If this is supposed to be a distraction, it's the wrong sort!*

I used my exasperated voice to say, "I've got it, Robbie. Please go and sit down and let me actually give it a try." He looked unwilling to let go, and for a second I thought he would refuse, but he held his hands up in surrender.

"As you wish," he said, making me think of Westley. *Not helpful!* But rather than sit down, he stood near in case I went flailing into the river and left the boat unmanned. He was so close. My head was still spinning from the smell of cologne, sweat, and Robbie.

I thought of his girlfriend. I tried to picture her. Then the light caught his eyes, and he sent me a look that made it very clear that he was remembering our kiss in the rain, and I forgot all about her.

I was going to need to nip this in the bud before we ended up in a sweaty heap on the floor. I would need to look for an opportunity to talk to him alone tonight and make it clear that I wasn't interested in pursuing anything. Maybe over dinner. Or back at the inn. For now, all I had to do was act natural.

WHOA! I nearly got swept off my feet. *This thing is so freaking heavy! Why didn't anyone warn me?* I kept a plastic smile plastered to my face while I tried to regain control without snapping my ankle off at the sock line. It was no small mercy that the river was shallow and slow and that we were on a straight course, but even still, the job was surprisingly difficult. Not least because the mischievous Cambridge winds were blinding me with my own hair. It whipped me in the face, blew into my mouth, and covered my eyes entirely at times. I tried to blow it out of my eyes, then tried a swipe with one hand while holding on for dear life with the other. No use.

I saw Robbie get up and go for the pastry box, where he found a light blue string that once held the box closed with a little bow. He picked it up and brought it over to me.

"Captain." He held it out. "For your mutinous mane."

I grabbed it gratefully, and he manned the pole while I tied my hair back in a short, messy ponytail at the nape of my neck, like an eighteenth-century pirate.

"Thank you. Now back to the poop deck with you!" I flashed him a genuine smile.

"Aye, aye, captain."

I really enjoyed myself once I got the hang of it. We coasted along slowly in the sun, and I did rather well. Luckily, I didn't have to make any turns, because with my ankle the way it was, I wouldn't have managed it. The few times I suddenly put weight on it for balance I was quickly and severely chastised by shooting pain all the way to my back teeth.

But I didn't drown anyone, I didn't make a fool of myself, and I tried something new—I'd successfully punted a ship on the River Cam in Cambridge, England, and I was rather pleased with myself. After a while, I left my station to sit back down. The ladies applauded me, and as I whipped the string from my hair, I took several sweeping bows. Robbie clapped right along with them and let out a whistle. As memories went, I knew this would be one that would stick to me sweetly like icing on my fingers.

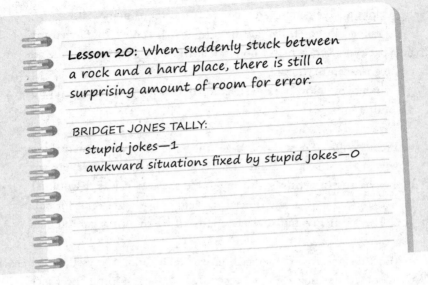

CHAPTER 20

Lesson 20: When suddenly stuck between a rock and a hard place, there is still a surprising amount of room for error.

BRIDGET JONES TALLY:
  stupid jokes—1
  awkward situations fixed by stupid jokes—0

We were staying in Cambridge town that night and arrived at our inn tired, sun-kissed, and grinning from ear to ear. As we parted to freshen up for dinner, I watched carefully and noted Robbie's room number.

I changed quickly into jeans, boots, and a modest sweater; I brushed my teeth, reapplied lip tint and mascara, and ran a hand through my messy hair. Then I headed over.

My every muscle was tense. I had to give myself a little pep talk before I could bring myself to knock. I planned to make a flippant remark or two through the half-open doorway, making a very casual point of the fact that what had happened between us was just a silly moment of irrationality. I was sure he'd be relieved that I was letting him off the hook and that there wouldn't be any mess to clean up.

Waiting for him to open the door felt like an eternity.

"Alice Cooper." This time my name was something else, something sensual. A wide, wolfish grin spread across his face, eyes alight. He had a quick look down the hall to ensure that we weren't being watched, and then, so swiftly, before I had any idea what was happening, he grabbed my hand, twirled me inside, closed the door behind me and backed me gently against it. His body pressed in closer down the length of mine. I caught my breath, suddenly drunk and spinning.

"I've been dreaming of holding you all day long." His face was an inch from my own, and I thought he would kiss me then, but instead he locked his blue eyes on mine and pinned me down with an intense stare that sent my heart pounding like timpani in my chest.

I couldn't speak, but after a second I collected myself and put my hands up, pressing them against him: not quite pushing him away, but letting him know that I wanted space. He backed up immediately, a confused apology on his face. This was not going as I had expected. I was totally off guard. I thought all I would need was a quick comment or two and we would laugh awkwardly, and then I could leave and it would all be behind us, a hot memory.

"I'm sorry," he said, taking another step back and letting out a breath. He rubbed a hand across his forehead and through his hair, looking puzzled and a bit sheepish.

"No, don't be. I was just . . . surprised. That's all." I cleared my throat and walked away into the center of the room where I could be safe from the smell of his cologne. Where I'd have to cover more ground if the memory of that kiss got the better of me.

There were two ways of doing this: I could sit him down and we could have a somewhat serious and horribly awkward chat about what happened and the boundaries that we would have to respect from here on out, or I could make a stupid joke of it. True to form, I opted for the latter.

"So," I started seriously. "I'm becoming a nun. I wanted you to be the first to know."

His brow twisted.

"I just wanted to kiss a man once before I got married to the Lord."

"What?"

"And turns out it was . . . gross," I said, making an apologetic face. "Really gross. Disgusting, in fact. Even if I hadn't already wanted to take a vow of celibacy, kissing you would have cinched it for me." I gave a sympathetic look.

He began to laugh. "You're an absolute nutter!" His face was confused but tickled. But the mood had lightened, as I'd hoped, so I changed pace.

"Yeah, so I just came here to say that I'm really sorry about yesterday. I got swept up by the castle and the rain and the adrenaline, and I got totally carried away. It was a silly mistake."

He looked like he might protest, so I hurried along quickly. I didn't want to sit and have a conversation about his relationship status, my messy life, his undisclosed girlfriend, or any of the rest of it. I didn't want to have to confess that I'd overheard him making plans to Netflix and chill with his girlfriend in her sexy new nightgown or whatever as soon as we got back to Edinburgh.

"I should never have started anything. You're a professional trying to do your job, and I basically held you captive and mauled you." He started to shake his head to contradict me, but I pushed on. "I don't want to make things messy for us. Can you forgive me? Let's just go back to how things were."

He stopped. Whatever was on his lips stayed there. After a moment of what looked like internal debate, he looked resolved. I hadn't left him any room for discussion. Finally, his features cleared into a neutral expression, and he stuck his hand in mine.

"Sure."

"Goodness! Can you imagine? With the way we fight, it would be outright carnage. Double homicide by the end of the week." I laughed, and he laughed too, though the smile didn't reach his eyes.

"Oh, gosh, it's nearly eight. We'd better get down to the lobby. Would you mind leaving a few minutes after me? Arriving together might look a bit suspicious. Also," I added, looking around the room to avoid his eyes, "could I ask you not to be so familiar with me in front of the ladies?"

"What?"

I knew this wasn't fair. It felt horrible. But I could hardly tell him that when he smiled at me the way he did, my entire body blushed, or that when he got close enough for me to catch the scent of him, my mouth watered, or that when he put his hand on my lower back today that I thought my knees would buckle. Far better to avoid any potential swooning triggers altogether. As my beloved Oscar Wilde put it: "I can resist anything but temptation."

"It's just, I don't want anyone to see us and get the wrong idea."

He looked stung. I felt worse.

"I don't think I've been anything but professional in front of the others. Have I?"

"Well, you know. If you could just be a little less . . . friendly."

"Less friendly?" He blinked. His face was hard, and we stared at each other for a moment, the atmosphere in the room chilled. "Right. No problem."

I had to stop myself from squirming. I hated this. I needed to slither out of there before things got worse. "Right. I knew you'd feel the same. Thanks again, Robbie." When I said his name this time, I thought I saw a hint of a flinch on his face.

He opened the door to escort me out in the universal gesture of "Don't let the door hit your ass on the way out."

There. It was done.

God, I need a drink.

HE WAS QUIET that night at dinner. Withdrawn. Usually, he was a natural at getting everyone to have a laugh, inciting book debates, making sure no one felt left out. This dinner was decidedly more tame without his merrymaking. Was he hurt, angry, annoyed, feeling guilty about cheating on his girlfriend, or simply distracted? It was hard to tell.

Flossie, on the other hand, was in rare form: telling us wild tales that Agatha tried her very best to prevent. Failing utterly, Agatha decided instead to provide a running commentary in the hopes of dampening Flossie's madcap claims and overall shock factor.

"The year was 1961. And Johnny Kennedy was sneaking out of Buckingham Palace to see me."

"What rubbish!"

"I was a sweet young girl of nineteen and wearing nothing but a pink bikini."

"Christ in a canoe! We're all going to hell in a handbag!"

THE NEXT MORNING, we were up bright and early and off to Canterbury, where sixteenth-century timber-framed houses crowded and hung over the narrow lanes, tilting forward on ancient beams like old men leaning in to hear one another. I loved it.

Robbie's tour about the history of the town and, of course, the legendary *Canterbury Tales* was fascinating. His historical knowledge never ceased to amaze me. I wondered where he had learned it all. There never seemed to be much that he couldn't answer. I tested this from time to time, trying to stump him with penetrating questions, but he only seemed delighted with the challenge and never once faltered.

At tea that afternoon, I took the only free seat at the table, which happened to be next to Robbie. I had read a historical fiction novel called *Katherine* by Anya Seton in which Chaucer was related through marriage to John of Gaunt, and I had some questions about Chaucer's life and his role at court. Robbie answered me politely and informatively, but when I tried to segue into something less formal, I was met with a steely gaze.

"Wow. You people with your tea. I've never seen anything like it."

"And the Americans are better with their coffee?"

"No, I suppose not. But we tend to get one Venti gallon jug for twenty-seven dollars at Starbucks and call it a day, while here people average dozens of cups of tea like a constant IV drip."

"How fascinating. If you'll excuse me." He stood, picked up his tea, and left the café to stand outside and make another phone call. *To his girlfriend, probably.*

I was disappointed, though not surprised. I had hoped that we could ease into a distanced but companionable acquaintanceship for the rest of the trip, but perhaps ignoring each other was the best we could do.

Helena saw the empty seat and walked over to fill it.

"Well, hello dear. Would you be interested in some company?"

"I'd love some."

"You've no idea how relieved I am to hear you say so, darling. Agatha has been droning on for the better part of an hour, bemoaning the rising cost of tea in Britain."

"Helena, we've only been here for ten minutes." I smiled.

"Really?" She looked at her gold watch. "Well, you know that time is relative, dear, and it slows down relative to the length at which Agatha airs her grievances."

We chuckled together.

"How have you been, love? You seem a bit steadier since last we spoke. Except for that ankle, of course."

"I think I am," I answered honestly. I hadn't really noticed it myself, but she was right. "I mean, I'm still just as confused, but I'm happier. I'm excited to finally be traveling. And it feels good to have you ladies around me. Like being wrapped up in a big, cozy, British blanket of good advice."

"Well, between us we've got about five hundred years of experience, so it's good to hear that we've learned a thing or two along the way." She made a show of pushing her reading glasses up her nose.

My eyes went reflexively to the window where Robbie could still be seen on the phone, laughing and joking while he leaned back against the building.

"Something catch your eye, dear?"

"Hmm?" I said, turning back to see her watching me with a measuring look. "Oh, I'm sorry. I just . . . drifted off. That's so rude. I'm sorry."

"Don't be. I don't blame you with such an irresistible view out the window."

"Yes!" I yipped like a dog whose tail had been stepped on. "Such a gorgeous town. Incredible architecture," I said all too quickly, and watched a smile curl her lips into a bow.

USELESS THINGS THAT I PACKED AND DRAGGED WITH ME ACROSS THE ATLANTIC AND AROUND THE UK:

1. That stupid purple skirt that wrinkled up like an accordion
2. My 4.5-inch stiletto heels
3. All warm-weather clothes (including two pairs of shorts, a pair of flip-flops, and two floral summer dresses)
4. Cashier's checks
5. One of those hideous beige strap-on pouches for traveling that you're supposed to wear around your

middle so that the thieves of London can't get at your big bills

6. *Antidiarrheals (thank you, God)*
7. *Three thongs*
8. *Sunblock (I mean, really!)*
9. *A written list of emergency phone numbers*
10. *Pepper spray, which I found out is illegal in Britain (!) and was thereafter too frightened to carry anywhere in case it fell out of my bag and I was arrested and deported on the spot*
11. *Two full boxes of tampons, obviously, because on day one they had shot out of my bag like bullets on a mission and were lost to me forever*

THE NIGHT AFTER the best Indian food I'd ever eaten, we found a perfect little place called Bramleys around the corner. Most were ready for bed, and Robbie was grumpy, but Helena, Madge, Lorna, and I decided to go in for a nightcap.

The place was adorable. I wanted to take it home in my pocket. There were strings of tiny lights and candles sparkling in the dim like the night sky. There were wingback chairs and frilly lampshades for chandeliers hanging from a ceiling covered in billowy fabric, like some magical tent that had popped up to fulfill our innermost dreams just as we wished for it. A small band softly played acoustic indie folk with a throaty, thirties-style vibrato. We found a velvet-tufted settee and the four of us sat on it smashed together, giddy and holding some masterfully made cocktails.

Somehow we all got on the topic of drunken shenanigans. Lorna and Madge were cute together: bickering away over old story details while they held hands. As we told our stories of intoxicated self-humiliation and the drunken failures of our friends and loved ones, I learned more about the three of them, and they learned more about me. It left us feeling warm and close—bonded as we were over the evening.

"Thank you," I said, holding my second cocktail high. "To the heavens for smiling on me and letting me be here tonight, a world away from home, with you amazing women. And thank you, ladies, for being such marvelous new friends. You are turning my sand to pearl."

They clinked their glasses to mine and gave me a group hug on the little sofa. This was the female camaraderie that the website promised. It was everything I hoped for when I booked this tour. How had I not seen it sooner?

CHAPTER 21

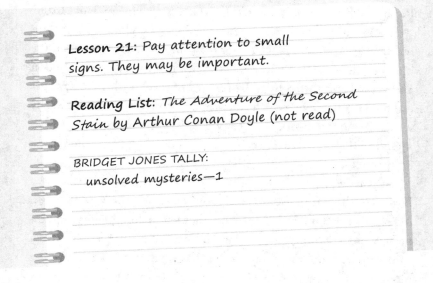

Lesson 21: Pay attention to small signs. They may be important.

Reading List: *The Adventure of the Second Stain* by Arthur Conan Doyle (not read)

BRIDGET JONES TALLY:
  unsolved mysteries—1

It was a day that would live in infamy—its horrors forever emblazoned on my memory like an acid burn. The sights and the smells of that morning will haunt me for the rest of my days and perhaps beyond, raking up fresh terror every time I am reminded of it. When some gruesome sight flashes before my eyes, or heinous odor curls menacingly up my nostrils, or even without any elicitation at all, the remembrance will hunt me down, it will find me, and it will traumatize me anew.

Who is to blame? I may never know. And in its eternal mystery, the memory grows stronger. Always there. Always clawing at me. Always triggering my gag reflex.

My alarm radio woke me at 4:45 a.m. with "Sweet Caroline"—I thought I had been shot through the heart. I rolled out of bed, put on a comfy traveling dress and leggings, and hobbled down to the new, modern tour bus. I threw Robbie's canvas duffel bag inside the luggage hold underneath, rather than stacking it behind the bus for Robbie to Tetris into the back as he would have done with old Rosie.

It was still pitch-black out, and there was a chilly nip in the air, but we were trying to make up for the time we had lost between the bus breakdown and the hospital visit. We had to make it to London and get fed and sorted for a 7 a.m. tour of the British Library's special books collections, which Robbie had arranged for us unofficially with a friend who worked there. We had a fully packed day, then a night in London, and sightseeing all the following day before setting off for Oxford.

The bus was dark and the heaters were blasting away, adding a *whoosh* to the soft sound of Vivaldi on the radio. *Ahhh. Sweet, sweet bus shut-eye*, I thought for a passing moment before I fell asleep under my coat, leaning back in my high-tech reclining seat with my cardigan for a pillow. I could never have fathomed then, in those moments of ignorant innocence, that I would soon be uncommonly grateful for my makeshift bedding.

For one heavenly hour, I slept like a narcoleptic baby sung to sleep by Julie Andrews. But then I woke, cajoled awake by some unseen unpleasantness. I didn't think it scientifically possible that a smell could wake a soundly sleeping person. Alas, this was no ordinary smell. This was an unearthly stink so fierce and so foul as to burn my nose hairs clean off. Soon it had filled every corner of the bus. It spread like an epidemic, waking sleepers and turning dreams to nightmares.

A few of us looked around, bleary-eyed, but no one seemed forthcomingly apologetic. I wrapped my scarf around my nose and mouth and eventually willed myself back to sleep, most likely to dream of rotting carcasses and sewage spills.

When we arrived, the sun was shining, I felt amazing, and we were in London. The London, England, of the movies. The London, England, of Dickens and Sherlock Holmes, of Shakespeare and Tennyson and T. S. Eliot. The London, England, of my dreams. I couldn't wait to get going.

The schedule was tight. We were to drop our things off at the inn, change clothes, grab a free crumpet, inhale a cup of fortifying tea, and then hurry to the library looking somewhat smart and less sleep-creased, if at all possible. We had forty minutes to get there, and the tube would take at least twenty. It was nearly impossible, but we were up to the task.

I went to retrieve my bag. While Robbie was assisting the ladies with their luggage, I spotted mine and grabbed it. As I pulled it out, I noticed it was a bit wet. *That's strange—did it rain?* I looked around at the dry road and the dry bus and decided that it didn't look like it had. But the canvas duffel Robbie had loaned me was certainly wet, and I opened it to find that the damp had soaked through the fabric. *Crap. That's a shame. Maybe I can take a couple of extra minutes to hang some of my clothes in my room to dry out.*

I zipped it back up. Then something hit me.

Something heinous. And yet intimately familiar.

That smell.

What was it? I dropped the bag, unbelieving, and looked back under the bus for answers. There above the spot where my bag had been was a tube. And on the tube was a little sign. A sign that said TOILET DUMP VALVE. My brain hemorrhaged.

What? Toilet dump valve? I very calmly moved in closer to read it again in case I was hallucinating, or in case it actually said TROPICAL DRINKS VAULT or TORCHLIT DUCK VULVA and I was just overreacting. But no. Not only had I read it correctly the first time, now I was close enough to see that the pipe was open and uncovered, its filthy, gaping maw still slowly dripping with sewage.

With great control, I carefully pulled my torso back into the fresh air, inhaled slowly, and turned my head with the grave look of a newscaster delivering the message that Earth would soon be destroyed by a flaming meteor.

"Robert."

He made a strange face. No one called him Robert, but "Robbie" seemed too light and jolly a nickname for such a situation.

"I need you to come here now, please."

He saw the look on my face and hurried over, concerned. All I could do when he arrived was point at the valve.

"What's the matter?" It took him a moment. "Whoa—this thing is open! Good thing you caught it! That could have ended very badly." He laughed. "Can you imagine?"

"I didn't catch it," I responded flatly.

"Huh?"

I pointed at my bag. Now that I knew what had happened, I could see that within the wetness, there were small bits of wet toilet paper clinging on to the canvas. *And . . . Oh God. Oh God, no. A smear. Several SMEARS!*

But there was no God. I knew that for certain now.

Robbie gasped.

"Burn it." I choked. "We'll have to burn it."

He stood there with his mouth open for a moment. Then he stood up straighter, squaring his shoulders in resolve.

"No, I'm sure we can just . . ." He stepped closer, but as he leaned down to unzip the bag, he stopped in midair, just hovering there for a moment, hands outstretched. Then he came to his senses, straightened, and returned to stand a little further off, rubbing his unsullied hands together as if to clean off imaginary germs.

Percy jogged right on over, took a sniff, and tried to flop down and roll in it before Robbie, with a speed like I've never seen, grabbed the handle on Percy's harness and lifted his entire body up off the ground in one swift movement before carrying him off to be leashed.

"Okay. I'm going to go inside and get some gloves and some disinfectant spray, and then we'll wash what we can salvage with super-hot water . . . and maybe some bleach?"

"Hot water? We don't need hot water. We need an exorcism."

We both looked down at the bag, the silence gathering between us.

"I touched it," I whispered, a pained confession I didn't want to be true. "I touched it with the skin of my hands." I held them out in front of me to show him, wishing that I could have them both cut off at the wrists in one clean chop. He pulled away from the threat of contact. I had just touched a bit of the wetness on the outside of my bag, but to me it felt like I may as well have been making a vase out of turds on a pottery wheel.

I blinked many times, looking from my hands to my bag and then back to Robbie.

"Okay, Alice. Let's deal with this thing one bit at a time. This is horrible. I can't believe this happened to you. I'm so sorry. That's the first thing." He waited a beat. "The next thing is that, I'm really sorry to say it, but we have to leave here very shortly, and we don't have time to wait. Would you prefer to stay here and wash and gather yourself and come meet us in town later?"

I didn't want to be left behind and miss out on the London itinerary just so I could stay at the hotel alone to wallow in an air thick with poo and self-pity.

"No."

"Okay. Then go wash your hands, and come down and grab some breakfast. We'll deal with this when we get back later. It can hardly get any worse, can it? I'll talk to the hotel and figure out what to do with your bag in the meantime."

"I can't, uhh . . . I can't touch anything with my hands."

"Right. I'll help you." He led me inside, got the key, and let me in the room. In the bathroom, he turned the faucet on for me and adjusted the temperature to near scalding, but not quite burn-your-skin-off. He pushed the soap dispenser several times and then left me to the undignified business of washing another person's feces off my hands.

I wanted to wash myself in boiling bleach and then put clean clothes on, but I didn't have any clean clothes. Basically everything I brought with me was soiled—quite literally.

That smell. *What if that smell clings to me like a parasite on a host body?*

I scrubbed ten times with three different types of soap, then dug the sanitizing gel out of my purse and rubbed on the entire bottle, from fingernail to elbow like a surgeon. I would have lit my hands on fire like I'd seen doctors do in historical dramas, but I couldn't find an open flame in time before it dried. Then I looked in the mirror, took a few breaths, tried not to think of all my favorite tops and bras and jeans and dresses I would have to say goodbye to forever, gagged a little bit one more time, and then went downstairs to join the group in stoic silence.

I did not eat crumpets.

"Here's what I'm thinking. We get some disposable gloves, put your bag on a plastic tarp, and go through it, separating what can be spared and washed, and what will need to be thrown in the bin." When I came down to breakfast, Robbie had been working on a game plan.

I looked at him—baffled, incredulous. "I can't keep anything in there," I explained as if he were a little slow. "That is not the kind of toilet water I like to wear."

He was going to argue, and then his shoulders dropped and he let out a breath. "I don't blame you."

"But, Robbie. We've got another two weeks of this tour, and I won't have anything to wear but the hideous thing I've got on right now. I'm going to have to get a new wardrobe, and since we don't often have a chance to do laundry, I'll have to buy enough to last until the end of the tour. Please tell me that you have insurance that can cover things like this."

His pained expression said it all. "The insurance covers theft and personal injury, but it wouldn't cover damaged luggage. No. I'm sorry. That's why the website said it was mandatory to purchase your own travel insurance. Did you do that before you left?"

Oh no.

"Well. I thought everything was covered."

His face fell. "Oh, Alice. How could you leave without travel insurance?" At the look on my face, he stopped. "Okay. I'm sorry. I will call the auto insurance company today, explain the situation, and see if there's any way they can cover some of your expenses. But Alice, even if they agree, which is a slim chance, it may take months for the money to come through." His face scrunched up again.

"What am I going to do, Robbie?"

"Well," he said, his face brightening a little. "I think we'll just have to have to shop creatively. Could be fun."

I scowled. "Don't you dare try to find a silver lining, you monster. Once someone poops in your bag, there is no silver lining. Okay. When can I buy something else to wear? Today?"

"Today is totally packed. If you don't have any particular interest in the British Library or Baker Street and you want to skip it and meet up with us later, that would be fine. Otherwise, you'd have to wait at least a few days until we have some free time in Oxford, or maybe Bath."

"I definitely don't want to miss anything."

"Okay. I'll finagle the schedule. I still think it's a good idea to go through your bag when we get back today."

I slumped. "Fine."

"Good girl!" he said, and I glared at him, but it was toothless, and a little bit of humor creeped in against my will.

"That smell was outrageous," he said, sounding shaken. "It made my eyes water."

"If only it could have been harnessed for good instead of evil. It could have powered Tokyo for a week."

CHAPTER 22

Lesson: None, obviously

BRIDGET JONES TALLY:
nipples—2

When we got back from our whistle-stop tour of London—the British Library, Poets' Corner at Westminster Abbey, lunch at Fitzroy Tavern, followed by the Sherlock Holmes Museum on Baker Street—I was exhausted. I'd have loved nothing more than a pre-dinner disco nap, but I knew there was no hiding from the task ahead. I would have to stare that poop in the face and take it down.

"I've got a little announcement." Helena's lovely face was alive with mischief. "I've spoken with an old friend of mine who has a new up-and-coming restaurant here in London, and if Robbie doesn't mind a last-minute amendment to our itinerary, then I'd like to invite you all to dinner tonight at Agate."

Some of the ladies gasped, and others clapped.

"Wow, Agate," Robbie said. "That would be amazing, Helena."

"Capital. Reservation's at eight, so put on your glad rags and meet in the lobby at seven-thirty sharp!" she said with a little giddy squeeze of her shoulders.

For a very brief moment, I had almost forgotten about my lost wardrobe. So many fallen friends lost in the Battle of the Bulging Bowels. My singular remaining outfit, the hobo muumuu I was wearing, was not *glad*. It was just *rags*. It had come from Target and was fit only for scooping out a litter box or for convincing persistent men you're not attracted to them. I had only brought it because it didn't wrinkle. I had paired it with leggings and sneakers, and to add insult to injury, I had caught my leggings on the corner of a table and ripped a little hole in the back. Perhaps they could set up a small table for one in the ladies' restroom to keep me from unsettling the other customers.

Robbie collected me solemnly and brought me to the back garden, where my bag sat waiting in the middle of a plastic tarp. He handed me some rubber gloves and put his on like a doctor on a kids' show, snapping them dramatically at the wrist.

I hiccupped a little laugh at that, and tried to be strong. "It's go time, fuckers."

"Yeah! Wait, who are the fuckers in this scenario?"

"Umm, I don't know. I just wanted to sound tough. The dirty clothes?"

"Aye, alright. I can get onboard with that."

We knelt down and started taking out the items one by one. The process was tragic, but I tried my best to be cold and impartial.

- Sweaters? Poop sponges. Too many nooks and crannies for the poop to hide. Trash.
- Jeans and blouses? Too close to the skin. Too easy to stain. Trash.
- Pajamas? I'd rather be thrashed unconscious by Michael Bolton's hair. Trash.

- White bodycon dress, now with brown "water" spots and blue chemical stains? Trash.
- Toothbrush? No comment.
- Contact lenses and case? A petri dish of pink eye just waiting to happen. Trash!

Oh God. I forgot about the lingerie.

The process of pulling out my toilet-dump-valve-sullied underwear in front of Robbie was mortifying. I had packed a broad range of panties, from French call girl to oversized faded period undies that looked as if they were family heirlooms.

He lifted up a pink G-string, pinching it between his gloved fingers and stretching the elastic with his thumbs hooked in the straps. "Do you want to keep your slingshot here? You know you're not supposed to fly with weapons."

I felt a hot scarlet blush cover my entire face and tried to snatch it out of his hands. Unfortunately, the straps were caught on his fingers, so they just stretched comically like rubber bands when I tried to wrestle it away.

"Christ! You've got enough knickers here to outfit an army! What did you plan on doing with all of these?" he said, pulling them out one by one and stacking them on the side to make a small monument to my humiliation.

"Clean undies are essential. Not that you would understand, you barbarian. You've probably been wearing the same pair since we left Edinburgh."

"Alice, I had no idea you'd been thinking on my pants this whole time. Need I remind you about the professional distance that we've agreed to keep?" I scoffed and rolled my eyes.

Luckily he drew the line at my notably small-cupped bras—like someone had split a lemon lengthways, hollowed it out, and sewn the pieces together—probably deciding that there was no safe way to tease a woman about her bras, thank goodness.

"Shoes!"

My shoes were all in zippered plastic bags. I had never liked the idea of dirty shoes rubbing up on my clothes and pajamas and unmentionables as they danced about in my luggage, so I always stored them in separate plastic bags. They were saved! Nestled between them sat my makeup case—in another plastic bag to prevent an oil spill should my face lotion feel rebellious. I extracted them carefully, unzipped, and checked for dampness. They looked clean to me! I would investigate more carefully from my room, but for now, I was elated. This was a victory!

We finished up, and I scurried to my room quickly to scrub the living daylights out of my hands and then shower in scalding water. We had dinner reservations soon. At least I would have decent shoes!

JUST AS I stepped out of the shower, I heard a tap at the door. My heart skipped a beat thinking it might be Robbie. I tightened the towel around me, and my neck grew hot at the thought of having him here in the room with me, damp and naked. I looked in the mirror and scolded my libido soundly into submission.

To my surprise, it was Helena.

"Alice, dear. I've got a little delivery for you." She sneaked in with a look on her face as if we were in on a little secret together. In her hand swung a garment bag with SELFRIDGES printed on it.

"Oh, Helena, you're amazing, but I couldn't possibly borrow anything of yours! What if I spill wine on it, or spatter pasta sauce down the front?"

"It's not a loan, darling. I told my daughter, Pippa, about your utterly horrifying ordeal, and she wanted to help. She's one of the head buyers at Selfridges, so she had a few things lying about and sent over a little care package. I had to guess at your size, but hopefully I have just the thing for tonight."

I stood stupefied. "No, Helena. You shouldn't have. This is too much. I can't accept."

"Don't be silly. Of course you can. Anyway, at least see what we've got before you decide." She gave me a solicitous wink. "I happen to think this dress might be your soulmate."

She pulled at a hanger, and something expensive slinked out. She turned it around so I could take it in and then held it up against my body to see how it might fit. My breath caught. It was silk in the most incredible shade of green—something between emerald and a dark jade, changing hues ever so slightly as it moved in the light.

"Oh, Helena. It's gorgeous."

"And it'll be gorgeous on you. Well, at least that's tonight settled then."

"How can I ever thank you? And your daughter? We've never even met!"

"Seeing the look on every man's face when you walk in tonight will be thanks enough, darling."

I blushed a bit at that, and she smiled, looking satisfied at having won the battle.

"Have you got any shoes, or shall I bring some of mine over?"

"I do have a pair of beige pumps, actually. Or black. All my shoes were in plastic bags, luckily. Which do you think?"

"We'll try them both. Now run get changed, and let's have a look at you."

I nipped into the bathroom and wiggled into the dress. That's when I realized half of it was missing—it was completely backless. The back scooped down low past the curve of my waist where the fabric hung open slightly, draping prettily before crossing in a vintage style, with three silk-covered buttons at the base of my lower back. The dress tightened then, fitting around the hips and bottom before flowing out from there to the hem. The front was fairly simple and modest, and the hemline was midcalf and the neckline high, but the silk showed every lump and curve of my body, every seam of my underwear.

I couldn't wear this dress without a sturdy infrastructure. The top wasn't tight, and you could see my nipples protesting the chill. Worse still, the slightest movement sent the silk rippling over my skin like water, and at the right angle you could see the shape of my breasts in their entirety.

Even a thong would have shown through this fabric, and what I was currently wearing was a forlorn, full-bottomed, gray cotton brief that rode a little too high and had been washed more than the floor of a fishmonger's.

No, it just wouldn't work. Oh God, Helena had gone through all this trouble, and I would have to wear my ugly dress and torn leggings after all.

"Let's see, pet," Helena called from the other side of the door.

I cracked the door and stuck my head out. "Oh, Helena. I'm so sorry. I can't wear this tonight."

"What's the trouble? Doesn't it fit?"

"Well, actually, it fits like a glove, but I don't have a backless bra or Spanx or those sticky nipple petals or anything, and everything is just, you know, there . . . on display."

"But it's silk. You're not supposed to wear anything underneath silk. It's made to caress your body in gentle waves, not to show off the cut of your knickers."

"You haven't seen it. I could pose for a life-drawing class in that dress."

"Come on out of there, you muppet. It's only me."

I creaked the door open and took a tentative step out into the room. Helena took a little breath in and covered her mouth.

"I know. As soon as I can, I'm going to buy the right underwear and—"

"It is absolute perfection," she said slowly.

"No, really. I don't think you—" I turned in a circle.

"It's even more beautiful than I thought. You're stunning."

"But I couldn't."

"Alice, it's silk. It's made to be a little bit . . . suggestive, in a chic, sophisticated way, of course. You have the perfect figure for it, and the green is incredible on you. Now dry your hair and put a little rouge on. We don't want to be late." She gave me a serious look. "Yes?"

I inhaled deeply and consulted the mirror again. I straightened my posture and steeled my reserve. "Yes. Good pep talk. I'll see you downstairs in fifteen minutes. I'll be the one with my headlights on."

"Atta girl!"

I HAD MY coat on when I met the others downstairs. At least it would buy me some time before disrobing dramatically at the restaurant, but already the ladies were telling me how nice I looked, just to be in heels and a little more preened than usual. The heels would be a bit tricky to navigate with the twisted ankle, but I knew we didn't have far to walk. My ankle had been feeling stronger lately, and I could hardly wear my sneakers. I would just have to take someone's arm when needed.

The ladies looked amazing, many of them wearing dresses I hadn't yet seen. I let out a low whistle. "Look out, London. Here we come!" We all cheered.

As we walked in, we let out a collective sigh. The restaurant was situated above the London skyline on a rooftop, enclosed in a glass conservatory framed in white Victorian ironwork. There was one central tree strung with lights in an immense porcelain pot, four simple chandeliers, and basically no other decorations apart from the peonies and candles at each table. In its simplicity, there was sumptuous abundance.

A gentleman came to take our coats. I held my breath, peeled it off, and handed it over. I happened to see Robbie behind me in the mirror. He stopped in the middle of unbuttoning and stood stock-still until the gentleman cleared his throat. The look on Robbie's face uncoiled something in my heart for a beat, then another slow, heavy beat. I blushed. There were gasps and lavish compliments from the ladies and a look of smug gratification from Helena as I was led toward a table facing the river.

I had decided to leave my crutches with my coat and make my way to the table gingerly in what I hoped was a sexy, slinky way. Helena put my hand in the crook of her elbow—lest all her good work be shattered by a ruinous moment that left me sprawling on the tiled floor sans panties.

Everyone in the restaurant was achingly fashionable, from the impeccably beautiful to the sharp and edgy. Of our dazzling cavalcade of gussied-up octogenarians, Berrta was the one exception. She wore pleated chinos, a brown sweater, and orthopedic walking shoes that looked very supportive. She didn't look the least bit self-conscious. In fact, she looked pleased and perfectly comfortable, and I loved her all the more for it.

We were utterly spoiled. Helena ordered three bottles of champagne to start and the chef's personal tasting menu for the entire table, alongside glittering wine pairings that we knew we would never taste again. She waved away our protestations. "It's much too beautiful a night to worry ourselves with foolish moderation."

London stretched out around us in every direction, and Helena had timed it perfectly so we would arrive just as the sun was finishing its descent, setting fire to the Thames and its bridge. The London Eye was lit up in an outstanding show, and even the iconic

Big Ben was in view, its face beginning to glow in the fading light. Everything around us changed from golden orange and pink to indigo, and then to inky, star-studded velvet. I couldn't believe that anything could be so marvelous.

A few times I happened to catch Robbie's eye, and when I did, the look on his face made my heart pound. He looked so handsome. He didn't often wear much color, but tonight he was in a royal blue cashmere sweater that made his eyes sparkle.

It was almost as if we were both in costume. Almost as if we could be other people, out at a beautiful restaurant, meeting for the first time. I wanted to forget all the arguments and battling egos, the phone calls to the secret girlfriend, and just enjoy the way it made me feel when he looked at me the way he did. Even though I knew I couldn't.

During one of the dessert courses, Doris began to cough, and downed the rest of the water in her glass. I got up quickly to retrieve another one from the bar, and remembered halfway there that heels, champagne, and twisted ankles make for poor companions. Just as I slowed down with a wobble, I felt Robbie's hands on my arm, holding me steady. He escorted me the few remaining feet to the bar.

"Sit here for a second, and take the weight off your ankle. I'll be right back." He hurried the glass of water to Doris.

"Hi" was all he said when he returned a minute later.

"Hi," I repeated, and we sat for a few moments, the music swelling in the air.

"Is Doris okay?"

"Good as new." He turned to me, and we both sipped at our waters. The silence grew thick and hungry between us. His eyes seemed to search me, trying to figure me out. It was too much. I broke first.

"Well, I have to say that I, for one, am disappointed in this place. I was really hoping for something more Medieval Times–themed, with wenches serving watery beer, and where we could eat turkey legs and ham hocks with our bare hands and then toss the bones to the floor while people jousted below. You know—the real London."

"My God, Alice, you're beautiful."

It was nothing, really, just a compliment from a handsome man, nothing more. The fact that it lit my nerves on fire and engulfed me so completely that I could no longer breathe was irrelevant. I swallowed, blinked, breathed in a shaking breath and gathered jokes about me like armor against this relentless onslaught of charm.

"Oh, this old thing?" I gestured to my fabulous dress. "Everything else I own is a biohazard, so I guess I made the right choice. Wouldn't you agree?"

He looked at me unguardedly for a moment.

"I think it's probably not a good idea for me to make any comments about the way you look in that dress tonight." His eyes caught mine. "They would definitely not be professional in nature."

My stomach flipped. I kept my face very calm so that he wouldn't see the hurricane he was causing. "Oh? And what about telling me I was beautiful just a moment ago?"

"Purely professional." His deadpan delivery shocked a laugh out of me.

"Really? Is this a service that I paid for?"

"It's all in the tour package you purchased. In fact, I just told Doris she was sizzling hot in that trouser suit, and gave Agatha a pinch on the bum. You shouldn't take these things to heart."

I laughed. "Wow. Lucky ladies! Is the whole group getting the same treatment?"

"No, not everyone. Lorna and Madge got a refund. Berrta paid double."

I gasped and laughed.

"What does that get her?"

"My client contracts are strictly confidential, I'm afraid. You only got the introductory package, so you've had your lot for the rest of the trip."

"What a rip-off. At least at Medieval Times I could expect a serf to whistle lewd remarks at me, or a knight to offer me a grope of his codpiece."

"Oh, aye, but that's English codpiece. Not worth the trouble."

"Oh really? And is this conclusion the result of rigorous study, Mr. Brodie?"

"Course not. Flossie told me."

I laughed in outrage. "She did not!"

"Oh, she most certainly did. I believe the comparison she used was dachshunds and Dobermans."

"She did not!" I laughed. It did sound like her. "I don't believe a word of it! What utter nonsense."

"Only one way to be sure." He gave me a salacious sideways look. "Ask Berrta." I laughed so loud that some of the ladies glanced over at us. "After her pickleball excursions, she could publish a peer-reviewed study."

I couldn't hold back the saucy smile warming my face, and we just looked at each other for a heavy moment and grinned. "So what package would I have to buy to take your arm and have you walk me back to the table?" His eyebrow cocked and he looked at me sidelong.

"Well, that all depends where you're wanting me to put my hand."

AFTER DINNER, WE had tickets for *Hamlet* at the Globe. As we filed in and shuffled down the row of wooden benches, I realized I would be sitting next to Robbie, and my heart gave a little lurch before I told it to be quiet.

It was open-air and the night was chilly, so I was happy to be sandwiched between Robbie and Helena. The play was incredible.

The benches, however, were terribly uncomfortable—you know, so that we could pretend we lived in the Middle Ages. My bottom became completely numb, like I was sitting on a slab of cold beef. I hugged my coat so tightly around me that the seams strained. Robbie unfurled his scarf and, soundlessly leaning over, he wrapped it around my neck, looping it twice and tucking the ends in, as if it was the most natural thing in the world. The scarf was still warm from his neck, and the intoxicating smell of him took me over. My eyelids fluttered closed.

For the rest of the play, like a stupid schoolgirl, I could notice nothing but the warm length of Robbie's leg pressing against my own. I could feel his muscles move when he shifted in his seat, and it made my skin tingle. Every second strung out into an eternity. It was all I could do to remember to watch to the play.

Hamlet thinks he *has questions? He doesn't know the half of it.*

CHAPTER 23

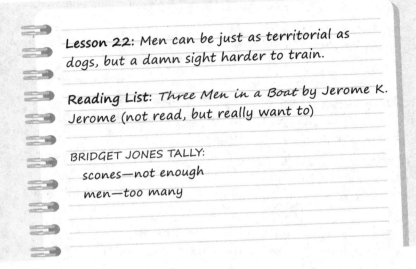

Lesson 22: Men can be just as territorial as dogs, but a damn sight harder to train.

Reading List: *Three Men in a Boat* by Jerome K. Jerome (not read, but really want to)

BRIDGET JONES TALLY:
scones—not enough
men—too many

I slept beautifully that night after my evening in the clouds. It was one of the best nights I'd had in years.

The next morning when I came down to breakfast, Robbie was on the phone. I could just make out the end of the conversation while I poured myself some orange juice.

"Alright, gorgeous. You look after yourself. Love you."

"Oh, is that Isla?" Helena called from next to me, where she was steeping her tea. "Send her my love, won't you, dear? Oh! Tell her that Poppy set aside a pair of kitten heels that we thought she'd like. We can post them up."

My stomach curdled. Was I the only one on the planet who hadn't known about Robbie's girlfriend?

I was sitting down with my cereal when Robbie made his way over to me. His face had a serious slant to it.

"Alice. I'm glad you're up. I've been wanting to talk to you." He sat down and lowered his voice. "I'm sorry if last night . . . well, I realize that I was . . . too familiar. It's all my fault. I got a bit swept away. I hope I didn't make you uncomfortable."

I was caught off guard. I took a sip of juice and thought for a moment.

This was the guilt then. I didn't like the taste of it. I took a bite of cold toast to collect myself. What could I possibly say to that?

"It's fine. It's not your fault. In fact, you know whose fault it is? Helena's! With all her bottles of free champagne, and slinky dresses . . . she owes us both an apology, don't you think?" He gave me a small, grateful smile.

"You're right. How dare she spoil us rotten? It was definitely all her fault."

My voice, when it came out, was a little too soft around the edges. "You really didn't make me uncomfortable. Nothing to apologize for." I cleared it from my throat. Then I stuck my hand out and added a boisterous "Enemies?"

"Enemies," he confirmed with a smile, and shook my hand firmly. And just like that, we were back on solid ground.

As WE SPED off in the direction of Oxford, Helena came over to sit by me.

"So I just got off the phone with my son, and he's made a little time for us so that he can show us around Oxford."

"Really? That's exciting. I didn't know you had a son in Oxford, Helena."

"I do. My youngest, Tristan."

"Is he studying there?"

It would be interesting to meet one of Helena's children. Someone from her world outside of the tour. We were getting to know all about one another's lives, but the more closely I bonded with the ladies, the more difficult it became to imagine them having any life, or existing at all, outside of this tour. The sensation made me passionately curious to catch a glimpse, however small, of the relics of this other parallel universe.

"He's a physicist. A fellow in medical physics, actually."

"Wow! That sounds impressive."

"He's always been very studious. Always has his head in some book or other. My other two boys were more athletic, but Tristan was the bookish one. It made him shy around other people, especially girls."

Oh, God. Oh God no. Please don't do this, Helena. Don't say it.

"As a matter of fact," she went on, "you two would have a lot to talk about. He's just accepted a position at Harvard and will be moving in autumn, so you can tell him all about Boston. Give him the inside scoop!" She waggled her eyebrows.

"Oh," I floundered. "I haven't been home in such a long time for anything other than seeing my parents. I'm sure a quick search online would be much better for the inside scoop."

"Nonsense. I'm sure you're a font of knowledge. Maybe you can even meet him there and show him around a bit one weekend. You know, to help him get acquainted. I think you two would really hit it off."

And there it is.

"Oh, you know, Helena. He sounds great, but . . ."

"Just keep it in the back of your mind." She flapped a hand to ward off any contrary notions buzzing around. "That's all I'm asking. You may be perfect for each other. He needs a strong woman to pull him out of his shell a bit."

Well, crap. An unathletic, socially inept man who is afraid of women. And she thinks he'll be perfect for me.

I'd been set up by beautiful mothers before, when I still lived with my parents. It had never once gone well. Genes did not always get passed down favorably. And they all had mommy issues, each and every one. I wouldn't fall for it again. I could imagine him with grisly clarity: doughy, bad skin, and thick saliva that crisscrossed his mouth when he spoke. He would smell of soup and loneliness.

And what kind of a name is *Tristan*, anyway? The name of a pale milksop with an Oedipus complex, that's what kind of a name it was. Embarrassingly theatrical. "This is my boyfriend, Tristan," I would say at a cocktail party, and people would immediately disperse like soap on oil to defriend me from their Facebook accounts.

Besides, I was emphatically *not* there to date. *Do you hear that, Universe? Stop flinging men at me!*

WE ENTERED THE city from the south, crossing the river, and Oxford began to unfold and show her secrets to us as we parked and began on foot through the narrow, cobbled city streets. Each step cast a spell on me.

How to describe Oxford? Is it possible, when a place so closely resembles your dreams, to put it into words? It's called the City of Dreaming Spires, and these spires I have dreamed of since I was a child.

The University of Oxford has thirty-nine colleges, like the Hogwarts houses, and each has its own charming character: Many were Gothic piles, generous of adornment and splendor, while others were all stately Georgian simplicity dabbled sparingly with just a touch of flourish, while yet others looked like old rough castles hewn from stone and heaped upon the old town walls, ready to defend against invaders. They were magnificent, and I understood why Oxford's students had labored so ardently to deserve them.

We wove through carved gray stone and leaded windows until the beating heart of Oxford opened up in front of us—where ancient, hulking libraries called our names in a papery whisper, and strange and curious heads peered down from lofty pillars, watching our every step with bulging eyes. The sun shone. Students cycled past, scarves flapping behind them.

"Oh, there's Tristan!" Helena waved.

I looked over, and there he was. Just as I had imagined. He was leaning back against the rails, though "slumping in a bulbous bundle" would be more accurate. He was everything I had dreaded, but with long oily coils of curling hair thrown in for good measure. I locked eyes with his waxen, sweaty face against my will, the way a person might find it impossible to look away from a horror scene. He caught me staring and smoothed a hand over his hair. When I didn't—*couldn't*—look away, he bit his lip in a salacious entreaty that he clearly expected to be met with equal rapture.

Hellfire! She's told him. She's told him that we were made for each other, and now he's salivating over the prospect of undressing me with his sweaty little hands. I could practically smell his hot, yellow vinegar breath from thirty paces away.

Helena dashed toward him, much in the way a panther might if it were in a mild hurry, but as she moved forward she grabbed hold of a random bystander and appeared to be squeezing him with her body. Was she being attacked while her son stood aside and looked unflinchingly at my body with a nauseating appetite? I was confused.

Helena grasped the stranger's hand, and they sauntered over to us—*two* panthers in a casual ballet. That's when I snapped the fuck out of it, and my jaw swung open with a squeak.

Tristan, obviously, was tall and beautifully proportioned, with a lean, sinewy body that was both graceful and masculine. He was dressed like something out of a catalog, yet somehow it appeared to be effortless. His mother probably picked it out. I didn't care.

That face! He had haunting gray eyes and chestnut hair. Some of it dangled over his eyes, and he had to brush it away in the most unwitting display of sensuality I'd seen since Poldark in a tricorn hat.

Glasses lent character to what would otherwise have been saccharine perfection, and a three-day-old dusting of stubble gave the impression that he had been far too busy to remember to shave. *What had he been too busy doing? Curing cancer? Seducing women? Writing tumultuous poetry?* The mind boggled.

He smiled, and the sun shone more brightly and the birds began to sing. And they were singing Barry White.

"Wow. What's going on here then? It looks like you've caught someone's eye." A Scottish voice, much closer than expected, broke me from my stupor.

"What? Huh?" I blushed hotly, my face burning. *Great. Now I look like a blotchy tomato. So much for a sexy first impression.* "Oh? Do you think so?"

"Be careful, Alice Cooper. He looks like a lady-killer."

Well, that's fair.

I followed his gaze, and my smile dropped. Robbie was referring to the pimpled lecher who had clearly mistaken my momentary attention for irrepressible lust. He caught me looking at him again and licked his lips . . . for my benefit. Robbie barked with laughter.

"Oh, shut up."

He laughed all the more heartily. "Don't let's be coy. Should I wave him over?"

"If you do not step away from me this instant, I will peel your face away with my fingernails."

He raised his hands in surrender and backed away slowly, pleased with himself.

Helena and her son joined us, with Helena making thoughtful introductions.

"And this is the lovely Alice, who is over from DC, where she takes the nonprofit sector by storm."

"Hi, Alice. It's nice to meet you. I'm Tristan." Oh, that gorgeous English accent. Now I knew what kind of name Tristan was—the name of a mythical warrior king, the name of a Greek god carefully wrapped in English tweed.

"It's nice to meet you too." *Quick! Say something charming!* "I hope you've come prepared to tell us all of your mother's most embarrassing stories—we're starting to believe she's flawless." He was even better close up. He was Prince William with hair, he was Michael Fassbender naked, he was Jude Law before the nanny incident.

He smiled. I nearly fell over.

"My mother said you were funny." We shook hands. I changed from tomato red to maroon. Blushing any further could be a medical emergency. "Well, I'm very happy you're all here, and that you've been looking after my mother so well. I begged her to let me show you around today, and she finally relented, luckily for me." I heard the ladies giggle and mumble among themselves. I wasn't the only one whom Tristan was winning over. "That is, if it doesn't spoil your itinerary too much, of course, Robbie."

"Oh, I think the ladies would be thrilled to get the insiders' tour. Thank you, we're looking forward to it." Robbie matched his friendly tone, but there was a nearly imperceptible something in his voice that caught my attention. I suppose he hated to give up the limelight even for one afternoon.

"Wonderful. It's all settled then. I was thinking we'd start here, nip into the Sheldonian Theatre, then I'll sneak us into the Radcliffe Camera—I hear you're all rather fond of books—and then go round to some of my favorite colleges. Does that sound like it'll do?"

The ladies were jubilant. Flossie began to clap. Percy ran in a circle around Tristan, yapping with excitement.

"Well then, first things first: tea and scones. We have a busy day ahead."

Vaults & Garden was a gorgeous café right in Radcliffe Square that had once been part of the cathedral, and inside it was bright and charming with vaulted ceilings and tall Gothic windows. The smell of delectable cakes and teas curled out into the square and lured hapless students in by the nose, leaving their research, no doubt, for another time.

Tristan was in line behind me as I perused the options.

"How can I pick just one thing? Any recommendations?"

He looked down at his tray, smiled sweetly, and pushed his glasses up on his nose.

"Well, I happen to think that they have the best cream tea in Oxford, if you fancy it." His voice was soft, and it melted over me.

Cream tea? Well, that sounds stupid. Is it just creamy tea? I want a pastry. "It's a major decision," I teased. "Are you sure that I can trust you?"

"I think so. How about this—if you're not convinced, then I'll have your cream tea and buy you an assortment of other things to make up for it."

"You know what, Tristan, I think we're going to get along just fine." He laughed, but didn't respond.

I ordered a cream tea as instructed. They offered me my choice of scones, still warm from the oven—*yay!*—and fresh local jam. I chose raspberry. It was served with a pot of delicious tea and, to my sheer delight, a ramekin containing a mountainous dollop of thick clotted cream for the scone.

Watching Tristan for direction, I split my scone and piled it high with jam and cream and bit down into heaven. I closed my eyes and inhaled deeply as I chewed that first bite. It was warm and cakey, buttery, so creamy, and just the right amount of sweet. It melded perfectly with the tea. I did a quick calculation of how many scones with cream I could conceivably cram down before we had to leave Oxford.

I smiled at Tristan. "You're off the hook."

THE HISTORY OF the place had a palpable, physical presence. As Tristan strode us through the cobbled streets, he intrigued us with stories from some of history's greatest thinkers, Oxonian traditions, brutal tales about the conflict between "towns" and "gowns," and hilarious and absurd student pranks on rival colleges going back for hundreds of years.

Tristan had been there since undergrad and was now a fellow at Brasenose College, and it would appear he made it his business to absorb every fascinating fact he had ever heard about Oxford. He spoke softly, but we hung on his every word.

At Christ Church College, we saw the Hogwarts dining hall—though we were told that the food served was so bad that it was sinister—and Tristan had even made arrangements to bring us to a restricted library high in the college where we were the only people save one librarian. Ancient leather-bound volumes were protected by a cage of actual laser beams, and there was a small collection of treasures like a Bible that had belonged to Queen Elizabeth I, Cardinal Wolsey's felt hat, and a jeweled box with an eerily humanesque mandrake inside.

Robbie, for his part, played the good sport. Somehow, impossibly, I got the feeling he didn't much like Tristan. Despite this, he didn't seem to be able to stop himself from asking Tristan lots of interesting historical questions throughout the day, and this made for a fascinating back-and-forth for us ladies to watch. I enjoyed having Robbie on the tourist side, because his mind worked in beautiful ways when it came to history, and his questions pulled at threads I never would have thought to feel for. I did also enjoy the fact that he had to take a back seat while some other man took control of his tour. It clearly rankled him, which filled me with joy.

When finally, late afternoon, we turned into the vine-covered doorway of our charming bed-and-breakfast, Tristan caught my attention.

"Hi, Alice," he said sweetly. "I had reservations to bring my mom to formal dinner tonight at my college, but she said she was too tired to make it. She, um, suggested you might be interested. Maybe you would like to come? You don't have to answer right away, but—"

"Yes! That sounds amazing."

He smiled and looked away.

"Great. That's great. I'll come by and scoop you up here at seven, if that's alright. Drinks and canapés start at half seven. Does that suit?"

"I'll be there with bells on."

"Lovely." We stood there for a moment, staring at each other, both pleased with the exchange but not quite sure what to say. "Right then." He adjusted his glasses. "See you at seven then. Good."

"Oh, Tristan!" I stopped him just as something terrible occurred to me. "What does one wear to a formal dinner at Brasenose College?"

"Ahh. Yes, right. I almost forgot. My mother said she had something for you, actually. Formal dinner tends to be . . . well, a little bit formal, but you'll . . . I'm sure you'll fit right in no matter what you wear, so wear whatever you like. I'll see if I can borrow a subfusc from a friend. I have spares, but I think they may be a tad long for you. Don't worry—leave it to me."

Helena has something for me? And what the hell was that word he just said? I decided to simply nod gravely, as if I absolutely knew what the heck he was talking about.

We said our brief and bumbling goodbyes, and then I watched him walk away—far more intently than was proper for an honorable young lady.

As I HEADED into the B&B, I ran into Robbie in the foyer. When he saw me, he gave a furtive glance to the window with a drawn brow. *Looking to see if Tristan had left,* I supposed. *Has he been waiting here for me?*

"Hey. So Tristan invited me to formal dinner at his college tonight. I'm sorry to miss our evening group plans, but it just seems too special an opportunity to pass up."

Robbie's face transformed. "Really? Are you going to be okay on your own with that guy? He seems dead sleazy to me."

I laughed outright, in his face, taken completely by surprise.

"*That guy? Sleazy?* You mean Tristan, who we spent our day with? The one who took time out to show us all over the city and held Doris's arm to keep her steady over the cobbles? Shy, soft-spoken Tristan, who is a fellow at Oxford? Helena's son, Tristan?" I laughed, hardly able to get the words out, enjoying myself immensely while he stood there, arms crossed and unamused. His little scowl made me laugh all the more. "Do you have a Taser I can borrow? Or perhaps a small switchblade?"

"Alice, you don't know him. Just because he seems nice doesn't mean he's trustworthy where women are concerned. I know what these public school boys can be like."

I laughed even harder.

"No doubt he has designs on Doris too, the pervert!"

His sharp blue eyes narrowed. "You know what? You're totally right. I was worrying over nothing. The minute you open your mouth, he'll be dragging you back to return you. The good news is, I'm sure you'll have the rest of your evening free to join the group for dinner. As planned."

He turned and started up the stairs, but I couldn't stop laughing.

"Wait," I called after him, giggling helplessly. "Robbie, wait!" He stopped midway up a step but didn't turn around. "Do you think you could help me go over some kung fu moves? In case he tries to hold the door open for me." He carried on without looking back. "Robbie, don't go! Where can I buy some brass knuckles?"

HELENA MAGICALLY HAD a second dress for me. She said she had gotten it as a backup for the backless goddess dress but kept it on reserve, because she knew if I'd had a more modest option, I would have chickened out.

I called her my fairy godmother and kissed her on the cheek. It was simple, black, and Jackie O in a classic but also perfectly modern way, and of course, because Helena had had something to do with it, was incredibly flattering.

After a long deliberation, I decided not to bring my crutches. I was going to a formal dinner at Oxford on a starlit night with a gorgeous man. Crutches just didn't fit with the imagery. Besides, I had managed dinner in London without them, and my ankle, while still sore, had been feeling much better. I did, however, tuck my black flats into my handbag just in case there would be lots of walking.

I sat in the lobby to wait, and within a minute or two, Robbie had jogged down the stairs on his way out. He stopped when he saw me cross-legged on the armchair, a small smile on my lips and smoky eyes imploring him to give me another reason to tease him.

His gaze dragged from my heels to my hair to my lips. An unguarded flash of longing made my stomach flutter before it disappeared. He nodded curtly and moved along. *You're the lothario I need to watch out for*, I thought as he walked out. *What a hypocrite. A man with a girlfriend definitely shouldn't be looking at me as if he'd like to ravish me on the wingback.*

CHAPTER 24

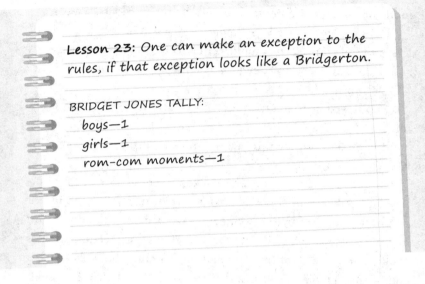

Lesson 23: One can make an exception to the rules, if that exception looks like a Bridgerton.

BRIDGET JONES TALLY:
boys—1
girls—1
rom-com moments—1

Tristan arrived at seven on the dot. Gorgeous *and* punctual.

"Wow. Alice. You look lovely." He smiled and gave me a chaste kiss on the cheek.

We walked to Brasenose despite his repeated offers to call us a cab, but I put my time in with my heels now, showing my legs to their best advantage, safe in the knowledge that I could switch to flats on the way home. It also gave me an excuse to clasp onto his elbow and hold tight to his arm. He was a bit awkward at first, but I made an extra effort to draw him out.

The city was somehow even more magical by lamplight. The old street lamps turned the great imposing stone castles of the city into spun gold against a darkening sapphire sky. We approached Radcliffe Square, this time from the other side, and when the Radcliffe Camera appeared into view, it was lit up and glowing: a thing divine.

We curled around the corner and into Brasenose, and in the ten minutes we had remaining Tristan snuck me in to visit some of the more interesting things that were restricted to outsiders.

"Here you go." He held a strange sleeveless robe out to me, with long strips of fabric at the shoulders that seemed to be entirely useless and that hung all the way down to the knee. "Your subfusc, my lady."

"Oh, wow. This is so cool." It really was.

"I borrowed it from a friend so you wouldn't be swallowed up in mine."

"That makes you the third person in your family to dress me this week."

He forced a laugh, and as he ducked his head to focus on putting on his own robe, I noticed his neck reddening. I hadn't meant anything untoward by the comment, but I suppose it had put him in mind of dressing me or undressing me. On some men, the shyness could seem weak or off-putting, but on Tristan, who looked like a goddamned movie star, it was delicious. It left me scheming about how to get more of it.

Dinner was impeccably laid out and steeped in ancient traditions about high table and who was allowed to eat when, etc. Tristan and I spoke easily enough—not quite old friends, but interested new ones, at least.

We spoke about our hobbies, our work, his new job, and his upcoming move to Boston. He was obviously intelligent, but not boastfully so. He laughed at all my jokes, and though he didn't really make any of his own, he seemed to enjoy my odd sense of humor.

I changed into my flats, and we walked the winding paths and crooked trails of the city's glowing streets. We ducked into some colleges on the way back, just to take a turn around their quads by moonlight, and then went for a drink at Freud's, a really cool bar in an abandoned church. All in all, it was a more dreamlike first date than I'd ever had.

When we got back to my B&B in Jericho, he asked me if I would be interested in seeing Port Meadow: a nearby park with a river and pubs. I didn't even bother to check my watch.

After a short walk, we went through a kissing gate into a rolling green space where cattle roamed freely. A tendril of the Thames thinned into a quiet creek that meandered lackadaisically through the trees, keeping painted lock boats afloat.

The moon was full that night, and we didn't need a flashlight to stroll through the meadow and traipse up the little wooden bridges that arched charmingly over the knobby fingers of the Thames. Something caught my eye. A twinkling in the distance—magic, surely. After all, Oxford is where some of Hogwarts was kept, where Narnia was born and Middle-earth was forged, and where Alice couldn't help but follow that rabbit down the rabbit hole.

The sparkling was Christmas lights, it turned out. They were wrapped around arched vines, and we entered through a little gate and ducked down a narrow hedge path until a garden opened up before us. It was a tiny thatched-roof cottage in the woods of the meadow called the Perch, and it had a fish painted on its wooden sign.

We got local ales and sat under a huge tree in the twinkling garden until it got too chilly, and then we went inside, ordered a final drink, and stocked up on heat on a leather club sofa by a massive fireplace blazing with warmth.

On the way home, we stopped under a canopy of arching oaks. Tristan turned to face me. In the quiet of the night, with his eyes large and dark, he asked me a question.

"Can I kiss you good night? I don't want to wait until we get back to your bed-and-breakfast in case we get interrupted there." He brushed his hair out of his face. "Also because I don't want to wait that long."

No one had ever asked to kiss me so politely before. I smiled and stepped to him, turning my face up in answer. He put his arms around my waist and dragged me in, no longer shy. When he finally put his lips on mine, it was the last scene of a rom-com—much anticipated, sweetly satisfying. He opened my lips with his, and my body softened into his arms. Sensuously gentle and warm, the kiss was a delicate thing—a moth's wings brushing a candle flame. He was a talented kisser, and when it was over and we walked the few remaining blocks to the B&B, I felt quiet, soothed, safe, and warm throughout.

ALONE IN MY bed, I drifted contentedly. A date with Tristan had sent me into a tailspin. How much of these feelings were for a glittering Oxford evening, and how much was for Tristan? Robbie was there also, hunkered down in the quiet eye of the storm, a string tied to his finger that wouldn't let me go.

I wondered if who I was—and who I thought I was, and who I allowed myself to be—might be changing. I certainly had a new perspective on some things because of the trip. Perhaps that might go some way to explaining my confusion—how might I know who would be a good match for me, if I wasn't really certain who *me* was anymore.

CHAPTER 25

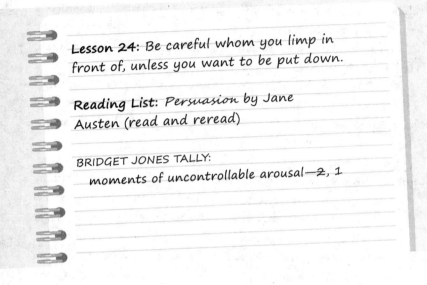

Lesson 24: Be careful whom you limp in front of, unless you want to be put down.

Reading List: *Persuasion* by Jane Austen (read and reread)

BRIDGET JONES TALLY:
moments of uncontrollable arousal—~~2~~, 1

We went to see the Bodleian Library in the morning, which was essentially a Gothic castle in the middle of Oxford that was built in the Middle Ages, housing thirteen million books and encompassing rooms upon rooms upon glorious rooms of books to read and research in. This included Duke Humfrey's Library: a low-lit medieval masterpiece carved and painted, ceiling to floorboards, and filled with leather-bound books, like something that had sprung from the pages of a fantasy novel. My mind swam thinking who might have sat in that room over the centuries and what they might have read. Robbie led us on the tour, and as always, enlivened centuries of historical information with fascinating asides and witty jokes.

Then we went to Merton College, which can be traced back to the 1260s—a year, not an address!—and where J. R. R. Tolkien was a professor. Here we got to visit Merton's library, a small, wood-paneled, barrel-ceilinged room with ancient celestial globes and archaic books attached to their shelves with old chains, as if someone wanted to prevent them from wandering off or attacking the guests.

To cap it off, we went for lunch at the Eagle and Child, a small, dark pub where the Inklings, a literary group that included Tolkien and C. S. Lewis, used to meet to discuss mysterious bookish things. How lucky was I to sip a pint with my butt in a seat that might once have supported Tolkien's butt? I wiggled a little, thrilled by the notion.

I was also happy to take the weight off my ankle, which had begun to throb with the day's exertions. I knew that I had overdone it on my nocturnal escapade, with the heels and the long walks through the streets and meadows. But I never liked to be the one at fault, so I decided it was probably gout.

Tristan turned up for a drink to say a quick goodbye to us before we set off for Bath. *Is it possible that he has somehow beautified overnight?* I, on the other hand, was back in my less-than-clean hobo muumuu and shuffled like something out of *The Walking Dead*.

Robbie said something and sat staring at me expectantly. He looked over his shoulder and spotted Tristan, and suddenly his tone sharpened.

"Hmm? What's that?"

"Well, actually, I asked you what things you needed to buy so that we could make a game plan for the shopping excursion. But you don't seem to be listening, or even the least bit interested in replacing your sewage suits."

"I was just zoning out. I've got a lot on my mind. You wouldn't understand. The only activity in your brain is the tumbleweed rolling around."

"Oh, I think it's abundantly clear to us all just what variety of thoughts are tumbling around in *your* mind." He kept his voice quiet enough to not be overheard, but I felt my face flush nonetheless. "Would you like a bib?"

I just hate him so much! Why was I so soft on him last night? Late-night insanity.

"Oh, shut up. You're the one who needs a bib, you big baby!"

Before he could say some other stupid annoying thing, I got up and hobbled full-speed over to Tristan to catch him before our time was up.

"Hey."

I hoped the one word would carry more than its weight.

"Hey." He had a sad half smile on his lips. "I hate to go, but I just wanted to duck my head in. I know you ladies need to get a head start if you've got to drive all the way to Bath today."

"Oh, it's only an hour and a half away. That's nothing by American standards. I've driven further than that for french fries."

He smiled. "I suppose it's not that far." He ran a hand through his hair and it fell back into his eyes. "Well, Bath is a lovely city. I'm sure you'll really like it."

"Thank you for last night. It was incredible. I feel like I would have missed so much of Oxford if you hadn't shown it to me."

"No, no. I'm the one who's grateful. I haven't had that much fun in months." He blushed slightly, probably fearing how the admission made him sound. "So I'll be moving this July. Would it be alright if I kept in touch? Maybe I'll be dropping by DC sometime."

"Of course!" I laughed. How could he have felt he needed to ask? "And let me know if you need any information, or if there's anything I can help with. I'd be happy to show you around Boston. I think you're going to like it!"

"I think I will too." His eyes glistened. "I hope I see you soon, Alice." He leaned in and kissed me softly on the cheek. The brush of his lips on my skin reminded me of our kiss the night before, and I felt my face pinken.

I turned away just in time to catch Robbie in midscowl.

Jackass.

I FELT LIKE Catherine Morland in Bath. It was a sweet, white wedding cake of a city: perfectly measured and planned, tiered and decorated with a careful, restrained Georgian hand. I wandered around, bright-eyed and happy, snapping shots of all the beautiful views. I would have swung my bonnet by its ribbons if I'd had one. So many of my favorite books and movies had been set in Bath that it felt like meeting an old pen pal for the first time: someone you had grown to know intimately over the years, but hadn't the chance to see with your own eyes.

After a whistle-stop tour that took us to the Roman Baths, the breathtaking Royal Crescent (where I had seen a breathless Sally Hawkins run countless times in search of her Captain Wentworth), and Jane Austen's House museum (where we dressed in period costume and giggled our pantaloons off), we meandered our way to one of the oldest houses in Bath—Sally Lunn's, circa 1482—for their famous Sally Lunn bun.

Afterward Robbie was to meet with Rosie, who was now supposedly back in tip-top condition (sarcasm) and trade back the more modern (nameless) replacement bus (that had pooped all over my things). The other ladies were to doddle about town soaking up the charming ambiance, while I, after four days of wearing the same abominable ensemble—clothes that I hoped never to see again, clothes that by now could probably stand unaided and waltz themselves down to the Roman Baths—would finally be able to shop for a few new things.

I decided that the first place to start would be the charity shops. Doris had suggested it, and I had to admit it did sound much more sensible than buying a brand-new wardrobe. I was delighted to find that British charity shops were small and curated—rather unlike

American industrial-barn-size Goodwills—and each one provided funds to a different charity, so you could feel good about your purchases.

The first two shops yielded nothing more than a nice plaid scarf and a plain black top, despite trying on several different items. Unfortunately, I was beginning to remember just how tiring shopping could be. I wished for what was probably the first time in my entire life that I had not brought my camera with me, as it was like a millstone around my neck. My ankle was really killing me in earnest now, and I dreamed wistfully of being in the filthy bowels of a Walmart, where I might take a leisurely ride on a motorized shopping cart from which I would select a variety of one-size-fits-all attire.

The shopping was taking rather longer than expected, particularly when each step sent little slivers of pain crackling up my leg. I didn't think I was being all that choosy, but I promised myself that I would succeed in purchasing *something* that didn't present me to the British public at large as an awkward teenage boy in a training bra nor a lumpy Amish schoolmarm with body odor.

After about an hour and a half and three different shops, Robbie happened upon me lumbering to my next stop. He hung up the phone and made his way over.

"You're limping worse than Doris." I was taken aback by his accusatory tone. "What have you done to yourself?"

"Well, all I'm saying is that Bath could do with a few more escalators, maybe a people mover here and there."

It wasn't a great joke, but I expected to get a chuckle, or at the very least a grudging smirk. Instead his face looked annoyed, and he ignored my flippancy altogether.

"So you're just going to continue making it worse? Is that the plan?"

With the pain in my ankle, and now a headache that was beginning to throb, I didn't also need a pain in my ass. Usually, his jibes and harassment were at least partially good-natured, but his mood since the morning had been unaccountably sour.

"Well, I'm disappointed to have to explain this to you, but to exist within the culturally mandated social norms of the region, I am expected to wear clothing to cover my body, and I don't think that there will be any luck retrieving my poop suits from London at this juncture, so yes, I am compelled to shop," I replied haughtily. "Shop until I drop, if I must, though I feel very unfortunate at having been forced to say such a thing out loud." I hoped that I was irritating him at least as much as was irritating me. I hoped that I was the gritty, impossible-to-fish-out eggshell in his bite of omelet.

"You're going to end up back in hospital, and we've wasted enough time on this tour as it is without another trip to see the doctor."

"Well, honestly, Robbie, what are you expecting me to do? Shall I just wear this hideous dress every day until it fuses to my body or dissipates in the wind?"

"Never one for drama, are we, Alice? There are other alternatives, obviously. For a start, I'm going to get your crutches from the bus, so you can take some of the weight off that ankle."

"But how am I supposed to shop with crutches? It's difficult enough as it is. Then there's my camera, and the shopping bags to carry . . ."

"Then I'll come along and help. I can help carry stuff, and we can use the bus for longer distances." It was nice, but the way he said it didn't make it sound very generous.

"Thanks, but I already have enough trouble without adding a cranky Scottish pack mule to my list."

He frowned at that. "Do you have a better plan?"

"Hmm. Oh, I don't know. Go about my business and look after myself like a grown woman? That usually works just fine." I heaped on the sass, and it made me feel better. I didn't need looking after. A sore ankle never killed anyone (*except for maybe unfortunates who got gangrene, or those multitudes of Victorian explorers who went to the Amazon and never came back).*

I didn't like the way this made me feel. I was the person who looked after other people, not the one who needed looking after. It was embarrassing that on more than one occasion I had needed Robbie's help so far on this this trip, and even Helena's.

"No, Alice Cooper, if it was working just fine, then you wouldn't be limping around Bath like a horse that needed to be shot. If you won't look after yourself, then I'll do it for you. So unless you've got a better idea, then I'm coming along."

Normal Robbie could be tolerable, probably even fun to shop with, but today's sour mood would render him insufferable. "Where are you headed next?" he asked, shutting down the debate portion of our conversation. I looked sideways at him, my mouth ready to make some excuse. "You're not getting out of this one, so don't even try. I'll throw you over my shoulder and carry you there if I have to."

Some small, repugnant part of myself did a cartwheel as I looked up into his stormy face. It was sexy, moody, intense. My mind tumbled headfirst into a vivid image of him throwing me over his shoulder and carrying me off to the bus.

He had sat next to me on the bench, close enough that I could see browns and reds in his dark stubble as the light hit it. The sudden jolt of his proximity confirmed that, despite my evening with Tristan, something still stirred in my chest for Robbie . . . and probably elsewhere.

His eyes rolled over my face like a thunderstorm. I couldn't help it—my gaze lingered on his lips, wanting to feel the scrape of his stubble on my neck, salty skin, pulses racing, the heat of his mouth on mine, biting, demanding, and insistent. I imagined a public display on this little bench in the very proper and refined center of Bath.

The kiss we had shared had been so electrifying that I hadn't been able to stop playing it over and over in my mind since it had happened. I was a junkie for the little butterflies it sent fluttering in the pit of my stomach. Even now that I had been kissed well by another man, Robbie's kiss was something that I couldn't let go of, no matter how much I had tried. It had been more alive somehow, hungrier. And I hungered back. I involuntarily sucked in my bottom lip, wishing there was still some part of the kiss left to taste. I looked up into his blue eyes, and I saw it there too—it was unsettling him. I knew what he was thinking. We didn't need language anymore.

"Well, I've got to pee."

Okay—I guess not.

"I'll find a loo on the way back to the bus, grab your crutches, and meet you here in ten minutes." He turned his head and looked at me a little askance. "Why don't you grab a coffee from that café while you're waiting for me? You look a bit rough."

Well, that's just great.

"Alright," I said. "You win." My voice crackled out in a husky rasp like a phone sex operator, and I felt my face flush with the embarrassment of my fantasizing.

"Alice?" he said in a fatherly tone. "Are you going to be sick?"

God. Is that what my aroused face looks like? Nausea?

"No." I used my bratty teenager voice.

"Alright then. If you're sure." He stood to go. Then, with no half measure of annoyance, he said, "I know you had a late one last night, but do try to stay awake, would you?"

He left me there alone on the cold bench, wishing I could vigorously slap myself about the face without drawing too much attention.

CHAPTER 26

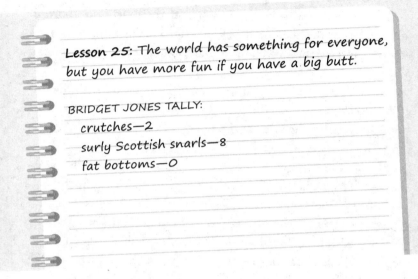

Lesson 25: The world has something for everyone, but you have more fun if you have a big butt.

BRIDGET JONES TALLY:
crutches—2
surly Scottish snarls—8
fat bottoms—0

Rather than Robbie taking a back-seated approach to the shopping excursion and sitting quietly in the chair with a magazine, like bored husbands the world over, he decided that it would be more efficient to "help." This could be achieved, in his estimation, by asking me what I needed, zipping through the racks with single-minded determination, and then testily thrusting at me any item that he deemed sufficient.

I actually left the shop with a set of waterproof hiking pants and a warm, waterproof jacket in a charming eggplant color for thirteen pounds. I couldn't tell if I owed this success to Robbie's assistance or in spite of it, but his churlish attitude made sure that I didn't waste any time enjoying myself.

As we made our crooked way to the next stop, I baited him. It was a little treat for myself—something I realized I enjoyed no matter what the occasion. Some girls prefer chocolate.

"Is this the Scottish immersion part of the tour? You know, to prepare me for the Scottish leg of our trip, where people are threateningly cantankerous, difficult to understand, and loathe spending money?"

"No, Alice Cooper. As you went above and beyond with the English immersion part of the tour, I didn't think it necessary." His voice was a barb as he held the door open for me to get into the next shop.

"Hmm. The question is, are *all* the English more friendly, pleasant, and patient than the Scots, or is my sample size too small?"

"Yes, well, the day is young. We have a few more hours in Bath if you want to find a few more men to bat your eyelashes at."

I laughed. He shriveled me with a look and then went through the door himself, leaving me behind to scoot through the closing door with my crutches. Though, at the speed it closed, I could have waited to heal completely and then tap-danced through. I smiled when I caught him turning back to make sure I made it through alright.

Now that I had what I needed for my outdoorsing, and I had two formal dresses thanks to my fairy godmother, all I really needed was a decent pair of jeans and a couple of casual, adaptable pieces that could hold up to the unpredictable weather and be comfy to travel in. *Not too bad. We'll be out of here in no time, and he can go be grumpy all over someone else.*

While I was looking in the women's section, Robbie was off elsewhere, leaving me to my own devices. This gave me both a sense of relief and a twinge of disappointment. I had prepared for antagonism. I had plans for torture.

After ten minutes or so of peaceful browsing and a somewhat

promising selection of items, I found my way over to a little locked glass case, which held some of the more precious items that had been donated. There was a set of gilded china at the bottom, some jewelry, two antique profiles in oval frames, and a handful of old books, beautifully bound and deemed worthy of the glass case. I spied a gorgeous edition of the poetical works of Walter Scott and asked the lady if I might see it. I don't typically go for poetry, but this one had a leather binding that was marvelously marbled on the outside and accented by amber leather corners and spine. It was a work of art.

The moment I put my hands on the impossibly smooth leather and smelled the breath of the paper, I was dragged back to the library at Abbotsford. I could feel the floor under me, smell smoke from the fire, as if I were about to curl up in a leather wingback in the bay window overlooking that River Tweed and read my afternoon away. It was magic, nothing less.

The price inside reflected this magic, however. I knew I couldn't justify forty-nine pounds. Really, the entire trip had been an extravagance, and I had promised myself I would take it easy on the wallet while I was here. The woman turned her back, and I took my moment to caress the binding, running my hands over its cool, smooth skin, inhaling the scent of its long years.

I backed into someone, bulky as I was with the crutches, and turned to find Robbie standing there, a stark look drawing in his features.

"Alice Cooper," he said formally.

"Mr. Mussolini," I said with a little half bow. I saw something flash across his face—humor or annoyance, I wasn't sure, but both options pleased me, so I took it for a win.

"What are you doing?"

"I am in the middle of a very passionate embrace. For goodness' sake, have the decency to look away and give us some privacy."

For a moment, I thought I saw his face soften, and I thought I had finally cracked him and he would give me a laugh. But instead he cleared his throat and sounded even more severe than before.

"Are you taking this seriously? I hope that you are. We have to meet the others in less than an hour, and there may not be another opportunity to shop." With a stern look, he grabbed my stack of try-on clothes from their position over my arm bracketed by the crutch. "Here, these will be in the dressing room. Waiting for you. Hurry up."

Wow. What do I have to do to make this guy smile?

I handed the book back to the lady with a sigh and went to the dressing room, as I had been ordered to do. When I moved a long coat from the peg, I saw an unusual item hidden behind it in the middle of my rack of clothes. *Unusual* is putting it lightly. This thing was bizarre and hideous beyond all reason. It was some sort of onesie from the seventies in ugly-wallpaper beige: long pants with not one but three layers of ruffles at the bottom, balloon sleeves, and a ruffled high-neck collar. I let out a high-pitched bark of laughter and heard Robbie's chastising voice immediately from right on the other side of the curtain.

"Will you hurry up in there." I laughed again. "Since you seem to need help, come on out and show me."

I looked at the hanging beige monstrosity and giggled helplessly, nearly out of breath at the thought of actually putting the thing on.

"Alice Cooper," he warned in his best headmaster voice. "Come on now. Make it snappy."

I unzipped about three feet of back zipper and wiggled into the polyester casing: some parts very tight, and some parts oversized and sagging. Laughing hysterically, I zipped the thing up with its long, whiplike zipper cord. When I saw the full effect in the mirror, I nearly collapsed dead on the spot.

I heard Robbie clear his throat outside, and I straightened up, wiped the tears from my eyes, and put on a serious catwalk face. I flung the curtain aside dramatically, prepared to do a runway walk down the aisle, but I saw him standing there with his hands on his hips, and I went weak in the knees. I had to steady my body against the wall, so wracked with shaking laughs that it actually hurt.

His face was all business. He was wearing short leather lederhosen with a neon-pink net tank top, cowboy boots, and a pair of gold-rimmed seventies prescription glasses that took up half his face and created a goggle effect. He had topped this with a fascinator—a stupidly tiny hat studded with silk flowers. Now I knew exactly how this ridiculous thing had magically appeared in the middle of my clothes rack.

"Hmm . . . yes, yes. Nice lines." He looked me over and blinked, wide-eyed through his massive glasses. "Excellent color for your skin tone—gives a nice jaundiced pallor. Turn," he said, pushing his glasses down his nose to stare over the rims and spinning his finger in a circle. "Sturdy zipper, and a baggy rear end like a deflated balloon, just the way we like it." I was wheezing at this point, unable to say or do anything else. "Well, it's a yes from me. I've never seen you look better."

I collapsed against the wall.

"Stop! You're hurting me!" I gasped out.

His face crumpled, and he finally succumbed to the laugh he'd been holding back. The sound of it had been well worth waiting for. It was infectious, contagious, it filled my veins with champagne bubbles.

When I could breathe again, I looked him over. "You look like a nearsighted Bavarian who was big on the eighties club scene going to a rodeo-themed wedding!"

He laughed until he was wiping tears away. I placed my hands on my hips and posed, waiting for his assessment.

"Hmm . . . you look like one of the Bee Gees got big into flamenco dancing and then went to a Victorian celibacy rally . . . after a buttock reduction surgery."

I laughed until I had to cross my legs like Doris at Pemberley.

"Honestly," I choked out between gasps, wiping my own tears. "Why was this thing ever made? This." I lifted my leg and fluffed at the ruffles. "Someone—a person—designed this item. To be worn." I tugged at my shoulder-to-wrist balloon sleeve. "*This* was some designer's magnum opus." I put my hands under the sag of fabric at my derriere, cupping it with both hands and gave it a couple of suggestive baggy lifts before looking over my shoulder and waggling my eyebrows.

When I could move again, I went and stood next to him, taking my camera from the backpack he had carried for me, and took a picture of us striking poses side by side in the mirror of the dressing room.

On the way to the till to purchase some jeans and sweaters that did nicely, we dropped the fascinator back on the hat rack. We had nearly left before Robbie found a sixties pillbox hat with a veil that he had to try on, and then a series of bowler hats and flatcaps, most of which looked quite sexy on him. Less so the lacy Lizzy Bennet bonnet I tied under his chin. I tried on a selection myself, much to his amusement, and then found on a nearby shelf a genuine antique silk top hat. It was small, so I cocked it at an angle over one eye and then gave him a saucy wink while I ran my fingers along the brim cabaret-style.

He swallowed visibly and cleared his throat, looking away to give his attention back to the hats.

"Well?" I asked.

"Well what?"

"Well, what do you think of this one?"

"Don't ask me that question. Just take it off before you give me a heart attack."

I was elated to find one of those tourist novelty Scottish plaid hats with the messy ginger hair attached. I laughed and held it out to him.

"Christ, no."

"Oh, come on, Robbie. Be a good sport."

"No. Never will I." His tone was deep and stern. That made me want it all the more. Forgetting my ankle entirely, I chased him around the hat stand with the express intention to wrestle it on top of his head. I cornered him at one point and got pretty close, but he grabbed my waist in both big hands, twirled me around and ran off, leaving me breathless from the exertion—and in truth, from the feel of his hands on me.

"Och. I'm trying to get her out of here, I promise!" he said to the lady behind the counter. "She's worse than a bag of ferrets!"

The woman laughed. "All the best ones are." She gave us a wink.

I limped toward the counter, my ankle protesting now, and made my purchases. I was pleased to leave with a bulging bag. I had even found a brand-new double pack of Smartwool hiking socks for four pounds.

Robbie grabbed my bags from me. "Alright, you hellion. Let's get you off that ankle and get some hot tea down you."

WE FOUND A sweet little café, covered in lace and flowers and clearly kitted out to appeal to Austen-loving women everywhere. As we sat down, Robbie blew on his tea and met my eye.

"Hey. I'm sorry that I was such a dick with you today. And last night . . . I was . . ." He thought for a quiet moment, but then seemed to decide against whatever he was going to say. "Well, I had my head firmly up my own arse."

"Oh, it's no surprise really. I've gotten used to you being a *baw-bag*," I said, trying out my new vocabulary.

He laughed. "Watch it. This is a respectable establishment. They wouldn't hesitate to turn out an unchaperoned lady of loose morals."

"I'll just explain that I'm practicing for Scotland."

"You're nearly ready then!" He sipped his tea. "Honestly, though. I haven't laughed like this with anyone in years. I know I laugh a lot, but . . . not like this. Can we . . ."—he scrunched his nose and bit his lip—"be friends? Actual friends? Not just mutual tormentors? It would be really nice to actually get to know you a little better."

And it was that word, *friends*—that one syllable laden with meaning and purpose—that struck me like a blow to the stomach. I didn't want to be Robbie's friend.

Anything more was hopeless, I knew, but at least I was going to stop lying to myself. Just the wanting of him was proof of the healing I had done. I was becoming myself again: a woman who was strong enough to care for someone who could not be hers, positive and likable enough to make new friends who sought out her company, and confident enough to be admired and desired in her own right. For more than half the year, these things had seemed inconceivable, at odds with my state of mind. But now, here I was, feeling almost at home in my skin again.

"I'd like that." My response was simple and honest. In part, at least.

CHAPTER 27

Lesson 26: If you don't open your eyes, you may miss what's right in front of you.

BRIDGET JONES TALLY:
teas—2
cakes—2
friends—2

We sat for a good while before we had to leave to meet the others, and we talked. We talked about everything. I hadn't planned to, but I told him about my failed engagement, my lost job, and how Hunter had already moved on, and it felt like knots being unwound. He didn't offer advice or commentary on my choices. Sometimes he was angry for me, or supportive, but mostly he just listened.

"Aye. I know what it's like to have the rug swept out from under you."

"Do you?"

"Yeah. I was midway through my dissertation when my mom got ill."

"Oh, Robbie."

"Breast cancer. Late detection."

My heart sank. "No."

"Against her wishes, I dropped everything to move back to Glasgow to be with her. She needed surgery. We didn't have time to waste. And then after the surgery, there was the chemo . . . and the radiation." He rubbed a hand over his face. "It broke her. It broke both of us."

"Oh my God. I'm so sorry." We sat in silence for a beat as the words filled the air around us. "I can't even imagine."

"So I can commiserate with you. Because I lost my PhD, my job offer, my girlfriend, and my flat all in about the space of three months while I cared for my ma."

"Your girlfriend too?"

"Yeah. I'd had a serious girlfriend then, three years. She tried to be supportive, but she couldn't just take a back seat to my mom's illness for who knows how long. I don't blame her, really. I just disappeared. I didn't handle things the right way."

I took a deep breath. It seemed horrible that someone would leave you for caring for your dying mother.

"What about your dad?"

"I've never even met him. They were divorced by my first birthday." Robbie smirked. "He obviously knew there was trouble on the way."

We laughed a little. It felt good for the mood to lighten for a moment.

"After chemo, we started taking trips. She said that if she had to go, she wanted to see as much of Scotland as she could before her time was up." The look in Robbie's eyes made mine sting.

"She had always wanted to move to Edinburgh, so we found a ground-floor flat in a quiet area with a garden entrance, and I moved her in. The first trip we took was nearby, to North Berwick, where Lorna and Madge stay. We saw Tantallon Castle and Bass Rock and the puffins, got lunch by the sea. She really brightened up that day, even if she was exhausted. The next trip was to the Borders. I brushed up on my local history to dazzle her, and found that I was enjoying it as much as she was."

I gave him a sad smile. He was so brave. "It sounds lovely."

"It was. It was a really special time. When you're about to lose someone, it really makes you appreciate the joy of every moment shared together. I savored them. Every tiny detail. I was grateful."

We poured a bit more tea. He reached over and took a forkful of my homemade tea cake, pushing over his slice of strawberry sponge for me to try.

"You're much stronger than I am."

"Nah. Don't say that. You're just in the middle of it, that's all. I was just doing the only thing I *could* do. I needed somewhere to focus all my energy. To do everything I could to make her happy and comfortable. Take as much control of the situation as possible."

"It takes a rare sort of person to take tragedy and heartbreak and be inspired to turn it into something beautiful."

He looked at me for a moment, and our eyes held. Some unspoken emotional thing passed between us, and I felt his heart squeeze in his chest, just as mine did. He cleared his throat and took another bite of his cake to shake the intensity of the moment off.

"So then, I bought a little old bus with enough space for me to fold up her wheelchair and store it in the back, and to give Mom more room so that she could lay down and sleep while I was driving."

"What a great idea."

Why had I never realized before that Boadicea Adventures was his company? I was a blind idiot. I should have guessed. I should have *asked*.

"Then she decided that, with all the room on the bus, she may as well invite a few friends along, you know? She wanted to see them all, say goodbye in person before she was gone. Things sort of took off from there. Twice a month we would plan a short excursion. Soon her friends were calling to ask when the next one was."

"She told me that her favorite thing about those trips was the female companionship. The nonjudgmental support and ease of being around other women. She said that the dynamic always changes somehow when men enter the picture. On her best days, or worst days, she didn't have to shut herself in or put on a brave face or care what she looked like or that her hair was falling out in clumps. The other women held her up.

"I figured that there were probably other ladies out there who might feel the same. So I tarted up the bus and started a little side business to help cover expenses at home. It just spread from word of mouth, which is why the clientele are all so . . . similar." He gave me a crooked smile.

"I see. I had wondered why an all-woman tour. She was right, though. The group dynamic is just simpler somehow. Closer, I think. I loved that you developed a business out of something that makes people feel safe and happy."

"I could never have done it without ma." His face was so open and emotional. I couldn't believe he trusted me enough for such an intimate, vulnerable conversation. He looked down and pushed whipped cream with his fork.

"What about now? Are you happy? Do you like the tours?"

"I love them. I suppose I started this at first as a way to honor her. This wasn't ever what I wanted for myself, but believe it or not, it makes me happier than I think I would have been on my own path. Instead of academia—researching and publishing from a dusty desk somewhere—I get to share in people's lives. I get to talk about history, and learn, and teach, and travel to new places, and occasionally help someone like mum who is going through a tough time. Being with them reminds me of her."

It was heartbreaking—listening to him refer to his mother in the past tense, listening to him be strong. My own parents were in their sixties, and we weren't as close as we could be, but even still, I don't know what I would do if I lost them. My eyes watered from the thought of it. Losing some of those same things had broken my spirit. But I hadn't had cancer to contend with. I hadn't had the loss of a parent. And yet he had made something good out of it all. Set up a new life and career.

I sucked in a breath and held it, trying to retain control and keep the tears at bay. I poured us some more tea and gave a soft smile.

"So what's next for Boadicea Adventures then? Europe? Egypt? Nudist tours? Please tell me that it's nudist tours."

He laughed a little. "You'd like that, wouldn't you?" His smile faded. "No, I told you, I just take it a day at a time."

"So you don't have any plans?" He may as well have said that he got bored of breathing so he doesn't do it anymore.

"I stopped making plans for my future years ago." He shrugged a bit and cleared his throat of its softer tones. "I mean . . . I have ideas. But, you know. You can't plan, really, can you? Life just comes and takes what it wants from you. Better to focus on what you have. Make the best out of the present."

It was the same life motto he'd shared with me on the night of the sandwiches. It had seemed so worldly and wise then. Focusing on the present and enjoying the beauty of life as you live it—it was what we all wanted, wasn't it? Something I needed to learn how to do. But now that I knew his past, I could hear the fear underneath it. It wasn't just about being a happier person and living in the present. It was a trauma response, born of the fear of losing everything again.

My voice came out soft. I didn't want to push too hard. "What kind of ideas?"

He gave a humorless smile. He didn't really want to answer, I thought, but he did, for me. "Well, I have a few. But the one that's most pressing really is starting up some new tours that are entirely wheelchair accessible. See, Doris . . . well, Doris has been on every tour of mine since I started, but she won't be able to get by much longer with just her cane. She uses a chair at home sometimes, but brings just the cane on our trips. It takes its toll on her. If I had another bus with a lift, it would be so much better for her. And I imagine there are other women that would like to travel but struggle to find anything that would truly work with a chair. Men too. There are a few accessible tours out there, but either you have to wait back while the others go for the more physical excursions, or they have some specialty tours but they cost an absolute fortune. Like four thousand quid for five days or something mad like that. But I know I could build a really exciting itinerary where they wouldn't miss out on anything." He stopped himself with a quick shake of the head. He was getting excited, more animated.

"Robbie. This is an incredible idea. My God, Doris would love that."

"Sure, ideas are fun. But something like this would take a huge investment, a massive risk, loads of time and planning. I just . . . well, I don't really have it in me. And it's just me here in this business—I don't have a safety net." He shook his head again. "I've thought about it. I've thought about it a lot. But it's just a big change. And it may not work. Life doesn't usually follow your plans."

"But sometimes it does." I still believed that. I had to. Otherwise life was nothing but chaos.

He was staring intently at his tea and busying his hands. I could see that he didn't want to be pushed any further and steered the conversation to safer ground.

"I'm really happy with what I have right now. I'm really lucky for having all this. That's what I'm going to focus on. I can honestly say that each day I work brings me joy. That's a rare and beautiful thing.

And I won't risk it. Those women out there have given me more than a new career—they've given me a new family. Maybe that sounds too sappy."

"You're right. It does. I can loan you one of my new blouses if you like." He laughed and ate my last bite of tea cake with vengeful relish.

CHAPTER 28

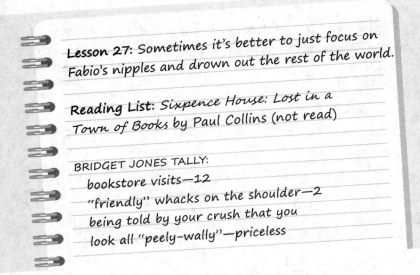

Lesson 27: Sometimes it's better to just focus on Fabio's nipples and drown out the rest of the world.

Reading List: *Sixpence House: Lost in a Town of Books* by Paul Collins (not read)

BRIDGET JONES TALLY:
bookstore visits—12
"friendly" whacks on the shoulder—2
being told by your crush that you
look all "peely-wally"—priceless

And with the return of the old bus, so too did the old folk music return to us. Though I rolled my eyes in Robbie's rearview mirror, the sound of it filled me with a happy, homey feeling, and I was glad to have it spicing the atmosphere of our tour once more. I wasn't sad to see the new bus take its leave. It had been with us only a few days, and though it had offered comfortable temperatures and at least *some* amenities of the twenty-first century, it had also excreted a toilet full of crap onto my luggage. As busses went, that bus was my all-time least favorite.

Lorna requested more of *The Moth*, and as we rode we listened to stories of triumph and failure and mortifying, unplanned nudity.

The intimate afternoon that Robbie and I had shared stuck with me like a scratchy sweater, close to the skin, always reminding me that it was there. It felt as if we had a secret from the others, this newfound closeness. The thought of it warmed me and sent a little thrill through my stomach that, in turn, made me uneasy in equal measure.

It had been the first real conversation we'd had since the night of the sandwiches. We had been through ridiculous and dramatic events together, he had looked after me, we had fought and played and even shared an exquisite kiss in the rain, but we hadn't really *talked* since that night in the kitchen.

Over the next few days, I realized that the nature of our relationship had subtly but perceptibly shifted. We understood each other better and respected each other more. We were no longer just two people who got under each other's skin and whose capacity to deal maturely with issues took a back seat to contempt, competitive goading, or sexual tension. We were, God help us, *human* to each other now. Meaning and care had sprung like weeds in the place that antipathy had left fallow.

We still teased one another, and perhaps to outsiders things looked the same as before, but they were more tender now. We talked in the brief pieces of stolen time that we found to be alone, and we shared thoughts, not just jibes, and tried to learn more about the other's life.

"I've seen that look before, Alice. It would be a hell of a thing to waste." Helena had caught me again, staring after Robbie as he took Percy for a walk to save Doris's knees.

"Oh no. It's not like that. He's got . . . we're just friends."

She laughed. "You're not fooling anyone, Miss Cooper. It's those warm blue eyes, isn't it?"

I smirked. "Has he got blue eyes? I didn't notice."

"Yes. I caught you not noticing just now." She sipped her tea and her voice softened. "Sometimes we're not ready for the things that come our way. Perhaps you're not ready to focus on anyone but yourself right now, and that's not a bad thing." She looked at me a little closer for a moment. "But then again, we shouldn't close our hearts to everything that doesn't arrive on schedule."

"But. I thought you might have been trying to . . . you know, introduce me to Tristan." I blushed. *Oh my God! Did I imagine that?*

"Oh, I was. I think you'd get on famously. But I think it's good for a lady to have options. Besides, men do seem to thrive on a bit of competition, don't they?"

Yes, well, Robbie *certainly has options.*

"Women too."

I wouldn't knowingly participate in cheating, especially not after Hunter. Surely that wasn't what she was suggesting. She winked, smiled a smile full of mischief, and left me to wonder.

ROSIE TRUNDLED US up to the Welsh capital, Cardiff, Roald Dahl's hometown. I loved it. It was green and beautiful, and it thrummed with life both young and old. *And* it had a collection of castles right there in the city. That just seemed greedy when DC didn't have any. Old Roald always knew the good stuff.

After that, we wound our way up to Hay-on-Wye, a sleepy Welsh village known as the first "book town" in the world, where more than thirty bookshops nestled along its picturesque little streets, stacked higgledy-piggledy like books on a shelf. Any bookworm in the world might feel their soul lived here.

And indeed, mine nearly escaped my body and stayed there forever after my heart shuddered to a gurgling stop in the cozy isles of Richard Booth's Bookshop.

"Isla is coming to see you?" Helena all but squealed.

Robbie laughed. "I know. She only just told me. I can't wait."

Helena gasped. "What's the plan?"

"Well, sadly, she won't be able to make it for dinner at the castle, but she'll meet us for the ceilidh afterward, stay with me, and then head back to Edinburgh in the morning."

"Of course. She couldn't miss the opportunity to get twirled around the dance floor by her big, strong man." He laughed, and my face puckered in an involuntary scowl. "She must have been missing you."

"I've been the one missing her, Helena. Three weeks is a long time to be away."

"Tell me about it! I haven't seen her since Hogmanay. Tell her that I simply cannot wait to see that gorgeous smile of hers."

I put down the book I had been pretending to read—a topless Fabio coloring book, *oh my God!*—and backed away slowly, like I could go back in time and unhear the most heinous combination of words to cross my path since *toilet, dump,* and *valve.*

I ran outside, took some deep breaths, gulped down some water, cursed out loud as some nice family happened to walk by, and then slapped myself back into the real world.

It was going to be fine. Of course it was. It was just Robbie's beautiful girlfriend coming to meet us. That's all. With her stupid beautiful smile. Totally normal. So that they could dance together at the ceilidh and stay together in a beautiful room in the castle. It was fine. Totally fine. People had girlfriends all the time. Big stupid deal! What did I care?

It ruined my day. That night at the pub (which was also an adorable bookstore), I listened to what I assume was a fantastic set of book readings from various authors with only half an ear. I decided to ask Robbie about it. Straight out.

Why not? I may as well prepare myself. Get used to the idea. I could handle it. I couldn't have him anyway. What difference did it make to me if somebody else had him . . . over and over again in the four-poster bed of a romantic Scottish castle where I would be trying to sleep in the next room?

I grabbed my beer and sidled over to Robbie, playing it real cool.

"Hey. So did I overhear you and Helena saying that Isla is coming to the ceilidh?" *He'll say no. I probably heard it wrong from the other side of Fabio's colorless nipples.*

He whirled around with a massive, beaming smile. "Aye, ya did! I've only just found out myself. Isn't it wonderful?" He grabbed my hand. "Alice, I can't wait for you to meet her. You two are going to get on like a house on fire!"

Whatever that feeling was in my chest dropped all the way down to the pit of my stomach. Why did it have to be "Isla"? Isla was such a damned sexy name. Visions of Isla Fisher and her incredible body danced through my mind.

"Oh?" I worked to make my voice as casual as I could. "You think so?"

"Are you kidding? She's going to love you." His eyes sparkled. It was so warm and generous a statement. The woman whom he loved would love me. And, if one were to extrapolate, it might be surmised that he himself loved me as well.

As a friend. Just like his hot girlfriend Isla would.

I pulled my hand from his, took a long swig of beer, and cleared my throat. "So what's she like?"

"Actually, you two are a lot alike." *He did not just say that.* "She's funny. And sassy. She has a rapier-sharp tongue and loves to rip me to shreds with it. And she too has a great messy mane of red hair!" He reached out and gave my hair a little tussle. It felt like he'd swung a 2x4 and whacked me in the stomach.

I have actually died and gone to hell, haven't I?

He laughed, delighted. So she was me, essentially. But probably funnier, employed, and with better boobs. I fought to compose myself and think of something funny to say, because apparently I was *so* funny. But he was too excited to wait.

"It was just a happy coincidence, really. She and her friends are in Malta just now, volunteering on a seahorse survey."

I rolled my eyes. *Great. She volunteered somewhere she could look sexy in a bikini while saving the planet, one goddamn seahorse at a time.* "But she'll be flying into Prestwick Saturday, and she told me she'd be close enough to hop on a train and meet us at the castle to cut a rug." He laughed again. I was beginning to hate the sound of it. "She said she could never resist kilted men who smelled of whisky." He rolled his eyes in playful exasperation. I began wishing that I would pass out on the spot and not have to hear any more. Maybe I would get lucky, and we'd be attacked by terrorists from a rival bookstore. "Though if I had any say in the matter, she'd be going straight to bed the moment she arrived." I dry-heaved.

Scratch that. Just shoot me now.

I nodded. Pretending that I was totally alright and that this was a healthy conversation between two friends. Because we were friends, weren't we? We *had* become friends, and despite all those stolen moments alone, those intimate conversations, the sharing of our lives, nothing else romantic had happened between us. No holding hands, no room invitations, no other needy, bone-melting kisses in the rain or otherwise. His unguarded excitement to see his girlfriend confirmed what I clearly needed to see—that everything I had started to feel for him, things I hadn't felt in years—or more truthfully, that perhaps I had never felt before—had been one-sided.

"Uh-huh. So is she coming with us for the rest of the trip?" That would probably be the worst thing I could imagine.

"Sadly, no. This'll just be a wee quickie. Knowing her, she'll just be in long enough to give me a bollocking and then shoot off again."

Ew! Oh my God. Is that what they called it here? *I'm going to throw up right here in the self-help section.* "Please. Spare me the details."

He laughed. "If you say so." He put a hand on my shoulder. "Are you feeling alright, duck? You've gone all peely-wally."

I cleared the bile from my throat. "I'm fine. It's probably just shock." *Act normal.* "The notion that any woman would voluntarily choose to spend so much time with you is making me feel seasick."

He laughed and whacked me on the shoulder. "Oh, she's no choice in the matter. She's stuck with me for the long haul."

Long haul? The words sliced. Burned. So I supposed they weren't teetering on the edge of a breakup, after which he would immediately realize that what he was looking for all along was a bossy, tightly wound American woman with a boyish figure.

He whacked me on the shoulder again like I was his old bar buddy. "Come on, Alice Cooper. You don't look so good. Let's go and get you a drink."

CHAPTER 29

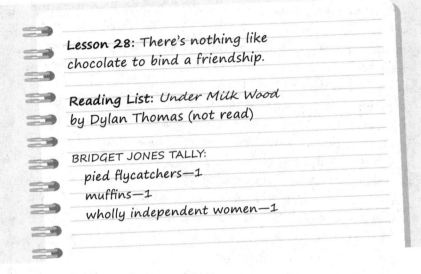

Lesson 28: There's nothing like chocolate to bind a friendship.

Reading List: *Under Milk Wood* by Dylan Thomas (not read)

BRIDGET JONES TALLY:
pied flycatchers—1
muffins—1
wholly independent women—1

We drove up through the spellbinding Brecon Beacons, where we trekked slowly through the wind and the mountains. Robbie read to us from *The Hobbit* as we envisioned ourselves in Middle-earth, which in that setting, did not require a vivid imagination.

Traveling further northward, we slept in rooms in Gladstone's Library, getting in early one rainy afternoon and spending all of a long and quiet evening under the canopy of vaulted beams spelunking the library's boundless depths and uncovering hidden nooks to retire with a few books and plunge ourselves in. It was a recharge day for tired book lovers.

These little solitary respites from the gaggle formation were welcomed for their stillness, but seemed only to prepare us for crashing back into one another at high speed, as if the hours apart had been the stretching of an elastic cord. We had become a little tour family.

We shared and bickered and laughed and supported and loved like family. It could have gone another way, but it didn't.

Whether I told them, or someone else did, they all knew my full backstory by the time we got to North Wales. But I wasn't sorry for it and did not pine for my privacy. I felt supported and listened to. Advice, when it was given, was done so with care and warmth. Those ladies were a veritable cabinet of wisdom, and I was not dumb enough to ignore it. Some things I wrote down in my notebook for fear of losing my grasp on the notion, or the memory of the way it was said. I asked questions, and for more stories, and teased out meaning. I was thirsty for it. I was building myself again—becoming stronger by weaving their shared wisdom into my threadbare spots.

I suppose in this way, I was organizing my recovery—making a controlled and measured effort, just as it was my nature to do. It was a research project with practical applications that I intended to employ upon returning to real life.

With my trusty camera, I kept a second journal—a visual poem, trying to capture, as I grew to know the character of each woman more intimately, the condensed essence of each individual, their quintessence. It would comfort me when I returned back to DC. I also had plans to send each person a little curated collection of photos, a love letter in my own language.

Looking through my shots, I was proud of what I had amassed. Pouring myself into a creative endeavor gave my cramped mind a good stretch and left it buzzing with excitement and new growth. As the sun set each night and rose each morning, my upset and anxiety about meeting Isla faded. It might not have done so of its own accord, but I worked at it. I helped it along; I tried to utilize sage advice and embody the growth I wanted to see.

It was going to be good for me, I decided. Once I met her and she became human to me and I saw how good they were together, all the rest of it would just disappear. My feelings for Robbie would morph into a stout and sturdy friendship type of love.

It was out in the gardens of the library that I chased Berrta from a safe distance—"Berrta-watching" while she bird-watched. I had taken some beautiful photos I thought she'd like. She looked so happy out there in the chilly gray morning with her binoculars that I wanted to join her. She gave me a wave when she saw me approach, sliding over and patting the seat on the bench next to her.

"Look there," she whispered, bringing her head close to mine and handing me her binoculars. I heard something chitter in the trees and tried to locate it with Berrta's help. This was surprisingly difficult. It took some real effort on both our parts for me to spot it. When I finally did, I felt all the more rewarded. It sang again: a simple, lazy little song that made me feel soothed and happy. I watched it through the binoculars, puffing its tiny little chest out and opening its beak wide. The wind blew and shook the leaves, adding two new instruments to the morning song.

"Oh, how wonderful." I hadn't expected the effect such a simple encounter was having on me. "What is it?"

"That's a male pied flycatcher. Not the rarest of sightings, sure, but quite the charming little fellow, isn't he?"

"Oh, he is. I think I could watch him for hours, if I had a hot mug of coffee." I handed Berrta her binoculars back and added sincerely, "Thank you, Berrta."

"You are most velcome." Looking pleased, she puffed up, not unlike the little flycatcher. I lifted my camera and took a few photos before it flew away.

"I think I'm beginning to understand why you love them so much."

"Ahh. Then today I have already done something good."

"You have." I smiled, digging into my coat pocket for a hastily napkin-wrapped bundle. "Can I repay the favor with half a chocolate muffin I stole from the breakfast room?"

"Ja, bitte!"

I smiled warmly, split the muffin, and handed her the half with the bigger chocolate chips.

"Vhat are you doing out so early?" she asked, chewing.

"Taking pictures. This time of day is perfect for the light. I saw the fog from my window and didn't want to miss out." I didn't add that I was taking photos of her looking cute with her binoculars on the bench, wrapped snugly in her scarf.

"It is a good hobby, and you are good at it, I think." She nodded confidently. "There is passion there."

"Well, thanks, Berrta. That's sweet of you to say."

"I do not say things for sweet. I say things ven they are true." She took another bite of muffin. I smiled my thanks at her and bit into mine as well. "If you do not have a job now, perhaps can you do something vith photography?"

She was very blunt, but I found I didn't mind—particularly from Berrta, who knew no other language, whether others wanted to hear it or not.

"Oh, I don't know. I don't think I'm *that* good. It's just a little hobby. I have a degree in international development."

"Ah well. You do vhat you love. But do not be afraid to reinvent yourself if you discover that you do not love it any longer."

I tried to quiet my immediate arguments to think about what she said. "What about you, Berrta? Have you always loved birding?"

"No, no. It is a new passion. Three years now."

"Oh, wow. Is that all? You seem so knowledgeable."

"Yes. I am knowledgeable. It is very easy to learn when you like something. I try to always find something new. The internet has everything. And also, I have been back to university three times over the years."

"Three times! Berrta!" I laughed. "How did you have time for it all?"

"There is always time. We grow old and stale if we do not push ourselves to keep moving and learning. It is a choice. I know vhat I choose. Ve must make time for ourselves and make room to grow."

"That sounds like very good advice. I haven't been in the habit of making much time for anything but working long hours and trying to advance my career, to be honest with you."

"Well, for some people, that is just vhat they need. For me, it was not. And I think not for you too." She brushed some muffin crumbs from her lap and looked at me before carrying on in her matter-of-fact tone. "I think perhaps you vould not have lost so much if you had given more to yourself instead of to others. It is only one man and only one job, yes? There are many others of both."

I laughed at how easy and relaxed she was about my losing everything. "Berrta, you're not wrong."

"I know. Things like this, they might come and go. You must fill yourself up. Make your own self happy, and then nothing can bring you down for long."

It was an interesting concept. I had always felt that I controlled my own happiness by working hard toward the next achievement. But if I failed, or that achievement was somehow beyond reach, it hurt. I punished myself for it. I had never really thought about internalizing happiness, whatever that meant.

"Isn't that just for Buddhists? They can just float above it all."

She laughed. "Hmm. Buddhists, yes, but me too, and maybe you."

"I guess I just feel like you build your own happiness outside—it's the outside that you built that makes you happy *inside*, you know? If you want a husband, you have to go out and find one."

"Yes, but sometimes you do that, and sometimes then your husband leaves you or finds someone else to sleep vith. Right? Happens a lot. No one should be responsible for your happiness but you, my girl. Happy must be built in here." She pounded firmly on my chest with an open palm. "I will not say that ve are born alone and ve will die alone, but . . ." She thought for a moment. "Ve are on a book tour, yes? I vill say like this—you write your own story. If others vish to contribute to your story, that is nice. And if they do not, then it should not matter. You make your way on, vith or vithout them. And you write your story how you vant it."

I thought about that. From another woman, it might have sounded jaded, but it didn't feel that way coming from Berrta.

"I don't even think I would know how to do that. Like . . . I've always wanted to travel. Always. But this is my first real trip abroad, you know . . ."

"Mm-hm." She nodded and took another bite of muffin. "This is good! Find your passions. Seek them. Try things. Learn vat makes you happy and vat does not, and then focus on making more of the good and less of the bad. This is true independence. And. Not only vill this make you strong"—she pointed a finger in the air—"but you vill see, it vill make you irresistible to men!" We both laughed.

"What are you two birds up to out here in the cold?" A Scottish voice came from behind us and Berrta waggled her eyebrows in silent punctuation. "We are just sitting down for breakfast if you'd care to join us, and then we'll be northward bound."

I smiled. I was excited to get back to Scotland. I couldn't help but picture the opening credits of *Outlander*, the camera sweeping over the rugged Scottish mountains. That might also have brought to mind an image of a kilted Robbie on the top of said mountain, wind in his hair, squinting heroically into the distance.

"Ja, Robbie. I am hungry. The birds are off to find their vorms, and so ve should be too."

She stood, then smiled down at me and offered her hand to help me up.

Trust Berrta to be so efficient. She had taught me a new hobby, delivered wisdom, and made me question my reality all in the time it took to eat half of a chocolate muffin.

As ROSIE'S LITTLE tires bumped us up yet another set of hills, I settled into a cozy stretch of editing the photos on my camera, deleting duplicates and blurry shots. The ladies napped and read, and Percy scratched at his ear and made his collar jingle. The sun streamed through the window and warmed my skin as the radio played soothing traditional music between announcements in rolling Welsh.

There were so many photos of Robbie. Photos where the light had struck him just so, photos where his smile lit his whole face up, candid photos where his eyes were deep and pensive. Photos I could not have stopped myself from taking.

In the moments in between—moments when the ladies took their time at a gift shop, or writing postcards, moments snatched in line at a café as we eyed the cinnamon rolls, moments when the ladies' conversations had turned in on themselves and left us conveniently unobserved—something real had been blossoming. I was enjoying the sensation of having a new friend. A real one.

Robbie and I talked often about our favorite books, movies, and bingeable series. Music was another fun thing to share and argue about. Robbie had an old iPod, and we would split the headphones, or he would pass it over to me to listen while he drove, keeping mental lists of the things he wanted me to listen to—sometimes an achingly beautiful macabre love song from Hozier, and sometimes the sexy swaying jangle of West African pop or the haunting minor key acapella harmonies from Bulgaria. He was so excited to share it all with me and to watch me listen for the first time.

The more I learned of Robbie, the more I liked. Yes, he was intelligent and quick-witted, but he was also thoughtful and caring. I noticed more how supportive and protective he was of the ladies, always looking out for them, always trying to facilitate friendships between them, and forever trying to make them smile.

He was caring with me too. He asked me sincerely how I was, and after taking some time to assess, I discovered that much of the time, I felt like me—something I had nearly forgotten the sensation of.

It was a friendship, and I was happy for it. Yes, this closeness made me acutely aware of my growing feelings for him—no longer just lust now, but genuine affection, longing, admiration . . . and a heaping serving of lust. I felt like I glowed when I was around him— like I was a little flesh lantern, and someone had lit my candle. But now, hopefully, I was becoming strong enough to handle these feelings and keep a level head.

Sometimes we even spoke of Isla. He grew more excited to see her as the ceilidh approached, and he made no effort to hide it. We might be talking about films, and I would ask, "What sort of movies does Isla like?" In this way, I could ease myself in. And when I asked about her, it always made him smile. "Oh, she's a purist. She likes the old classics. *Charade*, *Breakfast at Tiffany's*—absolutely anything with Audrey Hepburn." I held back an eyeroll.

He still spoke to her every day, even though she was now in Malta. If one was unfortunate enough to overhear it, you'd find that it usually started with *Hello, gorgeous!* and always ended with a heartfelt *I love you* and *Wish you were here*, which served to keep me firmly at a distance.

I certainly didn't notice that he smelled like a cedar forest after a rain. Or get goosebumps when he looked at me with those blue eyes that seared straight through to my soul. I hardly noticed at all when he casually put his hands on me, for some innocuous reason or other, and I felt like I'd been tenderly electrocuted.

It was going to be fine. I was going to be fine.

CHAPTER 30

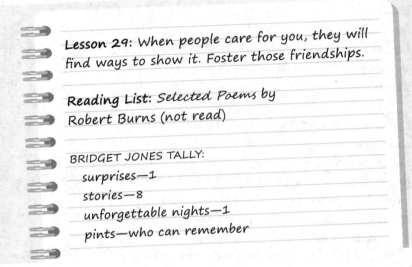

With so much going on within and without, it's no wonder I lost my sense of time and date. It came as a blindsiding shock, then, when the group surprised me for my birthday.

Once back in Scotland, we had stopped in Dumfries (home of Robert Burns) on the westerly side of the Scottish Borders, and went straight to the Globe Inn for supper at a time that was nearer to lunch.

It seemed a bit early for a pint, but everyone else at the table had ordered drinks, and it took me no time at all to decide to follow suit. I chose a deliciously nutty milk stout to go with my wild mushroom, thyme, and Wensleydale pie that was so decadently savory I nearly blacked out at first bite.

The conversation over dinner bubbled like a brook in a hurry. I wondered if perhaps it was just the booze, but it felt like there was a buzz of excitement coursing through our little gaggle. It was all I could do to keep up with the messy flow of several diverging and converging conversations. It was fun! I buzzed right along with them. Looking back on that first day in Edinburgh, I wondered how I could have peered into that fluffy cloud of white hair and seen tired and boring. They made me feel more alive just to be around them, reminding me every day that life is for the living.

After dinner, rather than going back to the B&B, I followed the crowd into another cozier room in the pub, ordering another round and settled in by the fire—lit and fully roaring, despite it being the raging ides of spring (this was Scotland, after all). We sipped our drinks and chatted away, and after some furtive glances between the ladies that confused me, Madge stood up and parked herself in front of the fire, warming her hands, clearing her throat, and then turning around to address us.

"Right." Her voice was loud and definitive. She looked squarely at me for a beat, during which I feared that I had perhaps been found guilty of some heinous social crime or other and was about to be publicly exposed. *Did I use the word* pants *incorrectly again?*

"Today is our Alice's birthday." I gasped and put my hand to my gaping carp mouth, and everyone giggled delightedly. *How on earth did they know? How on earth had I forgotten?* Once everyone quieted down again, she went on. I flushed with emotion.

"And so we thought, what better opportunity than tonight to take a moment and enjoy how lucky we are to have her?"

"Hear! Hear!" someone shouted. Others hooted, and there was an uproarious noise of adulation, tapping on glasses and stomping feet. You would have thought I had just ran and won the Kentucky Derby topless in flip-flops.

I felt a prickle behind my eyes. Some of the strangers in the pub joined along in the clapping and shouting, seemingly unbothered by the scene we were making at 6 p.m. in this otherwise perfectly respectable pub.

"So we're going to start by embarrassing you. Alice, you are an absolute ray of sunshine! Even when shit gets bad, and we all know that the *shit* got bad for you on this trip"—unreserved laughter at my expense—"you somehow manage to keep laughing. You are helpful, thoughtful, caring, intelligent, and generous, but most of all, you like to listen, and boy, do we like to talk!" More hooting. "You've made each of us feel as if you truly care about our lives and our stories, and that's why we came up with this little idea. Well, it was collaborative, really—we all put our heads together to make it happen.

"So for you, Alice, for one night only, *The Moth*—UK amateur edition—comes to Dumfries!" I gasped again. The ladies went wild with applause. I was laughing so much that my face hurt.

"Alice, we all know your life has had some ups and downs lately, and we've all felt the pain you have gone through—all the more keenly because, in our many, *many* combined years, we've been there several times over. Spending every waking hour in one another's pockets the way we have these past weeks, we've all seen you grow during this trip. We know you like to have things organized and under control, with a plan firmly in place, but as I'm sure you now know, life doesn't seem to care much about your schedule. But when plans get ripped asunder, that's the best time to start fresh, to build something beautiful from the wreckage. And we can all see that you're well on your way!" A lump started to gather in my throat.

"So without further ado—I've always wanted to say that—the theme tonight is 'When Life Didn't Follow the Plan.' All the ladies have been notified in advance and prepared something for you."

Madge addressed the other patrons then.

"Thank you, to all you poor bystanders out there who are tuning in, whether or you want to or no. We're all going to tell some stories from our lives. They can be no longer than five minutes. Chatty ladies, *you know who you are*, we will be tapping our glasses like so at the three-minute mark"—Madge paused to lightly clang a glass— "and then again at four, and finally we will drag you off by your hair at five. Now, all these stories are one-hundred-percent true, but you don't have to take our word for it—just ask our therapists!"

Madge was loving this, which made it all the more fun to watch. There was lots of applause, both from our group and outsiders. Then Madge took Robbie's flatcap from the table, dropped in slips of paper, swirled them slowly to great dramatic effect, and finally pulled one out.

"Well . . . the lovely Lorna, looks like you're up!"

"Oh heavens," she said. "Up first?" But up she stood, and moved into position in front of the fire. Then she walked back to her seat, picked up her pint, and took a giant swig as she brought it back to her position, to the sound of cheers from the ladies. It was a good start. I held my breath. I couldn't believe they were doing this for me.

"Well. I'm going to start the night with a serious one," she said apologetically. "This may come as a shock to all of you, but . . ." She paused for a beat. "I'm gay." We all laughed at her delivery.

"Some of you look surprised," she lied. ". . . so was my husband." From that point, the story took a turn and became more sincere, and deeply moving. They had gotten together very young and stayed together for thirteen years, tried to start a family, miscarried. She wove us through love and loss, and the unforgettable and unforgivable feeling of breaking another person's heart. In the end, she told us that if she had it all to do over again, she would do everything just the same, and not change a thing, because we are what love and pain and joy makes of us, and she was a product of a beautiful life, flawed though it was. All of it had brought her to Madge and the happy life they had shared together for nearly thirty years.

When she was done, I really wasn't sure how much time had passed. I had to wake myself up from the story. I felt like crying, but somehow found myself smiling instead. When she left the spot of privilege to regain her seat, I stood and swept her up in a great big hug.

"Thank you," I whispered. "That was beautiful. You're beautiful." She stroked my hair until her applause died down and then sat next to me, her hand on my knee, as we waited to see who would be called next.

Doris was next. She told a hilarious story about her great-grandson's eighth birthday, when she had planned to take them all to the city to visit an escape room as a birthday surprise. Upon arrival at an establishment called the Booby Trap, they emerged through a dark mysterious hallway to find themselves at a strip club at 2 p.m. on a Tuesday afternoon, where a woman was entertaining "naked as a jaybird." Of course, little Artie saw everything.

Doris had clearly told this story many times before, and her comic timing was impeccable. We were wild with laughter. When she finished, I swept her up in a hug that shook with giggles.

One by one they went up, and I fell forward into their stories, feeling their joys and sorrows along with them: my friends, my role models. Then I gathered each one into a hug and tried to press all my gratitude into them.

When Flossie got up, I thought it would be another wild mermaid story, but while some of it did seem to be a tall tale, a strong thread ran through it that was remarkably poignant—about the loss of her first love. She said that she had run away from home and a tyrannical father at sixteen and was found by a sultan. They toured the world together, she said, and she spoke of tents and lanterns, a large menagerie of wild beasts, and the beautiful glittering gowns that he had given her to wear. After they had circled the globe and returned home to her father, the sultan had asked for Flossie's hand in marriage. But her father had flown into a rage and threatened to kill the sultan, and they never saw each other again.

It was a beautiful, sad story. The way she spoke about falling in love and having it torn away sounded every bit as real to me as anything else. I'd never seen Flossie look hurt or sad, but the emotion washed raw across her face and left me quite moved.

"Maybe she's remembering past lives," I heard Lorna whisper. When I hugged Flossie she clung to me, and I clung to her too.

When it was Agatha's turn, she got up and told us that Flossie's story was "hogwash," which felt unfair but not unexpected. Then she told a story about a neighbor who moved into the cottage next door and was sneaking over at night to cut Agatha's roses that she had grown for the flower show. I was surprised and touched that Agatha had actually played along. I hugged her stiff little body that seemed to be all elbows and shoulders before she waved me off, but I thought I caught a small smile on her lips when she thought no one was looking.

Berrta told us a thrilling story about coming across a bear in the woods when she visited Canada on a wilderness tour, very much to her surprise and to the bear's. Berrta did not need glass-clanking reminders to finish her story on time.

Helena's story was about a mishap in her university years that saw her going to the wrong room for a life drawing class and disrobing in front of an architecture seminar. Once the professor arrived, she realized her mistake. She was mortified, but had refused to show it. Instead she had slung her robe over her shoulder and walked out naked with her head held high. It was a hilarious tale.

I could not get enough. I wished I had time to write everything down.

With only two stories left, Madge got up and told us about discovering the child abuse of a young Glaswegian girl that led her to work in social care, where she would spend many long and rewarding years looking after people who could not speak for themselves. I cried, and when I hugged her, I sobbed more into her scarf.

"Thank you, ladies," Robbie said as he walked to the fire. "It's the end of the night, and I won't take much of your time, but I thought I'd let you know how we all ended up here. Now, most of you know that I live a very adventurous life filled with danger. As is the case for most historians. But what you might *not* know was that I was originally on track to be an astronaut. Yes, a real-life astronaut with grand plans to travel to outer space and discover new planets, make friends with aliens, and fly through a black hole. I was ten at the time, but I could wait.

"That year I begged and begged my mother to let me go to space camp. I had asked around and done my research, and I discovered that there was a space camp down in Gloucestershire.

"Now, at ten years old, you'll no be surprised to hear that I was a selfish wee bastard, and it had never occurred to me that my single mum and I didn't have a whole lot between us, and that she may not be able to afford a fancy weeklong space camp in England.

"When my birthday came round, she told me the news, that I would be going to summer camp. And there was much rejoicing. But. I would *not* be going to space camp. I was going instead about an hour away to the ruins of a castle in Dunure, with two very old archeologists and six other nerdy weirdo kids. We'd be there for five days, and we'd camp out in tents on the rocks in the cold sea air and spend our days learning about stupid history that I didn't care a damn thing about, and digging in the dirt for old junk. And get this—we weren't even allowed to keep the old junk we found! It was history camp. And it was the very worst thing I could imagine.

"I moped for a full month. That's probably where I got these wee scowl lines right here. I begged my mum not to make me go, but nothin' doing. I dragged my feet and whined the whole way there.

"Well, we camped, we cooked outside, we played games and dug for treasure, we made hot chocolate over the fire, and we learned a lot about history. And to my surprise, I loved every damn minute of it.

"It was a fluke. Mum couldn't afford space camp, so she picked something cheaper. I was pure gutted. It was the most devastated that I had ever been in all my ten years. But it was when I was denied what I wanted most in the world that fate—and my mum—instead gave me a smack on the backside that changed my life forever. History became my passion. That trip set my life on a different course. That terrible summer—when I had the worst luck, when I drew the short straw—it changed my life forever. After that, I went to more history camps. I made history friends. I went on to read history at university and eventually to start my own historical tourism business.

"But luckily for you ladies, there's no camping outside, and Percy is the only one who digs in the dirt for buried treasure."

Everyone roared with applause. It was the last tale, and we were several pints in. It was a sweet end to a magical evening. I couldn't help but picture a whip-smart, grumpy little ten-year-old with big blue eyes and messy hair.

I had loved his story. I had loved all the stories. There was so much wisdom there, so much laughter and pain, and so many things that I wanted to write in my notebook and never forget. They had all given me pieces of themselves as birthday gifts, and they were more precious to me than they could imagine.

I asked a gentleman at a nearby table to take a photo of all of us by the fire. And it was only then, with a smile stretched wide across my rosy cheeks, that I realized I had completely forgotten to be depressed about a day that I had been dreading for nearly a year.

I PADDED SLEEPILY back to my room across the carpet of the inn, smiling gently to myself. I had had a lot of wonderful birthdays in my time, but none so deeply moving, nor so memorable.

I was grateful to Robbie and the ladies for caring enough to organize something for me and making it so special, and grateful to the ale that made me feel like I was floating along the hall like a feather caught in a lazy draft.

As I turned the corner, I stopped short to see Robbie by my door, straightening up after putting down a little parcel for me on the floor. He took a step away and then came back to fix the bow, making sure that it looked perfect. Before he stood up again, I had crossed the distance quietly and was standing just behind his shoulder. He bumped into me and then gave a start and a sharp gasp.

"Bloody hell, Alice, you creeper!" He grabbed both of my arms and laughed. "What are you doing sneaking around in the shadows like? Waiting to cut my heart out, I suppose."

"Nah. The black market only wants healthy, red-blooded organs." I smirked.

He laughed, then sighed. His warm breath carried with it the spice of honey and whisky. It stirred my messy wisps of hair and made my skin tingle.

"Well, I just wanted to leave a little something for you." He ducked his head and cleared his throat.

He hadn't yet let me go. He was staring at me. And for a blessedly long moment I thought he was going to kiss me. And for that moment, all the reasons why we shouldn't completely disappeared.

But he didn't.

"Did you have a nice time tonight, duck?" Each word was as tender and intimate as the kiss that I had hoped for. I nodded silently. A few strands of hair fell into my eyes and he let go of me then to brush it from my face.

"Tonight was . . ." I sighed, unsure how to put it into words. I closed my eyes to remember, shook my head, and grinned like a Cheshire cat without saying another word.

"Good. You deserve a bit of a spoiling."

I tried to think back to the last time anyone had done something so nice for me, and he must have seen the shadow of it in my eyes, because he gathered me up into a hug. We stood there outside my door and held each other, breathing steadily, comfort and alcohol coursing through our blood. I tucked my nose into the hollow made by his collarbone and the crook of his neck. I inhaled him and forgot about time, perfectly content.

"Alright, madam. Off to sleep with ye."

"Should I open this now?"

He looked away for a moment and sucked a bit of air through his teeth. "Nah. You open it on your own."

"Is it anthrax?" I mumbled sleepily, and then yawned.

He laughed. "Close. Special edition of *The Name of the Rose*, complete with poisoned ink. Good night, you." He kissed me on the forehead.

"Good night, you," I repeated, and closed the door softly behind me.

I put on my new flannel pajamas, brushed my teeth, and then sat back on the bed to examine my gift more closely. It was charmingly wrapped with a scrap of tartan fabric rather than paper, neatly folded around what was obviously a book. It was tied with twine, and the knot held a small, fresh-cut thistle loosely in place. When I plucked it out, I noticed that the thorns had been snipped off, and I smiled.

The wrapping came away easily, and my breath caught—it was the beautifully marbled Scott book that I had cherished at the charity shop in Bath. He'd remembered, and had gone back to get it and surprise me. That day in Bath was the day everything had changed between us. I slid my hand over the leather binding like caressing the skin of a lover and inhaled the smell that wafted from the old paper as I flipped the pages. It was beautiful. And it would remind me always of that day we shared together.

As I was looking at the illustration and roman numerals on the front plate, I noticed a little slip of paper that came loose. A note written in a neat, angular hand.

"Look back, and smile on perils past." —*Walter Scott*

Dear Alice Cooper,

Your trip here has already been quite perilous, and we are not yet nearly finished with you. I hope that every time you thumb through the pages of this book, or see its marbled binding out of the corner of your eye, that you'll think of the time you traveled across the sea to have an epic adventure. That you'll think of us. That you'll think of me.

> *With love on your birthday.*
> *Yours, Robbie*

I hugged a pillow and smiled myself to sleep.

CHAPTER 31

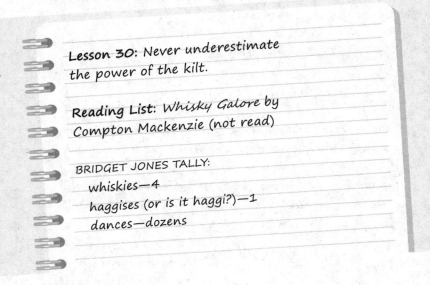

Lesson 30: Never underestimate the power of the kilt.

Reading List: *Whisky Galore* by Compton Mackenzie (not read)

BRIDGET JONES TALLY:
  whiskies—4
  haggises (or is it haggi?)—1
  dances—dozens

Then came The Day.

I'd seen ceilidhs in movies and TV, but had never danced in one before. I was determined to throw myself in with wild abandon and have the night of my life. I had been resting my ankle for days in preparation, and it felt strong. It felt like it could hold me up against an onslaught of Highland warriors who had no other purpose but to twirl me silly.

It was early evening when our little Rosie puttered up to Glenapp Castle, an immense baronial pile complete with turrets and towers. It earned a great round of whooping and applause when it came into view from the windows of our little bus, nestled regally within a leafy wooded estate—a Victorian vision of a Gothic fantasy.

Tonight was a fundraiser for the Scottish Book Trust. Dramatic flaming torches had been lit to welcome guests; it made me giddy with anticipation. A flag flew on the wind from the highest tower, and scores of great, eyelike windows peered down upon us, already starting to glow in the fading light. Thick gnarls of lush, twisted vines toiled up one side of the sandstone, trying jealously to claim it for the forest. It was romance incarnate. It was Northanger Abbey meets Castle Leoch. I squealed.

We were shown to our rooms to freshen up before dinner. My room was immense, with a huge bed, carefully chosen antiques, and beautiful windows. I put my bag down, walked to the window, and leaned against the sill. The view swept over the estate, and in the distance, a gray turbulent sea lashed against a rocky island. I breathed out, a long sigh that blossomed a puff of fog in the window, and relaxed into my bliss.

After a long, drawn-out, deliciously steamy shower, I wrapped my ankle, then set about making myself look like the lady of the manor as best I could. I ached to be corseted up in a huge period costume, festooned with tartan, layers of lace, and skirts upon skirts. I was grateful to at least be able to outfit myself in the elegant black dress that Helena had given me, and I decided to leave my red hair down and windswept, as a nod to my distant Scottish heritage. I slid on ballet flats for dancing, plus my plaid scarf for warmth and added Scottishness. I checked myself in the mirror. Then I checked my inner self.

I was alright. Like my ankle, my inner self was a bit bruised, perhaps, and something I should probably be careful with, but it felt strong and sturdy enough. I had prepared for tonight, and I could weather it. What's more, I was determined to have a great time.

As I made my way down the staircase, I saw that many of the ladies were already in the foyer, looking beautiful and sipping champagne. Then I saw Robbie. He was in a kilt—one less formal than some of the others, with their black dress jackets and horsehair sporrans. Robbie wore a beautiful soft blue tartan with a snug gray sweater, sleeves casually pushed up despite the chill of the old stone, a simple leather sporran, and brown leather boots below his socks. His calves, his back, his shoulders, the sporran chain tight across his hips—all were difficult to look away from.

He turned and smiled up at me. I had to stop for a moment, swallow hard, and remind myself to breathe. *What is he wearing under there?* Had I been a daintier lady of a more delicate disposition, I would have fainted on the spot, roused only by a walloping whiff of smelling salts. But I wasn't, so instead I imagined all manner of inappropriate kilt-centric scenarios as I glided down the final steps.

We ladies congratulated ourselves on how nice we'd scrubbed up, and Robbie said that all the men would be jealous of him. As we went in for supper, he and I fell into place, as we often did these days, at the back of the line.

"Hold it there a wee breath, lass." He thickened his brogue to a pea soup consistency, a rumbly growl that made my toes curl.

I stood stock-still, unsure of what was happening. He had a devilish grin on his face, eyebrow cocked as he came toward me slowly—a lion closing in on its prey.

"Ach, dinna fash, lassie," he rolled low in his throat. "This willna hurt a bit."

He came closer, and my eyes darted between us wildly, wondering what was about to happen. He slowly reached up and slid his hand under my plaid scarf and dragged it off my shoulders. *Oh my God.* Then he bent down and removed a pin from the bottom of his kilt, eyes flicking back to me. Coming near again, he paused for a moment, eyes intense but playful, in a gesture laced with so much sexual innuendo I wondered if I would need a pregnancy test afterward.

He spread the scarf over one shoulder and across my body like a sash and pinned it together at my hip.

"There."

"Does this mean I'm properly kitted out for the haggis?"

"Aye, you are. Aye, you are." He offered me his elbow. But as we started to walk after the others, he added, "Best to acquaint yourself with my arms now, ye ken, because they'll be swingin' you off the floor later tonight."

Whoa.

What the hell does that mean?

Is he talking about dancing? Because I've never heard anything so dirty in all my life.

"Promises, promises," I teased coquettishly. He tightened his mouth and kept his eyes straight ahead.

TURNS OUT, I'M a haggis girl! Who would have guessed that I'd be elbow-deep in sheep's stomach stuffed with lightly peppered innards and loving every minute of it? What the hell was a neep? Who cares!

Afterward there was cheese and oatcakes and some salted caramel fancy layered mousse kinda thing that looked like it came with its own Michelin star and tasted like an angel spun it out of kitten dreams.

We followed the rest of the group—and about sixty or so others, mostly middle-aged and older (though I did happen to notice a few rugged Scotsmen who appeared to be closer to my age)—to sit down on leather and velvet tufted sofas in a room where the fire crackled in its hearth, surrounded on all sides with wood paneling, lush garnet curtains, and various tartans on the rug and cushions. If one were to imagine a room to drink whisky in, it would be this room, and so that's just what we did.

Cheeks warm with cheer and easy smiles, we were as ready as we'd ever be for the dancing. A refined-looking gentleman came in and invited us all to the ballroom, where we could already hear the band striking the iron.

The band consisted of five handsome men dressed in kilts, and when they played, my blood rushed and thudded so that I felt dizzy. Even if we hadn't been here to dance, I couldn't have helped it. My legs itched for it, and my feet added a percussive rattle to the jigs and reels. Fiddle, guitar, whistle, accordion, drum, and even occasionally bagpipes carried us forward to the dance floor—and could have marched us happily off a cliff if they'd wanted to. We would have died twirling each other to the rocks below.

Isla had not yet arrived, and I had decided not to worry about it.

The first dance that I tried was the military two-step. Robbie pulled me over when they told us to couple up.

"Do you think you can dance on that rickety hoof you've got there?"

"Of course. You'll see. I'll be the last one standing at the end of the night."

"Is that because you will have stomped and elbowed all the other dancers to a pulp?"

I scoffed. "Hmm. Maybe I should find a more agreeable partner." I scanned the room.

He laughed and pulled me close with a tight arm around my waist. "Nae chance."

The band called out the steps for the dancers to learn before we all made a mockery of age-old tradition. Robbie took it easy on me, helping me by pushing and pulling me to the right places to be swung by the next partner and to loop back around without colliding with any merrymakers.

"Manhandling is by invitation only," I shouted between gulps of air while we took our places for the next dance.

"Och, you're only a wee helpless Yank. You need all the help you can get. Besides, it's my civic duty to stop you from crippling all the nice older gentlemen."

I was relieved to find that the atmosphere was light and easy. No one minded if you made mistakes, and many of the others there, even those with Scottish accents, were learning and missing steps along with the rest of us. We were all in it together, and it was such roaring fun!

I danced to every tune I could. Each dance was different, and I didn't want to miss one. I thought my ankle would demand breaks, but it felt surprisingly strong, and I felt as light as a feather. Sometimes I danced with strangers, sometimes with the other ladies, but most often with Robbie, the band whipping us into a sweating, breathless fury.

We teased each other as we swung around on each other's arms, grinning like punch-drunk fools, laughing at every falter and misstep. We laughed when it worked like clockwork too, because of the sheer joy of it. The music coursed through our veins like a drug we were already addicted to.

"Ladies and gentlemen, we're going to have a wee break, so please go and freshen your drinks," the bandleader announced. "To keep us all going, I'd like to invite a special guest to the stage. An old bandmate and dear friend, Robbie Brodie."

I looked around, confused. His were common Scottish names; surely there was another Robbie Brodie in the audience. But no, after a few refusals and some peer pressure, Robbie got up and joined the others. My mouth hung open on its hinges.

He stepped up to the mic and greeted the room easily.

"Now, while you're all catching your breath and bending your arm, I might sing a little song, if that's alright." Everyone clapped. "Thank you. This one's called 'The Lowlands of Holland.'"

He sang alone, a slow, haunting song about a young bride whose lover was lost to the sea. Robbie's voice was deep and earthy and filled with emotion, tripping and dragging single syllables into a cascade of notes in the way only the Celts could do. The honeyed rasp rang off the high wooden ceiling and raised the hair on every inch of my skin. I sipped my whisky and breathed deeply, utterly hypnotized, the spell only broken when the audience erupted into wild applause.

Then they handed him the fiddle. They struck up a set of tunes so fast that it was breaking the horsehairs on his bow. I was dumbstruck. My every nerve was buzzing. He was gorgeous up there. Powerful, confident, and oh-so-heartbreakingly talented. I caught myself holding my breath, while my heart took wing at the trill of the strings.

My head reminded my feet to root. This man was clearly still a stranger to me. I had told him everything. I had answered every question, and offered up every tiny piece to him. I had flayed myself open for his benefit, while all this—and much more—he had kept secret. I wasn't angry, really, or even upset. I was happy, mostly, at being here to see him perform. I just felt as if the rug had been swept out from under me.

Nothing is so dangerous for falling in love than watching a talented person do what they're good at. My mind raced ahead. I knew that tonight would hurt, and that I would fly home heartsore. But at least I knew I still had a heart that knew how to love. There were worse fates.

The band finished a tune, and I heard Robbie over the mic again.

"What an audience! Thank you!" Then he started laughing. And then: "Oh! *Hello, gorgeous!*" He laughed, smiling out into the crowd. And my world splintered apart.

CHAPTER 32

Lesson 31: Never ceilidh in anger.

BRIDGET JONES TALLY:
what's my name again?

Fuck. She's here.

My heart pounded so hard it hurt. My stomach dropped into my feet. My throat twisted. I scanned the room frantically. I couldn't find her. There weren't many women younger than fifty out there, and even fewer redheads.

"Well, I'd better stop hogging the stage before I get a skelping!" People laughed. He jumped offstage and hurried into the crowd. I moved closer, trying to catch a glimpse of her. I dodged through clusters of people and arrived to find him in an embrace, swinging around a petite woman with a chin-length mess of ginger hair. He put her down and held her out by her elbows. My jaw dropped. A chin-length mess of *graying* ginger hair.

Was this . . . ? But she . . .

She was a small middle-aged woman with intelligent, ice-blue eyes and a smile so big and proud it must have hurt. And she looked just like him.

Helena swooped in. "Isla! Took you long enough!" She laughed. "Come here and give us a squeeze."

I watched from the sidelines as Robbie rushed around making introductions.

"Doris you know, of course, and there's old Percy. Berrta is here from Germany. Berrta, this is my mom."

My vision blurred. *His* mom? I was dizzy. How the hell did I get everything *so* wrong?

After introducing all the ladies, Robbie slung his arm around his mom's shoulder and gave her another hug. He looked up to scan the crowd for me, but I held back out of sight. I needed to get a handle on the relentless waves of incomprehension lashing the shores of my memory.

I thought his mom died of cancer. Didn't he say she died? I thought back to the conversations that we'd had. We often used vague, abstract language to discuss the death of Robbie's mom, in the way that people tend to do to soften painful things. I *thought* they had been discussions about death. He had talked about her being sick, and about the fear of losing her, but perhaps he never actually said that she had died. Was that possible?

I left through a side door and found a place to sit out of the way, to regain my composure and sort through the deluge of thoughts and emotions. They struck me heavily one at a time in the following order:

She was the one on the phone.

He didn't have a girlfriend.

He'd been free the entire trip.

Somehow, this wasn't the relief it should have been. As if falling for a man who was unavailable wasn't bad enough, now it turned out that he *had* been available the whole time. So much had changed between us since I had asked him for space. That was long forgotten between us. He could have made a move on me any time he wanted. I had ached every painful second that I held myself back from him. He clearly wasn't fighting the same battle.

Oh, I knew he cared about me. That much was obvious. He made such an effort to cultivate our friendship. But he must have wanted me as a friend and little more. The flirting, or what had felt like flirting to me, must have been just a bit of fun.

I had added two and two and made six.

"Aliiice Cooooper!" He came laughing and rushing toward me. "Come on, lass. Come meet my ma!" He looked so happy. He grabbed my hand, and I went with him as he dragged me back to the ballroom, practically running.

When I finally met Isla, she greeted me with an honest smile that made glittering blue crescents of her eyes.

"Alice, this is my mom, Isla."

"Alice, dear." She clutched my hand snugly in both of hers. "Robbie's told me all about you."

"Maaaaa," Robbie whined, rolling his eyes and pretending at the role of embarrassed teenager, which made his mother laugh.

"How's that ankle of yours, Alice?"

"Much better, thank you."

"I see that. I saw you dancing earlier. You looked lovely out there. You're picking it up rather well."

"That's a little too generous of you." I smiled and tried harder. "I nearly took Robbie's big toe off a couple of times."

"Aye," he said. "But what a way for it to go!" He gave me a little wink. "Right then. Only one thing could improve on this. Who's up for a nip of something? My shout!" Robbie took orders from all the ladies, then turned to me. "I could use a bit of help with the glasses. Why don't you make yourself useful?"

I gave him a frosty look. It surprised me. I hadn't really meant to.

His brows drew quizzically, but he put his warm hand on my back and led me through the crowd.

He looked over his shoulder and then leaned into my hair and hummed conspiratorially in my ear. "How's about a little shot while we're here doing all this thirsty work?"

I shrugged noncommittally, but yes, I could drink the whole damned bottle.

"Are you okay? Tired? Is your ankle hurting you?"

"I'm fine," I said flatly. The classic feminine manifesto of the decidedly un-fine.

He ordered two shots of Jameson with a dash of Baileys. I threw mine back. I was angry. I knew it wasn't fair, that he hadn't really done anything wrong, but that didn't matter.

This guy. With that voice and his fiddle and those eyes, he was something otherworldly tonight: a prince, a celebrity, a fairy king in a story that had a dark ending. I was spiraling, falling for him harder than ever, and there was nothing I could do to stop it. And yet, he was clearly a complete stranger to me. And he was single, and he sure wasn't falling for me.

I wanted off this roller coaster. I would not continue to throw myself at a man who wanted me only for my friendship and personality! *How dare he? What a grade A asshole!*

I slammed my glass down aggressively, asking the barman for another. Robbie was surprised and confused. "What's gotten into you? I thought you were having a good time tonight." He took my hand. Concern was written over his face in a way that made my heart hiccup. I clenched my jaw and took the moment to ignore him as my shot arrived and I threw it back.

He wanted to know what had gotten into me? Well, I could help him out with that. I turned to face him slowly and gave my cold stare the dramatic moment that it deserved.

"Robbie. I thought your mom was dead."

He let out a small, shocked puff of air.

"What?"

"Yeah."

"Why?"

"What do you mean *why*? The way you spoke about her. The things you told me. The fear and pain of losing her."

He gave one short mirthless laugh and rubbed a hand over his face.

"I *did* almost lose her. It *was* very painful. They told me that she didn't have much time left. We said our goodbyes, we even had Christmas early. But . . . she beat it." He searched my face, looking for the source of my upset, then he laughed again. "Alice, she's fine now. She's perfectly fine."

I looked down at the bar. I didn't know how to respond. How could I explain that I was angry that his mother didn't die—because, ipso facto, it meant he didn't want me?

He swept me up into a big hug.

"You numpty." He laughed into my hair. The sudden heat of him spread through my body, right up my neck, and into my face. The smell of him. *Like whisky and manly capability, as if he's just come in from chopping enough wood to see us through winter, goddamnit!*

I pushed back a bit, and he released me but held me by the elbows. I tried again, reining it in a bit.

"I don't know how I could have gotten it so wrong. Of course, I'm obviously very happy that your mom is here . . . and well, you know, not dead." He barked a shocked laugh at the insanity of the conversation. "She seems wonderful." I stopped, but he knew there was more, and he searched my face silently, patiently waiting for me to drag it out. "It's just. All this." I gestured, waving my hand dumbly at the stage and his mom. My uncontrollable attraction to him, rampant now that I had added glittering talent to the intelligence, the smile, the calves, and the kilt. It was so unfair.

It sounded stupid to say, but I was going to blurt it out it anyway.

"It's just that I thought we were friends, but it turns out that I don't really know you at all."

His eyes widened.

Oh God. I sound like a stupid teenager.

I didn't want to hear what he had to say. I couldn't possibly bring myself to tell him the stupidity of the rest of my assumptions—that I thought his mom was his girlfriend and that I was mad that he was single and had not tried harder to get me, to kiss me again, to take me to bed. That I was hurt and embarrassed to discover that the feelings I was having—the struggle *every day* not to run flat-out until I collided with him and kissed him breathless—was one-sided. That the overwhelming romantic connection between us was little more than a product of my fevered imagination.

Before he could say anything, I went on. I just wanted it to be over.

"Look. Forget it. It was my mistake. It's only been a few weeks. It's not like we're best friends. It just took me by surprise, that's all."

Cheeks burning, unable to face him any longer, I grabbed a few of the glasses, whipped around, and headed back to the group before he could object. He couldn't pull me back without spilling the drinks, but he raced to cut me off as I blazed a trail through the dancers. He stood in front of me, drinks filling his hands, as close as we could be without dropping everything.

"Alice. What are you talking about? Of course you know me."

"Clearly."

"No. Don't do that. These past weeks I've gotten closer to you than I am to some of my oldest friends. Search me for why we've gotten along so quickly." A cheeky grin danced on his lips. "You're an unholy terror, but we're friends, and there's nothing I can do to stop that now. I care about you. You're a person in my life. So maybe it's only been a few weeks and we're still discovering things about each other. That's not a bad thing."

Ugh. Curse him for crafting a perfect response. It was sentimental, complimentary, insulting, and sensible in equal measure. *Friends, though. He said we were friends.*

"So I'm not an orphan, and I have the voice of an angel. I can also bake the best sticky toffee pudding that you've ever put in your mouth. But you'll get used to my being perfect. I promise."

I scoffed. At a loss for what to do next, I shoved him slightly, and he spilled a bit of the drinks on his arms. I grinned smugly and hurried back to the group. But I didn't feel any better. His little speech had only succeeded in bringing more emotions to the messy battlefield of my mind.

Somewhere, the levelheaded part of me reminded myself that in the morning, all this would look like very little. But I grabbed that reasonable idiot by the scruff of the neck, and I drowned her in the whisky lake currently sloshing in my head. He was doing all the right things, which made me like him more, and the more I liked him, the more I felt like a complete idiot. The only smart thing to do was to cling to that fury with both hands and not give in to the threatening desire to swoon.

"Thank you, dear," Robbie's mom said as I handed her a drink. "So tell me. How have you been liking your trip?"

"Oh," I said dumbly. I hadn't been prepared to transition to polite conversation. My eyes ran over the ladies, and I softened. I couldn't help but answer honestly, and the truth of it made my heart ache a little bit. "It's been wonderful. Truly wonderful."

"And what are your thoughts on this concept of all-woman tours?"

"Well, I'll be honest. When I arrived, it wasn't what I had expected, and I wasn't convinced that it was the right choice for me." I started haltingly, trying to be diplomatic. "But I couldn't have been more wrong. I do think that being an all-woman tour gave us a different dynamic. More space to bond. And I adore these ladies." I stopped for a moment, but Isla didn't jump in. Finally, I shared a bit too much under her warm, astute gaze. "They've been a balm to my burns."

Her eyes narrowed, and she put a hand between my shoulder blades, rubbing roughly the way one would soothe a large barnyard animal. It made me want to lean down and nestle into the warm softness of her shoulder and have a cry.

"Aye. It's done that for me before too."

We sat there in companionable silence, for a few moments listening to the musicians as they struck up again, her hand still on my back.

"Ma!" Robbie's stern voice came from behind us. "No manhandling Alice Cooper. She doesn't like to be manhandled, or so she says." He added this little chestnut in a lower tone and shot me a look that made the statement feel shockingly suggestive. I pinkened.

"She's doing nothing of the kind," I defended.

"And just what are you two conspiring about then?"

"Well, Alice was just telling me how she was enjoying the tour."

"Oh, she was, was she? And has she confessed that the bit she loves best is torturing me? Sure, she's cute, but she's more trouble than a badger in a basket!"

Isla gasped in mock horror. "Robert Brodie! You can't speak about a lady that way."

"She's no lady, ma—she's a stinging nettle." That earned him a swat from his mother. It was a ruse. He was trying to goad me into playing with him, to slip into our easy teasing, and she played right along with him. Normally, I would have eaten it up, but tonight it felt like salt on a paper cut; something I wanted to be part of but couldn't be. At least not in the way I wanted.

"Ignore him. He's a brute! What was your favorite part of the trip so far, Alice? I'm curious."

"Well . . ." I furrowed my brow as images of the trip spun through my head. It was honestly hard to say, I had loved so much of it.

"Oh, I think you'll find her favorite activity so far was at Kenilworth Castle. I've never seen her more enthusiastic about getting a hands-on experience in the British countryside."

I went crimson all the way to my toes. My only hope was that the lighting was too low for his mom to notice. When she turned her head to say something to Doris, I shot him a glare of pure, unadulterated hatred.

I had wanted him so much the day that we kissed that something had snapped inside of me and never recovered. I had thought he had wanted me with the same fervor, but he had just been going along with it, opportunistically kissing any old American who threw themselves at him. White-hot humiliation burned a kiln inside of my chest.

"Dashing White Sergeant!" the bandleader called out.

Robbie's mom grabbed my hand. "We need sets of three for this. Come on. Let's go kick our heels up!"

Robbie, Isla, and I made up a group of three where Robbie essentially played the center position of the dashing young sergeant courting us both. We stood across from Lorna, Madge, and Berrta. I was not in the mood to dance with Robbie, but his mom looked so pleased that I didn't want to disappoint her.

Robbie alternated partners: dancing to his mom, spinning her around, and then switching to me for the same before going back to her. We would hold hands with the other three across from us; spin around in a circle of six in one direction, and then the next; and eventually, after the spinning and switching and weaving, we would leave the ladies and join another set of three, making our way around to all the groups in the room. It was an age-old scheme to get people to mix and no doubt end up married before the end of the season.

What this meant to me was that I had only the very briefest flashes of opportunity to show Robbie the full force of my searing displeasure. Obviously, I didn't want his lovely mother or the other ladies to see me giving him the stink eye or cursing into his ear. So I had to be stealthy. I had to be two-faced. And I had to have rhythm.

Happy face at the ready, I Jekyll-and-Hyded myself around the dance floor at warp speed—smiling, scowling, hooting, clapping, baring my teeth.

"Robbie," I hissed, and then was slingshotted to the other side and back again.

"Yes, dear?" he replied pleasantly, just to piss me off. Then he held tight to my arm and spun me around so fast that my feet flew off the ground and a little yelp escaped me.

Discombobulated, I danced a little bit in place, laughing and clapping as I faced his mom.

"Would you—" I scowled back at him. We wove merrily in and out in little happy steps and skips. "Stop—"

"Can't stop now!" he sang when he got close again, a mischievous shit-eating grin splashed across his face.

If looks could maim, he would have been castrated on the spot. Unfortunately, they couldn't. *Maybe I could do it with a knee instead.*

He laughed, delighting in my frustration, his joy only multiplied by my inability to tear him limb from limb while gracefully and competently skipping, twirling, and clapping. My elegance and agility were taking a hit.

"I hate you," I said quickly as he happily danced a pas de basque across from me.

He smiled. "No, you don't."

"Yes, I do! Oh—sorry, Lorna."

"No, you don't."

I tried to swing my elbow at him and make it look like part of the dance, but he just skipped away, leaving me to look like a teapot on my own. I plastered a smile on my face, put my other elbow up, and did a few little kicks so no one would notice.

"Ooo!" Berrta said, clearly impressed, and did something similar in an effort to match me. *Oh God. We look so stupid!*

Defeated, disoriented, and looking like a complete idiot, I focused on my dancing for the few bars left. When it was done, I walked away in a storm.

Lorna came to grab me for the next dance, and I didn't resist. She was so happy, viewing the world through a merry whisky haze, that she didn't notice my shift in mood. I didn't want anyone to, really. It was such a beautiful, perfect night that I didn't want to spoil it for anyone. Only for Robbie. I could very happily ruin his evening as well as his ability to ever sire children and call it a night.

The dance after that was something called the Gay Gordons. As I walked toward Berrta, Robbie grabbed my waist from behind and spun me into the circle. It turned out that this one was danced very closely, as he knew it would be. My back was pressed to his front, and our two sets of hands clasped above my shoulders. It involved being close at all times: switching directions back-and-forth while not letting go of the handhold. It was a fast dance, clearly designed to make one feel dizzy and giddy and to give couples an excuse to rub up against each other.

Robbie used this as an opportunity to keep me from running away. I instead chose to use it as an opportunity for revenge. As we switched directions, I took special care to flick him in the face with my hair. As we went backward, I stepped on his toe, and one time even managed to land a blind kick back on his shin. He squeezed my hands, but looked down at me with curiosity, amusement, and barely a trace of the pain and annoyance that I had hoped for.

As we spun, moving backward and forward around the dance

floor, his breath came faster, our bodies bumping and rubbing accidentally as the dance picked up speed. The feel of him took me over, and I had to close my eyes for a moment, letting him take control. His hands were large and warm and strong, and wouldn't let mine go for anything as he guided me. It made my head swim. I wanted to kill him, but that task was made especially difficult when I was weak in the knees.

"What's going on with you tonight?" The music was loud, but he was close enough to put his lips to my ear.

"Just stop toying with me! I'm not your plaything to pick up whenever you're bored."

"But you love it when I toy with you, Alice Cooper."

"No. I don't. I'm sick of it!" I was shouting now. The music swelled and drowned us out.

The moment the music stopped, I tried to go, but he kept a very firm hold of one hand and marched me out behind him, weaving purposefully through the crowd as the dancers assembled for the next dance. He was leading me out of the room.

CHAPTER 33

Lesson 32: I am a raging idiot.

BRIDGET JONES TALLY:
OH—1
MY—1
GOD—1

It was all well and good, causing trouble and airing my discontent, but I did *not* want to have a sit-down heart-to-heart. I was fairly drunk now, but even if I hadn't been, what would I say? How could I possibly explain? I loved the friendship that had been growing between us: it was a joy and a comfort. I had found myself waking every morning in a hurry to spend as much time in the warm glow of his hilarious company as possible, waiting for the precious few moments we snatched alone together.

How could I talk about my anger tonight without ripping the foundation of our friendship to shreds, and irredeemably humiliating myself in the process? We'd never recover. And then, before I knew it, I would be back to the US, and we'd be grateful not to have to awkwardly keep in touch. The thought was a slow knife to the gut.

I jerked at my hand, but he wasn't giving an inch. I felt like an animal with its leg in a trap. The more I pulled, the more his grip tightened, and the more furious I became.

We turned the corner swiftly into an empty room. My eyes blinked at the darkness. A bit of light spilled in from the hallway and illuminated rows of empty chairs. I stopped dead in my tracks, and managed to stop him as well. But he changed track too quickly for me to think. Rather than jerking me over to the chairs like a rag doll, he swung around, closed the space between us in one stride, and backed me against the wall. His body pressed on mine to keep me in place. His hand, still encircling my wrist, pinned it to the wall next to my face, his other arm caging me in.

He stared at me so intensely for a moment that it burned inside of me. In the shadows I saw emotion chase over his face: confusion, irritation, determination, and a flash of wry amusement. The air was thick and heavy as we both breathed hard into the silence. He searched my eyes as if he might find some answer there.

Then he lowered his face. Our warm, heavy breath mingled in the air together, much louder now than the sounds of the band playing in another room.

"Alright." His voice was a low rumble, steady and dangerous. "What is this?" He looked stern. Then something softer crossed his face, an entreaty, a promise that he would listen.

"Nothing. It's nothing."

"Alice." A warning.

I tried to turn things around. "I was just annoyed. I told you before. We've already talked about this." His chest squeezed against mine, pinning me closer, and his jaw tightened.

"So. Let me get this straight. You're *this* upset with me because my mom is alive, and I can play the fiddle?" His voice was flat and even, willing me to stand up for myself, to explain.

Instead I looked away. His face was so close to mine that when I turned, his lips brushed my cheekbone. My skin prickled with heat that made me squirm. "Alice," he said more softly. With his free hand he took my chin and moved my face back to his, searching again. "Please."

He waited, our chests rising and falling in unison, our eyes locked together with so much tension that my entire body hummed from the force of it.

I sighed and my resolve crumbled.

"I thought your mom was your girlfriend."

He started to laugh, but then he looked angry, and let out an annoyed gust of air through his nose. "What?" he asked very slowly, forcing himself to stay calm.

"I thought. Well, I thought . . . you're always on the phone all the time." He cocked his head, as if to tell me that this wasn't making any sense and I had better hurry up with a clear explanation. "You're always talking to a woman on the phone, and calling her gorgeous, and telling her that you love her."

"And so? It couldn't be anyone else?"

"You told me that you wanted to take her straight to bed!"

"What? No, I didn't!"

"At the pub."

"No. I said that *she* should go straight to bed. Because she'd be tired from all the traveling, and I still worry about her doing too much."

"Well, I thought you were going to ravish your sexy girlfriend."

"Ew, Alice. Jesus!"

"But then, you called your mom gorgeous tonight and, well, I thought your mom was dead, but anyway, then I thought maybe you didn't have a girlfriend after all."

He stared at me. His blue eyes were wide and dark.

"Well?" I huffed when he refused to speak. "Do you have a girlfriend?" I had wanted it to sound firm and accusatory, but that's not how it sounded at all. I had to look away. I tried limply to wriggle out again, to get a bit of space, to get away from his eyes, but he held me like steel shackles.

"No. Of course not." He ground it out. "So . . . you're upset because I *don't* have a girlfriend?"

"Yes!" I finally shouted in exasperation, breaking the oppressive quiet of the room. "*Yes*, okay?" I thrashed now and pushed him away. He gave a few inches, no more. "Because if you don't have—because I thought you . . . obviously—"

His eyes widened and he sucked in a breath. Suddenly I was slammed back into the wall and his mouth was on mine, his hand around the back of my head, holding me closer. He kissed me hard and deep—an angry, frustrated kiss, pulling me into him like the oxygen he needed to live.

I was rigid with shock for a moment. Then I kissed him back.

It was hungry and desperate, blind to everything else. He grabbed my other wrist and pinned it up, one on each side, keeping me firmly in place until he would decide that the kiss was finished. I heard a small sound escape from low in my throat. It was an animalistic cry muffled against his open mouth. He hardened in response. He deepened his kiss, devouring me. His stubble scratched against me, and my pulse pounded in my ears.

My body arched to bring my hips closer to his, and he let go of my wrists, his hands sliding down my body. Grabbing me by the waist, he lifted me and held me up against the wall until my legs locked around his hips and drew him in closer. I bit his lip, and he gasped, moving his hands to my stockinged thighs, and pushing my bunched-up dress back to get his hands on either side, holding me up with my legs spread wide around him.

I moved one hand into his hair, the soft black hair that I'd wanted to touch every day since I could remember. I tangled my fingers through the thick mess of it and grabbed a fistful tightly. My other hand was on his arm, the muscles hard and smooth moving under his skin as he pushed his hands down my thighs. The sensation of it burned inside of me. I dug my nails in, wracked with a tightening longing, losing control, desperate for more of him, as he growled deep in his chest. We pushed against each other. Needy. Panting. Grasping.

I do not know how long we kissed like that in the dark, but I know that he did not stop until I was shaking, and we were both struggling to catch our breath.

When he finally lowered me down, my legs were too weak and shaky to walk. He supported me, his arms around me until I regained my strength. My dress slithered back down over my hips, my stockings still in place—though, I would discover later, with a telltale run where his fingers had torn through, now laddering down my thigh.

He pressed his forehead against mine and closed his eyes. Breathing me in in ragged breaths, kissing me gently on the nose, the forehead, the soft space where my eyelashes met near my temple.

He started to laugh then. Slowly at first, and then losing himself to it. The jumping of his chest shook us both.

"Alice. Surely." His voice was slow and hazy. "Surely, you must have known." He opened his eyes and searched my face.

"I . . ." I said breathlessly, but nothing else would come.

"You're far too clever to have imagined that I wanted to do anything else but this since the moment you walked up to my bus and started swearing at me."

"But then why . . ."

"You're recovering from a breakup, sweetheart. You told me to back off. I didn't want to push you."

"Oh."

It was all I could say as my world turned itself inside out.

CHAPTER 34

Lesson 33: Exciting new opportunities
should be grabbed with both hands.

BRIDGET JONES TALLY:
knowing looks—1,000
PDA—yes
silk robes—1

We staggered our entrance back, as if that would fool anyone. I went
to the ladies' room and did my best to make myself look less as if I
had just narrowly survived an encounter with a randy stag. I also did
my best to wipe the dopey puppy-love look off my face, to no avail. I
looked in the mirror and gave myself a stern talking to.

AAAHHHH!!! Oh my God! Oh my God! Oh my God!

It didn't help.

Walking back into the room, I saw that the band was taking a
break. Several of the ladies turned their heads when I reappeared—
each one, it seemed, with a knowing smile. I had tried to stop myself
from looking at Robbie as soon as I entered the room. When my
eyes finally made their way to his direction, I found him talking to
his mom and Helena. But his eyes were glued to me. It was written all over his face, from his hair (messier even than usual tornado

standard) to his slightly askew sporran and his sloppy grin and the love-lost twinkle in his big blue eyes. To anyone who was looking, it was clear to see.

I wandered nonchalantly to the Scottish Book Trust table for sign-ups and donations, deciding that it was probably the safest place from prying questions. A little crowd had gathered at the table, including a very animated Flossie, empty champagne flute in hand. She was leaning over the table in conversation with the volunteers, explaining how to do magic tricks. Adorable.

I sidled over and put my hand on Flossie's arm to say hello without breaking her conversation. Next to her, an older man in a kilt moved over to make room for me.

"Good evening," he said. "It would seem we have a mutual friend."

"It certainly would. I'm Alice—nice to meet you."

"Lovely to meet you, Alice. I'm Sidney. An old friend of Flossie's. Are ya havin' a nice night?"

"Oh, I'm having a spectacular night." He had no idea.

"Is it your first ceilidh then? Or are you an old pro?"

"It's my first. I'm surprised I haven't stepped on your toes yet!"

"Ha! I take it you're visiting from America?"

"I am. Washington, DC. What about yourself?"

Flossie's voice rose. "Now, I've found that when you're wearing almost nothing, the crowd hardly notices the rabbit." I grinned. Agatha was soundly asleep in a chair on the other side of the room. I was happy to see Flossie holding court and enjoying herself.

The man leaned in. "I'm from up north. I've moved around, but I stay in Bonar Bridge now."

A laugh burst out of me. I tried to cover it up with a cough. "Where?"

"And the saw is real. One-hundred-percent. But a good magician is always careful with a nice set of legs," said Flossie.

"Bonar Bridge," he answered. "Northeast."

"*Boner* Bridge?"

"Aye, that's right."

No. Surely it can't be. I swayed a little and tried very hard to school my face into seriousness.

"Boner Bridge? Must be . . ." *A very small river,* I started to say. Thankfully, I stopped myself just in time. ". . . beautiful. It must be beautiful." *Either that or Flossie was right about the dachshunds and Dobermans!* I started to laugh again, losing the battle. *With any luck I'll be finding out later tonight.*

"Sid!" said a woman newly arrived on the other side of the table. "Would you look at this turnout?"

"I almost couldn't believe it. Well done, you. Almost double what we had last year."

"Well, we certainly couldn't have done it without your help! Oh, just a second, Sid. I've got to grab Hector before he heads home."

Flossie had barely noticed I was there. She was having a grand time. I took the moment to extricate myself. "Well, it's so nice to meet you. I'm afraid I promised someone a dance."

"Lucky someone," the man said, and gave a gentlemanly little bow.

The tune changed, and I saw Robbie making his way over to me with determination. I rushed toward him laughing. I hid my face in his shoulder as he pulled me in close and moved us toward the dance floor. We danced most of the other dances together, spinning around each other like courting butterflies on a summer breeze, indiscreet now about what had probably been clear to everyone else for some time.

The band asked Robbie to come up and sing and play a few more tunes. This time he sang "Ae Fond Kiss." I danced with Berrta and Madge and Flossie, who kept up remarkably well with the steps, oftentimes better than I did! It was curious how sometimes Flossie seemed more present than the rest of us put together.

As the evening wound down, Robbie and I couldn't help but

send more and more frequent glances in each other's direction—questioning and expectant. The way you do when your friend has half a slice of cake on her plate and appears to be full. My stomach flipped each time he caught my eye. After all this time of wanting something that we thought we couldn't have, we finally understood each other, and we knew that the only thing left between us now was time. How much time was the question.

The ceilidh whipped itself into a climatic whirlwind finish with the Orcadian Strip the Willow. The entire party stood in two long lines facing one another. The couple at the top would spin together, advancing down the entire line, stopping at each new couple to take a quick spin with them before going back to their partner to spin down to the next couple. What this meant was a hell of a lot of spinning.

The band started fast and then sped onward, relentlessly faster and faster, issuing a challenge, daring us to keep up.

It was sheer insanity. The burly men in the line did their best to lift their partners and spin them fast enough to get their feet off of the ground, which was equal parts terrifying, exhilarating, and sexy as hell. Most of the time I couldn't even see straight enough to find the person who was spinning me next, but they didn't wait to come grab me by the elbow and spin me before passing me back to Robbie to be spun again, who rather than spinning me at an elbow's distance would grab me close around the waist, lifting my feet off the floor, while making me feel secure and tightly held. He had deliciously strong arms and a firm grip, which I was very grateful for, because I was dizzier than a wino on a Tilt-A-Whirl.

I was exhausted and elated. I couldn't remember the last time I had so much fun. Everyone clapped and yelled and whistled, and we did the same, panting from exertion, our heads still whirling. Robbie turned to me with a wild grin on his face and planted a celebratory peck full on my mouth for God and everyone to see. It was a surprise, and I didn't know if it was the danger of being caught by the others or the thrill of not caring, but the electricity it generated curled my toes.

A little bit sweaty, messily attired, and hair suitably tussled, our group found one another afterward, laughed and yelled, and clinked glasses. Some of the women, like Doris, had sat out the faster dances and looked as if they were exhausted just from watching us. Some, I noticed, were still carrying on conversations with a few of the dapper older gentlemen who were circling around. After all, what is a ceilidh if not a place to flirt and meet people?

I helped Doris up from her chair. "Well! Percy and I are going up to our princess bedroom to get some kip. We'll need to sleep for a year after this!"

Helena grinned. "Be careful. You may need a kiss from a prince to wake you up." She waggled her eyebrows.

"Hmph. Only a frog would kiss that face," said Agatha. Doris hooted and clapped her on the back, much to Agatha's chagrin.

There were hugs all around, including a long, warm hug from Isla, who asked me to come back to Edinburgh soon so she could take me to lunch in the gallery gardens.

They all peeled off to their respective bedrooms, laughing and singing and recounting incidents from the evening. Robbie and I began to make our way back, walking like our shoes were soled with honey.

"So," he said.

"So," I said.

He grabbed my hand as we strolled slowly, lacing his fingers with mine. This was a particularly intimate gesture for me, one I reserved for long-term relationships, but from him somehow it felt as if we'd been holding hands for years. Its warm comfort unfurled in my center and stroked gently at the fire in my belly.

"So," he said again.

When can we make out again? I asked myself. *How about now?*

"Can I walk you to your door?" It was a gentlemanly offer, one that I hoped would lead to more making out. *Can I ask him to carry me to bed instead?*

"Of course, but I don't have any money for a tip. Would you accept a buttock grope or an abdominal fondle in lieu?"

"Mmm . . . that all depends. Would I be on the giving or receiving end of this transaction?"

"Oh, I'd be open to negotiations. For instance: two grabs for a fondle, or one pinch for three nuzzles, or a tweak for a grope."

"Interesting. I believe your currency conversion may be off. You see, here, one good winching would be the equivalent of—"

We were at my door, and I cut him off by pulling him against me and kissing him like the world was about to end. Everything else floated away from me, and my mind went quiet, meditating devoutly on the shifting points of contact between Robbie's body and mine. His tongue, his teeth, his breath, his hands, his hips, his arms, his thighs. My body was ringing with the intensity of it. So sweet and intoxicating. A longing almost to the point of pain.

He slowed and pulled away slightly, giving enough distance so that he could talk. I opened my eyes, and when he finally opened his as well, they were dark and hazy. He spoke so closely that his lips moved against mine when he finally said, "I think I should probably let you get some sleep."

I was in shock. *Sleep?! Aphrodite after a few margaritas would be more interested in sleep than I am right now!*

I stayed silent for a moment to give myself some time to think. I didn't want to be pushy. Maybe he wanted to wait. Maybe he was tired. Maybe he was worried that we'd had too much to drink. Although every inch of his body was telling me he was ready to take me to bed immediately before he lost his patience and decided the hallway was an acceptable alternative.

"Alright," I heard myself say sweetly from a long way off. *You idiot!*

"I'm just . . . I'm just down the hall if you need me for anything."

He kissed me again, tenderly, sweetly, but reining in the passion. I wanted to cling to him. I wanted to wrap my legs around him. I wanted to consume him body and soul.

But I didn't. I kissed him back, and then I let him glide away, the heavy wool kilt swaying down the hall to his bedroom.

I opened my door with a shaky hand, and the decadent luxury of the interior failed to even take my notice. I paced. Then I brushed my teeth while I paced. I took my dress and stockings off and paced some more. My mind was in a hazy blur trying to grasp at a strategy for getting him back. I pinned my hair up into a messy bun and hopped into the shower. I stood for a few long minutes under the hot cascade, steam swirling around me and fogging up the room.

Then I shut the water off with a decisive swipe. Before I could stop to think, before I could question myself, I got out and looked for something to wear, grabbing a satin robe in a soft ashy rose shade, GLENAPP CASTLE embroidered on the breast. It could have been a paper bag or a giant piece of aluminum foil for all I cared. I covered my body with it and tied the knot around my waist as I raced from the room, leaving the door open behind me: barefoot, wet, and with single-minded intent written in every line of my body.

CHAPTER 35

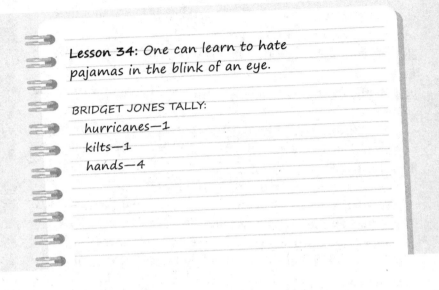

Lesson 34: One can learn to hate pajamas in the blink of an eye.

BRIDGET JONES TALLY:
hurricanes—1
kilts—1
hands—4

I stormed down the hall like a hurricane, not even knowing what I would say when he opened the door. The only thing I did know was that I refused to go to sleep thinking of him, the way I had done every night since the day that I'd arrived. I couldn't have stopped myself if I'd wanted to.

I wasn't exactly sure where his room was, but it didn't deter me. I'd knock on them all if I had to.

I turned the corner, and to my surprise, there he was, walking toward me. My feet began to run, and I didn't stop until I crashed into him. He grabbed me so tightly that we couldn't breathe, then lifted me up and spun me around, laughing deep in his chest while I covered his face with kisses.

"Miss Cooper," he said politely, holding me a foot off the ground.

"Mister Brodie."

"I wondered if we could maybe have a chat—"

I slid down his body and stopped him with another searing kiss that made my knees weak. Then I grabbed his hand and dragged him back to my room. The door was still open, and I slammed it shut behind us. I went after him, kissing him ferociously, as we backed our way to the bed.

I sat him down and straddled his lap. Then I noticed what he had in his hands.

"What is this?" It was plaid pajama bottoms and a soft T-shirt.

"Umm." He wore a smile that flushed at the corners. "Well. What I wanted to say was—"

"Before you were interrupted."

"Yes. Before I was interrupted." He smirked, but then grew serious. "What I wanted to say was this. Alice, I don't want to waste any more time. I know that you'll be going home soon, and I will kick myself for every minute that I wasn't near you. I don't want to be presumptuous. I brought some pajamas. See?" He held them up to show me. "Nothing has to happen, but I wanted to ask if maybe I could come to bed with you. Just to . . . to sleep next to you. Hold you, if you'd let me. If you'd want me to." He looked up at me through his eyelashes, having made an overture, and waited for my response. I stared at him, locking eyes with his, dark and honest now, not glittering with their usually cheeky mischief.

"To hell with that plan." I grabbed his pajamas and threw them across the room. Then I grabbed his sweater and dragged it over his head. He laughed as I pushed his half-naked body down beneath me and planted a kiss on him that left no lingering question as to how I wanted the rest of the evening to go.

"Christ," he exhaled.

"Is this an acceptable alternative?"

"Aye. Very acceptable."

When I sat up and finally looked down at his body, I let out an appreciative breath.

"Holy crap!"

I ran my splayed hands over his beautiful torso. I had been spoiled. His broad, muscular shoulders tapered down to a narrow waist, and the muscles of his chest, arms, and stomach stood out. They were solid without being sculpted—the body of a strong, active, outdoorsy man, rather than one who spent hours at the gym every day. His skin was smooth and perfect, and the feel of soft skin over hard muscle made my head spin. He had a thatch of hair across the middle of his chest, which was soft and manly, and when I ran my hands over it, the butterflies in my stomach went into tornado mode. He could not have been more perfect for me had I constructed him myself, from star stuff and fevered sex dreams.

I wanted my mouth on him. I took my time kissing and tasting my way from his neck, across his flat stomach, to his hips where he still wore his kilt. He took deep breaths and grumbled softly. I sat up and ran my hands across his arms. His hands came up and encircled my waist and then slid up the silky satin of my robe to my breasts, where my hard nipples yearned for his touch. He growled, a painful sound, as if he couldn't take much more, and sat up to kiss me, but I pushed him down again and coquettishly slid one shoulder out of my robe. It glided down my arm and then, slowly, off of my breast. The weight of it pulled at my other shoulder, and a little wiggle had the other side sliding down to pool at the sash at my waist.

He groaned and took me in his hands, and my body writhed in exquisite anguish.

"My God, you're perfect, Alice." I shut him up with my mouth.

His kilt and my robe may as well have been sewn from wrapping paper for how long they lasted after that.

We spent the next six hours devouring each other in an Olympic tangle of recurring orgasms that paid reverent homage to the six-teen long days of frustrated foreplay that we had been bludgeoning each other with. These tantric sessions were punctuated by bouts of laughing at each other's jokes, short naps, and hungry, exhausted cuddling, which led, of course, to more sex.

The physical chemistry between us was electric. Explosive. I have no idea how we had managed two weeks without ripping each other's clothes off. Yes, it was raw, animalistic passion at its best, but there was an underlying tenderness there as well: a sweetness and an eagerness to make sure that the other was comfortable and happy. We cared about each other. He was very careful to listen to my cues and seemed to intuit everything that I would like. When we napped, we held on tightly, unwilling to let go even in sleep. He smelled so good. We fit together. It felt natural.

WE WERE VERY fortunate indeed that a late start was scheduled for the next day. Robbie had correctly assumed that we ladies would enjoy the luxury of sleeping in that morning to spend more time in the castle rooms and gardens. Isla had left at some dark early hour and sent a knowing text to Robbie, thanking him for selflessly giv-ing her the entire room for the night, and telling him to sleep late and drink some water.

By the time we got up, we could see from the window that some of the early risers were out walking the grounds, or sipping tea and coffee in the sunshine and birdsong-saturated garden. It was spring, after all, and it was good to see that Scotland occasionally remem-bered it.

We, however, did not soak up the sights and sounds of our beautiful surroundings. Instead we soaked in a steamy clawfoot tub together and enjoyed very different sights and sounds indeed. Af-terward, as we got dressed for brunch—and my goodness, we were starving!—I heard Robbie curse from the other room.

"Something the matter?" I asked, as I applied a little mascara.

He laughed ruefully. "I didn't think to bring anything but my kilt and my pajamas! Ugh. The walk of shame is especially dangerous when you happen to know half the guests in the hotel."

"Well, there's always this . . ." I said, dangling the silky pink robe from a finger. He scoffed. I secretly hoped he would bump into at least one or two of the ladies so that he would have a funny story to tell me later.

"Maybe I'll just go bare-arsed. Tell them that I'm doing research for my upcoming nude history tour."

"Ooh—yes please! I vote for that option."

"Oh, you'll pay for that, Alice Cooper. If you thought for even one moment that I had forgotten about those pictures that Berrta showed me, then you are sorely mistaken, darlin'."

I stepped closer to distract him with a kiss and then whipped his towel off.

He growled low in his throat and kissed me back, pressing his naked body against my clothed one, showing obvious signs of interest.

"Dinnea get me started again, ya wee hellcat." He thickened his accent knowing that it turned me on no end.

"Fine then. Go on back to your own room. If we stay here any longer, we'll not only be late for brunch, but you'll have to carry me down to it, because I'm already having enough trouble walking as it is."

"Hmm . . . Okay." He shoved me backward onto the bed with a smile. "I'll carry you down then." He jumped on top of me, ignoring any pleas of protest I managed to squeak out between fits of laughter as he kissed his way up my body, tickling my waist with deft fingers and my neck with his overgrown stubble. "Not a bad bargain for me, truth be told. Hurry up. Get your kit off." He bit my ear lobe and reached down to tickle my knees.

"Never!" I wheezed. "I'll call the police and have you arrested for undue temptation and titillation!"

"Ahh, but you're a Yank. You'll not know the phone number."

"Pfft! 999. Come on, you'll have to try harder than that."

"Hmm . . . harder, she says . . ." He kissed me passionately for a few seconds, pressing against me in a way that was making my head spin. Then he stopped abruptly. "No, you don't! We've got to go get some brunch before we pass out. It would be an embarrassing thing to explain to the paramedics." He stood up, pulling me up with him before wrapping his kilt around his lithe body and pulling his sweater on. He clipped his sporran over the worst of it and gave me a chaste peck on the cheek. "Wish me luck."

Fifteen minutes later when I strolled into brunch, I realized—as everyone else had, no doubt—that the huge, goofy smile I was sporting hadn't left my face since the evening before.

Brunch was amazing in every way, and yet I remember almost nothing about it but the way Robbie looked at me.

CHAPTER 36

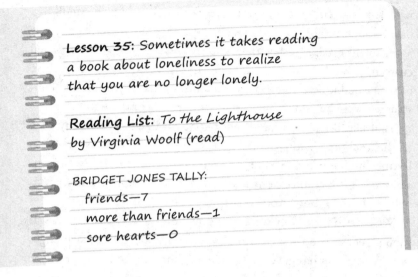

Lesson 35: Sometimes it takes reading a book about loneliness to realize that you are no longer lonely.

Reading List: *To the Lighthouse* by Virginia Woolf (read)

BRIDGET JONES TALLY:
friends—7
more than friends—1
sore hearts—0

After the giddy heights of postcoital mimosas, we headed north through the Trossachs National Park and Loch Lomond, making several stops for photos, walks, and snacks along the way to take in the stunning scenery.

I couldn't quite put my finger on it, but Scotland had a different feel to it. We had been through some of the most beautiful landscapes that I had ever seen in England and Wales, but somehow, in some ineffable way, Scotland simply sat differently on the skin—or under the skin, in my case. It seeped gently into every pore and took hold of me in a possessive way that I understood, even then, that I would never shake.

As we sat on the bank of Loch Lomond, Robbie discreetly took my hand, reminding my butterflies that they had something to flap about. After the night before, we weren't trying to hide anything, but neither were we trying to make anyone feel shocked with an overexposure to canoodling. Instead we tried to lavish each other with tiny, careful moments of tenderness—a hand on the small of a back, a look prolonged for a second or two, a warm smile, a gentle joke, softly teasing rather than the sharp slice that was our usual custom. It felt private and intimate, and in the present atmosphere of unspeakable awe and beauty, the hurdles that my brain had constructed were being forcibly torn down, letting in the light.

That felt like something. It felt big. It felt like loosening my hold of the anchors I had clutched so tightly, even as they sank. I was letting life happen and take me with it, even if it didn't seem sensible. Even if it seemed contrary to my plans. Even if it was scary as hell. At least for now. And, smart or not, it felt like living.

We carried on to Oban for a stopover on the way to Skye. It was such a gentle, coddling evening, perfect to smooth the sharp edges of any lingering hangovers. We strolled along the strip between the pastel storefronts and the choppy bay and watched the sun set. We treated ourselves to a long, languid dinner with a charming view, and perhaps a cheeky bottle of rosé or two, for the table, of course. It felt like a cozy evening with family.

Through every elongated, treasured moment, I knew the evening was bringing me a second closer to going to bed with Robbie. But instead of heading straight up to bed when we got in, Robbie turned to me after the others had said their good nights.

"Do you fancy a stroll in the moonlight, beautiful?"

"Are you trying to get rid of me? Dump my body in the bay?" I stepped into him and slid my arms around his waist.

"Nah. If I thought it was that easy to trick the devil, you would have been in my bed on day one."

I sank into his arms and mumbled sweetly into his chest. "If you had tried it, I would have desexed you with one of Berrta's Birkenstocks."

We walked softly along the shoreline, holding hands. When we took each other to bed later that night, the tenderness of the evening stayed at the forefront. He stared into my eyes like his heart was breaking and mending at the same time. We didn't have time for jokes as we peeled each other's clothes off, button by button, worshipping each touch of the lips, each inch of warm skin. The way he touched my body with his brushing fingertips made me shudder. Places that I hadn't before thought of as particularly sensual—the side of my ribcage, the inside of my elbow, the ridge of my clavicle, the back of the knee—were suddenly erogenous. His hand slowly glided over every inch of me in feather-light deification. It made each nerve ending feel closer to the skin. By the time he got to my nipples, they seemed so much more sensitive. He was gentle when he stroked my breasts and rubbed his thumb over them. I panted and cried out. He worked his lips all the way down my torso, and I felt his warm breath on me for a moment, nothing else, then the softest brush of lips, and then his tongue. It sent me careening into waves of climax.

Later we made love gently, tauntingly slowly and perfectly in tune, a ballet that was somehow more passionate and more meaningful than the night before, and then we fell asleep in each other's arms.

WE SET OUT early in the morning. Robbie had pulled himself away from my sleepy embrace with an unwilling groan. It was well worth getting up before the sun, I decided, as we made it to Glencoe for the sunrise. I am not sure that I had ever seen anything so moving.

Robbie told the heart-wrenching story of the Massacre of Glencoe, and we felt more grounded in this unreal landscape, as the air bit at us with its frosty teeth, and we thought how lucky we all were to be there. Then we packed up, wrapped ourselves in Rosie's woolen blankets, and set off for Skye.

If fairies exist, they are forged in Skye. Skye: where the wind had whipped the mountains into stiff meringue peaks that rose and curled back on themselves in a garden of uncanny vistas and hallows. Hearty, sure-footed sheep dotted the slopes and danced along craggy cliffs, looking wise and capable with thick, curling horns. Dense clouds rode quickly on the back of wind and painted the emerald green land below in shadow and light, rippling like water while crystalline shards of sun pierced through and stretched down to meet cold earth.

We started with warm, strong cups of tea and sat on the cold rocks by the churning sea. Birds sang and swooped in gray salt air not yet yellowed by the heat of the afternoon sun. There we talked about Virginia Woolf's *To the Lighthouse*, which was set in Skye. We discussed its feelings of solitude and how it tied itself to the landscape, emotions that I would have embodied weeks ago, but now, I reflected, could not feel more foreign to me as I sat hip-to-hip with my friends for heat while listening to the warming cadence of Robbie's voice.

"'It was odd, she thought, how if one was alone, one leant to inanimate things; trees, streams, flowers; felt they expressed one; felt they became one; felt they knew one, in a sense were one; felt an irrational tenderness thus (she looked at that long steady light) as for oneself.'"

Robbie read from the book, but the full-mouthed roaring of the wind and the waves demanded that he deliver a performance, head and voice raised to conquer the wild space. I gazed at him, and my heart beat a little louder.

Many of us took the hike up the Old Man of Storr. From that height, mountains, waterfalls, lochs, and cerulean sea spread out in such unreserved beauty that my breath caught, and my cheeks grew cold with freshly sprung tears. Next to me something stirred, and a familiar hand threaded its fingers with mine, warm and generous.

"You alright, darlin'?"

I breathed out slowly. "Oh yes. I'm just happy."

THAT NIGHT AFTER Robbie had fallen asleep, I lifted his book from his chest: *The Shadow of the Wind*, one of my recommendations. I slipped the bookmark into place and moved it to the bedside table. Something slid out from between the pages. It was the light blue string that I had used to pull back my hair on the punting trip in Cambridge. It still had the bow that I had hastily tied. My heart squeezed in my chest. He had saved it and pressed it into his book as a keepsake.

WE WENT TO the Fairy Glen our second day on Skye. It was a valley of strange, miniature emerald hills, nearly conical in shape, clustered charmingly around the sheep whose ancestors had explored the grassy dunes so often that they had worn little levels and steps in hoof-size rings around the sides of them. There was a proportionately small loch and some craggy cliffs and outcroppings, which might have looked dramatic and foreboding had they not been so adorably Lilliputian. We wandered around, cradling hot cups and leaving trails of pastry crumbs, releasing puffs of tea-warmed ghosts into the crisp air as we laughed, absorbing what sun we could, and having a minikin adventure in a Hobbiton landscape where even Doris could climb to the top and loom large as king of the mountain.

Next we took a break from the wind at Talisker Distillery. The warm honey of its whisky burned down my throat. I took a moment to remember the flavor, so that the next time I tasted it, I could close my eyes for a moment and be transported back to that most magical of islands, where I had been so very happy.

The last hour of sunshine was enjoyed at the Fairy Pools. We followed along a hidden hollow, where a seam of water cascaded down one small waterfall into another, collecting in little turquoise pools, rounding and polishing smooth arches and basins in the stone. When it began to drizzle, a rainbow unfurled in front of our eyes for a brief, wet moment, arcing gracefully over the jewel-colored Fairy Pools before fading away again. It was the third rainbow I'd seen that day. Who could complain about a bit of rain when it put on such a show? When we turned around, the sun had begun to set, and we walked back through the golden glow under a raspberry sky.

Never was a bed more comfortable, more warm, nor more welcoming than our bed that night.

CHAPTER 37

Lesson 36: Always carry a Biscoff.

Reading List: *Outlander* by Diana Gabaldon (read, multiple times)

BRIDGET JONES TALLY:
dogs—1
rabbits—1
grass stains—3

THINGS I'VE LEARNED SO FAR IN THE UK:

1. British food isn't bad; it's quite tasty, in fact, but it has lots of gravy.
2. British teeth are bad.
3. "Juice" is basically any cold nonalcoholic drink in Scotland. So Coke is a juice, despite not having ever been squeezed from a fruit or vegetable.
4. People use the "c-word" a lot over here, even sweet old ladies. Breasts are most often referred to as ~~tits~~ without shame or equivocation.
5. Everything can be a pie, and pies aren't sweet.
6. Any dessert is called a pudding even if it's nothing like a pudding.

7. Separate taps are standard, and seek to infuriate me at every turn.

8. There is a lot less water in the toilets here, which is both a good thing and a bad thing.

9. They typically put average-looking people on TV, which seems healthier than American television but is also less fun to watch.

10. People in Scotland always seem pleased if you ask to pet their dog, whereas people in England sometimes make a face not dissimilar to the face that they might make if you requested to cup their bottom.

11. Accents are still sexy. This novelty does not seem to degrade with time.

We scooped down, stopping at Loch Ness, and slept in Inverness, a beautiful little city on a river, but also the city where Claire Fraser goes for her honeymoon and later disappears through the standing stones. The following day we began our journey south.

"Now, I know that some of you are fans of the *Outlander* books or telly series, or both." Robbie laughed as the ladies hooted, like topless Jamie had just walked on to the bus. "Well, you're not the only ones. Tourism has doubled in Scotland since the series was released. I was very reluctant to start watching myself, and now . . . well, I have to confess to having watched every single episode and season one twice."

Doris chimed in. "Oh, I could happily watch that Jamie open a tin of sardines. No plot required."

"Or fixing that watermill on a loop for three hours," Helena said.

"So what do you ladies say if we take an early picnic to some nearby standing stones? We'll see if any rugged Jacobites emerge to carry us away to another century."

This was a popular option. As he drove us away from Inverness and into the farmland not far from the city, he gave us a brief talk on eighteenth-century Scotland and the Jacobite rising, and then prompted us with reading group questions while we animatedly spouted our opinions on both the books and the television series.

EVERYTHING WAS GREEN with farmland and wooded patches, and we were greeted by two low stone circles that stood in a quiet wood owned by the farm. It looked as if they had sat here quietly century after century, happy not to be often bothered by visitors.

The sun was shining and the birds singing, and we sat on the stones and ate some tasty sandwiches from the nearby farm shop. Lorna looked to be a little extra cautious with the stones and decided to sit on the grass instead, which I found strange and cute. Agatha had complained of being tired and decided to take a little nap on the bus, so the rest of us just leaned back on the warm stones and enjoyed the sounds of nature. It was all very peaceful.

Or at least it started out peacefully. Before all hell broke loose.

Hell, in this case, was conjured by Percy. Percy and a rabbit, to be exact. He wasn't on the leash, of course, because for some curious reason, Doris thought he could be trusted. Initially, his explorations extended only to peeing on historically and spiritually significant stones, begging for sandwich scraps, and attempting to steal Madge's bag of crisps. But when a young rabbit made the mistake of quietly nibbling the grass nearby, Percy moved with a speed I didn't know he possessed. They were both off like lightning to the sounds of Doris's cries.

"Oh, Robbie. Could you, dear? I'm sorry, but I'm no match for him with these knees of mine."

"Of course, love," he said, already up.

"Typical male." Flossie smiled, leaning back to sun her face. "Always chasing a bit of tail."

"Alice, why don't you go along with Robbie, lovely?" Doris asked me. "Percy can be a tricky bugger. I'm sure Robbie could use an extra hand or two."

"Yes, of course!" I was eager to help, but then Doris gave me a little wink that made me feel like the statement was far more salacious than I had given her credit for.

"And once you've found him, take him for a little walk, would you? Burn off some of that energy."

We set off at a jog. There was farmland and woods as far as the eye could see, and if Percy had enough of a head start, he could get properly lost and cause us some real trouble. We called and called after him, but the scruffy little terrier wasn't often the obedient type, despite what his vest said.

"We don't even know which way he went at this point."

"I know. But that rabbit is faster than Percy, and she'll have out-smarted him long ago and gone down a hole somewhere. He should have slowed down by now, I would think, and will just be exploring at his own pace."

Robbie was right, luckily. It wasn't long before we spied Percy down the gentle slope of a hill. We ran down to him, and he promptly took off. He knew we were there to catch him and wasn't ready to give up his newfound freedom. We ran after him into the heather, trying not to get tripped up on the stones and roots as we went.

"Hey! You be careful with that ankle there, Alice Cooper. I'll not have you breaking it this time. No running, right?" Robbie pinned me in a serious gaze from several feet away that stopped me in my tracks, mostly because I loved it when he was serious.

"It looks like you need all the help you can get."

"Alice."

"And anyway, if I broke my ankle, you might need to pick me

up and carry me to safety." He smirked sideways at me. "Last time wasn't half bad, I seem to remember."

"Oh, it wasn't, was it? You cheeky wee devil. Just you let me deal with one troublemaker at a time, will you? I'll catch Percy, and then I'll be back to deal with you."

The way he said it made my hair curl. I could die happily here in the heather after being smoldered to death.

The fact that Percy was a bit of a lazy dog worked to our advantage. There were plenty of things to stop and smell, and that gave us time to catch up. But just as Robbie was closing in on him, he dodged out of Robbie's grasp and ran off again. We both called out to him some more, Robbie adding some choice words, but none of it helped.

"Right. I'm going to loop around this way and head him off if I can. You just keep walking steadily that way, and we'll see if we can nab the silly bugger."

Robbie circled around him, and I advanced from behind, calling his name in my friendliest "good boy" voice. We got close and locked eyes on each other. Percy was in the middle snacking on a little pile of rabbit droppings as we closed in on him.

"There's a good boy, Percy. Let's go home and see your Doris, shall we? You see. There's nowhere for you to go."

But of course there was. Sideways. Percy knew that, and off he trotted.

"Ah! Bugger me!" Robbie laughed, frustrated, and then came in for a quick kiss before running off after the dog.

"Sure," I called after him. "We can try that next."

"Wait. Have you got any food on you?" he called back.

"I don't think so. Let me check." I dug around in my new jacket's various pockets. There was the distinctive rattle of a plastic wrapper. Percy's ears perked up. It was an extra Biscoff that I'd been given at a café the day before.

"Good boy, Percy. Who wants a treat?"

His tail wagged. Game over.

WE WALKED SLOWLY through a lovely shady area, near a little burn where the stream made a comforting sound.

"I reckon we ought to respect Doris's wishes and have a little stroll before we head back. What do you say?" With Percy's leash in one hand, Robbie laced the fingers of the other with mine, and warmth blossomed in my chest.

This new thing, whatever it was, was only a few days old, and I felt like a schoolgirl, with the blushing and the butterflies and the not being able to think of anything else but him. His hand was warm and wide and slightly callused from instrument strings and heavy suitcases, and when my hand was in his, I felt like somehow everything in the world was just as it should be.

I smiled. "Well, she did ask us nicely."

He stepped in front of me and put a tight arm around my waist, pressing my body in close, leaving just a breath between our lips.

"It's nice to have you all to myself." His voice was low and provocative. Being this close to him made my whole body tingle with recent muscle memory. I looked up at him, but couldn't think of any sassy reply as he slid his hand behind my head and brought me that last inch closer for a long, slow kiss.

By the time he let me go, I had to take a few deep breaths to steady myself. At least I tried to behave, but was surprised to find myself lowering down to the grass and pulling him down with me. He laughed. It was a throaty, gruff thing that made me lose control.

Percy had long since collapsed into the grass, as if he had just run the length of Britain, and gone to sleep. Robbie tied his leash nice and tight against a nearby tree.

I grabbed his shirt, pulled him down on top of me, and kissed him ferociously.

"Should we get back?" I asked, out of breath. "The ladies might be waiting."

"It hasn't been long, and we don't have a busy day planned. Agatha is napping, and Berrta is off with her binoculars. They'll all be relaxing in the sun. Don't worry."

I kissed him hard. "Are you sure? Maybe we should get back," my voice said, while my body screamed at me to shut the hell up.

"We're fine. And it doesn't seem like you're quite ready to leave," he said, running his hand over my sweater, making my back arch to meet it. "I think I could get used to your mixed signals."

"Alright, but just ten minutes." I pointed at him. "And only over the clothes stuff. Agreed?"

"I can live with that." He kissed me again with a smile on his lips.

"Good. Because I'm not sure I can. And I'm going to need you to keep me in line."

CHAPTER 38

Lesson 37: A dirty mind is a
terrible thing to waste.

BRIDGET JONES TALLY:
  dicks—2
  cocks—4
  boners—1

We found our way sheepishly back to the group. I felt guilty on both our behalves, and I hoped the ladies didn't notice that my lips had been kissed until they were plump and pink.

When we arrived, the gaggle looked just as relaxed and contented as Robbie had promised they'd be. Most of them were sitting sleepily in the sun. Berrta was off with her binoculars, as promised, and Helena, for some reason, had a pair of tweezers and was plucking whiskers from Doris's chin.

Doris's face split in a relieved smile when she saw us. "Oh, there's my boy! Thank you, you two. You've done your good deed for the day." Helena stood back, tweezers at the ready in case she should be called back into action, and Percy jumped right up into Doris's lap to lick her face.

"I wouldn't—" I started.

"Oh, it's okay. I love it."

I smiled and shrugged. If she didn't care a bit what he'd been snacking on, then neither did I.

"Right. How is everyone feeling? Are we ready to move on southward to ever so slightly warmer climes?"

"Yes. I think ve are ready. It was a good day. I saw a Scottish crossbill!"

We all piled on to the bus, where Agatha was sleeping with her mouth open and an angry expression on her face, yelling at a neighbor in her dreams, no doubt.

"Well, the bus is still here, so it's not 1743," said Robbie. "More's the pity. But then again I'm fairly certain that they didn't have fish-and-chips in 1743, so it's not all bad. Now is everyone in and ready? No one has left any bags behind?"

"Flossie," Agatha croaked through a dry throat.

"Pardon me?"

"Flossie," she repeated. "Where's Flossie?"

"What?" He turned around in his seat, brow pinched. "Don't worry. I'm sure she'll be right outside." He jumped off the bus to look, a little faster than his casual tone would warrant.

Within ten minutes we were all back down calling her name and spreading out to look in the nearby woods. Poor Agatha was frantic. I could understand.

"Where was she? Who was looking after her? When did you last see her?"

"Well, she was definitely here when we ate our sandwiches. She sat just there," offered Helena.

"How long ago was that?" Robbie asked.

"About an hour and a half, I'd say."

"Merciful heavens." Agatha turned to Robbie. "How could you let this happen? Where were you?" My stomach sank. If we'd come straight back, this might not have happened.

Doris stopped him before he could take the blame. "Oh, that's my fault, Agatha. Percy ran off into the woods, and I sent Robbie and Alice off after him. The rest of us were all here, but she was so quiet. She just . . . snuck away."

"You imbeciles!"

"Right. Did anyone notice anything that might help us figure out where she went or what she was doing?" Robbie asked.

"She did look extra nice today," said Lorna. "She had on a pretty dress, and her hair was super bouncy."

Agatha turned on her. "Her hair? How could that possibly help us? I guess we can let the police know that her hairdo was extra bouncy today when they're drawing her picture for the six o'clock news!"

"Well, they would probably just use an actual photo—"

"She's gone! She never does anything like this. I don't know if someone took her, or she wandered off a cliff, or is floating dead in a river somewhere!"

Things were spiraling. That wouldn't help. His voice was even, but I saw the look in his eyes. He felt responsible. He was scared. He doted on Flossie, and he knew that sometimes she was totally there, but then sometimes she wasn't. I stepped in. "Robbie, can you please get the bus and check that she's not heading down the road? Check the side roads too."

"Good idea."

"I'll organize the ladies into search parties, and we'll go out in groups to search the area."

"Can you do that?"

"Yes. We will call you from Helena's phone if we find anything. That'll be your direct line to us. I'm going to set up a WhatsApp chat for those of us who have data so the groups can all communicate."

"Thank you, Alice. We'll find her. I'm sure she's absolutely fine."

I stepped closer to Agatha, trying to stop the tidal wave of panic before it crashed in on her. "It's okay. I'm sure she couldn't have gone far. She must have just gotten a little bit turned around, is all. We'll find her. There are eight of us and one of her. There's nothing particularly dangerous in those woods. We're going to be strategic. We'll spread out and work together, and she'll be back on the bus in no time."

"I never should have taken that nap."

"This is not your fault. It's going to be absolutely fine. You'll see."

Having a plan seemed to calm Agatha. But when I reached to take her hand, she didn't yank it back—she clasped on for dear life. That worried me more than anything.

WE ALL CHECKED our phones to see which ones still had a strong enough signal for calls and GPS. Then I split the ladies up in groups, each with a working phone, and we all swapped numbers. I created a group chat that included Robbie so we could all keep updated instantly.

"Doris, can you stay here please, in case she comes back to the bus? Keep your phone in your hand and your ringer on, please. We need one group over here, one in this area, and another here." We circled around, and I showed them the areas on the phone GPS. I took a screenshot, color-coded each section, and sent it to the group. "We'll go out and call her name, and try not to stray too far from the paths so that no one else gets lost. In thirty minutes, we will all turn around and head back. I'll send out a message as a reminder, so we should all be back here at the standing stones in exactly one hour—or hopefully sooner, when we find Flossie. I'll honk when I get back in case anyone gets turned around."

WE RETURNED AN hour later, empty-handed. It was worse than we had expected. I could tell that Robbie was working to keep a calm demeanor for the others.

"What if Percy could help?" Doris suggested. "You never know."

"Not a bad idea," Robbie said. "Anything is worth a try."

Percy was made to sniff Flossie's scarf, and for a moment, he pulled on the leash with a frantic determination.

"I think he's got it! He's on to something!"

Robbie took the leash from Doris, and we all followed quickly behind, hot on the trail.

Then the terrier made a sharp turn, snuffled around in the bushes, and sat his plump little hindquarters down to eat someone's discarded sandwich crusts.

"I just knew someone would end up dead on this trip," Agatha said. "I warned you all, didn't I?"

Robbie's face collapsed. "I'm so sorry, Agatha. But I promise you that we're going to find her. I'm going to call the police, check at the farm shop, and I'm going to let the farmers know what's going on—ask if they can spare some people to help, hopefully on vehicles."

Doubt and dread were beginning to creep into my thoughts in earnest. I began to picture all the terrible things that could have happened.

Helena's logical voice broke in. "How could we not have found her? It's just so odd that she could have gone so far on foot that she isn't able to find her way back to hear us calling in any direction. Maybe we're missing something here."

"Well, I thought . . ." Lorna's gaze shifted worriedly to the largest of the standing stones. "Couldn't it . . . well, maybe—"

Madge grabbed her hand and said quietly, "No, darling. It couldn't."

"But she was all dressed up like she was going somewhere. And she had her emerald earrings on. She brought gemstones! I mean, I know it sounds crazy, but unexplained things happen all the time, and we shouldn't discount anything at this point. Right?" She paced a bit, but couldn't stop herself. She lifted her hands to one of the smaller, less threatening stones, but didn't touch it. "Has anyone heard a . . . a buzzing?"

"Wait!" Agatha raised her voice above us. "Look. There's a note. She left a note! It was in my handbag." She held up a sheet of floral stationery and waved it in the air.

"What does it say?" asked Berrta.

"I'm just getting to that, if you'd give me a blasted moment," Agatha snapped. "It says, 'Dear Aggie, I have run away. I have been picked up in a car and will be very far away by the time you wake up and read this. Do not try to find me. I have taken a jar of rhubarb preserves and a spoon from the breakfast room at the inn in Inverness to keep my strength up. I will pay for it by post. At least, I will pay for the jam, but not the spoon, because I plan to return the spoon in its original condition. It was slightly bent. Flossie Philipson.'"

We stared at one another. No one dared break the silence.

A yelp escaped Agatha. "Blethering fool!"

"Is that all of it?" Lorna asked.

"Yes, of course that's all of it!"

"But where did she go?" asked Madge.

"This note is not helpful to us," said Berrta matter-of-factly.

"No. It is not. Thank you for the confirmation!" shouted Agatha.

"If I vere going to leave a note," said Berrta, "I vould not go on so much about spoons."

"If you ran away, no one would bother to read your note!" Agatha snapped.

"Yes. I am really sure my husband vould read it."

We all stared at one another again in utter shock for a full sixty seconds. *Berrta has a husband?* Lorna's mouth was actually open. Berrta had never mentioned a husband. We had all just assumed.

"But—" Lorna started to say.

"You're married, Berrta?" Doris couldn't help herself.

"Naturally. Otto. He cooks an excellent rouladen," she answered unflappably.

Madge brought us all to our senses. "Let's stay focused. What are we going to do?"

Robbie rushed back from a phone call with the police. We updated him on the note.

"And then we found out that Berrta is married!" Lorna chimed in, still in shock. "Did you know that Berrta was married?"

Robbie ignored this. "Well, a note is good news, isn't it? That means she's not hurt or lost in the woods. Alright, Agatha. Think. Is there anything else you can give us? She said she was in a car. Who could have picked her up all the way out here? And how could they have done it without anyone noticing?" Everyone chattered, but no one seemed to have any ideas. "Well, we know she's not here at least. That's something. Let's all get into the bus and head to the farm shop and see if they saw anything."

"Oh, yes. A lovely lady came through here and met up with an older gentleman . . . oh, about two hours ago now, I'd say."

"Jesus wept," Agatha said.

Robbie sucked in a breath and held it for a second. "Alright. Did they mention where they were going?"

"I'm afraid not."

"Who was the man? Have you ever seen him before? Did you catch his name? Or see what kind of car he was driving?"

"No. I'm sorry. I've never seen him before. He looked like a nice older man. Well-dressed. Very respectable."

"Could he have been a cab driver?" Robbie asked.

"No, not a cabbie. The lady looked very happy to see him. Had a warm hug when he arrived, like old friends."

"He is a kidnapper and a predator!" Agatha shouted.

"A friend?" Robbie said. "Does that ring any bells, Agatha? Who could that be?"

"No one! Flossie hasn't got any friends. I am the only person she knows."

"Well . . ." I started, trying to think back past the whisky haze that clouded my memory. "I think maybe she had a friend at the ceilidh. At least, it seemed that way."

"Oh, yes," said Helena, brightening. "She did, didn't she! Clever girl. There was a nice gentleman she spoke to a lot that night at the ceilidh. I wasn't introduced, but I couldn't help but notice how attentive he was." Helena's antennae were always wiggling for any hint of romantic gossip.

"What? When?" Agatha's cheeks pinkened. She had had quite a lot to drink the night of the ceilidh and had dozed in and out between sips while seated in a comfy armchair.

"Yes, she stood up with him many times to dance," Doris agreed. "Quite a dapper gentleman."

"That's got to be it!" said Lorna.

"Well, we've got nothing else to go on. It's worth a shot," agreed Robbie. "But who was he? How do we find him?"

"I thought he told me they had known each other a long time, but we didn't say much more than that," I replied.

"They haven't," Agatha insisted.

Robbie turned to me. His eyes were wide. Flossie had run off with some strange man. "Alice, you spoke to him? What else can you remember?"

"I don't know," I said helplessly. "I'm sorry. I'd had a few drinks by that point."

"What did he look like?" he asked.

Doris answered. "Small chap, about her size. White hair. Mustache. Medium build. Blue eyes. Smartly dressed—in a kilt, so probably Scottish."

He turned to the lady at the counter. "Does that sound like the same man?"

"Yes, that's him exactly."

"I'm so sorry that I can't remember more," I said. "I think he had an old-fashioned name. I think it started with an *S*. Maybe Sylvester or Spencer or something like that."

"Sounds like a pervert," said Agatha.

I ignored that and went on. "He chatted to the people at the sign-up table. I think they knew him, and maybe he even helped with the event?"

"That's something. I can get hold of the event organizers to see if they have any information. Trouble is, there were quite a few white-haired Scottish gentlemen helping the Trust at the ceilidh, and without a name . . . What about where he lived? Did he live close to Glenapp? Glasgow? Edinburgh? Or was he northern? Which direction?"

"Jesus, I don't know. Up north maybe? I'm not sure. I'd even have trouble pointing out Edinburgh on a map."

"Damn." Robbie was pacing. The others began to talk and ask questions among themselves.

"There's . . ." I started and stopped. "I can't," I stumbled. "Never mind."

"Huh?" Robbie asked, his face taut.

"Well. It's just. I kind of remember something about the town he said he lived in. I wasn't paying much attention, and I was tipsy. But I remember because it had something to do with . . ."

"Yes?"

"No. Forget it. It's not helpful."

"Everything is helpful right now, Alice. What is it?"

"Penises." I let out the word in a gush. "It had something to do with penises." At that, everyone stopped and turned to me slowly. No one breathed. You could have heard a mouse fart.

"What?" Robbie stuck his neck out, hoping that maybe he had misheard. I died.

"Never mind. I don't know. I just . . . I remember that I was going to make a penis joke, and then decided that it might be inappropriate."

"What? Penises? Are you serious, Alice? *Penises*?"

I wished fervently that he would stop saying *penises* in this wholesome little farm shop where the nice worried lady behind the counter was clutching her pearls.

"Umm. Okay. Are there any places near here that sound like penis?"

The shop lady flushed scarlet and started cleaning the countertop with great determination.

"Peniston?" asked Helena, taking it seriously. "Could that have been it? But that's in Yorkshire."

"Upper Dicker," someone said.

"There's Cockburn in Edinburgh," Lorna said. "But that's not how it's pronounced, so that's probably not it."

"Dicks Mount?"

The ladies were becoming very animated.

"I've heard of a place called the Knob, and one called Bell End, but I think they're both in England," said Doris. "Why are all of these todger places in England?"

"I don't know," said Helena. "Brown Willy is in Cornwall. Too far away."

"Ooo—there's a Twatt! There's a Twatt in Orkney!" Lorna said, excited. "That's right up there in the north. Could it have been a twat instead of a penis?"

"No, no." I shook my head, trying desperately to remember while a room full of sweet old ladies shouted lewd words at one another.

"I have a friend in Worcestershire who lives on Minge Lane," said Doris. "That's the God's honest truth. I post letters to her all the time, and I always get a smirk from the postie. She bought her semi-detached for a song!"

Helena turned to Doris and said, "Tristan used to let a flat on Crotch Crescent in Oxford. I always told him he should buy the place—for the address if nothing else."

We were getting off topic.

"What is the matter with you people?" spat Agatha. "A woman is missing, and all you fools can talk about is private parts!"

"Google says that there's a place called Cockshoot," Madge broke in, scrolling furiously on her phone. "But I don't know where it is yet. Let me look it up."

"That's not it. I would have remembered that one for sure."

"You're right. That's in England too. Interesting."

"Oh! How about Cockermouth?" Lorna did a little hop of excitement as she shouted this. "Cockermouth is really lovely. Everyone should go to Cockermouth. Come to think of it, Wordsworth was born there, so it really should have been part of the trip, Robbie."

This was only making things worse. I tried to keep us on topic. "Something about . . . an erection maybe? Does that ring any bells? It wasn't so literal. Slang maybe—like a stiffy, or a boner, or . . . something with wood maybe? I don't know." I stopped myself before I said anything worse.

"Boner!" Madge slapped her hand on the counter and made everyone jump. "Bonar Bridge! Is that it?"

"Yes! Boner Bridge! Yes, that's it! Oh, thank God."

Robbie was all business. "Bonar Bridge is about an hour north of here. He could easily have driven down to meet her."

Agatha was soon to dampen our spirits. "What help is any of this childish nonsense? We still have nothing to go on. By the time you idiots get anything done, that Scottish pervert will already have her in some cheap love motel!"

"Doesn't sound so bad," Doris mumbled.

"Right, we've got a physical description and a location. That's got to be good enough," Robbie said.

"You call the organizers at the Trust. I'll borrow someone's phone to call Glenapp and see if they might have any contact details they would be willing to give out. I can try the police if they won't give it to me."

We got on our phones and went to work. The castle was a dead end, but less than five minutes later, Robbie's voice was raising to a shout. "Sidney Richie! Wonderful. Thank you, Shona, I can't tell you how grateful we are. Yes, I will absolutely take that number now, please."

"Thank goodness he's a friend, at least," Lorna told Agatha.

"He's never met her before, I tell you. He's just a chancer! Poor Flossie isn't all there, and he saw an opportunity to take advantage. He's probably got her at the bank right now emptying out her safe deposit box."

"Surely she wouldn't have a deposit box here in Inverness?" offered Lorna.

"That's beside the point!"

"Hello?" Robbie said on the phone. "I'm looking for Mr. Sidney Richie. It is? Thank God. My name is Robbie Brodie, and I'm calling about a woman who's gone missing this morning. Flossie Philipson. With you? *She's there*," he said for our benefit and nodded to Agatha. "Where are you? Okay. Is that the one on Planefield Road? Good. Can I speak to her, please? Flossie, love. Are you alright? We've all been worried sick. Oh, I know. I know. It's okay. Yes, I'm afraid I do have to tell her. Look, we're going to head down now and meet you at the green. Can you just stay put, please? Thank you, dear. No, no one is angry about the spoon. See you there in just a moment." He hung up and turned. "They're at the bowling green back in Inverness. It's not far from here. Let's all stick together and go now. Is that alright, Agatha?" She nodded her agreement.

Something crumpled in Agatha's face, and as she turned to me, I was surprised to see something there, a shadow of gratitude.

A bell chimed, and a few customers came in.

"Ooh. We forgot Cockfield. That's another one."

"Well, I've heard about a street in Lincolnshire called Fanny Hands Lane."

"Oh! Oh! I just remembered a Wetwang down in Yorkshire!"

"Wetwang? Really?"

"Will you kindly shut the hell up!" snapped Agatha.

CHAPTER 39

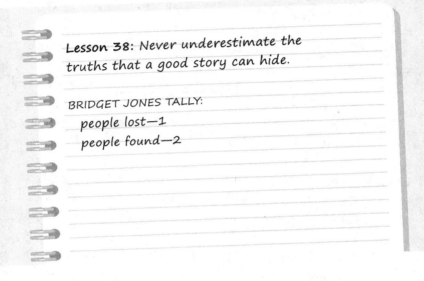

Lesson 38: Never underestimate the truths that a good story can hide.

BRIDGET JONES TALLY:
people lost—1
people found—2

When we arrived at the bowling green and found Flossie with Sidney Richie, the poor man looked so upset that I stopped being angry and actually felt sorry for him. It didn't hurt his case that he happened to be objectively adorable. He was small and lean, and he had dressed up nicely with a little tweed jacket and bow tie and a matching tweed flatcap on top of a messy tuft of white hair. In his buttonhole was a white rose tinged with peach, and I looked down to see that sticking out of Flossie's handbag was a beautiful bouquet of flowers, with clusters of berries, thistles, foxgloves, and matching roses.

"We're so sorry to have worried you all," Sidney said, wringing his hands.

"I'm not," said Flossie. "It's nice to be worried about from time to time."

"Oh, Flossie dear. Don't say that. I'm sure they had a terrible morning thinking that something had happened to you."

He turned to Agatha, approaching with a bravery that I would have been hard-pressed to find in his shoes.

"Agatha, forgive me. I had no idea she hadn't discussed this with you."

"Well," she said, her voice like a whip. "We've called the police, so you can make your excuses to them, you pervert."

Flossie stepped between them. "Sid hasn't done anything wrong. Don't speak to him like that."

"He's persuaded you to run away with him, a complete stranger, he plotted and schemed, and he's driven you off in a car and taken you . . ." She looked around quickly, and evidently decided she didn't want to say *He's taken you bowling!* for the obvious reason that it sounded so damn cute.

"He's taken you away from your tour group!"

"I'm not a child, Agatha, no matter what you might think."

"Then why are you acting like one? Why didn't you tell anyone where you were going?"

"Because you wouldn't have let me come."

"No, I wouldn't. And I would have been right, as always. You have no business sneaking away to run off with this filthy philanderer."

"Sid is not a complete stranger. I've known him for over fifty years. And he is not a philanthropist!"

"Well, actually, I do my best to make donations every month . . ." Sidney said quietly to no one in particular.

After Agatha stopped protesting and denying everything they said, a story unfolded piece by piece that seemed to be as much a surprise to Agatha as it was to the rest of us. We all sat down on the benches overlooking the bowling green in the sun, quieted our hungry stomachs, and listened intently. I was shocked that none of us had pieced it together sooner. If only we'd listened a little more carefully to Flossie, instead of always assuming that she was just away with the fairies.

Sidney was the man from the stories, of course. "The Spellbinding Sultan of Samarra."

"That was just a name for the stage. I'm only a butcher's son from Tain. But when I was eighteen, I decided that I wanted to see the world, so I joined the circus. At first I was just a dogsbody, helping to set up the tents and move them from place to place, but I picked up sleight of hand as we went along and learned whatever I could. Within a year I had my own act."

The circus had traveled through Flossie's town in Devon when she was seventeen. At the time, Agatha had been living and traveling as a companion to a wealthy aunt from the Lake District. Flossie had sneaked away from her father to see the circus and was completely dazzled by the spectacle.

"I saw her in the crowd that first night, and she was just the most beautiful thing I think I'd ever seen," Sidney said shyly. "I decided to do an illusion where I needed help from an audience member, and called her up to the stage."

"I stole away every night that week to go see him perform," Flossie added proudly. "It wasn't difficult. Father liked the drink."

When the week was over and they were moving on to the next town, Flossie had arrived with a bag packed and asked to go with him, and Sidney had talked the big boss into it.

"Once he took one look at Flossie, he wasn't hard to convince. She could draw a crowd."

They'd given her a sparkly costume, and she had begun as the sultan's assistant. After a time, they started asking her to help with the acrobatics show.

"She was a natural," Sid bragged. "Mavis the Marvelous, they called her."

"I loved it up there. The lights, the costumes, the crowds and applause. I felt like a queen."

Until one day she fell off a horse and broke her ankle.

"Sid offered to take me home, but I wouldn't go."

"Anyone who traveled with us had to contribute. With Flossie out of commission for a few months, it caused issues. But we struck a deal with Big John."

"We shared a caravan!"

Sidney went pink, and turned to Agatha. "We did, but it was all very proper. Nothing untoward."

"Sid hung a theater curtain down the middle of the trailer and slept on the floor, and nursed me back to health. It was very heroic."

The rest of the story wasn't as happy. Flossie's father had lost a leg to diabetes, and she'd gone home to look after him. He had kept her from Sid, of course. He didn't want her to leave, and Sid didn't have much money. He railed at her. Performing with the circus was for shameless harlots, and it would disgrace the family if word ever got out. He said that she'd been living in sin and made her promise never to speak of it again to anyone. And she had kept that promise.

"I never knew that Sid was looking for me."

"Of course I was. I went to her father's house, but he told me she had married and moved away. I thought maybe after I stopped performing, perhaps she'd realized that I wasn't so exciting after all. I wasn't a sultan from the Middle East, just a poor Scot without much to offer a new bride. I sent letters for a year or two, but when they were never returned, I didn't want to bother her."

"If this is true, how could you never have told me? In all these years?" Agatha's voice was still angry and defensive.

"Because you would have agreed with Father."

Flossie reached out and grabbed Sidney's hand. Agatha's face was drawn, but she didn't deny it. There was more there than just anger; to me she looked totally and utterly lost.

EVENTUALLY, WE MOVED our conversation to a café for a long, late lunch. None of us was eager to separate the two after such a touching reunion, and we were hungry for more of their story.

Shyly, Sidney took out a folder and, to our giddy delight, we pored over original posters that he had saved showing Flossie, a stunning bombshell, standing on the back of a camel, or hanging with arms outstretched from a trapeze, her sequined leotard glittering like jewels. They were color illustrations; even the mermaid was there, just as she'd said. There was also one where Flossie stood next to Sidney as a deck of playing cards floated in the air.

He looked strikingly handsome, and she looked like a movie star, all shining waves of blond hair and hourglass curves. He had also saved some news articles, and we passed them from person to person, greedily reading everything we could.

Agatha was quiet as the grave. I wondered how two sisters could share a life and have this secret between them. It was hard to imagine what she was feeling. Confusion, betrayal perhaps, jealousy certainly for an exceptional life lived, which she had had no part of. Perhaps she didn't know where she fit in with this new Flossie, or how they would carry on from here. Not quite the way they had been for so many decades, perhaps.

When we finally dragged ourselves away from Inverness, we were running quite a bit behind schedule. Sidney's face had looked crestfallen at saying goodbye to Flossie all over again. I tried to look away when I saw him clasp her hand in both of his.

"Seeing you again . . . well, it's brought me more happiness than I can say."

She didn't respond. Her eyes were misty with unshed tears, her hand wrapped around his, like she wouldn't let go for all the world.

"I wonder if I could write to you, and if maybe I might be able to come down to Somerset to visit. Maybe one day you might like to come back to the Highlands for a little holiday? There are so many beautiful things to see here. I have plenty of room for both you and Agatha to stay."

"Yes, I would. I would like that very much. I also need to return this spoon."

He turned to Agatha then. "I really hope that we can get to know each other better. Flossie used to speak of you so often that I felt I knew you. I can't apologize enough for today, but I hope you can find it in your heart to forgive me and let me make it up to you."

"We will see about that." Most of the bite had gone from her bark.

ACCORDING TO THE itinerary, it was the day that we were supposed to talk about *Once There Were Wolves* as we toured a reindeer park in the Cairngorms, and *The Winter Sea* as we visited Slains Castle for sunset, but we would have needed more time. Instead, Robbie drove us straight down to Dunkeld, where we checked into an adorable traditional inn.

When Robbie said that he was taking us to a deli, I had visions of a school cafeteria, complete with hairnets and brown plastic trays, but what we found was a charming award-winning restaurant with a stunning selection of gourmet deli items, a wall of spectacular wine, and a modern menu of Scottish tapas.

Sharing lots of small plates and bottles of wine lent itself to a chatty evening of shared stories, warmth, and laughter. Questions for Flossie bounced around the table like a pinball machine, and she glowed from the attention. We should never have discounted her stories. It was true sometimes she lapsed into befuddlement, or creative renderings of real experiences—tall tales from a woman whose personality was much larger than we knew, an adventuress in earnest. We began to adjust the way that we listened and asked questions. She'd been in our midst the whole trip, and we'd looked right past her.

THAT NIGHT ROBBIE and I collapsed into bed, exhausted and reflective. He lifted up the covers, and I crawled in and flopped down like a rag doll before he wrapped me up in legs and arms.

"Hey," he said. "Thank you for today. You were amazing. You kept such a level head. I honestly don't know what I would have done without you."

"Pfft. It was Flossie. I would have done anything. Besides, I love organizing things and implementing a plan. I know you were worried, but you did a great job keeping the ladies calm."

"Hmm. We make one dynamic duo, Miss Alice Cooper."

I took a moment and allowed the warmth of that statement to melt over me. Then I propped myself up on one elbow and kissed him, trying to press into him all the unsaid feelings I wasn't sure I would be able to put into words before I left.

We made love, but afterward, neither of us could settle.

"Hey." I stroked the hair back from his forehead. "Are you okay?"

"Yeah. Course." He let out a sigh. "I guess I'm a bit shaken up, to be honest."

"Me too."

"We could have lost her."

"Nah. She was always in good hands. And think about it—if she hadn't run away, we probably never would have known that she had this whole incredible secret life, and none of us saw it."

"It's just so tragic. My heart broke for them."

I sat up to get a better look at him.

"Really?"

"They found each other. They had everything they wanted, and it all got taken away. For nothing. They spent their whole lives apart believing that the love of their life had forgotten about them. Life can be so cruel."

I thought about that for a minute. It was odd to me that I had heard the same story and taken away something completely different. "I don't see it that way."

"Don't you?"

"They both took a risk when they were young—broke free and did something wild, completely off script for them. Maybe all the building blocks were in place for them to have this life where Flossie stayed home with family, and Sidney took over his father's business. But instead they were bold, and they lived their lives completely, even if only for a little while. And they were rewarded with this glorious adventure and true love, and enough memories to last a lifetime. I think that's a beautiful thing."

"But wouldn't it have been all the more painful then to lose it? What if they'd fought harder? Could they have found each other again? Could Flossie have left her father and found Sidney? Or Sid have come to her home and demanded to see her? Told her how much he loved her, said he wasn't going to just let her go?"

Robbie's eyes searched mine, clearly in pain. I was surprised by how emotional he was getting. It had happened so long ago.

"I don't know, Robbie. Maybe so. No one can know what might have happened if they took another path. But I'll bet if you asked them if they would take it all back and spare themselves the pain, they would tell you that they wouldn't give that time up for anything."

We laid back against the pillows and held each other. He was quiet for a while, and so was I, lost in my own thoughts. There was a bit of pain in my chest, and I tried to needle it out.

My voice came out soft and hesitant, as if I was making a confession. "Do you know what I kept thinking today when they told us their story? That I was jealous of them. I was jealous because they had this big, beautiful, epic adventure—like something out of a story-book. And . . ." I had to stop for a moment and take a few breaths to keep my voice from cracking. ". . . and I don't know. When is it my turn? When will I have a grand adventure? After the career and the husband and the kids? After the mortgage payments? When I retire?"

"Well, you're here, aren't you?" His voice wasn't defensive. Instead it was gentle. Comforting. The offering of a consolation prize.

"Yeah. Of course. But this was just a couple of weeks, and it's almost over. I'll be gone again in a few days."

He threaded his fingers with mine and held my hand in that way of his that could make me feel safe, gentle all my worries away, just with the curl of a few fingers. He opened his mouth, and I thought he would say something, but he didn't. Instead he shifted behind me and gathered me into him, wrapping his big arms around my chest and holding me tight.

"I'm thirty now, and it all happened so fast that I can't even re-member how I got here," I said. "I never ran away. I never broke free of my story. What if I was supposed to? What if I missed my chance?"

"You didn't."

"I'll wake up tomorrow, and I'll be fifty. And sixty the day after that." It sounded silly, dramatic, but tears swam in the corners of my eyes.

Robbie shifted and put his mouth next to my ear. "Alice Cooper. I've never met anyone more capable of deciding what they want for their life, and making it happen."

I couldn't accept that. The words were so very wrong that all the old familiar pains and insecurities resurfaced. "But I haven't. I messed everything up. And I'm so confused."

"You're adjusting, that's all. Give yourself time, sweetheart."

I felt a tear slip down, and then another. He brushed it away with the soft pad of his thumb and kissed my damp cheek.

"Besides. It's never too late. The circus will always be looking to hire people like you."

I laughed and hiccupped my tears back in. "Would you buy tickets to my show?"

"I'd heckle you from the stands. Say it was false advertising and demand my money back."

I smiled, and the tears dried on my hot cheeks, salt pulling at the skin. "You wouldn't dare. I'd be waiting for you. With my clown posse."

We slid down and curled into each other. Thoughts drifted as I faded closer to sleep, sometimes solid, sometimes diaphanous wisps of gossamer smoke I could not grasp hold of. But in the darkness, something tugged at me and wouldn't quite let me drift off until I spoke it aloud.

"Robbie?" His breathing was heavy and regular. "Robbie?"

"Hmm?"

"Will you promise me something?"

"Anything."

"You know that dream you have of a wheelchair accessible tour?"

"Yeah?"

"It's wonderful. Make it happen. You're building something beautiful here. What you want is right in front of you. Don't let fear stop you from reaching out and grabbing it. Don't let this get away. Fight for it."

Maybe it was something I'd been wanting to say. Maybe it was something he needed to hear. Or maybe it was just the emotional melodrama of someone who'd had a very long, dramatic day. But I meant it.

His arms closed tighter. "I think . . . I might be done with letting things get away from me," he said into my skin, and then we slept.

CHAPTER 40

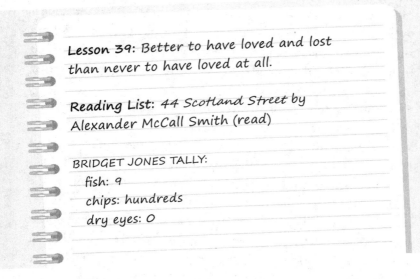

Lesson 39: Better to have loved and lost than never to have loved at all.

Reading List: *44 Scotland Street* by Alexander McCall Smith (read)

BRIDGET JONES TALLY:
fish: 9
chips: hundreds
dry eyes: 0

BOOKS THAT *SHOULD* HAVE BEEN INCLUDED
ON THE TOUR READING LIST:

1. *Men Are from Mars, Women Are from Venus* by John Gray
2. *Auto Repair for Dummies* by Deanna Sclar
3. *Water for Elephants* by Sara Gruen
4. *Cesar's Rules: Your Way to Train a Well-Behaved Dog* by Cesar Millan
5. *Rude Britain: The 100 Rudest Place Names in Britain* by Rob Bailey and Ed Hurst

As we neared Edinburgh, I approached it with fifty percent mounting excitement for a climactic ending to an incredible trip, and fifty percent as if my toenails were being slowly wrenched away one by one by a blind sadist with a tremor. Robbie and I had spent practically every hour of every day together for three weeks, and soon I would be handing over my luggage—most likely to be torn limb from limb, set aflame, and then partially digested by a wildcat and regurgitated directly upon the baggage carousel—and then getting on a plane and flying home.

Home. The thought of it stirred trepidation and discomfort. Getting my life on track was going to be hard.

I was proud to say the trip had done many of the things that I had hoped it might, and many other things that I hadn't expected. I felt more in touch with my feelings. I was more capable of living in the present. I was beginning to see the beauty now in life's unchartered territories and the joys of spontaneity, and the value of having great friends along the way. Learning from others, embracing mistakes—I was seeing the world with a fresh lens, and I wanted to make sure that going home wouldn't mean going back to who I was before and losing sight of all that.

The idea of leaving Robbie was torture. But I knew that it had always had an expiration date, and so did he. We had become a couple in the space of a week. I hoped I would be up to the task of telling him what that meant to me. He had helped me to feel more like myself than I had in a long time, perhaps more than I ever had. Still healing—yes. Still a mess—maybe. But a beautiful mess who was learning to adapt, who was learning to take life for all it had to offer, to be able to learn from the hardships and move on: suck all the chocolate off, spit the raisin out, and walk away.

I wasn't really sure how things would be between us when I got home—how we would settle into a long-distance friendship, how often we would call or message or send little gifts—but I knew without question that we would. Even if it would be years before we saw each other again, it wouldn't matter; it would feel as if no time at all had passed. I felt proud of myself for being able to open up to the joyful experience of caring about someone new without a long-term agenda or plan for the future in sight. For others it might have been a free and easy no-strings holiday romance—for me it took strength and courage.

EDINBURGH UP CLOSE was even more beautiful than I had dreamed. Like my favorite books, it was an intriguing mixture of light and dark. The ancient sandstone wore varying shades of gray, some buildings having turned completely black over the many hundreds of years of soot and grime and time. These huge Gothic structures towered over the landscape, making everything feel a little bit creepier, and inspiring thoughts of all the things they had witnessed in their years: wonders and horrors, celebrations, wars won, witch drownings, conquering armies, plagues, kings and queens come and gone. Dark, mossy cobbled paths snaked their way between crooked buildings, making shortcuts for those on foot who would experience damp, cold, dripping passageways that opened to sunny squares, cathedral spires, and what must be some of the most beautiful streets and buildings in the world.

The weather obligingly went along with the theme, moodily mercurial. The locals warned that you would get all four seasons in one day: gray and stormy one minute, warm and sunny the next. Between the cold stone of the buildings and the gray, rocky mountains they hunched upon, the city was awash with daffodils and roses and trees heavy with sweet blossom in a joyous spectrum of color.

I happened to like my ethereal beauty with a dash of ghoulish macabre, and found that the aesthetic of the city appealed to me immensely. It was a photographer's fantasy of moody shadows and crooked angles.

If the city looked lofty, grand, and darkly mysterious, then the vibe couldn't have been more different. It was a happy city where, despite the weather, people busily bustled on foot, were quick with smiles as you passed, and were always pleased to help with directions if needed. It would be a great place to live. There were lots of cool pubs to meet friends for drinks, as well as music, art, and festivals. And all of those mountains and steep streets would be great for your derriere.

"HEY, SO I'VE been thinking," Robbie began that morning, as I stretched and started stirring back to life. I wished that he would get naked and come back to bed. "I know you have tonight booked in the Grassmarket, but I was wondering if you would want to cancel your room tomorrow for your last night, and come and stay at mine instead."

It was a lovely, thoughtful idea. Even better, it would sate my ravenous curiosity.

"Hmm . . ." I said, making him work for it. "Is it up to hotel standards? Because I feel like it'll be filthy."

"It's revolting."

"Rats?"

"Oh, yes. Beautiful, plump things. I've been fattening them up on butter pats and tiny shortbreads. I think you'll approve."

"Good. What about the views? Nice views are important."

"Well, I can promise rather a nice view of my arse if you ask politely." *Don't mind if I do.*

"Done. Is it centrally located?"

"You'll be located in the very heart of my bedroom, just steps away from your every desire." He smiled and added, "Provided that they are purely carnal in nature, and that you don't need for *literally* anything else, because other than that, I can offer zero amenities."

"*Alright,*" I droned out, like a child being forced to clean her room. Really I could think of nothing better. "I guess so. I'll hate it, but at least I'll save some money."

"Oh, you'll pay for it alright," he said lasciviously.

I smacked him on the bum. "Deal."

"Excellent!" He was excited. His eyes sparkled. "Can I make you dinner, or would you rather go out? I thought you might like something home-cooked after all this traveling, but there are lots of good restaurants nearby if you prefer."

"I'm the type of woman who lives for adventure now, so I'll take my life in my hands and go for the home-cooked meal, thanks."

"Perfect! Do you like French food? Because there's a good patch of snails living in the bathroom that I've been meaning to get rid of."

THERE WAS SO very much to see and eat in Edinburgh, and we tried to do it all! We spent a good hour in the incredible little mansion set back from the Royal Mile that had been turned into a Scottish writers' museum. We went through the ancient, gnarled cemetery Greyfriars Kirk and heard about its famous little dog, Bobby. We went to the fabulous Armchair Books, where there were so many secondhand and antique books that stacks of them crowded in from the walls and made a cave of wonders one could delve into and never want to leave. We passed by the castle and the palace, both incredibly beautiful, and the Elephant House café where J. K. Rowling was said to have written *Harry Potter* at the window with a cup of tea in hand. We also popped into the National Library of Scotland to see their treasures, including some unique sculptures carved from the pages of old books, characters springing from the binding into life and capturing the imagination.

High tea at the secret garden room at the Witchery was sheer, dreamlike decadence. Old Gothic architecture framed beautiful views, and green vines and flowers grew indoors, coiling in from every direction and snaking along the rafters, reaching out to ensnare and ensorcel the guests. Tiered silver towers were heavily laden with tiny treats both sweet and savory, and we all took our time eating and chatting and relishing one another's company, knowing it would soon be missed. Even Percy was well-behaved, and the staff brought him a silver water bowl and a fancy doggie cookie. It was a grand highlight for the end of our tour.

Afterward, on the way down the Royal Mile, I nipped quickly into a café and bought a treat to hide in my bag. Robbie loved surprises, and he always woke up hungry. I had gotten into the habit of secretly squirreling something away during the day to leave on top of his bag at night as a little surprise to keep him going through the busy morning tasks. On lucky days it might be a pain au chocolat from a café we'd been to, on less lucky days it might be a banana I'd stolen from the breakfast room the evening before, or if that failed, a Kinder Bueno, a Mars bar, or one of the copious chocolate bars that I knew him to eat to keep his insatiable sweet tooth at bay. He loved it, and it made me happy to know that he would discover it in the cold dark of morning and have something to look forward to.

That day I had quietly purchased a millionaire's shortbread to go. I knew it would be the last one I would buy for him, and it pulled at my stomach with a hollowness that made my nose sting before I could blink it away.

When it came time for our final meal together, Robbie left it up to us, listing a few options: upscale Scottish cuisine, locally renowned Indian restaurants, lively gastropubs. Several of us were on our phones looking at online reviews and photos when Lorna broke in.

"You know, it would be a shame to hide from this incandescent sunshine. What if we just sit in the grass and eat right here in the park?"

"Oh, I do like that idea," said Doris. "And so does Percy. We could get some takeaway. Fish-and-chips and pizza sound good to anyone?"

So that's just what we did. We found our own little corner of Princes Street Gardens, and we all lowered down to the lush, green grass. The castle was on its great rock in front of us, the gilded mermaid fountain bubbling prettily nearby as the flowers nodded in the breeze around us. We laughed and chatted as we sipped cold cider that tasted like liquid sunshine and ate crispy, hot fish with fat, potatoey chips. I got mine with salt and Edinburgh sauce, as per Robbie's recommendation, and it was sharp and malty as I licked it from my fingers.

The days were longer in Scotland than down south, but when the sun finally set, we were treated to a show, as the castle burst into light, orange and pink and golden.

Robbie asked the group which part of the trip we liked best, and we all took turns describing our favorite moments in detail. I said that mine was the moment in Skye when I realized I wasn't lonely anymore, which made us all a little bit more teary.

Robbie held up his bottle. "Can I just say, that I meet a lot of charming ladies on these tours." Madge wolf whistled, and we all laughed. "But this trip has been a real adventure, with rowdy nights on the town, bodily injuries, surprise parties, dog chases, grand mysteries, incredible revelations uncovered, friendly debates, and a whole book's worth of stories . . . even a bit of romance." He gave me a little wink. I blushed hotly while they whistled and cheered. "I've rarely seen another group grow as close as this one. Despite all our differences, you've been caring and supportive of one another, and a true joy to be around." We all clapped at this, tipsy and sentimental. Maybe it was just tiredness, but in the dimming light, I thought Robbie's eyes looked a little pink. He found goodbyes hard.

"I hope you've all enjoyed it as much as I have. You've done more than make my job easy; you've made it difficult, because I know it's time now to say goodbye, and I'm going to miss the hell out of you. So here's to you, each and every one. Thank you." He raised his cider and drank a long draft, and we all did the same.

"Well, I'm sure the ladies won't mind me saying thank you on all our behalves," said Doris. "Robbie, we learned, we laughed, we lived. You've been our captain and our hero. And even when we were ignoring *another* history lesson, you were always oh-so-nice to look at!" She broke off with a cackle.

"Hear! Hear!" We all drank again.

I squeezed Robbie's hand and gave him a little look. I recognized pride blossoming in my belly. He held on and gave me a look back that made me feel perfectly complete, and my heart ached all the more for it.

We talked books and travel and future plans and drank more cider until dusk pulled over her blanket of stars and the castle lit up with a silvery light. The ribbon of chill in the air became more persistent. We knew we could not put it off forever.

There were hugs all around as we said our final goodbyes on Princes Street, some hopping on the tram, some getting cabs, and some walking up the hill, or down the hill, all starting the first steps of our own journeys home.

Berrta surprised me with a sturdy hug and a round of solid pats on the back. "Auf wiedersehen, Alice. I am happy to know you."

"Aww. I am so happy to know you too, Berrta. Thank you. I hope next time you're birding in the States, we can plan to see each other."

"Yes, good." Just like that, she said goodbyes to whoever was left on her round, turned on her sensible orthopedic shoes, and started walking.

Helena came and hugged me for several long minutes.

"Helena." I let out a big breath. "What can I possibly say? How can I thank you? For everything. And not just the dresses. You've held me up and kept me going—"

"Shh, shh. Hush now or you'll ruin my mascara. This isn't really goodbye." She gave me a little look. "I've no doubt I'll be seeing you soon. Very soon." She gave me a kiss, another hug, and then shot

Robbie a meaningful look before she took him a few steps away for a quick heart-to-heart.

Lorna and Madge came over together. "Alice!" cried Lorna. "Oh, do say we'll see you soon. I know! Why don't you meet us in Santa Fe?"

"We don't have plans to go to Santa Fe, my love." Madge turned to me. "But please come stay with us at the studio in North Berwick. You can stay as long as you like. Weeks. Months!"

"Yes, move right in!" said Lorna.

"I would love that!" I laughed. "And I can't wait to see what wonderful things you do with your new art outreach program. You'll hear from me soon. I'm going to call you to talk over some fundraising ideas I've had."

"Oh! Hear that, Madge? Professional help! Just so long as you know we can only pay you in scones." We laughed. "I'm going to miss you, Alice. Did I tell you that dream I had about you?"

"Yes, you did, darling. Yesterday." Madge put a supportive arm around Lorna's shoulder and said gently, "Come on along, love. Pumpkin time."

Lorna put a hankie to her nose and blew. "Oh, alright, alright, we'd better go before I fall to pieces. I just can't help it, can I, sweetie?"

"No, you can't, love. You and your big, soft heart."

We grabbed one another in a hug triangle, and I promised to email them soon.

Agatha approached and handed me her address. "In case you want to write, Alice." She shook my hand—formal at first, but then she put her other hand on top, like a little hand hug.

"Oh, I will. Thank you, Agatha. In fact, I have a little something I plan to send you." If I'm not mistaken, her cheeks colored a little.

I found Flossie having an animated chat with Doris and moved to join them.

"But if I hadn't pulled the fire alarm, they would have caught me with my trousers down!" said Flossie, and Doris laughed.

"I hate to break this up," I said. "But I wanted to say goodbye, and each minute I stay here, it gets harder and harder to leave."

"Oh, she's in a hurry to get back to bed, I'd wager," Flossie said with a wink. "Just remember to always keep at least *one* article of clothing on, to maintain an air of mystery. I suggest a hat."

I pulled her in for a hug and laughed. "Flossie, I'm going to miss you and your stories! I'm going to do a little hunting online and see if I can't find anything interesting about your circus days. Would that be okay?"

"Oh, that would be grand! It feels good to connect to the past. It's . . . grounding. You know what I mean?"

"I think I do, Flossie." I gave her another hug. "Agatha gave me your address, so I'll let you know what I find."

Doris parked her cane to the side, and shuffled over to grab me with both arms. She had ketchup on her top, of course, but I hugged her all the tighter for it. "Well, I guess I owe Robbie another thank-you," she said into my ear.

"Why's that?" I laughed.

"I was a little worried after our chat in Cambridge. Now I can rest easy in the knowledge that you have been *thoroughly* romanced."

"Doris!" I laughed, and she grabbed me tighter. Percy jumped on us, jealous for all the attention that he had to share. "I'm really going to miss you, Doris." I leaned down and scrubbed Percy's ears. He jumped up and I gave him a little hug. My eyes grew cloudy. What would I do without them all? "Doris, can I just call you every single time I need life advice? Or have to decide anything at all?"

"I'd be cross if you didn't."

"Good. In the meantime, when I miss you too much, I'll just pop on 'It's Not Unusual' and think of you. And of epic, passionate romance." I gave her a smile, and she hooted and gave me a smack on the rump. "Or 'She's a Lady'! Is that about you, Doris? Are you *the* lady?"

"My lips are sealed. Now go on, me love. You've spent enough time with us old bags. It's time to ride off into the sunset with that strapping young man of yours."

I had a little cry on the walk back to the hotel. These weren't the same tears of grief and dread I'd cried on my own night after night in my apartment; they weren't the fearful tears I'd cried in the bathroom in Whitby. These were sweet. Tears just for the joy of knowing these women. Yes, homesickness already settling in for the time I knew we would spend apart. But also comfort for knowing that this wasn't the end of our story together.

Robbie had tissues. Because of course he did.

ROBBIE STAYED WITH me in my beautiful room in the Grassmarket. We made passionate love and had a long bath together. We said little—neither of us wanted to face our reality. We just wanted to live in the moment. We stayed awake, wrapped naked in each other's arms all night. We watched the sun rise behind the castle through the window, and Robbie ordered room service, which we ate in bed, and then finally went to sleep, wrapped up and full.

CHAPTER 41

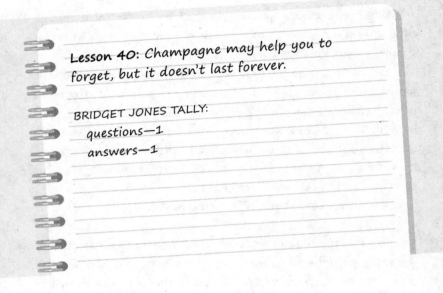

Lesson 40: Champagne may help you to forget, but it doesn't last forever.

BRIDGET JONES TALLY:
questions—1
answers—1

We slept until noon and then had a slow day. We had a tasty brunch on the West Bow of the Grassmarket and then strolled down into New Town, hit up a couple of antique shops and bookshops that Robbie wanted to show me, then took a break from the city and strolled the magical green valley of the Water of Leith Walkway to Dean Village and back. We held hands under the leafy trees and beautifully arched bridges, and listened to the birds sing and the river babble beside us.

Robbie's flat was in Stockbridge, an adorable little hamlet of Edinburgh situated along the river and positively filthy with boutiques, cool cafés, eateries, and charming bookstores.

"Home sweet home, at long last." Robbie opened the door and revealed a space that gave my heart a little palpitation. "Get comfy, I've been training up the rats for a little parade in your honor."

"I'm not surprised. This place is a hovel. It's gross. I definitely can't get naked in here. Ever."

It wasn't. I loved it.

He laughed. "Oh, is that so?" He snatched my hand and yanked me until I crashed into him, his back against the closed door. He wrapped his strong arms around my waist and took my breath away, his mouth hungry on mine. "I take that as a personal challenge, Miss Cooper." I sighed and kept my eyes closed as a supernova gathered in my tummy.

"Give me the grand tour then."

"Nae chance. I'm off duty."

"Do you work for tips?"

He gave me a dark look. "I might be persuaded."

He tugged at my hand, and I forced myself to remain mostly composed while he showed me around. He had an entire wall of bookshelves and several good reading nooks. He even had one of those antique chairs with a curved back and top that canopied over the sitter like a giant hood. It sat looking out over a big window, perfect for losing yourself in a great story.

The flat was historical, probably a hundred and fifty years or more, and it had retained many of the original period features. Some were a bit crumbly, like bits of missing cornicing or the squeaky hardwood floor planks that came loose and set out to stub your toe, but no less charming for the gentle dilapidation.

The ceilings were high, with crown molding and huge sash windows with those old foldaway wooden shutters that were so neat. The living room was painted an interesting fern color. From the ceiling hung a lighting fixture made from an old piano soundboard, and there were various instruments, of course, hung in cases or leaning against furniture. The walls were hung with old maps, no doubt scavenged from antique shops around town.

Most of the furniture was antique. Not so much of the type

that was purchasable from polished showrooms in the fancy part of town, but rather the bits that were dug out from the crammed old junk shop on the corner, dusted off, and loved all the more for their nicks and chipping paint. He had houseplants too, but most were of the desert variety, probably because he could leave them for a month and they wouldn't judge him for it. His kitchen was small but clean, and the spices and appliances made it clear that he liked to cook. Everywhere I looked, there were little pieces of him, and I ate up every morsel.

As we walked around, and he pointed things out, I slowly undressed myself, starting with my cardigan, taking items off one at a time and dropping them on the floor where they fell.

By the time my top was off, he got muddled, and tried clearing his throat several times while he took me around more slowly. "And here is some stuff." He stared at my bra with single-minded intent as he waved his hand at a collection of things that looked like they probably came from an archeological dig. "It's all good stuff." He reached out a hand, and I slapped it away. On the way to the bookshelf, I slid out of my jeans and stepped over them in a new lacy red thong, similar to what I had been wearing that drunken night in Whitby.

He made an uncomfortable grumble.

"And some other stuff. With . . . pages." I slid my hands over my bra suggestively and then slipped a strap down. He inhaled a long, pained breath, and his eyes widened.

"Oh, and you should see the umm . . . this . . . uh." He looked around, and then pointed at a painting. "This junk, whatever it is."

I unhooked my bra, gave him a little smile, took my time slipping it off, and hung a strap from the corner of a painting's frame. He made a low appreciative sound, and his eyes grew dark.

"Would you like to check out my cupboards?"

"Oh, absolutely. But it is pretty chilly in here."

"Mmm. I can see that." He stepped in closer. And then he

swooped down and picked me up just like he had done at the castle, and I rested my head against his shoulder and pressed slow kisses into his neck as he carried me to the bedroom. "Let me see if there's anything I can do to help."

WE GOT DRESSED and swung by a few pretty shops and bakeries for groceries, where Robbie spoiled me with a lovely bottle of full-bodied red wine, olives, a selection of life-altering cheeses, and an incredible bottle of cava. We opened the red, put on an old scratchy Billie Holiday record, and cooked together, dancing and tasting as we went, in no particular hurry to sit down.

We spent hours at the table until the candles burned low. We laughed and drank, and he told me embarrassing horror stories from his past tours, and I told him about my foolish university hijinks. I talked about my plans for the future, about the type of job I hoped to find.

I was surprised when I found myself saying that this trip was making me question my plans in ways that I hadn't expected. Talking about it was helpful. Robbie's face was tight. I got the feeling that he didn't much like talking about my plans for going home but had resolved himself to doing the best he could to be supportive and insightful for my sake.

I would need to take stock and do some real soul-searching when I got home.

"Will you think some more about the new bus?" I asked gently. "You sounded like you might have been coming around to the idea the other day."

He didn't answer right away.

"I think I've started to come round to the idea of planning for *some* things, but I don't know that I'm quite ready for that."

"Okay." I tried not to be too pushy. It did not come naturally. "Would you maybe consider letting me do some research for you?"

"That's sweet. Sure. And I can promise that I'll do some of my own as well. But I think that's all I can promise at this point." I was content with that. The rules we live our lives by seldom change overnight. I was proof of that. He cleared his throat. "Anyway, this unplanned life of mine brought you to me—delivered you right to Rosie's door looking for a fight. And you sure look bonnie when you're angry."

"Oh, I do, do I?"

"That's right. That's why I didn't mind waiting while you lost your temper outside the bus on day one. I knew you'd eventually give in. At least I had a show while I waited."

"Uh-huh. Well, I'm about to get real bonnie in a minute here if you keep this up."

"Wonderful. Why don't we move this to the sofa in that case." I threw a cork at him, and then he pulled me over to his lap for a kiss.

It was perfect in every way, and that in itself was excruciating. Then the strawberries and cava led us back to bed, and for a time I forgot everything else, including how difficult the next day was going to be.

IN THE MORNING when I woke, Robbie was already up. I stretched and yawned myself into life, and he smiled down at me.

"Alice Cooper. Are you finally awake?"

"Mmm."

"Good, because I have another question."

I stretched again and wrapped my arms around him, pressing kisses along his jaw and letting my hands roam.

"Are you paying attention? It doesn't feel like you're paying attention."

"Mmm." Both my hands cupped his bottom.

"Well, maybe this is better, come to think of it. Go ahead and get a handful. So." He pulled away far enough to look me in the eyes.

"What I want to say is . . . stay." We both waited for a moment, not daring to breathe.

"Stay," he repeated. "At least for a little while. Maybe a few months?" Before I could respond, he rushed on. "You could stay here with me. You won't need a visa, and we can cook, and spend the summer together, and I can show you around Edinburgh, you could come on my next tour if you wanted to stay that long, and we can just . . . we can just be together."

I breathed and took a minute.

"What would I do here?" I asked softly after a while.

"Why do you have to do anything? Can't you just take a few months off?"

"Robbie, I've *had* a few months off. I've had six. I need a job. I need to go home and get my life in order. I know this is hard, but—"

"Please think it over. I know it's not your plan, but . . . Alice, you've changed everything. You challenge me. You've woken up this part of me that I had cut away years ago. Being with you makes me realize I want this back. I don't want to be Sidney." He put a hand on each side of my face and stared into my soul. He forced me to look at him, to see how vulnerable he was. "I don't want to let this go. We can make a new plan. Let's make time to see where this goes, instead of letting it slip through our fingers. Let's fight for this."

My heart burned from the inside out into a cinder. The champagne glow from the night before had worn off. I knew that I couldn't stay. I mean, maybe I could stay a few more weeks, maybe a month, but that would only make it harder to leave when the time came.

I had no life here. I also knew that with his mom in Edinburgh, Robbie wouldn't leave Scotland any time soon. It's not as if he could drop his business and his mom and move to the States to be with me.

My eyes burned. My stomach felt like a black hole, dropping and pulling everything down into the darkness with it. I wasn't strong enough for this. But I had to be. I had prepared for it. I'd thought of little else since that night at Glenapp Castle. I had said it enough, over and over to myself. All I had to say was two words.

"Sweetheart." It was the first time I had called him that, and I saw him wince. He knew I was softening a blow. "I can't." I sighed. "You know I can't." I wrapped him up in my arms and held on to him. Hot tears broke free and made their way slowly down my burning cheeks. "I have to go and face my life now."

We clung to each other as if we were at sea and a storm was coming. And maybe we were.

ROBBIE WANTED TO drive me to the airport, but I couldn't stand the pain of a long goodbye. I called a cab, and on the ride over I dug out my little notebook and looked at my Trip Goals List.

UK BUS TRIP GOALS:

1. Crawl out of pajamas.
2. Get over cheating bastard and his stupid ironed jeans.
3. Have my first real adventure!
4. Achieve stability, strength, and growth.
5. Adjust life plan, and prepare to kick butt upon arrival home.

I took out a pen and started checking them off one by one. Then I made a new list.

THINGS LEARNED AND NEVER TO BE FORGOTTEN:

1. Stop and appreciate the moment, the small things, the roses. You will never be in this exact moment again.
2. Always listen and keep learning from others. Everyone has a story to tell.

3. Learn to listen to your heart when it speaks to you.

4. Sometimes it's okay to be the one who gets looked after. It does not make you weak.

5. Show people how much they mean to you.

6. Be ready for anything life has to throw at you. Embrace it. Adjust. Find the silver lining.

7. Happiness comes from within, so fill yourself up! Take up knitting, learn to sing, read more books, do something with your photographs.

8. Not everything has to happen by thirty. Life keeps going, and new, exciting things can happen at any age if you let them. Even thrilling new romances at seventy-six!

9. Life is what happens when you're busy making other plans.

I CRIED QUIETLY on the flight home, numbing myself with hamster-size bottles of wine and an endless stream of stupid movies I hadn't yet seen because they made me feel ashamed to be human—movies that featured, for instance, a time machine that was also a hot tub.

When I got home, I tried to cry myself to sleep, but the jet lag had turned me upside down, and I found that my body refused to be rocked to sleep by shaking misery. I allowed myself one night. One night to wallow in self-pity until my fingers got all pruney.

It was midnight. My allotted heartbreak time was officially over, and recognizing that the luxurious abyss of sleep was out of reach, I grabbed my book. When I opened it, a little scrap of paper lay tucked into the pages alongside my bookmark. In Robbie's tidy, slanted hand it said:

I love you, Alice Cooper.

And then a little lower down: *If you enjoyed your trip with Boadicea Adventures, please be sure to leave a glowing review on Tripadvisor.*

I laughed out loud alone in my empty room. The sound echoed off the walls as salt tears slid into my mouth.

Okay, another hour or two, I decided. *Another hour or two. And then I'll move on.*

CHAPTER 42

Lesson 41: None of us has a crystal ball.

BRIDGET JONES TALLY:
dates—2
surprise visits—1

July—three months later

We sat outside in the early evening under lush potted trees. Their gracefully arching limbs twinkled with glittering strings of bistro lights. I didn't usually order rosé, but it was rosé weather, and the crisp acidity mixed deliciously with the warm breeze and the buzz of the city.

"You look so lovely tonight. I'd almost forgotten how lovely you are."

"Aw. Thank you. Here's to you! To your big move!" We locked eyes, clinked glasses, and sipped for good luck. "Very bold, moving all the way across the Atlantic where there's a decided deficit of Tunnock's tea cakes and clotted cream."

He flashed a blinding smile. "I think I'll manage."

We strolled home, chatting easily, and for a moment, speaking to him made all the memories from my trip to Britain swim to the surface, more alive than they had in weeks.

"It's so good to see you, Alice. Thank you for a wonderful night. I haven't laughed this much in months."

"It was really great to see you too, Tristan. I'm glad that you're here in Boston. I mean, it's no Oxford, and you obviously made a *huge* mistake. But you have a pretty face, no one expects you to be bright as well."

We were outside my parents' brownstone now. He smiled, blushed, and adjusted his glasses, then he leaned in to me slowly. Our eyes met, softly stirring the butterflies in my stomach.

We shared a soft, sexy kiss. I breathed him in. My heart thudded, and my blood turned to honey. The butterflies fluttered. Then dropped and died on the wing.

IT HAD BEEN quite an eventful three months since returning home. My broken heart, and homesickness for Britain and all my newfound friends, was tantamount to sitting on a fire-ant hill in a pair of hot pants. I had set myself the goals to apply for at least five jobs daily—weekdays only, I'm not an animal—to call my parents every Sunday and Wednesday like clockwork, and to visit them once a month. I wanted more from them now. I wanted more from me.

I was building a life again, a home, and within two weeks of returning I had had four interviews lined up and was soon offered an interesting position at a growing grassroots NGO, which I accepted gratefully. Things were going just as planned.

I worked hard to rebuild a social life, rekindling old friendships, joining a book club and a hiking group, and reaching out to new people. I had more to offer now, I felt. Now I had stories to tell and photos to show. I was learning to be more open, and was shocked at how a night with a pizza and a friend to chat to could talk most problems right out of existence. I cooked for people, I invited them to cocktail bars I wanted to try, I remembered the little details of their life. I wanted to be the type of friend that the ladies had taught me to be: warm, bold, and generous.

Contrary to all my fears, things had actually improved quite a bit since the forcible dismantling of my life. I had a job that I preferred, and while I made a lower salary, there was more room for growth, travel, and opportunities to lead future projects. I was free of Hunter and his salmon polo shirts, and wondered now why we hadn't cut the cord sooner. It was honestly a relief. I had independence. I could date again if I wanted to, and now I knew that there were men out there whose company was fun, thrilling, passionate.

There was Tristan. We had been on two dates but hadn't rushed into either feelings or bed. I had done what I could to help him look for a new apartment in the fun parts of town and had emailed over some information about how to get around, good places to eat and drink, and other logistics.

I wasn't entirely sure what I was feeling for him. The predominant feeling was confusion. He had mentioned that he might like to visit DC. I had said something ambiguous like *That sounds fun* but hadn't attempted to solidify further. He hadn't pushed me. He was so perfect. What was wrong with me? Was this because I was not yet over Robbie, or was this because there was something innate missing between us? It was so new. I told myself not to worry the unripened fruit right off the tree.

Robbie and I kept in touch mostly by way of long-winded, story-like emails. I would pore over them several times, spending much of my week planning a worthy response. This was punctuated by brief WhatsApp messages and pictures of things we thought the other might find funny—the best so far being a candid shot of a woman in a ruffled pantsuit that, if you squinted, was not that unlike our saggy celibacy suit.

I also continued to encourage (see: pester) him about making his dream of a wheelchair accessible tour work. I sent him several websites for American tour companies who had done something similar for inspiration. And, because grant applications had always been one of my work responsibilities, I sent him info on UK grants he could apply for to help kit out a new bus with a lift, and other expensive logistics that might be holding him back.

We'd had a few video calls over the months, but though we talked long into the evening, and well past Robbie's bedtime, it left us feeling somehow lonelier and further apart afterward, as if we'd had to say goodbye all over again.

We briefly talked of visiting each other, but I certainly couldn't leave the country with my new job, and wouldn't yet be able to ask for any time off. So he'd have to fly all the way over to see me for just a few hours in the evenings and maybe a free Saturday and Sunday, if I was lucky. It would have been expensive and wouldn't have made sense. We knew that a transatlantic relationship wasn't sustainable. It only would have made it harder for us to move on.

When he went on tour, it was basically impossible for us to schedule a call, and he didn't have time for long emails, so things grew distant. It felt beyond our control. I had decided maybe that was for the best. There was a Robbie-shaped hole in my heart. But it would scab over soon. It had to, right?

I also kept in touch with the ladies. I had my photos printed, and I sent them all albums, each one specially curated for the recipient. I hand-bound them with ribbon and the type of luxury recycled paper with the little flower pieces embedded inside. The front covers were inscribed with a flourish: A MOST BODACIOUS SPRING.

Doris and I had had a few telephone calls during teatime, which was a good time in the morning for me to also have a cuppa, and we would pretend that we were having them together somewhere cozy.

Berrta sent me a weekly link for updates to her blog, which was in German and English and mostly about bird-spotting and the development of her up-and-coming bird-watching tour company. She included a short, personal note for each email. I read posts with a cup of coffee on a Sunday, and she seemed to really love getting my notes in the comment section.

I had gone online and to the library to research the Spellbinding Sultan of Samarra and Mavis the Marvelous, and found some images, a few glowing reviews, a beautiful photo of Flossie, and even a news story from Manchester on microfiche—an interview with the sultan. When I sent Flossie and Agatha their photo album, I included a folder of printouts and suggested they share them with Mr. Richie.

Not long after, I received a surprise parcel from Flossie and Agatha. It included a cookbook of British pastries, in which Agatha had written a warning against the imminent threat of fat thighs, and a sheath of lovely pressed flowers from Flossie that I arranged in a double-glass frame with the group photo from my birthday.

A month later, I got a postcard that said perfunctorily: "To Alice Cooper, from Flossie and Agatha Philipson." The interesting part of this was that the postcard was from Cawdor Castle. In Scotland. In the Highlands of Scotland, to be exact. And suspiciously near, one might think, to the infamous Bonar Bridge.

I had the most contact with Lorna and Madge. I arranged a few Zoom calls for them with contacts of mine who were fundraising big-hitters, and even one group who was very successfully running a similar art therapy project in the Bronx. They most often messaged me in unison, sometimes with adorable bickering included.

Helena was never too busy to send WhatsApp messages, sometimes just a photo or an emoji, but other times texts full of family stories and loaded with questions about my life, friends, new job— and of course, my love life. I tried to keep the last a bit restrained, as Tristan would have featured on the list. Although, in fairness, the list would have looked like this:

MEN IN MY LIFE:

1. *Tristan—2 dates*
2. *That fried rice deliveryman who winked at me that one time—0 dates*

Then one day, I got a text from Helena: *Bored stiff. Booked a ticket to Boston. Fancy a night on the town?*

I told her I'd be there with bells on. What I didn't tell her was that I had a secret agenda.

I HAD BARELY slept. I arrived, wild-eyed and folder in hand, to Boston's gorgeous Terra restaurant after a long night at my computer. I could barely stand the anticipation.

The minute the doors swung open, I saw Helena's silver hair gleaming in the stark slices of sun and shadow. If only I had time to get my camera out.

She rushed over, and we crashed together into a big hug.

"Alice!"

"Helena!" I breathed in her familiar perfume, and she kissed the top of my head, just like my mom used to do.

"Oh, I can't tell you how good it is to see you. Thank you for coming all this way."

"I wouldn't have been able to live with myself if you were in the States and I couldn't see your beautiful face in person." I gave her another squeeze and we rocked from side to side, because a regular hug wasn't enough.

As Helena and I broke apart, Tristan came in for a kiss on the cheek. I waited for the blush to heat my face, for the crackle of electricity to send little bolts of lightning to my fingertips, but they didn't come.

We talked about my train journey and Helena's flight, and ordered food. While we waited for it to arrive, she noticed me glancing nervously at the folder I'd brought.

"What have you got there?"

"Well. I'm glad you asked. So." I took a moment. I hoped it would work. "This is a gift, but it's also a . . . well, let's call it a challenge." Helena lifted an eyebrow. "When I got back home from Britain, I spent the first few weeks going through my photos. I had *a lot* of them. Almost two thousand." They gasped. "I know. I was in heaven. Anyway, the more I looked, well . . . I hope you won't mind me taking the liberty. Here."

I spun the folder around and opened it. A black-and-white close-up of Helena stared back at us. It was striking. Tristan picked it up.

"Alice. This is gorgeous."

"There's more." There were—about twenty of them, but it had been a tough choice to decide between a hundred or more that belonged in a damn magazine.

Helena was silent. By the time Tristan had gotten to the fourth photo, her hand was at her mouth.

"These are remarkable. Mom, you're so gorgeous. Did you know she was taking these?"

"No," I interrupted. "I always like to get candid shots, because most people look uncomfortable as soon as they know their picture is being taken. Although to be honest, had Helena posed, these may have been even more beautiful. She's a pro."

"Did you alter these?" Helena asked, finally breaking her silence.

"Of course not. Just the cropping and the focus. Changed those to black-and-white." I looked at her. "I didn't need to do anything."

Helena cleared her throat. "I . . . these are just . . . just so beautiful. I can't believe you did this for me. It almost feels like . . . well, it brings back memories."

"What's this?" Tristan had gotten to the printed page under the last photo.

"Well." I looked nervously at Helena. "I did a little research. Those are the names of some modeling agencies in the UK who I think would be very interested to receive these."

She gave me a look. "Oh, I couldn't."

"Oh yes you bloody well could," said Tristan. "You have Jemima at the shop now, and you've an empty nest, and Dad's always busy with his golf and woodworking. You were just telling me how you've been feeling bored and restless."

"Listen, it's your decision, obviously, but I brought my camera, and we have a tour of Boston planned for tomorrow . . ." I leaned in and whispered, "Why don't we have a little photoshoot?"

Warring emotions collided across her face as she looked between me, Tristan, and the photos: one minute wry, as if she might laugh us off; another teary and nostalgic. Finally it settled on excited.

"Oh, alright." She grinned. "Why the devil not?"

We cheered and clinked our glasses, and I smiled hard and held on to the table lest I float away to the ceiling.

HELENA AND I visited the Public Garden and then made our way over to some stops on the Freedom Trail. She was like I'd never seen her, fizzing with energy. Exhausted from all the walking, we finally gave in to our need for tea and refueling, and found a hipster coffee house with so many pretty potted plants that it was nearly a jungle.

"Sooo?" I tilted my head. "What do you think?"

"Lovely place. However did you find it?"

"Don't play coy with me, madam." Her mouth curled into a sly grin as she brought a hand-thrown mug to her lips. "What do you think about my idea?" I pushed her. "Don't tell me you didn't love it out there."

"I won't pretend. It was terrific fun! I haven't felt this alive in years."

"And? Do you think you'd like to send the shots out to some agencies?"

"Well. The demand for models my age is low, and it's been several lifetimes since I was working in the business. It's a long shot." She dragged out the moment for suspense. "But there's only one way to find out, isn't there?"

I gasped and grabbed her hand. "Really?"

"Yes! You win. I want back in."

We made excited plans to go back to Tristan's to take some headshots there. She smiled and gazed at me over our half-eaten cinnamon buns, studying my face.

"Have I told you how wonderful you look?"

"Really? This?" I looked down at my faded shirt and regretted not making a bit more effort.

"That's not what I mean, darling. You look happy. Your shoulders are back, your smile is easier, the shadows under your eyes have disappeared. You don't look like the same woman I met a few months ago."

I wasn't the same woman. Hearing her say so made me feel emotional but in a good way, a way that warmed me to my toes.

"You know, I *am* different."

"The new job, the new friends, the new hobbies, promising men in your life. It sounds to me like you have everything you said you wanted all those months ago." She smiled and leaned back contentedly in her oversized armchair, but I thought perhaps I'd heard a note of challenge in her voice.

"Well . . . I guess I do." I hadn't really seen it that way, but she wasn't wrong.

She put down her tea and searched me for a moment. "And? Are you happy?"

I sipped and considered. It was a big word. Maybe I didn't have quite *everything* I wanted yet, but this was the happiest I had been since I could remember.

"I am. At least, I think so." Helena tilted her head, and somehow I surprised myself by what I said next. "I mean, I'm *much* happier than I was before." She waited. "But maybe I still feel a little bit like there's . . . I don't know."

"Something missing?"

"Something missing." I had never really acknowledged it before. Not even to myself. I really *was* happy. I felt positive about my future for the first time in nearly a year. But somewhere in this new person that I was discovering was a tiny, niggling something missing.

We stared at each other for a drawn-out moment, but not with any demands or pressure; more as if we wished our souls might speak to each other and tease out the issue among themselves.

I spoke first. "Can I ask you something?"

"Anything."

"What do you think Flossie's life would have been like if she hadn't run away?"

Her brows drew. I could tell it wasn't what Helena had expected, but she quietly mulled it over.

"I don't think we can know that." She took another sip of tea. "But knowing what we do of the rest of her life, I would speculate that it may have been a more colorless and drab existence—taking care of that father of hers, perhaps never really getting her chance."

"And you? What if you had never left university?"

"Well, I daresay my poor sister would still be gone, and my trajectory would probably have been much the same in that regard. However, I would have missed out on that time of stepping into myself. Perhaps I might have been a different woman, perhaps not. But I would certainly have missed out on a whole world of experiences."

"When we were in Scotland, it really struck me how important that was. I've missed out on having adventure in my life. Although now seems like the wrong time—I finally have a new job and I'm settled again, building something here. But maybe it's something to plan for, you know? In a few years? What do you think?" I quieted the voice in my head that said I really should be having children within a year or two.

"These are big questions. Sounds like we need to stop drinking caffeine and switch to something a little more . . . philosophical."

I laughed. "You know, you might just be right. Let's go back to Tristan's and talk this out over a boozy photoshoot."

"You took the words right out of my mouth." We laughed and started to gather our things. But her gaze stopped me. It turned into something a little more solid, tangible, and sinewy. She held me in it.

"Are you going to talk to Tristan?"

She knew. Somehow she knew before I did.

"I . . ." I didn't know what to say. Pain lanced at my sides. It felt horrible. I felt guilty.

I looked at her and nodded. I felt the life where I had Tristan's gorgeous children and Helena for a mother-in-law slip away from me in that moment like a physical thing, even though it had never truly been mine, I knew.

She was right. I had everything I'd ever wanted, and it simply wasn't what I wanted anymore. It stung a little. But this time it didn't feel like grief or loss. It felt more like a growing pain.

I hoped that Helena wouldn't be angry or worse, disappointed with me. I wasn't prepared to lose this new pillar of my life, this new friend. "I'm so sorry."

She let out a breath. "That's alright, petal. We cannot captain our hearts. Quite the contrary is true, I'd say."

My throat tightened. She collected her bags and I followed suit, but before we left, she came to stand next to me, wrapped an arm around my shoulder, and pulled me into her side. "It'll all be alright. You'll see. Just, let him down easy, will you?"

CHAPTER 43

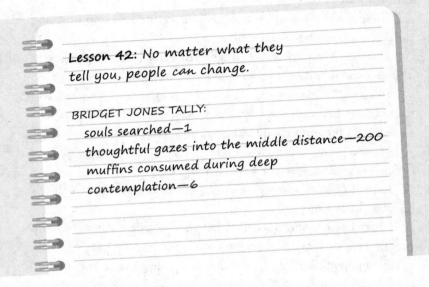

Lesson 42: No matter what they tell you, people can change.

BRIDGET JONES TALLY:
souls searched—1
thoughtful gazes into the middle distance—200
muffins consumed during deep contemplation—6

August

In August I found myself applying for a UK Ancestry visa. I don't know how it happened. I just came to with the pen in my hand. I swear.

But I'd never use it. It would just be a nice thing to have as, say, a memento. Or in case of a North American zombie apocalypse. Or if it turns out I need fish-and-chips to stay alive and my doctor demands that I move immediately.

ONE MORNING I received an email from Robbie. The subject line said *You're my inspiration*. The only thing inside was a link, which brought me to a new page of the Boadicea Adventures website: New

Tours for Accessibility. I scrolled down, and my heart leapt into my mouth at a photo of a brand-new bus—with a wheelchair lift.

"Boadicea Adventures is proud to offer new audio equipment for the hard of hearing. We are also in the process of planning wheelchair accessible tours for both women and men, boys and girls of all ages."

He was doing it. He had taken a risk, made the leap, and was planning for his future. My heart flooded with bittersweet pride. It made me miss him all the more.

I clicked through the website and found another new offering on the tours list.

Boadicea Adventures: History of Music and Folk Culture

Join us for a three-week musical voyage across Scotland and Ireland, where we'll scour every pub, festival, and ceilidh in search of the world's best craic!

As we travel across these remarkable landscapes, we will discuss the role of music in folk culture, investigate the history of Celtic music in centuries past, and learn about how traditional song has preserved an invaluable oral narrative of colourful stories.

Folk music today is a noisy, hip, thriving scene, growing daily with new innovations on century-old traditions and attracting listeners and musicians from all over the world.

Get ready for lively sessions! We warmly encourage you to bring along your whistle, bow, tipper, or set of pipes, to learn to sing a few songs or dance a few steps. There will be plenty of opportunities to sit in on tunes between sights and pints.

CHAPTER 44

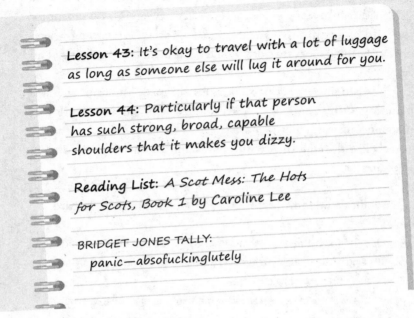

Lesson 43: It's okay to travel with a lot of luggage as long as someone else will lug it around for you.

Lesson 44: Particularly if that person has such strong, broad, capable shoulders that it makes you dizzy.

Reading List: *A Scot Mess: The Hots for Scots, Book 1* by Caroline Lee

BRIDGET JONES TALLY:
panic—absofuckinglutely

October

I never could have imagined that I would be so happy to see the inside of Edinburgh Airport. To set foot on British soil. To know that the wait was over. To be safe in the knowledge that, no matter what was about to happen, soon there would be chips.

I'm not sure that I had ever been quite so nervous and excited in all my life. My heart was in my mouth, butterflies were in my tummy, and I had to pee even though I'd just gone.

Robbie had no idea that I was coming. It was going to be a surprise. A great big surprise. But good surprise or bad surprise, only time would tell. We hadn't been able to speak very much the past few months because he had been busy with tours all summer, and I had been working my rear off to tie up all loose ends, hire my replacement and train him, pack up my apartment, store the majority of my worldly possessions in cardboard boxes in my parents' house, buy a new goddamned suitcase—well, two large ones and a two small ones, if I'm being honest, which would forever be to blame for my permanent squint and gnarled spine from lugging them around like Quasimodo taking his bells on vacation. I had sold everything I could, apart from my body, because I didn't want to die of syphilis after I had gone through all the hassle of packing. Yes, I was in it for the long haul, and I had hauled a lot.

I had almost no solid plans after my arrival. I would go on this amazing music-filled tour for the next three weeks; afterward, I was going to stay with Lorna and Madge in North Berwick for ten days and help where I could with event planning and getting some big grant applications in. The rest I would just have to play by ear. I had started reaching out to organizations with my résumé, and I was also looking into the possibility of a master's degree at the University of Edinburgh. But until something was sorted, I would need to find a bartending shift or a café job, probably a flatshare, and try very, very hard not to blow my savings on scones and clotted cream.

Perhaps I would move on to get my doctorate and become a professor; maybe I'd build my own grassroots start-up using photo essays to show the world what it is like to be a woman in a developing community in the Global South; or maybe I would open up my own bakery bookshop with boozy events, scone stamp cards, and weekly book club meetings. I didn't know. I could plan, I could dream, but just like every other person on the planet, I didn't know. And I was okay with that.

My *only* plan was to surprise Robbie. And now that I thought about it, *What in the flaming hell was I thinking!?* He could be seeing someone else (some leather-faced harlot, no doubt), he could have forgotten me (I would have), or it could be too much too soon (obviously). But I had envisioned his surprised face so many times now that I just couldn't bring myself to spoil it. Besides, I wanted to do something wild and spontaneous and huge for the first time in my life, and not have any future plans other than to follow my heart.

The way I saw it, this could have two possible outcomes: (1) From the passionate throes of picturesque marital bliss, I would congratulate myself, again and again, for making the best decision in recorded human history, *or* (2) I would fling myself onto a burning pyre and sizzle slowly, making sure I had ample time to lament loudly, and sing my tale of woe for all to hear while Robbie toasted s'mores on the flames. I'd probably be finding out if it was to be option 1 or option 2 in about an hour and a half sharp.

I dragged my Sisyphean heap of luggage into the bathroom for a bit of slapdash quality control. Listerine, mascara, deodorant: If I was going to tell Robbie that he was probably the love of my life, I didn't want to murder him with my breath before I could even finish asking if he'd have me.

Breathe, Alice.

Fuck, fuck, fuck.

There he was, in his usual parking spot. Punctual this time, looking like a vat of chocolate I wanted to dive into. Messy hair, blue eyes, cheeky grin, stubble, snug green sweater. *Holy crap! I'd forgotten he looked this good. I don't have a shot in hell!*

I had put my hood up and hidden myself across the street at Harvey Nichols. I was pretending to be busy with window shopping as I watched him call out names, hug old ladies, and help them on the bus. *Ohhh! Doris and Percy!* I had to hold myself back from running over and ruining the surprise.

My entire body was a live wire. I wanted to run full speed until I collided into him, knocked him over, and covered his helpless prostrate body with kisses in the street.

"Jean Simmons." I saw him stop, smirk at the name, and then scrub his face with his hand. I wondered if he was remembering a time six months before when he had been laughing at my name instead.

"Hellooo? Jean Simmons? Is Jean Simmons about somewhere?" He looked around, checked his watch, and then dug his phone out of his jeans and started to dial. That was my cue!

Leaving my luggage behind, I snuck up and cleared my throat. "Are you waiting for me?"

His face shot up at the sound of my voice, and he stared at me, completely frozen. Then he grabbed me quickly and suddenly, as if I might fly away, and hugged me so hard that I'm sure I heard a rib crack. When he finally let go, he searched my face, laughed, and then hugged me again.

"Alice, oh my God! What are you doing here?"

"Well, I have a tour booked."

"What? Is this you? Jean Simmons?" He laughed so hard that I felt it in every bone in my body. "I should have known! Are you really coming with us?"

"Yep!" My grin stretched into a smile so wide that it hurt.

"Jesus!" he said, sweeping me into another hug. "Oh my God. This is bloody brilliant! Christ! How did you get here? Why didn't you tell me? I can't believe this! You're really coming with us?"

"Yep! I'm really coming with you! I even learned a couple of songs to sing." He spun me around again and I giggled like a child. "Well, you know . . . I thought it was probably a good idea to learn a bit more about Scottish culture, now that I'm a local."

"Huh?" He frowned and cocked his head. "What do you mean?"

"I mean . . ." I pointed to the suitcases across the street. "That you'll have to lug around an extra suitcase or two this time. Because I'm moving in."

His brow creased. "Moving in?"

"Yep."

"You mean . . ."

"I just moved over. To Edinburgh. I live here now. As of about an hour ago."

This is it. This is the moment.

His smile dropped. "You're joking . . ." he said flatly.

"Nope."

"I don't believe you." His face grew tight and serious. "This is so sudden. You wouldn't just leave your life. Your new job . . ."

"I did."

"But . . ."

"But what?"

"Well . . ." The corner of his mouth quirked a fraction. "Did you even make a pros and cons list?"

"Of course I did. I made dozens."

"And how did I fare?"

"Oh, you lost every time." He laughed. "But, you see, the thing is . . . you make me frustrated, and a little nauseous, and like I have a whole hive of bees buzzing under my skin." He looked alarmed. My heart started to pound. "And when I'm with you, I feel like I'm standing at the top of a cliff and I have vertigo, and it makes me feel like if I just flapped my arms, I could fly. And I want to be touching you, like, all the time, and when I do, your skin gives me a literal contact high. And when I'm not with you, I can't stop thinking about you. Ever. I have tried so hard, and it never works." He didn't say anything. I didn't give him time. My heart was racing. I thought I might pass out. I started to lose it. "The thing is, I've never felt like this before. And I moved here for *me*, to have an adventure, and I know I didn't ask you, and if you don't want me here, that's okay. But, you know, if you *do*, well, being in love is an adventure I want to try, and . . ." I pumped the brakes and stopped myself before I imploded. "Well? Dear God, please say something."

He let out the breath he had been holding during my entire soliloquay. It looked painful. He swallowed hard. His eyes looked misty, if it wasn't the bracing October wind. He stared at me for a searching moment and then over at my mountain of luggage. He put a hand up to his forehead, grabbed a fist full of his hair and pulled at it before dropping his hand over his mouth.

"Oh, Alice. You've ruined everything."

I steadied myself against the bus. My soul left my body in one giant rip.

He shook his head. "I have been working so hard for months. Saving, planning, booking flights. I've made this whole grand plan to come win you back. It was going to be so romantic."

My heart flapped its wings in the cage of my chest. My nose stung. "You did?"

His blue eyes sparkled like sun on the sea. "But that's all ruined." He stepped closer. "I guess we'll need a new plan now."

I nodded and sniffed. A gaudy tear broke free and splashed on my cheek. "I can help with that."

"Well, you'd better start filling in your spreadsheets then. Because there'll be no getting rid of me now, Alice Cooper."

Then he stepped forward and wrapped me up in his arms. I closed my eyes, and behind them, the world exploded into color as he pulled me into the most passionate, most world-shattering, most soul-filling, most life-defining kiss since the invention of kissing.

When I could open them again, I wiped the tears away from my flushed cheeks and shot a look at the window to see every fluffy white head and bifocal pair of glasses pressed comically, mouths agog, against the windows.

"Wait a minute . . ." I said, as Robbie moved to collect my bags. "Is this an old lady tour?"

ACKNOWLEDGMENTS

Firstly, to my amazing agent who has made my dream job possible, Jane Dystel—who, despite being a titan in the industry, took the time to wade through the slush pile, pluck out my weirdo book, and say she was here for it. Thank you.

To my incredible editor, Tessa Woodward, who is unwaveringly sunshine and rainbows, and has cheerled me into making this book the best version of itself.

To the teams at Dystel, Goderich & Bourret; Avon Books; and HarperCollins, particularly my editing maven, Miriam Goderich; Kendall Berdinsky; Nataly Gruender; Madelyn Blaney; Mary Interdonati; DJ DeSmyter; and Danielle Bartlett; as well all the people who work tirelessly behind the scenes to make the magic happen.

To my very first I-think-maybe-I-wrote-a-book-and-could-you-please-read-it-and-tell-me-if-it's-anything beta readers: Jacqui Long (who inexplicably, and without solicitation, read it multiple times), Amanda Van Camp, and Neasa McGarrigle—lifelong friends and fellow book nerds, who were, and continue to be, incredibly supportive and helpful.

To my hilarious Comedy Cabinet whom I am forever asking, "Which is funnier here? A sex joke or a fart joke?": Matthew Williams, Denise Guay, Scott Burtness, and Caitlin Neal-Jones.

For general bookish support—my rom-com ladies: Deidra Duncan, Poppy Alexander, and Breea Keenan, as well as Jennifer Gold for all my industry questions, and Mila Kane for all my romance questions, and my whole crazy Vegas crew—you know who you are.

And especially to my plot wizard, writing partner, and blackberry crumble baker, whom I can *still* thank for all these extra pounds, Robbie Graham.

To my loving and supportive family—Stephanie, Juan, Steven, Michael, Amy, Oliver, and Nikky, who all love me despite the fact that I write books about exploding toilets and are supportive enough to listen to me talk endlessly about it without scowling. Especially Mom, who *always* told me that I was going to be a writer someday.

To everyone's shitty, ratbag ex-partners in the world out there— yes, them—may they continue to inadvertently push us to find the strength to build new, happier lives and stretch for stars we thought out of reach. My life was dismantled once, and this book is the direct result. It has been my happy place, my experiment in self-care, and a project in self-discovery. I hope that it might somehow provide a little extra encouragement to any readers who want to move on from unhappy situations and build shiny, exciting new ones.

And last, but most certainly not least, to Sarah-freaking-Jones, to whom the explosive bus toilet incident *actually* happened . . . in real life . . . right down to the toilet dump valve sign, on an overnight bus from Oxford to Edinburgh while we were in uni together. I *adore* the way you tell that story and will forever be grateful that you let me borrow it to make my own. Had your luggage not been shat upon so ingloriously, *Work in Progress* would probably have been mostly poopless, and that would have been a real shame.

ABOUT THE AUTHOR

Kat Mackenzie is an American who just happened to find herself living abroad for ten years and accidentally traveling to over forty countries in an attempt to taste all the food. She holds degrees from the University of Edinburgh and the University of Oxford, but has discovered that they serve her best collecting dust on the shelf while she pens comedy-forward stories about women who travel.